There is something about the love of men for men that speaks to the heart.

Masculinity in passion is more than muscle and attitude. It's in the mix of hardness and tenderness, the burning gaze and the soft caress. The struggle with expectation to be tough and the need to be vulnerable. There is something about these stories that show men opening–sometimes eagerly, sometimes reluctantly–to love.

For your pleasure, we offer you men who reclaim lost love, men who find themselves in the love of another man, and men who defy oppression for the sake of love. These are stories that show that an ending is not necessarily the end and that softness is not the same as weakness. In all, eleven stories of love and romance between men from ForbiddenFiction's top authors, including award-winners Julian Keys and Lynn Kelling. To you, our readers, we bring the love.

Also recommended...

You may also enjoy these other ForbiddenFiction works:

Leather Wishes, by Julian Keys

Mason, the leather top known at the Cockpit Bar as the Fancy Man, loves to create BDSM scenes for people—the more unusual the better. Charles brought him one of his tougher challenges, and the two have been together since. It hasn't always been easy, as they work out what they are to each other, both as dominant and submissive and as lovers. Now Mason and Charles work together to create BDSM experiences of intense emotion. As they help other people deal with broken hearts and long-buried desires, they also confront the possibilities in their own relationship. Partners in the scene and in the bed, the two men come to appreciate that they could be so much more together. (M/M)

Threshold, by Lynn Kelling

Seven stories from one of the masters of M/M erotic romance, Lynn Kelling. These stories give prequels and other insights into two of her most popular series, Deliver Us and Whatever the Cost—both in the world of The Society of Masters.

Bring the Love

Edited by Lon Sarver

ForbiddenFiction
www.forbiddenfiction.com

an imprint of

Fantastic Fiction Publishing
www.fantasticfictionpublishing.com

BRING THE LOVE

A ForbiddenFiction book

Fantastic Fiction Publishing Hayward, California

© Lon Sarver, 2017

CREDITS
Authors: Dorla Moorehouse, E.E. Grey, Jacqueline Brocker, Jamie Freeman, Julian Keys, Kailin Morgan, Lynn Kelling, Olivia Stone, P.L. Ripley
Editors: Lon Sarver, Rylan Hunter, and James L. Wolf
Cover Design: Siolnatine
Cover Art: Cover adapted from photos © Curaphotography and Ekhphoto at Dreamstime.
Inside Cover Design: D.M. Atkins, Carol Fiorillo, and Siolnatine
Inside Cover Art: Photos from Roman Sinichkin at Shutterstock and Timhesterphotography, Model photo by Curaphotography Photo by Dnf-style, Photos © Meggj and Stryjekat, and Photos from Anpet2000 and Janaka Dharmasena at Dreamstime. Benjamin Franklin Bridge photo By Ben Yanis [CC-BY-2.0, via Wikimedia Commons]. Adapted from photos © Cpio3 and Elena Rostunova and Photo by Naypong at Shutterstock. Photos by Lon Sarver.and Adriane @ Urband Images.
Production Editor: Kaye O'Malley
Proofreading: Aislinn, Blue Sapphire, CarvedWood, Jae Knight, JhP323, Kailin Morgan, Siolnatine, and Todd Michaels
Font: Wellrock Slab

SKU: SPC-1.100025-01 FFP
ISBN: 978-1-62234-329-4

Published in the United States of America

DISCLAIMER

Contents

Cigarette Burns

Cigarette Burns

The fog seems to press in around him, misting his jacket and the mess of unruly blond hair that falls into his eyes as he stares at the dark and dirty pavement below his feet. He tugs at the tips, dyed black only because he's too lazy to re-dye the rest or cut it off. The cigarette between his fingers smolders gently, the red tip bright against the darkness of the alley.

Fucking bars that don't let you smoke inside, is the only thing he's thinking as he raises the cigarette to his mouth and takes a long drag.

Shivering, Maddox releases the tip of his hair and stuffs his hand in his pocket, hunching his shoulders as if trying to sink into the brick wall behind him. He should go back inside, but there's nothing for him there. There's nothing for him out here either, just the slow burn of his cigarette and the flickering streetlamp a few feet away.

It's not that late out, barely midnight, but he's had more than a few drinks already. Honestly, he thinks he deserves it after the shit he's gone through lately. Despite the tingling warmth in his fingers, the rest of him is still cold as he takes another drag and sniffs from the way his nose is starting to go numb.

The mist settles decidedly in his hair and on the shoulders of his black jacket as he leans back against the brick wall, contemplating going back inside or just going to a liquor store and continuing the party on his own. It's not as if he has anyone to disappoint at this point aside from himself.

Flicking the cigarette away and watching it fizzle out in a puddle, he pulls out another and lights it slowly. The flame from his lighter dances in the darkness then disappears in a small click as he shuts it off and stuffs the lighter in his jeans' pocket.

1

E.E. Grey

A few people are walking down the street beyond—Maddox can hear them—and they seem to slow as their eyes pass over the alleyway with him hunched in the darkness.

He knows he doesn't look presentable, with his hair a fucking mess and the jagged edge of a tattoo peeking out from under his collar. There are bags under his hazel eyes and he hasn't showered in three days, but who's counting anyway? He smells like stale cigarettes now with a hint of cheap beer, and he's not even sure when the last time he changed his shirt was. What did it matter anyway? It isn't as if there is anyone to impress.

He can still hear Joel in his head, his pompous voice filling him as he tells him there's someone else, it's over and he's leaving.

"It's not you, Maddy. Well, actually it is. Sorry."

It's the 'sorry' that haunts him the most (and maybe the 'Maddy' too. He fucking hates that nickname). It hadn't been sincere in the least, and Maddox hadn't felt at all bad about accidentally dropping Joel's iPhone in the toilet five minutes later.

He knows he shouldn't be so upset about it considering how the last few months have gone, but Maddox is mad; at Joel and at himself. How could he not have known that Joel was fucking cheating on him for two months? He'd been so much happier, and it wasn't as if they'd been having sex at all. Seven months down the drain on an asshole like that. It makes him want to smash something that belongs to Joel or drown his sorrows in alcohol. He's chosen the latter, mostly because Joel had taken his things when he'd left two days ago.

Huffing to himself, and he can even see his breath now as it gets later and colder, Maddox sucks in the sweet nicotine of his cigarette. It's been months since he's had one, all because of Joel. He doesn't fucking care anymore though. He'd given up a lot for Joel and he's tired of it. At least with Joel gone he can finally be himself again, without the extra effort of trying to quit smoking or actually keeping the apartment clean. What pisses him off most is that despite how much he tried to change, in the end, it wasn't enough. Maybe he should never have bothered in the first place.

Pulling his sleeves down over his hands, Maddox raises the cigarette to his mouth again. He wishes he was drunker than he is; wishes he didn't have to think about any of this. He can't even

2

remember what he did before he met Joel. It seems so long ago now.

There's a noise down the alley, the sound of the bar door opening and someone stepping out. Maddox should really go home or at least somewhere warm like back inside, but he doesn't even care enough to get out of the cold at this point. Instead, he tongues his cigarette and shrinks back against the wall as someone comes his way.

It's a guy that had been in the bar. He was there when Maddox arrived, but he hadn't paid him much attention. He doesn't look cold in his own jacket and jeans. He stops a few feet from Maddox, sweeping back his dark brown hair out of his eyes and glancing down the alley as if waiting for someone.

Maddox ignores him, scrunching up further. He's still got half a pack of cigarettes to go through if he feels like it. He can do anything if he feels like it now. The thought should be liberating, but it just makes him angrier.

"Hey, can I bum a cigarette?"

The guy is next to Maddox now, hair falling back in his big, dark eyes. He's a few inches shorter than Maddox but built thicker with his square shoulders, the shape echoed in his jaw. He's got his hands stuffed in his jacket pockets now and he rocks back on his heels for a second as Maddox contemplates him.

Without a word, Maddox pulls out his crumpled box and taps out a cigarette, handing it over to the guy. The guy doesn't ask for a light, pulling a lighter from his back pocket instead.

Maddox's hair is damp and he can feel the mist on the back of his neck too now, colder when the breeze picks up down the alley. He fights back a shiver and takes a drag of his cigarette, eyes half on the guy next to him now.

The guy is decently attractive, he thinks, eyes flitting over his face, from his crooked nose to his pale, pink lips closed around the end of the cigarette. His hair is cut messily, like he did it himself, uneven lengths on different sides, too long in the front. He watches the guy's tongue dart out to wet his lips as he takes the cigarette away and leans his head back against the wall.

It's been too long, Maddox thinks. He watches the guy and wonders what it would take to get him to go down on him. He doesn't even know if the guy is interested in other guys, but it never hurt to ask. He can't bring himself to, though, and he looks away. No one would want to with him anyway; Joel had made that perfectly clear.

His cigarette is almost finished and he's just thinking about grabbing one last beer before going home to see if there's anything left of Joel's to break when the guy beside him shifts, shoving his hair out of his eyes again with a rough hand. When Maddox looks over he finds the guy watching him intently. It doesn't make him nervous or excited or anything. He's lost all ability to care. If apathy was a religion he'd be a god.

"Long day?" the guy asks.

Maddox scrunches up in his jacket in the cold, staring down at his cigarette instead. It's almost burned down to his fingertips but he doesn't smash it out yet.

He doesn't reply to the guy either. He doesn't need to reply. He's not going to spill his sob story to some random stranger he met in an alley between the trash cans and the stray dog rooting in the corner. It's pathetic enough that he even cares about all of this. He doesn't need to relive it again.

The guy moves first, turning towards Maddox as Maddox fingers his cigarette and wonders how much penalty there would be to break the lease on his apartment. Every fucking thing in it reminds him of Joel and how much of an asshole he really is.

"Hey," the guy says and Maddox glances at him, thinking he sees a flash of silver in the guy's mouth, maybe a tongue piercing. "You want to get another drink?"

Maddox pauses. He thinks maybe the guy is coming on to him, but maybe he's also hallucinating. It's been seven months since he's done this, even talked to another guy with sex as a possible outcome. In a way it had been nice, not having to guess, knowing he'd have someone to go home to. That had all been a joke.

"No," he mutters, finally replying to the guy, using his voice for what seems like the first time in days. It's rough from all the cigarettes, scratchy and low.

The guy isn't insulted, licking his lips again before raising the cigarette and taking a drag. Maddox watches him, watches the way his tongue flicks out first, dragging over his bottom lip. He hasn't been with anyone in months, and it's not like it would take much to get him going at this point.

4

"You wanna fuck then?" the guy asks, plain and simple as if asking for another cigarette. His eyes are big and dark (interested) in the flickering light of the streetlamp and Maddox watches him shove his hair back again, casually, as if he's said nothing out of the ordinary.

As blunt as it is, Maddox just contemplates it for a minute. He doesn't know this guy at all, and neither of them has even really expressed interest, but Maddox is a little drunk, and he's sure he could get into it.

The guy, on the other hand, takes a step towards Maddox, eyes roaming over his collarbone and the tattoo peeking out there. It's the look in his eyes, dark and purposeful, the flicker of something more than just a passing interest, as he meets Maddox's, that sends the first shiver down his back that's not due to the mist pressing in around him.

The guy's mouth curves slightly as he watches Maddox, fingers playing with his cigarette. "What do you say?" he asks, tongue flicking out to wet his bottom lip again.

Maddox feels something in his chest sort of seize up at the question, but he doesn't want to know why. He can do anything he wants now, and that includes fucking random guys he meets outside of bars.

"Okay," he says finally, stubbing out what's left of his cigarette on the wall behind him. The crumpled butt drops to the wet pavement. His fingers are cold and he pushes his hands into his pockets as the guy's mouth curls into a smirk and he nods towards the end of the alley.

Maddox doesn't reply but steps away from the wall and the guy joins him, rough fingers brushing against the bit of exposed skin at his wrist. His glance slides sideways, eyes on the guy's mouth, the way his hair is already back in his eyes. They don't need to speak as their eyes meet again and Maddox doesn't question his decision for a second as they leave the alleyway together.

They go to Maddox's apartment because it's closest, and, for the first time in three days, he's not thinking about Joel. He's not thinking of the cruel way he'd just said, 'By the way, I've been fucking someone else for two months.' He's thinking about the guy next to him, the one with the uneven, floppy hair that he periodically shoves out of his eyes. He's thinking that he doesn't even know his name but he doesn't care in the slightest.

They haven't even kissed, but the walk to his apartment is enough for Maddox. He likes that he knows nothing about this guy. He likes that he just wants to fuck him. He hasn't done that in a long time. It makes him feel free, like it doesn't fucking matter if he knows the guy or not.

He can feel himself growing warmer as they walk, a thrum of something exciting coursing through his body, the cold no longer affecting him as he starts to picture what it'll be like once they get to his place. His eyes are on the guy's fingers, the pads rough with calluses from he doesn't know what. He doesn't need to know, and that's the best part.

He wants another cigarette as they reach his building and he opens the door and the guy brushes up against him as he passes through, lingering a second too long against Maddox, and Maddox swallows slowly. It's like some kind of electric charge passes through his body at the touch that isn't even a real touch, barely there, a slight pressure against his side.

Letting out a breath, he leads the way to the elevator, hyper aware of every movement they're making now. His fingers still itch for a cigarette, but he masters the impulse as he presses the button to the elevator and takes a small, sharp breath as the guy presses up against his back, mouth barely brushing against his ear.

"What floor?" the guy asks, voice low, and Maddox wants to lean into the warmth of his breath on his ear. It's doing things to him as they stand there, the guy's hands sliding to his hips as if waiting for his invitation.

Maddox hasn't done this in a long time but he still remembers how it goes, how it used to go before Joel told him he was too much of a slut, before they'd actually started dating. Maybe he used to sleep around too much but it hadn't stopped him from being faithful.

As the anger builds again Maddox forces it away with the ding of the elevator. This isn't about Joel. This is about him and what he wants.

"Seventh," he replies as he steps inside, the guy following step for step, fingers brushing against a sliver of bare skin as Maddox pushes the button and the doors slide shut.

He shouldn't be surprised, but he is when the guy shoves him up against the back of the elevator as it starts to rumble upwards. For a second he's disoriented at the assault of feelings that flood his mind —a flash of shock, followed by guilt, then finally overridden by a burning desire to just stop feeling anything.

The elevator is rising and the guy's mouth is on his neck, hot and demanding, echoing the push of his hands under Maddox's shirt, rough, calloused fingers sliding over his stomach, and Maddox sucks in a breath. Reaching down, his fingers wrap around the guy's and he pushes, shoving him back so he's the one in control. He's sick of not being in control. The guy doesn't protest one bit, eyes darting eagerly over his face, mouth half open and breath hot against Maddox's lips as he presses their mouths together.

It's not a finessed kiss in any way, rough and raw, teeth biting and tongues sucking whatever heat they can find. Maddox's hand is still wrapped around the guy's wrist, pressing it into the elevator wall as they're rushed upwards.

"What-what's your name?" the guy pants.

Maddox pulls his mouth away to take a gulp of air and the elevator jerks to a stop. "Maddox," he mutters, jerking the guy's wrist forward as the doors slide open and they stumble out.

He glances down the hall but it's empty. His neighbors aren't much of night owls anyway.

His apartment is down a few doors, and he feels the guy behind him, his free hand sliding to his hip and squeezing. A strange thrill runs down Maddox's spine and he pulls his keys from his pocket and fits them into the lock.

"I'm Rory," the guy says without prompting, breath hot against Maddox's ear.

Maddox shoves the door open, barely pulling the keys from the lock before it's slammed shut. The dim, front hall light flips on. He's got Rory boxed up against the door.

Rory's eyes are a beautiful hazel color and his lips are a light, rose-pink. There's a dark freckle under his left eye just above his cheek and his hair falls unevenly into his eyes. Maddox thinks vaguely that he probably doesn't look much more put together

7

when the apartment behind him is strewn with takeout boxes, unclean shirts and mismatched shoes.

Maddox goes for Rory's mouth, wanting to feel it, feel the difference between him and Joel, even if he's not supposed to be thinking about Joel. There's a clear difference from the very beginning, as Rory doesn't hesitate to push at Maddox's clothes, pushing his jacket off and tearing off the dirty tee shirt underneath.

Rory's hands skim over Maddox's thin waist, the pale skin, brushing over the tattoo that rises up on his hip bone and swirls around his back, the cherry tree Joel used to laugh at. He knows Rory's fingers are tracing the petals even though he can't see, too busy biting at Rory's mouth, rough and hard, pressing him back against the door until he's close enough to feel the bulge in Rory's jeans.

Panting, he glances down, hating the squeeze of uncertainty that grips his heart for a moment, the thought that it can't be for him, but Rory chooses that moment to reach for Maddox's neck, steering it to the side so he can nip at his neck, teeth scraping down and a hot mouth closing over the skin and sucking until Maddox slips, pushing his hips into Rory's and groaning as a hot lick of friction darts through him.

"Mmm," Rory hums, mouth never leaving Maddox's neck as his hands go for the button on his jeans, jerking his hips forward unexpectedly. He gets the zipper down before Maddox even opens his eyes and his hand shoves underneath, cupping Maddox through his underwear.

Maddox's hands slip against where they're pressed against the door, boxing Rory in. One falls to Rory's hip, squeezing tightly and pulling him in flush even as Rory palms him, drawing out a low moan.

"Fuck," Rory mutters, and Maddox agrees, rutting into his hand.

He can feel the flush crawling up his skin, pink rushing up to his cheeks, the back of his neck, and, for the first time in months, he doesn't feel embarrassed about it.

Rory's mouth slides up quicker than Maddox expects, biting at his lower lip before sliding his tongue inside Maddox's mouth, exchanging hot air between them, a frantic motion that Maddox loses track of within seconds.

"I wanna suck you off," Rory pants a moment later, hand still wrapped around Maddox's cock, grip firm and hot, and Maddox would never argue. "Let me suck you off."

"Fuck yes," Maddox replies in one huffed breath, watching with a flicker of fascination as Rory drops to his knees without a second's hesitation, hands pulling Maddox's jeans down his thin hips to bunch around his ankles.

He almost feels exposed, standing in his living room, surrounded by last night's Chinese boxes, the couch that is currently buried in jackets and shirts, the stacks of unorganized DVDs strewn around the TV, but as soon as Rory licks a stripe up his cock he forgets everything.

His mind is cloudy and all he can feel is the hotness, the slick, wet slide of Rory's mouth on his cock. He bites down on his lip as he watches; watches Rory take him in, back and forth, sucking and licking. Rory's hand is wet when it wraps around the base of Maddox's cock, stroking and pulling, rubbing over the hard prick until Maddox can feel the heat rising all over his body.

"God, fuck," Maddox mumbles as Rory tongues the head of his cock, almost a teasing slide of his tongue. "Jesus Christ, your mouth, fucking fuck." He doesn't know what he's saying, reaching down to tangle his fingers in Rory's dark hair. It's soft to the touch, clean and shiny, and Maddox's fingers clench as he gasps sharply.

Rory's mouth is either extremely talented or Maddox has gone way too long without getting any, or it could be a little of both. Either way, Maddox clenches his teeth as he tries not to choke Rory, but a part of him, that little reckless part that even thought this was a good idea, doesn't care at all about this stranger.

Rory makes a noise, soft but insistent, and he pulls back before Maddox can protest, raising his eyes up and Maddox stares down. Rory's mouth is puffy and red, and Maddox just wants his cock back inside it, wants to fuck his throat until it's raw. Rory's staring up at him, though, hot breath puffing over his prick, and Maddox closes his eyes as blood thuds south.

"Fuck me," Rory pants, voice rough but firm.

Maddox opens his eyes, meeting Rory's eyes, and he hates that he hesitates, hates that he stops to think about it. He shouldn't be thinking about anything.

So he grabs Rory's upper arm and drags him off his knees, pushing him over to the couch. There's nowhere to sit on it, so Maddox steers him to the backside, pressing him against it. His hard cock rubs against Rory's ass slowly, torturously, and he wonders why Rory still has his pants on after all of this.

"Take off your pants," he orders him. "I'll be right back."

He won't admit to scrambling to the bathroom, glancing back only once to see Rory drop his pants unceremoniously and kick them away.

He fumbles through drawers, trying to find the right one, pushing aside combs and half-empty bottles of gel and toothpaste. In the furthest drawer from the door he finds the box that Joel left, probably as a hurtful reminder, but Maddox just rips it open and pulls out a condom. He snatches the lube out with it and hurries back to the living room.

Rory stands by the couch, completely naked, cock already hard and waiting as Maddox returns.

Pushing him back against the couch, Maddox gets the condom open and on before he flips open the lube. He fumbles when Rory presses back against him, ass rocking back against his cock. He needs to take control, he thinks, shoving Rory's hips back against the couch, tearing his eyes away from a freckle on Rory's hip. It's in the vague shape of Florida, he thinks, shaking himself and slicking his fingers with lube.

He doesn't go slow as he pushes in the first finger, watching Rory's back arch, hearing the moan he lets out, like he just can't get enough.

"Yeah, fuck, more," Rory says, pushing back against him. "Fuck yes, Madd, fuck yes."

Maddox pushes in a second finger despite the way Rory whines, like he just needs more. A shiver of something unfamiliar runs down Maddox's spine, dropping into his stomach as he watches Rory rock backwards. He shakes it away, though, pulling his fingers out and replacing them with his cock.

Rory is mumbling profanities as Maddox pushes in through the tight, throbbing muscles that clench around his already pulsing cock. He's hard as fuck, harder than he can remember ever being with Joel. He attributes it to this being the first time in months he's been inside anyone else, had anyone else gripping his thigh and begging him to move, to go faster, to fuck him as hard as he can.

Rory's not a quiet one, cursing every time Maddox moves, every time he slides in harder, rocks deeper inside him. He keeps up a stream of commentary on how fucking amazing Maddox's cock is, how good it feels, how much more he wants.

"Fuck, fuck, touch me, shit, please, holy shit," Rory mumbles, head bowed forward, and for the first time, Maddox notices a tattoo dropping below his hairline, hidden by his hair. He can't tell what it is exactly but it's all black, like a shadow etched onto his skin.

Rory rocks back onto Maddox's cock harder, forcing him to go faster, to fuck him deeply. The hot flush that spreads over Maddox's body is becoming nearly unbearable and he grits his teeth as he thrusts sharply into Rory. His hands are pressing long, red bruises into Rory's hips, but Rory isn't complaining. If anything, he seems to like the flare of pain, the reminder for later.

Maddox reaches for Rory's cock with barely any time to spare, gripping hard as Rory comes without warning, with only a hitch of breath, the hand clenched around the back of the couch going white as he grips the cushion.

"Fuck yes," Rory hisses, still pushing back onto Maddox's cock, and Maddox lets go then. He lets go of everything, anything he was holding back, pounding Rory against the couch, and Rory doesn't complain at all, groaning and panting down at the cushions.

"Shit!" Maddox bites out as his stomach clenches hotly and his fingers dig into Rory's hip, and he comes, hips jerking into Rory. It's a crashing wave of heat that washes over him, sweeping through his stomach and tingling in his fingertips as he finally releases Rory's hips. The red marks press into Rory's pale skin as Maddox steps away.

Rory is still cursing under his breath as he turns around, glancing at Maddox. "Shit, that was good," he says, a smile curling the corner of his mouth, and Maddox lets out a short breath.

Maddox wants a cigarette and he backtracks to where his jeans are bunched on the floor near the door. Digging in the pocket, he comes up with the dented pack and taps one out. When he glances back, Rory is just leaning against the couch, still completely naked, and he makes no effort to cover up but neither does Maddox.

"This place all yours?" Rory asks as Maddox lights the cigarette and takes a grateful inhale of nicotine.

Maddox's eyes are drawn to the messy room, the bedroom door ajar behind Rory, the coffee pot in the kitchen still half-full from that morning.

"I'm moving," he says instead because he realizes as he stands there that there's no way he wants to stay there.

Rory nods after a second and reaches for his shirt instead, pulling it on.

Maddox doesn't say anything as Rory dresses, buttoning his jeans and running a hand through his hair. It sticks up messily in places but Rory doesn't seem to care. Maddox takes another drag of his cigarette and watches Rory pick up his jacket and sling it over his shoulder.

Rory casts him a short glance before making a detour to the kitchen counter and scribbling something down on a piece of paper there.

He brings it over to Maddox and presses it into his free hand. Maddox arches a skeptical eyebrow, but Rory just smirks at him.

"Call me when you're in your new place," he says, stealing Maddox's cigarette for a second and taking a drag. Maddox stares for a second. "Seriously."

Rory saunters to the door and leaves with an interested quirk of his eyebrow before he disappears.

Maddox stares at his cigarette clutched between his fingers, and it takes him a second to grab his jeans and pull them on haphazardly. He flops down on the couch a minute later and reaches into the pile of newspapers that goes back the last three days, coming out with the classifieds.

Taking a drag of his cigarette, he flips it open to the apartments section and settles down, stuffing the crumpled note in his hand inside his pocket and he sinks into the darkness but it's not quite as dark as before.

If you enjoyed this story, you can sign up for a free membership at ForbiddenFiction.com and discuss it with other readers and the

author at the *Cigarette Burns* story page at
http://forbiddenfiction.com/story/EEG-1.000043.

We do our best to proof all our work, but if you spot a text error we missed,
please let us know via our website Contact Form at
http://forbiddenfiction.com/contact.

Naked in the Sun

Naked in the Sun

I held Daniel's hand as we walked down the steps of the ophthalmologist's office, although by now he no longer needed me to help him navigate, and I'd learned to stop assuming he always needed my hands or my eyes to get around. He'd grown adept at the cane as his eyesight had diminished. Holding hands was now as sign of affection again, rather than a way for Daniel to navigate his surroundings while acclimating himself to the rapid loss of eyesight. We were leaving the doctor's office after being told what we already knew: Daniel was now completely blind. He'd developed early-onset macular degeneration; not only had it hit early, it hit fast, and there were no treatment options available. Within a year, his vision was gone. We were stuck with this for the rest of our lives.

I reassured myself by remembering that it could have been worse —he could have developed cancer that went undiagnosed until it was too late. He could have been in a car accident, slipped into a coma, and I would have been at the mercy of his family over visitation rights, even though we had been together for over a decade. Daniel could no longer see me, but at least he was still here. Although we'd had to make some adjustments to our life, none of them felt like an inconvenience, because I was grateful that he was still with me.

Daniel was more silent about his own grieving and coping. I knew he was depressed. He'd spent fifteen years working as a computer programmer, and loved every minute of it. As his eyesight had deteriorated, his workplace had made a number of accommodations for him, but his visual decline happened so rapidly that they were unable to keep up. The human resources department had placed him on paid medical leave while the company finished upgrading his workstation and making other adaptations around the building to meet Daniel's needs. While his joblessness was temporary, it seemed to affect him even more than losing his sight. He hated being alone during the day. Usually, I came home on my lunch hour and dropped him off to spend the afternoon with his sister. Despite his obvious discontent, Daniel rarely complained, just grew more and more withdrawn. I did the best I could to support him, hoping one day he'd either be willing to see a therapist, or snap out of his depression.

As much as I wanted to pretend that this disease hadn't had some effect on our relationship, I could only be in so much denial. We were both helpless to stop the disease, and I'd overcompensated by overprotecting him. Losing his job and independence had been bad enough. Daniel wasn't thrilled to have me refusing to let him do chores, or attempting to cut his food for him, or assuming he couldn't get anywhere without my assistance. I'd only been trying to help, but I'd made the problem worse. It hadn't been enough to break us, but I still had to check my own behavior sometimes, and remember that the dynamic, strong man I'd fallen in love with hadn't changed just because he couldn't see.

Daniel's melancholia seemed surprisingly absent as we stepped out of the cool building and into the spring air. I had assumed he'd be downhearted at the finality of the diagnosis, but I thought I saw a smile as he lifted his face to the sun and took a deep breath. He was surveying the surroundings in his own way, exploring without sight the sprawling medical campus so large that it contained a park in the middle, complete with statues, a pond, benches, and food vendors.

"Can we stop and get some falafel?" Daniel asked.

At first, I was puzzled by his question, still forgetting that though he had lost his vision, he had his other senses, and that over time they had sharpened. Of course he could smell the falafel stand that I could still only see.

I checked my watch: one o'clock. I had taken a long lunch at noon in order to drive Daniel to the ophthalmologist, but needed to be back at the office by two for an important conference call. Still, we had time for a quick lunch, especially because his sister lived near the hospital, so it wouldn't be out of the way for me to drop him off.

"Sure. Do you want me to read the menu aloud for you? I doubt they have a braille one, but I can check."

"No, no, just order me some falafel. I'm not picky."

I pointed Daniel in the direction of a bench, then went and ordered our food. We ate in silence for a while. I watched Daniel; I had irrationally assumed that when he lost his sight, somehow his face would become blank, but his features were as expressive as ever. He ran his hand along the bench to take in the texture, giggled at a joke in the distance I could barely hear. Despite the finality of the doctor's words, he seemed more at peace than he'd been in months.

"Will you describe the park for me?"

"The sprinklers are spraying all the flower beds, which is ridiculous for this time of day; it should really be done in the morning or the evening. The peonies are in full bloom, pink and white. The grass has just been mowed. Can you smell it?"

"Yes, yes, I can. How many people are walking around?"

"Not too many. Mostly people hurrying back from their lunch breaks, a few students hanging around. It's not particularly crowded."

Daniel started tracing his hand up and down the inside of my thigh. Before I had time to ask what he was doing, my cock was fluttering, pressing uncomfortably against my fly.

"Andy, I'm horny."

At first, I was more surprised than aroused. As Daniel's vision waned, so did his sex drive. I was exhilarated to see part of his old self. But rather than seize the moment, I checked my watch. It was 1:20.

"I'm sorry. I wish we could go fool around, but I have to be on a conference call in forty minutes. I don't have time to drive all the way home and have sex before I need to be back at the office, especially if you want to spend the afternoon at your sister's place."

Daniel turned toward me and grinned. "Then I guess you'll have to fuck me here."

My mind started racing with what could go wrong if we got caught. "What? And risk getting thrown in jail for public indecency? You're being ridiculous." My job wouldn't approve, that's for sure. And I had no idea how Daniel would handle it if we got arrested and were taken to jail. Almost immediately, I mentally smacked myself for once again assuming he wouldn't be able to handle it.

"You're the one being ridiculous if you're going to pass up the first time I've been horny in two months."

I looked around. It really wasn't that crowded. We could probably get away with it. My mind was made up when I spied some large shrubbery a few feet away.

"Okay, but I want us to hide in some bushes. I don't want to miss this conference call because I got arrested."

"Fair enough."

I guided Daniel over to the shrubs, helped him to the ground. Once stable, he pounced, knocking me off balance, flat on my back, arms pinned to the earth. I was ashamed to realize that I was surprised by his assertiveness. It suddenly occurred to me how often my sexual fantasies had involved me being in control, and being excessively tender and gentle. I hurried to turn my thoughts back to Daniel and the attention he was giving me. This moment was too important to be ruined by my own distractions and insecurities.

Daniel started unbuttoning my shirt as his tongue delved between my teeth. His erection was pressed directly against mine, and I thought I was going to burst from joy and arousal. Daniel was grinding against me, his smooth fingers pinching my nipples, teeth taking greedy bites from my neck as I writhed. He couldn't see, but he had my body memorized.

"I want to suck you off," he whispered. "And then I want to fuck you in the ass."

I opened my mouth to speak, but Daniel shook his head. Placing three fingers under my chin, he pushed my lips closed. "I know what you're about to ask. Don't. Yes, this is exactly what I want to do. Just let go and have fun. Please."

I tried to unbuckle my belt, but Daniel, preferring to take control, pushed my hands away and removed my shoes and pants himself. I started to panic, realizing I was completely naked, in a public park on a medical complex. I tried to breathe, trust in the concealing powers of the shrubbery, and relaxed once I felt Daniel's tongue licking my cock. I moaned, but quickly stifled my voice, not wanting to draw attention to us. Daniel slid the tip of his tongue up and down the shaft, brushed his dry lips against the head, teased my balls with his fingers before finally giving me what I wanted: his entire mouth surround my dick. I gripped the grass, pulled it out of the dirt as I squirmed, got soil beneath my fingernails. Daniel thrust his head quickly, greedily making up for months of depressive celibacy.

As Daniel sucked and licked me, he pressed a finger up to my ass, putting pressure against the hole, refusing to enter, just teasing me. I felt hot sparks spread out through my muscles and skin, beads of sweat bursting out at my temples.

"Please, please put your finger inside me. I need it."

Daniel pulled his mouth off my cock. The breeze that went by left my dick throbbing for his warm mouth. I thrust my hips toward his face, silently begging for him to keep sucking.

"Nothing enters your ass except my cock, understand?"

"Yes."

"Good." Point made, he resumed his work, and I knew I didn't have much longer. When Daniel reached up towards my nipples again, I lost the ability to hold back. One twist, and I couldn't help but let out a yelp as I shot cum into Daniel's eager mouth.

Daniel stood up gently and slowly undressed, making sure I was paying attention as he revealed his chest, his ass, his cock, his entire gorgeous body to my eyes and to the bright afternoon sun.

"Get down!" I gasped. "You might fall."

My stomach tightened. I knew I'd said the wrong thing the second it slipped through my lips.

"My legs work just fine, you know." Daniel's tone was hard, and I was worried I'd completely killed the moment. My body was still throbbing with excitement, though. I didn't want to stop.

"I know, I know, I'm sorry. I just... look, please, get down."

"Why? Maybe I'm enjoying the way this feels, the way the sun hits my skin."

"Somebody might see you!"

"So what if they do?" he asked. He remained standing a few seconds longer, defiant, but finally dropped to the ground.

Another thought occurred to me. I hated to say anything about it, lest Daniel think I was being too nitpicky after my first outburst, but I knew I had to bring it up. "Hey, I don't mean to ruin the fun, but we don't have any lube."

Feeling around for his clothes, Daniel finally found his jacket and reached into a pocket, pulling out a sample-sized bottle.

"I've been horny from the minute I woke up, but you'd already left for the office. I could have masturbated, but I wanted to wait for you. I've had this bottle lying around for a while, and I grabbed it just in case I had the opportunity to use it." I watched him lube up his cock until it glistened in the sun. "Now turn over. I want to fuck you from behind."

I rolled onto my hands and knees, felt Daniel's cock slide inside me. I'd missed this feeling, the fullness. I'd missed the groan Daniel always made when entering me, the way his nails dug into my hips. I'd missed the feeling of his balls colliding with my ass, the particular *smack* they made on my flesh. As Daniel thrust into me, I could feel the sun beating down all over my skin, filling my body with even more heat.

Over the top of the hedge, I could see a woman walking past. Daniel let out a sharp grunt and she stopped, turning slightly in our direction. Part of me started to panic, thinking that we were about to be discovered and turned in to the police. But after a moment of listening, the woman turned back and went on her way. As I watched her wander off and knew we were safe, relief mixed with sexual energy made my ass start constricting with orgasm, the fullness overwhelming my body and my muscles quaking as the pure sex energy poured out of every pore. Thanks to the sudden spasm in my ass, Daniel's cock gave one final, huge throb and he shouted as he exploded inside me.

I curled up with Daniel briefly, but jumped back up when I realized I only had fifteen minutes before my conference call was scheduled to begin.

"Come on, we need to get going. Your sister will be wondering where we are, and I'm going to be late."

"My sister won't miss me. Call into work and tell them you got food poisoning. Or that some emergency came up with me while we were at the hospital."

"I can't do that!"

"You already broke one rule today. Why not one more? Play hooky. Let's not waste this beautiful day." He gave me a smile that was both teasing and pleading at the same time.

"How come you're so happy and playful? I thought that with the doctor's diagnosis, you'd be even more depressed than you were before."

"Actually, I feel free. Losing my sight was difficult, but now that the process is over, I'm liberated. There's no more waiting around for the inevitable, because the inevitable has already happened. I feel like I can begin my life again, and I want to celebrate."

"Then let's celebrate. I suppose they can make this conference call without me."

I helped up my beautiful partner and handed him his clothes. We drove home, and though he could navigate the house just fine, I carried Daniel into the bedroom.

If you enjoyed this story, you can sign up for a free membership at ForbiddenFiction.com and discuss it with other readers and the author at the *Naked in the Sun* story page at http://forbiddenfiction.com/story/DM1-1.000131.

We do our best to proof all our work, but if you spot a text error we missed, please let us know via our website Contact Form at http://forbiddenfiction.com/contact.

Bare Blue Steel

Chapter 1:
Poker Face

Leaning against the low wall, Jimmy tried to be still, but his leg kept juddering up and down, a tapping movement that scraped against the polyester of the sports bag at his feet. That rapid rustle was the only other sound apart from a quiet burring that came from the trees. Bird or insect, Jimmy wasn't sure, but here, on the vacant scrubby land, he could hear everything with a startling clarity.

How far does the sound of a gunshot travel? he wondered. This was still London. Not some lonely field with nothing but the birds to flap away when it went off. That's always what happened in movies, wasn't it? When a gun goes off, a flock of birds, flapping frantically, take to the air. Was it meant to, Jimmy wondered, symbolise death, the soul leaving the body, taking flight upwards to heaven?

Above him, the sky was gray, a block of indistinguishable cloud. Heavenly was not the right word. He'd heard somewhere once that Hell wasn't a place of fire and torture, but an absence of God, of no grace and beauty. Of numbness.

Hello Hell, Jimmy thought.

He looked at his watch. Still five minutes to go. He'd arrived ahead of schedule, an instinctive habit he was beginning to regret, because it meant more thinking time. Waiting time. Tom was a spot-on type; he'd always told Jimmy that if they wanted you there at 5 to 7, then they'd say 5 to 7. So Tom would arrive at 2.30 pm on the dot.

If he was coming.

It's a scenario that Jimmy'd seen played out in countless movies; right then he couldn't remember which ones, but the scene is awfully familiar. The tension, the drama of will-he-won't-he; or

23

maybe the audience was wondering who the bloke on screen was waiting for? What's going to happen in this bleak landscape? Like in the movies, there was no soundtrack, only amplified sounds of nature, or white noise, the buzz of a lifeless desert. But there were no funky camera angles in real life, no extreme close-ups. Just a heaviness on Jimmy's chest and shoulders.

Jimmy rubbed the bag with his foot. Something heavy shifted, eased its weight towards Jimmy. He pressed against it with his ankle, and knew it was the gun.

The gun had been sitting at the bottom of Tom's drawers in the bedroom, wrapped loosely in a light blue shirt. Jimmy had only seen Tom wear it once. Had Jimmy not been in a fit of ironing and cleaning, he'd never have found it, and perhaps Tom would have moved it elsewhere when Jimmy was at the pub on shift. All Jimmy had done was push some of Tom's folded shirts aside. The unusual weight of one of them, slightly crumpled, had raised Jimmy's eyebrow. He'd placed his hand on it, feeling the large lump, and lifted the shirt and the object it concealed. The material had rolled down like a curtain, and though it was still covered, it was clear from the outline that the object was a gun.

Tom was away for three days, something to do with work. Business deals, somewhere in the direction of Birmingham. Discussion of Tom's business was always nebulous, and a topic Jimmy had soon realised Tom didn't fancy talking about. He'd only ever complain about this wanker he had to call, or the daft muppet he was working with, but no names, no one ever brought back to the flat. That part Jimmy could understand—Tom wasn't very 'out', though he was more than ready to pop a dickhead in the mouth if they gave him lip about it.

Tom never had, not to Jimmy's knowledge, but he'd come pretty close. First time they'd gone to a club together. Mixed club; gay, straight, anyone was welcome, or so it had claimed. Some guy still had looked askance at Tom's large hand on Jimmy's back. Tom had rounded on him, rough words and chest forward like a rooster. The bloke had scampered off, and the act had cast an invisible shield over both of them for the rest of the night. Jimmy gave Tom the best blow job he'd probably ever had when they got home. But they never went back to that club.

It took Jimmy about half an hour to get the courage to unwrap the gun—it sat shrouded on the coffee table, in between the tissue box and the pile of local newspapers, as if it were a half-dried plate with a tea towel thrown over it, abandoned to answer the door.

When he did, he straightened his back, lowered himself carefully to the edge of the couch, and made sure his hands were steady. He picked up the bundle, and peeled back the material.

The shirt dropped away, and there it was: a black handgun, some kind of a revolver. Jimmy almost waited for the dramatic piano chord, the moment of the close-up on the actor's face, that pause where everything hung in the air. Jimmy's heart still kept beating, he still kept breathing, and the kitchen clock kept ticking, ticking, ticking.

It was both larger and smaller than Jimmy had ever imagined. Smooth metal of an industrial precision. He'd never seen a gun in real life. He didn't think of the muskets he saw that one time at some museum as weapons. Behind glass, with their carved handles and inlaid designs, they'd seemed bold and beautiful, but harmless; just props.

This one... The only way Jimmy knew it was real was its weight. Water pistols from childhood were as light as air—filled with water he could have still thrown it about casually. There was nothing casual about the one in his hands. Jimmy couldn't imagine the damage its bullets could do; this was heavy enough to hurt to someone if you hit them with it.

He didn't try and open it to see if it was loaded.

Jimmy put it down, and tucked his hands under his arm pits. He pressed his knees together, and breathed hard as the blinders he'd put on himself ebbed away in the stark light of the room.

When Jimmy and Tom met, Jimmy had just started working at the White Stag. The pub ran a monthly poker tournament, an event which the otherwise noisy Stag regarded with a pride and a touch of solemnity. Richard the manager shoved Jimmy into the section they cordoned off for it, telling him there would be little trouble, that the players were there for the game, not for some argy-bargy that the pool room tended to attract.

Jimmy first saw him saunter into the pub in a pin-stripe suit, and as Tom, thus far unnamed in Jimmy's mind, sat down, Jimmy noticed his shoulders. Broad, the kind you wanted to rest your head on, or squeeze, or worship. Next thing he saw was his hair. He wore it in the 70s style, thick and full, held in place with what might have been brylcreem once upon a time but was probably VO5. He emanated an aura of cool mystery, the perfect picture of a 1940s gangster, but without the dramatic black and white picture.

Not like he was an actual gangster. They, Jimmy reckoned, wouldn't be hanging out in a place like the White Stag. Kind of a pity, might have made the place that much cooler.

He mentally smacked himself for that thought. Daft bugger.

Tom shook hands with the players. Images from *The Cincinnati Kid* played through Jimmy's mind—there was a familiarity, but a calm, cool guardedness to the way they looked at each other. The game hadn't started and they were already sizing each other up. Only thing that was missing, for the most part, were the sharp suits and vests. Tom wore a vest with a blue satin front, and some of the much older blokes did as well, but others were in a variety of gear, from wide collared shirts and track suits to jeans. Tom sat with a straight back, perfect poise. Water could have rolled down the lines of his body in perfect, unbroken drops.

Jimmy knew bugger all about poker—just what he'd picked from stuff he'd seen on screen. Fold, showing your hand, something about matched pairs of cards and runs. Aces win. The game itself became dull to watch, but when Jimmy wasn't working, he looked at Tom's table. At Tom. Tom played with the steadiest face of all the players. Beneath all the others, Jimmy detected the shifts, mostly of annoyance, but nothing but a serene pleasantness exuded from Tom.

Still, he lost, and from the zero chips he had left at the end of the night, quite badly too it seemed. He didn't stay for a drink, but he left the pub with a secretive smile. Jimmy watched him go, checking out his shoulders, back, his arse... and thought *Oh well.*

Jimmy said to Richard, "Thought that bloke had it made."

"Tom you mean? Yeah, he's pretty good. Guess not tonight."

Jimmy repeated the name in his head five times to remember it. "He here often?"

"Yeah, a bit." Richard eyed Jimmy carefully. "You checking him out?"

Jimmy made no secret he was gay, but the White Stag wasn't a gay pub. So he just shrugged.

"Well, if you were, not going to be a problem. If you're his type, at least."

Richard winked, and left Jimmy to wipe up tables. A pleased flutter fell down his chest as he tidied up, giving consoling nods to the loser and smiles of congrats to the winners.

He hadn't expected to see Tom for days, but when he left the pub, ciggie in hand, preparing to light it, there Tom was, leaning back on the brick wall, staring up at the street light.

Richard's words in mind, Jimmy went up to him. Tom saw his approach, and gave a quick smile; only his lips, but it seemed to reach his eyes.

"You were at the game?" Jimmy ventured.

"Yeah. And you were at the bar."

Jimmy lit his ciggie, ignoring the excited bubble that the bloke had noticed him at all.

"Seemed a bad night for you," Jimmy said.

"Yeah, couldn't bluff my way out of it. Old fella at my table was pretty sharp."

"Sorry to hear it."

Tom shrugged. "You win some, you lose some." He regarded Jimmy again. "You just started here."

A statement, not a question. Jimmy said, "Yeah, few days back."

"Didn't think I'd seen you. What's your name?"

"Jimmy. Yourself?" Even though he knew it already.

Tom put his hand out. "Tom."

A solid pump of his hand, a strong grip.

Jimmy asked, "You a regular, then?"

"For the games. Play in the pool tournaments as well. Poker though, that's where it's really at for me."

Jimmy thought of Tom in a fitted waist coat and white shirt, bent over the pool table (that perfect position to grab a good feel of a bloke's arse), cue in hand, how his hand might glide over the polished wood, of its length, of the clatter of balls as they knocked each other. A gorgeous, steely grace. Bond, James Bond, by way of Caine as Jack Carter.

"You any good?"

"Fucking brilliant."

Jimmy sniggered. "Not shy about it, then."

"Why be modest when you can be honest? You got a spare one?"

Jimmy passed him the packet, and held his lighter for Tom, watching his lips purse and contract around the cigarette. Tom's eyes lifted up, and as orange blossomed at the ciggie's tip, those lips grinned, catching Jimmy like a sharp, sensuous hook.

Tom straightened up, inhaled, and breathed out a long slender stream of smoke. "You finished for the night?"

"Yeah."

"Want to get out of here?"

The question was very casual, as if he'd just asked Jimmy the time, but Tom played with the cigarette, slipped it between his lips, his tongue running down the filter end before sliding it back into his mouth.

Jimmy tried to respond in kind, and put his hand on the brick wall, leaning like a hustler, hips forward. "What were you thinking?"

"Got some scotch that could use some company back at mine." Another drag, another flash of the tongue. "If that's your sort of thing."

Jimmy had to stop himself from looking too excited. He said, blandly, "Yeah, that's my sort of thing."

On the walk back to Tom's flat, Tom kept a cool distance. Jimmy tried to match it, but kept thinking that his Converse probably made him look like a hipster twat. Once there, Tom poured the scotch, then put his hand on Jimmy's shoulder, lowering him to the peeling brown leather couch.

They wanked each other off, sipping the scotch and sometimes passing it between their mouths. Jimmy felt all of fourteen—grabby, puppy-eager, especially next to Tom's suave slickness. He even looked cool when he came, and Jimmy had been sure no bloke ever managed that. Afterwards, Tom stripped off Jimmy's clothes, made Jimmy lie with his head in Tom's lap, and with a maddening delicacy hovered his hand over Jimmy's body. His palm and finger tips scarcely touched the skin, raising only the fine hairs. Jimmy held his breath, nervous but entranced by the exploration.

"Wouldn't mind keeping you around, babe," Tom said. Jimmy kissed him, hungry, and started to get hard again.

Chapter 2:
Down the Barrel

That had been it. Jimmy had moved in two weeks later. He began divesting the apartment of the rest of the sagging furniture. Tom said as long Jimmy didn't overdo the Ikea look it was fine. And somehow Jimmy's desire for bean bags and fluffy cushions managed to work with what he thought of as Tom's style, clear lines, heavy colours, black with dark blue. Naturally Jimmy put up his film posters —*The Terminator, Enter the Dragon. The Matrix, Lock, Stock and Two Smoking Barrels, Butch Cassidy and the Sundance Kid.* That was the first lot—Tom would smirk when he'd come home and find another set had replaced them for the next month.

As an ironic gesture, Jimmy bought a print of the dogs playing poker, which got the first raucous laugh from Tom he'd ever had.

"Can take it back if you want," Jimmy said, feeling stupid.

"Nah, babe. It's cute. Really cute."

Tom taught Jimmy the basics of poker—using the strip variety rather than money or chips. Jimmy never mastered the poker face, and always found himself naked to Tom's still clothed body. Not that Tom minded, at all.

"You don't need to learn how, babe," Tom told him once. "I like knowing what you're thinking."

And Tom's unreadable, terribly cool expressions were a fair trade. He surprised Jimmy with random gifts, tasty tricks in bed, and impromptu romantic getaways. Jimmy could never guess what was coming next. Just as much as he never quite knew what Tom's business was up to; when he'd be away, and sometimes, for how long.

Which was... fine, really. It was a bit... odd sometimes when Tom seemed to leave only with wads of cash—he told Jimmy he didn't trust credit card companies and only ever had a savings account. Tom had his reasons, Jimmy told himself, even when he was a bit nervous about that much cash lying around the apartment.

Not that a break-in would have been easy—burglars would have needed a lorry to break through the locks at the front door. Tom told Jimmy that they couldn't be too careful—inner city living had its dangers. A fair point.

Jimmy did prefer it when he had some idea of when Tom was coming back. At the very least, whenever he was away, Tom did call him to check up, see if all was well, and tell him to keep his gorgeous self out of mischief. Which Jimmy thought was sweet, since mischief was never Jimmy's thing. The worse he got into was a bit of pot with friends on nights with the Play Station, or drinking a bit too much and blubbering at Tom how much he fucking loved him. At those times, Tom would brush his hair from his forehead, kiss his temple, and sometimes say it back.

One of those nights, Jimmy hadn't been that weepy, just overly affectionate, kissing Tom's jawline, his neck, when the buzzer rang. Jimmy sighed, murmuring disquietly as Tom eased out of his grasp and pressed the answer button near the door. Tom winked at Jimmy, who put on a pout, knowing full well it wouldn't speed up his return. A bloke's voice Jimmy didn't recognise came through the speaker.

Tom responded. "Hey, Gaz."

"Heya, Tom. Mind if I come up for a bit?" The question sounded like he was trying real hard to be casual.

"Na mate, not a good time. I'll come down to you."

It wasn't the first time Tom had had a conversation in the lobby. Jimmy folded his arms, and waited as Tom left him alone.

Once, when such a visit occurred during the day, Jimmy had crept to the window, peered down onto the carpark below. Tom had been talking with a bloke, tracksuited and blinged up all expressive gestures, while Tom had been doing his usual cool, easy thing. Jimmy had held up his hands as to frame them in a film shot, invent some dialogue in his head about a crazy scheme they were concocting.

This time, Jimmy heard a shout from the window, coming from downstairs. He jerked, broken from his fake sulk, and was about to get up when Tom came back, swiftly opened and closed a drawer, and left with an envelope that Jimmy knew contained one of those wads of cash. Jimmy sat on the edge of the couch until Tom came back.

"What was that about?"

Tom thought a second before saying, "Nothing to worry about, babe. All sorted."

Go on, ask, what's he really up to? a voice in his head said, teasing, intrigued. Jimmy almost heeded it, almost grinned and leaned back on the couch to coax it out of Tom.

Tell me all about it, he almost said, and his cock stirred.

Jimmy shook that away. What a daft thing that would have been. He opened his arms out, and Tom settled next to him, pulling Jimmy to him as he lay back on the couch.

In Tom's arms, head against those broad shoulders, Jimmy knew life was safe, secure, and good.

Why fuck that up by asking dumb questions?

Jimmy didn't put the gun back right away. Whenever he wasn't in the room, the shirt was over it, like a shade covering a bird cage. If he was on the couch, though, he kept the gun in full view. He ate breakfast on his lap, staring at it between bites of toast. Before he went to work in the evening, he hid it on the table's lower shelf. But during the day, the thought of it, like a perfect, frighteningly carved stone, waiting for a single touch to awaken it, dragged at his mind. Pressed at him.

Jimmy drifted through the days with a deep haze wrapped around his body. Each movement was slow. He said little to anyone at work. Customers asked him what the hell his problem was, and Richard wondered aloud if he were sick. Jimmy ignored it. Cigarettes were ashy in mouth.

In the moments when Jimmy was rational, the gun made sense. Practical sense. The door locks, the cash, the visitors—why wouldn't that world that Jimmy had been ignoring not be in the flat itself?

He hadn't really expected that it would be something as undeniable and solid.

So the gun itself was one thing. But the thought of Tom with a gun was something else.

Cops don't carry them over here, Jimmy thought. This is London, not L.A. Trigger-happy, power-mad British bastards at least only had a truncheon. It was the bad guys that had them, and then only some of them—you were more likely to get knifed than shot. Jimmy screwed up his face. Tom wasn't a bad guy. Some might have looked at him and thought he was too smooth, maybe a little dodgy, but he wasn't *really*...

Jimmy thought of Tom cuffing him gently on the cheek, of the way he leaned out the window, ciggie in his mouth, as if he were the squire surveying his lands, not a semi-professional poker player with a unnamed business glancing over the estates and tower blocks of east London. Always affectionate, yet always at a distance, a cool distance that made Tom feel... a little dangerous. Never dangerous with Jimmy, though. Always so sweet with him...

Thoughts came to Jimmy of everything he knew about guns. What little he knew, it turned out. On TV, at the movies, they were everywhere. All the time. Sidearms, rifles, handguns, pistols, automatics, semi-automatics, machine guns, uzis, derringers. The names that he knew where garnered from a host of fictional cops or gunslingers in Westerns, any side of the law. Magnum. Colt. Glock.

Jimmy got online and Googled 'gun'. The search results were too immense, so he got on to Wikipedia and typed in 'revolver '. It didn't take him long to find an exact picture. Smith & Wesson Model 29 in blue steel, .44 Magnum cartridges. Harry Callahan's preferred weapon. One of Travis Bickle's many guns.

How had he not known that?

It was Jimmy who picked the DVDs they watched, just as it was Tom who decided on the sports viewing (where sports included darts and snooker, naturally). Tom knew the Bond films, but it was Jimmy who sat him down for Coppolla, Ford, and Tarantino. Westerns, Easterns, the *Dollars Trilogy* and *The Magnificent Seven* versus *Yojimbo* and *Seven Samurai*. Tom laughed the most at Guy Ritchie's work—over the top, how not like London yet wouldn't it have been awesome if it was? Jimmy taught him how to pick the gay subtext, from *Ben Hur*

and *Spartacus* to Hitchcock's *Rope*. That had amused Tom, though he'd wondered aloud why they couldn't just be, you know, actually queer once in a while, and wasn't just noncing around in make-up and being all la-di-da. Jimmy shrugged, and said wait a couple of years—it might get better. Tom only smirked.

When Jimmy put up his poster of *Taxi Driver*, Tom announced he's never seen it. Jimmy determined to fix his education. They lay on the couch with a bottle of whiskey and Jimmy leaning on Tom's chest, trying his best not to keep talking; 'this is amazing, oh God, this part's good!' or pointing out Scorcese's two cameos, or how incredible Jodie Foster's performance was at that age. Tom let him anyway, chuckling in a way that made Jimmy feel both like a silly kid and utterly adored.

"This guy's *nuts*," Tom said when Bickle went crashing into the campaign office and scared the shit out of Cybill Shepherd.

"You pick that up?"

A gentle cuff to the head. "I'm serious. I thought he was meant to be about saving the kiddie, and look at him. And I thought he was meant to be cool! But... he's a bit of a loser."

Jimmy just rolled his eyes, and they kept watching.

Bickle was buying guns, talking to the mirror—you talkin' to me? Then he was strapping them to his body, naked from the waist up. Jimmy's neck always flushed; he'd seen this movie dozens of times, knew each camera angle, could anticipate each of Travis's moves, every flick of his wrist with one of his guns. But always...

Tom leant down to Jimmy's ear, his breath fire on Jimmy's already tingling neck. "He's got a body like yours, babe."

"You think so?" Jimmy asked, quietly.

"Oh yeah." Tom kissed the spot below Jimmy's ear. Flick, snap! Travis pointing the gun at the mirror. A flurry as he spun it, sliding it back into the holster.

Jimmy got hard; really, really hard. Tom slipped his hand down Jimmy's chest, and cupped Jimmy's cock and balls over the denim of his jeans. Jimmy murmured, and Tom squeezed.

Little by little, as the film progressed, Tom unzipped Jimmy's fly, and began stroking his cock through his boxers. Each move was slow, not at all hurried, but by the end, by the time Travis was mohawked and armed and shooting Sport and kicking down the door to the brothel, Jimmy was thrusting his hips into Tom's hand, groaning, begging under his breath. The shootout, blood everywhere, pimps and clients and Travis', and at last, with a final, solid jerk, Jimmy came. The camera panned back over the scene of carnage, and Tom was whispering in Jimmy's ear that he was much hotter than de Niro ever was.

After that, Jimmy's neck didn't just flush; he now couldn't see a still from the film without getting a hard-on.

It was one thing when it had been the film. When it had been celluloid and food dye blood, swaggers of the hips and thrusts of the hand, the angles of the body suggesting action on the verge of exploding into something... really fucking exciting.

Something Jimmy sure as hell shouldn't be feeling when it was real.

⚭⚭⚭

Two days later, Tom called, saying he was at Liverpool Street station, would be home in about fifteen minutes. Jimmy folded himself into the arm chair, and stared at the front door. It stood starkly, like a white wall in a hospital room, sterile yet menacing. He wondered if that was why Tom usually sat there—it had the best sight of the front door (Tom always insisted he see the door when they ate out. Even in the el-cheapo Turkish place around the corner.)

Jimmy considered that Tom's work might have been completely legit this time. He hadn't brought the Magnum with him. But then... maybe he had more.

Jimmy hadn't thought of that. And ten minutes wasn't really enough time to ransack the apartment to find out.

The door knob jangled. Jimmy jumped, and settled when he heard the key turn in the lock. Tom entered, small suitcase in one hand, jacket over one arm, and wearing that really sexy fedora. He looked every inch the 40s film star, except he had no spats on his shoes. Jimmy smiled at him. It was a struggle to keep his lips turned up.

Tom's smile was toothy, wide. "Hel-lo gorgeous."

Before Jimmy could speak, Tom was at his mouth, his hands on Jimmy's cheeks. He always kissed like this if they'd not seen each other for a while, and Jimmy usually responded with a chuckle through the kiss. This time, he opened his mouth and allowed Tom to plunder, slipping back further on the arm chair, Tom pressing closer and closer to him.

"Hey," he said when Tom released him.

"You right, babe?" Tom perched on the arm chair, hooking Jimmy's shoulders.

"Yeah, just..." Jimmy stroked Tom's knee, trying to rub away the blankness in his mind. "It's good to see you."

Tom plucked the fedora off his head and put it on Jimmy's. It was a little big for Jimmy, and sank right over Jimmy's ears and down his forehead. He forced a chuckle. Tom pinched the brim, and brought Jimmy's face back into the light.

"Really good to see you, babe. Really bloody good."

They hugged. That felt right. That felt *normal.* Even as Jimmy's lower stomach was as far from normal as ever.

Jimmy had to work that night, and Tom was off at a game somewhere, so Jimmy still beat him back to the apartment. When he got in the shower to wash the smell of the pub from him, he held his cock, hard and heavy, but not stroking it. If he tried to, he convulsed horribly, as if a slimy creature had slid down his stomach. After he crawled under the bed sheets, he lay very awake, looking at the drawers, the dark outline of a demon hunched and waiting in the dark.

It was like this that Tom found him. Jimmy didn't move as Tom ran his fingers over Jimmy's face.

Tom gave a final flick down Jimmy's nose. "Looking a little lonely there."

Jimmy blinked, and glanced up at Tom, and his cocky, plotting expression. Horny as all hell, Jimmy knew, aware of Tom's erection at his elbow.

"Keep me company, then," Jimmy said, cursing inwardly that it wasn't more than a whisper, thinking it was going to give him away very soon, that Tom would know Jimmy knew.

Tom unbuttoned and unzipped, folded his clothes over the back of his chair. Jimmy lay as still as a corpse, forcing Tom to pull back the duvet and slipped in alongside him. His side, away from the drawers. Jimmy became a barrier between the drawers and Tom. Between Tom, and the gun.

Tom suckled Jimmy's neck. His kissed his way from Jimmy's ear to the top of his shoulders, down that sinewy bit of muscle and nerve that always had Jimmy alight with arousal. Jimmy arched his back with a jerk. A strange snapping went through him. The thought of the gun tucked away, its long black length, and how it would look in Tom's hands, flashed into Jimmy's mind.

"Mmm... you like that, don't you?"

Jimmy breathed out a yes. Tom used two fingers on Jimmy's cheek to bring their mouths together, turning him firmly away from the drawers. Tom scooped out Jimmy's mouth with his tongue. Jimmy stretched into the kiss, pressing the length of his body right next to Tom's. He let himself be claimed by Tom, completely drawn into his arms.

Tom whispered, right in his ear, "God, I've been thinking about this for days. Jerked off before breakfast, every-fucking-day, thinking about your sweet body."

"Tom..."

Tom cupped either side of Jimmy's chest. He slid his hands downwards. Jimmy inhaled, his chest and stomach hollow. His torso a barrel, a barrel of the gun. Long, straight, slick. Tom squeezed, murmuring, pressing his hands up again, his thumbs finding Jimmy's nipples, and pushing into them. They became hard instantly. Jimmy bit his lip. He saw Tom rolling them around his thumb, Tom chewing his lip as Jimmy imagined him inspecting two metallic bullets, deciding which he would use; the one on the right, the one on the left, or perhaps both. A magic bullet, one with someone's name on it.

Tom lowered his mouth, and nipped at Jimmy's left one with his teeth. Jimmy whimpered, the pleasure also a little painful. Tom smiled around his bite, sucked hard, making Jimmy gasp and grab the back of Tom's head.

"Christ!"

"No, just me, babe."

Jimmy managed a laugh, somehow. Tom kissed him on the lips, and began the long trail back down Jimmy's body with his mouth.

Many murmured praises for Jimmy between kisses, sucks and licks. 'Hottest body, babe, fucking gorgeous, I could come just looking at you.' Jimmy swallowed, and as Tom's mouth and hands wandered further and further down, he saw Tom picking up the gun, thumb running down the length of the barrel. Saw him skim his fingers over the heel and handle, roll around the trigger. Jimmy shuddered at the thought, just as Tom bit that very arousing spot above his hip bone with gentle teeth.

Further and further down, until Tom kissed all around Jimmy's curly pubic hair, circling around until his tongue rubbed against Jimmy's cock. Kissing the barrel, kissing the top of the gun for good luck, Jimmy thought. Suddenly, Jimmy chest tensed, he clenched his fist. He couldn't stop the image, he wanted to stop it—but it slammed into his mind just as Tom sank his mouth on Jimmy's cock, the thought of him sucking the barrel. Licking it. Then... making Tom open up and lick the gun himself. Jimmy tried to meet Tom's eyes, trying to see his own cock sliding in and out of Tom's mouth. Oh fucking hell... he was as hard as the barrel, erect and long, and all he saw was black metal slick with saliva.

His cock... his weapon... his rifle... and Tom was loving and licking it. Tom wasn't going to let him come; he'd bring him to the brink, then dance away from it, nuzzling and murmuring while Jimmy rolled his head from side to side, the pulse of pleasure threatening to burst.

At last, Jimmy said, "Oh God, Tom, oil me up."

Tom gave one last, fierce suck, making Jimmy cry out as he pulled back. Tom chuckled. "I like how you say it. Oil... only got lube though."

Any gun needs oil, needs polishing to fire straight. Tom's had seemed clean and shiny. The sounds of the bottle of lube opening and squeezing came to Jimmy's ears. Tom knelt between his legs, and lifted Jimmy's right leg over his shoulder.

"Here you go, babe. Let's get you ready for me."

Tom spread the lube around Jimmy's hole, Jimmy flinching at the coldness. Cold like metal. It was soon warm on his body, and seconds later Tom inserted a finger, and began to stretch Jimmy. Rubbing him inside, rubbing the gun, polishing it, cleaning the gun powder away, smoothing the edges, making it bright and shiny and ready for action. Tom's finger, then the second one, widened and stretched Jimmy, getting his body used to the invasion of the length, of another person, of the promise of a bullet and of firing speed. The upward pressure on his hole made him keen loudly, words lost to him as he saw the final brushes of cloth against the blue steel of the barrel and the handle. His hips began to buck, his right leg almost unable to stay on Tom's shoulder, and Tom, above him, chuckled deviously.

"You want it so badly, don't you, babe?"

"Fuck... yes... Tom..." And the next words came before he could stop them. "Load me up, load me up, load me up."

Tom leaned over him, kissed him, tongue filling his mouth, before pulling back and asking, "How? Like this?"

Jimmy swallowed, knowing exactly how he wanted it. "From behind."

Tom smiled. He pulled his fingers out, let Jimmy lift his leg down, and with strong hands turned Jimmy onto his front. Jimmy braced himself on his palms, spread his knees, and waited for Tom to put the condom on.

Tom put his hands on Jimmy's shoulders, and slowly drew them down Jimmy's back. He squeezed the sides of his chest, fingers pressing to the edge of his stomach. Jimmy shivered, again his chest becoming the barrel, but now, on his knees, his arse and legs were the handle. He was bent over, cocked and ready. When Tom grasped his cock, Jimmy saw Tom's toying with the trigger, rubbing it, teasing, threatening, deciding.

"Please..." Jimmy whispered. "Load me up."

"Trust me, babe—you don't need to beg."

Tom angled his cock against Jimmy's hole, and pushed. Jimmy saw Tom's fingers sliding bullets into the cylinder, pictured him grinning as he flicked it, made it spin around. Tom thrust in all the way, and the cylinder snapped into place.

Jimmy groaned Tom's name. He was achingly hot, filled up, to the hilt, aimed, ready to fire.

"Oh babe, you're so tight, but..." Tom eased his cock a little way out, then slid it back in. "You're so smooth."

"Yes... you feel fantastic... Tom..."

Tom began moving his hips, and Jimmy's whole body engulfed with heat. He closed his eyes. He saw Tom and the gun, Tom in his sharp suit, fedora, running down a dark street—chasing, or being chased? It didn't matter. There was pursuit, the chase. Tom's harsh breaths of exertion, and Jimmy right with him, the perfect tool for destruction.

Every particle in Jimmy prickled with fire. Each thrust sent a juddering pulse from his tail bone to his neck, spiking out across his back and around his chest. All was excitement, thrill, a chase, a hunt, Tom in utter control and Jimmy his willing weapon. Tom leaned over Jimmy's back, still bucking into him, and reached around. Jimmy cried out, his cock so engorged that the touch made his body jerk, his head thrash. Tom stroked and pulled, thrust deeper and harder.

Jimmy shut his eyes. Tom stopped running, and saw his enemy looking right at him. His hand clenched around the gun. It was time.

Tom thrust short and sharp, then long and deep... raised the weapon, cocked it. Jimmy moaned. Almost there, almost there. The target was in sight, Tom aiming Jimmy, aiming the gun... and with a great tug, a curl of his finger, the gun fired, and Jimmy came.

The orgasm shot through him. Everything vanished from Jimmy's vision—he was the bullet released, pure burning fire, but now he had no target, no goal, just the scorching pleasure, just Tom holding him and pumping still as his hot cum spurted, as Tom moaned, thrust three more times into him, before releasing him, leaning his cheek on Jimmy's back, panting.

"Oh babe... oh babe... sweet Jesus, babe..."

Jimmy sagged, Tom's weight pushing them to the bed sheets, now wet from Jimmy's cum and their mingled sweat. Jimmy's whole body was pulsing, throbbing, and he felt Tom's heart beating on his back. They lay like that for a long while, before Tom pulled out and unrolled the condom. He lay down next to Jimmy, and drew him back to spoon him, so Jimmy was once again looking at the drawers.

"I missed you, love," Tom said, kissing Jimmy's sweaty shoulder.

"Yeah..." was all Jimmy could manage.

The downer after a high Jimmy knew a little about. The soaring heights before the crash of reality brought you a general sense of gray. That was not what happened as Jimmy lay curled next to Tom, their breathing slowly returning to normal rhythms. Instead, a deep pit opened up inside of Jimmy, full of everything he'd been trying to keep down for the past three days. It would not close, and Jimmy, seeing what had long been buried in him, knew it was going to stay open.

Jimmy pulled back from Tom, saying he was going to wash down. Tom let him go, winking at him, smug smirk at his lips.

Jimmy showered with his hand over his mouth, sobs crushed in his palm, and the water falling like hard pebbles onto his skin.

Chapter 3:
Final Target

"What's going on?"

The tea cup in Jimmy's hand tremble a little, so he put it on the coffee table, next to the flapjacks. Tom's own cup sat untouched, and Tom was hunched forward, eyes serious and demanding.

Jimmy shrunk back into the couch. "What do you—"

"Jimmy."

Tom never called him by his name. Jimmy pressed his lips together. Tom kept his gaze steady.

"I can see everything on your face. You know you're not good at hiding things, and you've been cagey with me since I got home. Then last night."

Jimmy's heart thumped. "What about last night?"

"Heard you in the shower. You were bawling your eyes out. So I've got to wonder what the hell is it I've done. Because... Jesus, did I hurt you? 'Cos babe, it was... bloody intense, and I'd hate myself if I did something like that to you."

There was so much concern on Tom's face that Jimmy wanted to lie, wanted to tell him no, it wasn't him, it was work, he was just relieved because last night was so good. It was fantastic, in fact.

But that was the problem, wasn't it?

Jimmy shook his head. Wordless, he left the living area, went into the bedroom, and brought out the Magnum. He placed it on the coffee table, right next to the flapjacks—*some gun powder with your tea?* he thought—and crossed his arms.

Never had Jimmy seen Tom anything beyond a little surprised. His face now was pure white shock; eyes wide, tense cheeks, skin threatening to draw back.

"Why did you go into the drawer?" Tom's voice was low, and almost dangerous, but Jimmy wasn't frightened by it. Should have been, but he wasn't.

The layers that Jimmy hoped to not peel back started to come off. "Just putting stuff away."

A sceptical expression. "Really?"

Jimmy sneered. "You think I was spying? Why would I? I've done a good job pretending that you were completely legit so far, why go changing it?"

Tom looked a little cut. "Don't pull that face, babe. Don't."

Jimmy didn't change his expression. "Why not?"

"It's... not you."

Jimmy pointed to the Magnum, lying coyly under the cloth like it was innocent. "Didn't think this was you either."

Tom shook his head, voice a little pleading. "It's not what it looks like."

"What's that mean? Jesus, Tom. What the hell is it that you do?"

The blunt, direct question that Jimmy had never asked and Tom had never shared, out there in the open, hovering between them and over the gun. Tom tried to give Jimmy a hard look, but Jimmy knew his was harder. At last Tom capitulated, with a tired sigh.

"Poker."

Jimmy rolled his eyes. "Tom, for fu—"

"That's the business as well. I'm not just a semi-pro. It's high-stakes games. So high that they aren't legal. You saw *Lock, Stock*, how they got themselves into the shit? That kind of thing."

That kind of thing meant four lads getting into deep shit, Jimmy thought. The kind of thing that's fucking funny when you're watching it but would scare the crap out of you if you were actually involved.

"So you play—"

"And organise. Bring folks together who've got the dosh. It's not... no one gets hurt."

"So you never shot someone?"

"Fuck no. How can you even—"

"How can I even what? Think it? What the hell am I supposed to think?"

Tom began to chuckle; unkind, sarcastic in its undertones. "Bloke goes off to work, doesn't tell you what's up, doesn't talk about he does, and you never asked? You're either naïve or you don't give a toss either way."

Jimmy reached down, grabbed Tom's shirt. "You bastard! You didn't bloody let me in close enough to know. You didn't want me to know."

Tom's chin indented, the way he always did when he was trying not to lose it. He gripped Jimmy's hands, tried to pry them off, but Jimmy held fast. Tom stood, tried to use his height to get Jimmy to step away, but they were nose to nose, his angry breath on Jimmy's chin.

"No. And you know why? I didn't want you touched by all that." Tom cupped Jimmy's cheek, and his voice cracked a little. "You're so fucking lovely, babe."

That single crack almost broke Jimmy. Christ, he thought, don't cry. Don't cry. His hands tightened so much he could have ripped Tom's shirt away entirely, but when Tom threw his arms around his back, Jimmy fell forward, and allowed himself to be held. Tom rocked him back and forth, gentle, soothing. Jimmy wanted it, craved it so much, and knew it wasn't deserved.

"Tom..."

"I'm sorry I scared you. So bloody sorry. It's just for protection. Just there in case."

Once more, Jimmy saw Tom with the gun. The pit yawned inside Jimmy, and he could have wept, but the knowing, the knowing that had gnawed at him all night and for the morning until now, was beginning to take a greater hold than the fear.

Jimmy swallowed, and said, "It wasn't you who scared me."

"What do you mean?"

"We shagged last night... you know what I was thinking about?"

Jimmy felt Tom's chest tense up, and his hand stilled on Jimmy's head. "Babe..."

Jimmy stepped back, and pointed hard at the gun. "This. This fucking thing here. And you know what? I enjoyed it. Really fucking enjoyed the idea of you with it, raising hell. Using it—"

"Don't talk like that."

Tom shook his head; emphatic, furious. Jimmy couldn't have stopped now. He knew his voice was getting harder, louder, and he kept on.

"Thinking about you firing it. Like it was some kind of bloody film. 'Cept no one gets up after this is used, do they?"

"Jimmy, shut—"

"And you know what? I *liked* it. I was as hard as a bloody rock thinking how hot you'd look using it. God, I could have come ten times if you'd fucked me hard enough—"

"Shut up!" Tom grabbed Jimmy's shirt, fists balling under his chin. "Just fucking shut your mouth and stop talking shit!"

As outraged as Tom sounded, his now red face looked more on the verge of tears. Jimmy's own eyes began to prickle, but dry and wretched rather than wet.

"I wish it were shit but it isn't! I wish... I didn't feel like that. I really do, Tom. I really fucking do. But it's there. It's in me. And I can't change it now. Can't shut it out."

Tom had never raised a hand to him. He didn't now, but there was a look in his eyes that made Jimmy swear he was going to hit him. Instead, Tom shoved him back, grabbed his jacket, and made for the door.

Jimmy's legs were concrete boots as he sank into a dark harbour. He couldn't turn to stop Tom from going, but as the door slammed shut, he collapsed to his knees, arms hooking around his chest to stop the sudden convulsive breathing that overcame him.

The text came two days later. Jimmy had bunked off work claiming illness, and spent it curled on the couch eating only dry crackers. The thought of alcohol seemed too terrible to contemplate; his brain was numb enough.

The Magnum stayed on the table, ignorant of the pain and the stagnant air in the flat. Jimmy avoided looking at it, but wouldn't move it either.

Jimmy had thought it would be him out the door, running from his gangster boyfriend, complete with an hourglass dress, furs around his neck, heels tat-a-tat tapping to the nearest taxi. Not Tom looking at him and realising Jimmy was in fact a whore all along. Except maybe that would have been better. You can explain whoring. You can't explain... this.

His phone had been buzzing with calls from a few friends and colleagues. Wondering where he was, he figured, but he ignored them all, letting the messages and texts bank up. He glanced at it sometimes, strangely hopeful but also deeply cynical, sure he would just sit there and nothing would ever come.

It was almost ten at night when the text came.

Sorry I ran like that. My turn to get scared. Call me?

Jimmy read it over and over again. He heard Tom's voice say it, true and upfront. He looked at the gun, the hole of the barrel poking through the cloth, doggy snout wanting a pat. Wanting attention.

Can't shut it out, Jimmy thought. Slowly, he got to his feet, washed his face, and pulled out his laptop. It took him half an hour to formulate the plan, and another fifteen minutes to get the right words to text back to Tom.

Jimmy heard the steady beat of footfalls before he saw the figure coming towards him. The slightly hunched, broad shoulders, hands stuffed in his pocket, and that light swagger could only have been Tom's.

Jimmy straightened up, but didn't move towards Tom. Tom was looking down. Maybe he hadn't seen Jimmy at all. When his head rose, he came to a stop, and Tom looked at Jimmy with amazement.

"You're *here*."

"You *came*."

"Well... the alternative was pretty dire."

"The alternative?"

Tom took a deep breath. "Losing you."

Jimmy's plan almost fell apart. He wanted right then to just run to Tom and throw himself into his arms, let Tom tell him it was ok, let them both pretend that nothing had changed, that they could go on with it all like before. Tom's shoulders, the ones he loved leaning on, those big hands to cradle the back of his skull, would make it all safe again.

An awful lump formed in Jimmy's throat. "Yeah... I don't want that either."

"So... what are we here for?"

Jimmy crouched, and opened the sports bag. The Magnum practically rolled into his hand. He stood, and let his arm drop by his side.

Tom's lips parted. A loud intake of breath, and Jimmy raised the gun.

Tom took a step back, hands going up defensively. "Jimmy..."

Jimmy flipped the Magnum in his hand, and held it out to Tom, the handle in his direction.

"Teach me."

Tom blinked, and it was a long minute before he breathed a harsh, "*What*?"

"Teach me how to use it."

"I heard you. Jesus Christ... *why*?"

"Because..." Jimmy swallowed. "It's part of you. Part of your life. And now it's part of me too. You want to lose me, really want to lose me? Keep me out of your life, then you will."

Tom's eyes went stone cold. "That some kind of threat? 'Tom, if you loved me, you would,' crap? Because babe—"

"It's not like that. Come on, Tom. We can't pretend nothing's happened, there is no bandaid to plaster on it. Whether you like it or not... I'm part of it now. Can't take it away."

Tom shook his head. "Babe... you're a sweet, sweet kid. Do you know what the people I work with are like?"

"No. But what if they come around to flat and you're not there? What if they find out about me and where I work, 'cos I sure bet you haven't mentioned me to any of them. Did you think that far?"

Jimmy knew he sounded very calm. But the hand that didn't hold the gun trembled.

"I..." Tom rubbed his eyes. "I can protect you."

"Tom... we've both seen that movie."

Tom growled. "Life isn't a bloody movie!"

"Yeah... that's what I realised when I found this."

There was no response to that. Tom put his hand over his mouth, inhaling deeply. Jimmy stepped closer, still holding the gun out. Tom shifted back, shaking his head again.

"Do you have any fucking clue what you're asking?"

Jimmy stepped closer, the Magnum now near Tom's chest. "Not really, but... If you want a saint, an angel, some little cherub to cherish or some other shit like that, you better get the fuck out of here. Because maybe I'm a sweet kid, but... there's other stuff there too. I don't know what to call it, but it's there, and it's not going away, and..." The calm suddenly left, and Jimmy's voice cracked. "And it scares me, and I wish it wasn't there, because you hate it, but... Jesus, Tom. I can't pretend it's not there. I just can't now. And you know... this is your life. It's not all guns, it's not all blood and bullets and violent crazy stuff, but it's part of it. And it's part of me too." Jimmy pressed the handle against Tom's ribs. "Let me in. Show me more."

A thin line of bright liquid formed along Tom's eyes.

Tom grabbed the gun, then Jimmy, and pulled him into his arms. Jimmy's cheek on Tom's shoulder, and he let out an awful sob, and it didn't stop. Tom's own hot tears fell on Jimmy's neck, but he was nodding, nodding and saying yes, he would, yes, he will, while the Magnum pressed into Jimmy's back.

"Tom... I love you."

Tom was still nodding, still crying, when he pulled back, and put the gun so it was in both their hands.

"That why we're out here? So I can show you?"

Jimmy sniffled, and said, "Gotta start somewhere." He pointed to a set of cans he'd lined up on arrival. Nothing so obvious like a line up, but targets nonetheless.

Tom made sure Jimmy had hold of the gun, and stood behind him. "Here."

Tom adjusted his arms, told him to tighten his shoulders, moved his elbows so they were at the right angle. He then slid his hands down Jimmy's arms, until they covered Jimmy's own completely. Moulded over Jimmy, locked against each other. Tom's fingers covered Jimmy's, matching his hold on the gun as much as he could. He told him to look down the barrel, to find his target, and not take his eye off it until after the bullet had hit it.

"You are sure about this?" Tom spoke right into Jimmy's ear.

Jimmy inhaled. He was holding the gun, and Tom was holding him. Once more, he was the gun, the perfectly aimed weapon. Jimmy felt his cock stir, just a little, but his heart beat was steady, his stomach calm.

Jimmy let his breath go. "Completely."

Tom whispered, and gripped Jimmy's hands. "Then fire."

Jimmy nodded, and pulled back the trigger.

If you enjoyed this story, you can sign up for a free membership at ForbiddenFiction.com and discuss it with other readers and the author at the *Bare Blue Steel* story page aat http://forbiddenfiction.com/story/JB1-1.000193.

We do our best to proof all our work, but if you spot a text error we missed, please let us know via our website Contact Form athttp://forbiddenfiction.com/contact..

Greasy Boy

Chapter 1:
Clean Getaway

The conference was supposed to go all day but Simon bolted at one o'clock. He had a three-hour drive back home and didn't relish the idea of spending his evening on the road. He wanted to get home before dark. To be home in case Peter came back.

He jogged out to his car, threw his briefcase in the backseat, pulled off his jacket and tossed that on top of the case. "Where the hell are you going?" a voice said from behind him. Simon turned to see Danny Weisman, one of his old college friends that now worked for the D.A.'s office, leaning against a BMW with a menthol cigarette jammed between his lips. "Cutting out kind of early, aren't you?" Danny said, the menthol bouncing up and down like a metronome, keeping time with his words.

"I'm going home," Simon snapped, the irritation obvious in his voice. Danny had a bad habit of telling the truth exactly as he saw it, which was an admirable quality most of the time, just not when it was directed at Simon himself. Simon could see what was coming. It was the same 'conversation' they had been having for months. The conversation about Peter.

He slid behind the wheel of his Lexus, rolled down the driver's side window with the push of a button and lit a Camel.

Simon had quit smoking a year ago, after months of Peter badgering him about it, then Peter turned around and quit him just a few months later. It hurt just thinking about it. The cigarettes came back not long after.

"He's not coming back, you know," Danny said as he pushed himself from the BMW and knelt next to Simon's open window. "No matter how much you hide in that apartment, he isn't coming back to you."

"What am I supposed to do? Just forget about him? We were together for five years."

"Yeah, forget about him. I'm sure he has forgotten you."

"Fuck you, Danny. I miss him," Simon said, and felt his throat tighten. He choked the ball of emotions back down, burying it in his chest where it would ferment and come back as heartburn. Like a zombie in a George Romero horror movie, the pain of losing Peter just wouldn't stay dead.

"I know you do. But, the only way to get over him is to start living again. Trust old Danny, I know what I'm talking about."

"Yeah, live like you do?" Simon scoffed. For all the years Simon knew Danny, his friend had never had a full time lover. There had been boyfriends, guys he dated now and again, but never a real, honest partnership. When he wasn't dating, he supplemented his sexual needs with trips to the back room of the leather bar or, when he was away from home, like now, he cruised well-traveled parks or highway rest areas.

"Maybe," Danny replied, smiling. "A back alley blowjob might just be what you need." He grinned when he said this and wiggled his eyebrows. They looked like two caterpillars squaring off for the fight of the century. Simon laughed, feeling the tension moving out of his shoulders. This was why they were friends; Danny told him what he didn't want to hear, but needed to, then made him laugh afterward. Danny was right and Simon knew it. He had to let go. He had to start living again. Now, if only he could figure out how to do that.

"What I need," Simon said, "is to get home. I need Peter to come back to me."

"No," Danny replied, grinding his cigarette out on the pavement between his feet. "That's what you want. Sometimes, what we want and what we need are two different things. What you need is to get your shit together. I love you, man, and that's why I'm telling you this. You need to move on. Go get laid. You'll feel better, or maybe you'll just feel less. Either way is good."

Simon sighed. Again, Danny was right. He did need to get laid. His balls had ached for days now; no matter how much he jerked off, it didn't relieve the pressure. In fact, it seemed to make it worse.

But, he didn't think he could live like Danny. Anonymous sex scared the hell out of him. Sex should not be casual, Simon felt. It should mean something to the participants more than just the inevitable orgasm. There had to be a connection there, a history that each could use to enhance the experience for the other. It should be tender and gentle and loving.

But, that was not what Peter had wanted. He'd wanted to "explore" his sexual limits, to "test his boundaries," was the way he had phrased it the last night they were together. Essentially, he'd wanted Simon to tie him up and flog the shit out of him with the assortment of leather toys he had brought home.

Simon couldn't do it, though. He couldn't inflict pain on Peter, even when Peter wanted him to. He couldn't allow himself to consent to this new kink that his lover had so recently become enamored with, this deviance of rough sex. And he couldn't live his life like Danny. He couldn't risk his reputation with public sex or fucking someone without even knowing their name, or as Danny often bragged, care. In Danny's world, names could be dangerous. Many of his partners were married or had high profile jobs that could be destroyed if others discovered what they did in their free time. So, the men were reduced to physical attributes. They became Mr. Curved Dick or Ol' Fuzzy Bottom.

A car pulled into the lot, parked. The engine ticked as it settled and began to cool. The driver opened the door and got out, a briefcase tucked under his arm. The driver was tall, handsome with a dark beard that was cut so close to his skin it seemed painted on. Simon and Danny watched the man, watched him confidently stride into the building, his head held high, shoulders back, firm chest lying just under the hard starched white shirt and conservative dark tie.

"Ooh, that's what I need," Danny said once the man was safely inside the building. "A little afternoon pick-me-up."

Simon started up the engine. "Go get him, Tiger." Simon laughed and shot Danny a quick wave then pulled the Lexus out of the parking lot.

When he got on I-95 South, Simon slipped his tie from around his neck, nearly fumbling his glasses off in the process, and dropped it in the passenger seat, where the tie coiled around itself like a snake, ready to pounce. He flipped through the radio stations, found nothing good, then shook another Camel from the pack in the passenger seat and lit it.

Simon pulled on the cigarette, feeling the warm smoke fill his lungs. The best taste in the world, except for maybe cock, he thought and felt a moan rise up in his throat.

Sex. It nearly drove him mad thinking about it. He hadn't been with anyone since Peter left and the many months of sexual prohibition were now starting to affect his mind, he feared. He no longer thought about Peter when he masturbated. He no longer saw Peter's smooth, tight little body writhing under his imagined tongue, squirming as daydream Simon licked him from his nipples to his hard ridged belly, then further down. He could no longer taste Peters cock in his mind as he caressed himself, one hand pulling the thick fold of foreskin over his own cock, warm, sweet precome oozing from the head, slickening his curled fingers and running down the long shaft to mire itself in the forest of blond pubic hair, while his other hand dipped down under his balls. The thick fingers dancing in and out of his ass, manipulating his prostate until he came with the force of a volcano.

Peter never entered his mind while he came. Instead, he saw himself in one of Danny's midnight trick tales or of a new cruising spot he had recently discovered. He saw himself, in the woods, on his knees, with a stranger before him. He imagined himself hungrily pulling the strangers pants down and feasting on the cock before him. He could almost smell the raw, sweaty funk of the man, taste the coppery tang of the engorged cock as it was thrust down his throat. He could hear the hard, happy grunts of the man as the stranger rushed on to orgasm. The threat of literally getting caught with his pants down, forcing the stranger to come far sooner than either wanted, yet adding to the excitement of what they were doing.

He thought of Peter afterward, while he lay in the bed, his arms wrapped around the otherwise unused pillow, the come drying on his belly. He thought about what Peter might be doing now. Then he remembered the hairy backed gorilla Peter had run off with. An investment banker from Boston who wore leather on the weekends. He could see them in his mind. Peter was so small and perfect. *They are always perfect when they are no longer around*, Simon thought, with that hulking monstrosity he had run off with, slithering up next to him. He saw Peter's beautiful body lying prone on a thick bed of feathers and satin sheets while the gorilla, lustfully panting, hot steam shooting from his nostrils, dipping his arm in a tub of Crisco, preparing his fist to enter Peter.

Of course, this was all in his mind. Peter probably was not into fisting, but he had wanted Simon to abuse him. He had wanted to be tied down and beaten and Simon couldn't do it. He couldn't do it then, and perhaps still couldn't. The thought of what Peter might be doing now, of Peter exploring his masochistic tendencies, was beginning to excite Simon. Public sex and sadism was finding its way into Simon's fantasies. He wondered, *Is this just because I am so god-damned horny, or is something else going on? Am I in fact, becoming like Peter? Or like Danny? Do I really want dangerous sex?*

In frustration he grit his teeth, forgetting about the Camel stuck between them and nearly severed the filter off. He pulled it from his mouth and mashed the stub out in the ashtray. He ran his fingers through his hair, platinum blond with just the tinniest hint of gray, and felt the grime of the road. He'd spent the morning sitting in an overheated conference room sipping cold coffee and eating heavily sugared pastries. The graying hair bothered him. He was only twenty-six and he wondered, what would it be when he was forty? Completely white, probably. Just like his father was at that age. His skin was still young though, smooth, blemish free and the pale color of ivory. He rarely went out in the sun, he couldn't tan anyway, but the sun aged skin. So did smoking, but it was easier to stay indoors than it was to give up nicotine. Especially when there was no one there to insist you quit the habit.

Another Camel found its way into his mouth and as he smoked, that sticky, tacky dry feeling smoking always did to his mouth and throat urged him to find something to wash the taste out.

A single empty water bottle rolled around in the passenger seat. A sign up ahead indicated the upcoming exit as having gas, food and lodging. It was a rural exit and the tall grass lining the exit seemed to wave at Simon as he pulled the Lexus off the highway, down into this tiny community. A single two-lane road met him. To the right, the Big Pine Motel, a dilapidated rest stop for the weary and not-very-choosy traveler. Several of the letters in its sign had long since disappeared so it now read, Bi Pin otel. On the left, a small service station with a single island of gas pumps.

He sat for a moment at the stop sign, checking both ways for traffic before pulling onto the narrow road. But there was no traffic. He could see a good distance beyond the motel on the right and the gas station on the left and there was not even the faintest hint of another body out there. It was as though he had come to the end of the Universe and he was the only visitor. The great pine trees that gave the motel its name reached up from both sides of the road, shading it so just tiny dapples of sunlight flickered on the pavement. He took the left and turned into the gas station.

Simon pulled up to the super-unleaded pump and jumped out of the Lexus, unscrewed the gas cap and slid the pump nozzle in the hole. He had more than half a tank of gas, but since he was here he might as well fill up. "Help ya?" a voice called, startling him into looking up at the source.

A young man walked out of the service bay, wiping his hands on a greasy towel. He looked to be about twenty with oily black hair and a matted goatee on his face. His shirt was open down to the navel and the wife beater undershirt covering his thin frame was covered in spots of oil, grease and sweat. He wore blue Dickies pants that hung from his thin hips as though they were defying gravity. How they stayed up was anyone's guess. Maybe he stapled them to his bones, Simon thought.

"I'll take it," the young man said, sliding his hand over Simon's to relieve him of the pump handle. His hands were blackened with oil and dirt stains. Simon pulled his own hand away. "Full service. You want me to fill it?" The tag on his shirt informed Simon that his name was Rick.

"Sure," Simon replied. "Can you check the oil too?"

"Yup." Rick smiled, revealing a mouth full of even white teeth with the exception of one front tooth that was chipped. Simon felt a stirring in him at that imperfection. It made the young man seem... vulnerable was the only word he could come up with, but that wasn't quite right. Vulnerable often meant weak and he appeared anything but that. He had a strength to him, a raw toughness to him that men in Simon's world of the overeducated and well-paid often lacked or kept well hidden.

No, he was not vulnerable but the chipped tooth did give him the appearance of a wounded man. A man who might have seen bad things and been hurt by them. It stirred in Simon that protective spirit that had, so long ago, urged him into a career in law. It was the big brother in him, the Florence Nightingale. The boy didn't need Simon's protection, but it was hot to think he might.

The gas station was small, two mechanics' bays and a small glass-fronted office. On the curb before the office door was a soda machine with one of its fluorescent bulbs flickering behind the plastic panel advertising the ice cold drinks inside. Simon threw a fistful of quarters in and a can of soda dropped into his hand. He pulled the tab and guzzled half of it down. The cold soda burned a sweet trail down his throat. Draining the can, Simon tossed the empty in a rusted oil drum that had been transformed into a garbage can. It clanged against the sides.

The soda had quenched his thirst but now he had to piss. Simon asked Rick, "You got a restroom here?"

The young man read the oil dipstick, then slid it back in its hole. He looked up and smiled at Simon, his hands still working the dipstick. He licked his bottom lip, his tongue rasping against the stubble on his chin. "Yup. Around the back." He pointed toward the left of the office. "Here's the key." He shoved his fist in his pants pocket, pushing the Dickies down slightly to reveal a heavy bush of dark pubic hair. Simon looked, then quickly pulled his eyes away before Rick noticed. He tossed the keys to Simon, then slammed the Lexus' hood shut. "Oil's fine."

Simon nodded, thought about pulling out his keys and hitting the little red security button to lock the doors before going off to the bathroom, then thought against it. He didn't want to look like an untrusting asshole in front of the guy. Men like Rick were tough, thick-skinned yet easy to offend. How a man was perceived by his fellow man was as important as he perceived himself. If a man was seen as untrustworthy by his neighbors then he might as well have moved to another town or lived up to his nefarious reputation because no matter what he did, how he was seen was what he was.

Simon didn't lock his car not only because he didn't want to offend the guy by inadvertently suggesting he might do something to the vehicle, but also because he realized he was attracted to the mechanic. Rick was a nice looking man and when he had smiled at

Simon, that chipped tooth flashing like a beacon, Simon felt something going on in his belly. Butterflies, or just the slightest quiver of excitement. He had been horny as hell since Peter left and the six month dry spell was making him near insane and this greasy mechanic, Rick, was sending his lust meter into the red. He would rather risk losing some meaningless object from the glove compartment or the handful of coins in the center console than offend Rick.

It's not like I have a chance with him, Simon thought. Rick was probably, likely, straight, but the probability of something happening between them was not the motivation of his concern for Rick's feelings. It was the possibility.

"Thank you," Simon said. He caught the key ring in his hands and watched as Rick pulled the loose Dickies up onto his hips again. He noticed the slight swell of his crotch, the lump that shifted down his left leg as he dropped the Lexus' hood back into place and moved back to the pump. Simon turned and walked around the back of the building to the bathroom. He unlocked the door and went in. It was small. There were two dirt-stained sinks ahead of him, with smoky mirrors above each. Oily fingerprints marred the glass surface. To the right were two toilet stalls. He chose one and felt his bowels churn, which meant he had to sit. He hated sitting on public toilets, especially one this dirty, but he was two hours from home and it wouldn't wait. Simon lined the seat with toilet paper, then pulled his pants and underwear down and gently sat on the paper.

The wall separating the stalls was filled with graffiti.

Suck my cock!

For a good time call....

Jane M. takes it up the ass and Jeffrey Dahmer burns in hell were some of the witticisms left by previous shithouse poets.

There was something else in the wall as well: a hole about waist-high that could easily swallow Simon's fist. He glanced through the portal and saw the toilet on the other side.

It was a glory hole. Simon chuckled under his breath. Danny would be thrilled to find this, he thought.

The hand carved addition in the wall slightly disturbed him, the thought of what went on here, and yet, he felt a rush of excitement in his belly as well. Scenarios from the Falcon videos he and Peter had rented came back to him. Hard muscled men engaging in anonymous sex that would be risky in the real world, but exciting in the make believe world of porn. He realized that rarely did a porn movie show a committed couple making love; most were strangers meeting for the first time by swallowing each other's cocks. Was porn programming gay men to act out these scenes, he often wondered, or were men naturally promiscuous and only restricted to relationships because society directed people in that direction?

He finished, flushed. Just then the restroom door opened and someone walked in. The newcomer entered the stall next to Simon's and he could hear the rustling of clothing, the familiar rasp of a zipper being undone. He glanced through the hole and saw blue Dickies hanging from thin hips slide down a pair of pale, hairy legs. A set of white briefs that had become gray with age and large dark yellow piss stains on the front, blushed dully in the dim light of the other stall. A large bulge slowly rose from the dirty cloth like a time-elapsed film of a volcano forming on a small island. It was Rick on the other side and he didn't seem to be in a hurry to do anything but massage himself. He didn't free himself to urinate and if there was ever an instance when the real world could resemble a cruising scene in a porn video, it was now. Simon's throat became as dry as the Sahara. His heart banged in his chest like it was trying to get out.

He watched as Rick slid a greasy hand over his basket and massaged it, toying with his balls until the bulge began to grow too large for his briefs to hold it in.

Rick slid a finger in his briefs and slowly pulled them down. He exposed the patch of wiry pubic hair Simon had seen earlier, then the stem of his cock. More and more, until his entire erection sprang out and slammed against the dirty wife beater undershirt with a muffled slap. He pushed his underwear to his ankles along with his pants, then wrapped a dirty hand around his dick and began tugging on it. It was about seven inches long, circumcised and weighted down with enormous hairy balls.

Simon pushed his face closer to the hole and felt revulsion at himself for doing so. He wasn't supposed to do something like that, he wasn't supposed to want to do something like that, but he did want it just the same.

Rick turned and lined up the thick cockhead with the hole in the wall and pushed it through.

P.L. Ripley

Simon leaned back as the hard cock came through to his side. He could smell the hot sweaty sex of the erect cock, the heavy cloud of pheromones with just the lightest hint of piss. It smelled heavenly. An aroma he had missed in the last six months of sexual isolation.

"Suck it!" Rick called from the other side of the wall.

Going down on a dirty dick is insane, he thought and ignored Rick. He wanted to suck it, though. Man, how he wanted to pull it down into his throat. The raw stench filled his nostrils, enveloping him in hot, wet lust. He wanted it, he wanted the sweaty, pissy cock in his mouth but still, his vanilla mind kept screaming at him, "NO!"

But another voice rose up beneath his own, a voice that demanded him to try it, just this once, let go and do something he wanted, instead of what he should. It was Danny's voice and he could almost see him, here in the stall, a menthol jammed between his lips, bouncing up and down as he egged him on.

"Do it," Danny said. "Who gives a fuck what other people think? Do it because you want to do it. Do it, because this opportunity won't come again."

"Suck it," Rick called again his voice deeper, gruffer than before, forceful even. "Do it!"

Chapter 2:
Getting Dirty

Simon slid from the toilet seat to the cement floor, his pants still around his ankles, his heart hammering in his chest as he nervously reached out to the mechanic's cock. He could feel the heat rising off the pulsating head as his fingers came dangerously close to making contact. Simon's breath came out in jagged gasps. He wanted it, he needed it but.... *Don't do this*, the rational voice in his head begged. *Don't cross that line.*

His fingers hovered just a breath away from this object of his lust. Hovered and waited and resisting the urge to back away, Simon ran his fingertips down the length of the cock. Rick moaned on the other side of the wall. Simon quickly pulled his hand back.

He could hear Danny cheering him on. "Feels good, doesn't it?"

It did. It felt real good to have another man quiver under his touch, no matter how light that touch was. And it felt... necessary, like this was the one thing that would keep him together for another week, another day, another minute. He was going mad with his sexual seclusion and now, finally, he had the opportunity for a reprieve. That is, if he could go through with it.

But, how could he do this? How could he shun a lifetime of strict relationship-based sex? How could he abandon his own vision of morality?

"Please," he heard Rick whisper from the next stall. He wanted to be touched as much as Simon wanted to touch. Perhaps he needed it as much as Simon. The protective spirit rose in him again. The big brother, here to take care of Rick, to ease his suffering, took over. Rick needed his help, HIS help. No one could take care of him but

Simon. No one could do this for him, right here, right now, but Simon.

He took the cock in his fist and felt his courage waver. This was insane, how could he allow himself to carry on like this? How could he dare wrap his hand around a strange man's cock in such a filthy place as this? How could he... then he heard the soft moan from the other side of the partition. An enticing quiver in Rick's voice. Simon slid his hand down over the glans, catching several droplets of pre-come, then slid back to the base, where the tuft of pubic hair curled up through the hole in the wall.

"Suck it," Rick said, a hopeful request with just a hint of aggression. A forcefulness to his voice, a rough demanding.

He couldn't do that. Touching was one thing. Holding it in his hand, stroking it, loving it. But, put it in his mouth? No, that was too much. That was going too far. If he knew him better, was in a safer, cleaner place, like the bedroom in his apartment, then he might be able to. But here?

"Oh, do it man." Rick called to him. The curious lust that had forced Simon to his knees in the filthy bathroom, that had pushed his eye against a hole where perhaps dozens or even hundreds of men had rubbed their filthy crotches or shoved lube-slickened assholes against, now pushed his tongue out to the wanting cock and curled it around the stinky dick-head. He tasted it, let the flavor of the boy dance in his mouth a moment then slid his tongue along the underside of the shaft. He pulled his tongue back up to the head and let it quiver over the head and in the piss-slit, then pulled the entire tool in his mouth.

The mechanics of the act was like second nature to him, and if he closed his eyes he could imagine he was somewhere familiar, back in his apartment, on his bed. But, when he opened his eyes to the wall before him, he could not pretend he was anywhere but there. And the man in his mouth was not someone he knew.

A strange sensation began to blossom inside Simon. The self-imposed restrictions that had guided his life to this point began to loosen, to break apart. The inhibitions that had been his moral grounding for his entire adult life were a sham, he realized. Restricting sex to a relationship did not give him the moral high ground; it was the result of his unwillingness to take a chance.

Yes, this was risky. Yes, this was illegal. *But holy shit*, he thought, *it's the most exciting sex I've ever had.* And he was beginning to feel, perhaps for the first time, free. He could do anything. He could give this man pleasure, and take it in return. He didn't have to know him, because he knew himself. There was no guilt. No need to reprimand or punish himself for this.

Rick moaned, breaking Simon from his own mind and turned his attention back to what he was doing. Simon smiled around the cock. It didn't taste as strong as it smelled. The musky scent from Rick's heavy balls filled Simon's head with a desire more powerful than a hurricane. He pulled the cock deeper into his mouth, letting it slide down his throat until he thought he would gag, then slid it back out. He pushed himself harder and faster down on the cock, soaking up every inch, until his nose mashed against the greasy boy's rank pubic hair. He inhaled deeply, taking in the piss and sweat stench of the wiry black mat.

Simon discovered that he loved this. The real man taste and smell beat the flavor of soap and cologne he had grown accustomed to. He reached down into his lap and found himself as hard as the mechanic. He tugged on his own cock a few times, pulling the thick, rubbery foreskin over the head then gave it up to concentrate on the cock in his mouth. *This is what sex is supposed to be like*, he thought. Raw, urgent, primal. He was beginning to understand Danny's appetite for this.

"Yeah, that's it," Rick cooed. "Take it all." He began to rock his hips, sliding the cock in and out of the glory hole. "You like that big meat in your face, don't you?"

He did. In fact, he loved it. Simon wrapped his fist around the cock and stroked it as he sucked. He wanted to see the mechanic come. He wanted to watch as Rick shot his load, see the shaft flex and jump as streams of warm jism erupted from it, splashing down onto the dirty floor.

Then, without any warning Rick pulled his cock from Simon's grasp and back through the hole. Simon just sat on his knees and stared as Rick dropped to the floor. They knelt, staring at one another for a second and Simon saw the burning lust in Rick's eyes, the same that Rick probably saw in his.

"Gimme yours," Rick demanded.

Simon stood on shaky legs. He lined himself with the hole, then paused. A thousand scenarios ran through his mind then, with a thousand different outcomes. All of them bad. What if, his mind asked, this was a set-up? What if he pushed through to the other side and Rick clamped something on him so he couldn't pull back out, then called the cops? Or what if he cut Simon, cut his dick off and let Simon bleed to death here on the floor of the out of the way bathroom at this gas station in the middle of nowhere? What if....

"Please man, give it to me," Rick wined from the other side of the wall. He had pressed his face against the hole and his hungry tongue came through, lapping at the air with just the tip making contact with Simon's cock.

A hot shiver ran through Simon. He steeled his courage and pushed his own hard dick through the hole. Rick immediately sucked it into his mouth.

His mouth was hot, wet and velvety smooth. The greasy kid toyed with the cock head, flicking his tongue over and under, and nibbled at the long shaft with his broken tooth. This was heavenly. After six months without another man's touch, this almost felt like his first time all over again. Immediately, Simon's nuts began to tighten, to twist in a hard knot under his slobbering cock. He didn't want to come, at least not yet.

He started pulling his cock back but Rick stopped him. The mechanic tightened his fist around the base of Simon's cock and held him there while he sucked on it. "Stop, man, I'm gonna come!" Simon squealed.

"Can you come again?" Rick asked slowly, his voice deep and husky. He licked the glistening, purple head after each word.

"Yeah. I just want it to last."

"Don't worry. I'm not through with you yet." Rick replied, then Simon felt the hot mouth engulf him again.

Simon gasped and felt that familiar tingle in his belly. His nuts rolled and churned and he could feel the come moving up through his shaft. "I'm coming!" Simon warned him. His entire crotch seemed to explode. He slammed his hips harder against the wall as waves of orgasm washed over him.

Bliss, sweet beautiful bliss. He felt his knees weaken and he grabbed the top of the divider to hold himself upright while his legs pleaded to give out from beneath him. Simon felt the mouth still on his cock as Rick swallowed every drop given him.

The mouth continued to tease his cock, sending spasms through his crotch. Simon wanted to tell him to stop, it was driving him insane, but he could only grunt and pant. Finally Rick pulled his mouth away with a last slurp and Simon pressed his face against the graffiti covered wall to catch his breath.

Simon felt pain then, not in his body—that was still quivering with post-coital delight—but in his mind. He had just participated in an act he had always seen as morally beneath him—anonymous sex with a man he didn't know, or quite frankly, care about. Yet, he enjoyed it just the same. What did that make him?

"It makes you human," he heard Danny's voice say. "You can climb down from your high horse now and join the rest of us peasants down here on Earth."

He heard Rick rise to his feet and then the jingle of keys and coins as he pulled up his pants. The stall door opened and softly banged closed. Simon pulled his dick back through the hole. It was still semi-hard but with the right touch could be fully erect and ready to go in just a matter of minutes. His own stall door opened and Rick stepped in, holding his pants up with a greasy fist. "You came in my mouth." Rick said.

A hot tingle of fear rose up Simon's spine. The mechanic looked pissed. His eyes were pressed into thin slit squints and his hands constricted to hard fists. This, Simon thought, was where he paid for his little fun. This was the retribution for crossing the ethical line, for sexual congress outside the restraints of a relationship. "I know, I'm... I'm sorry," he stammered. "I warned you I was coming. I've been tested, I'm negative."

"I wasn't complaining," Rick said and opened his fist, letting his Dickies fall to the floor. His spring-loaded hard-on bounced up and pointed at Simon. Rick grinned open mouthed, the chipped tooth shining out between his thin lips. "It likes you."

Simon smiled back. "I like it too." He took it in his hands, massaging the low-slung balls. The dark hair on them tickled his palms. Now that they were face-to-face, Simon felt a little less daring, a little shyer about what he wanted to do. There was some power to not seeing the man you were sucking off.

His eyes glanced over his watch as his fingers deftly manipulated Rick's balls. How long had they been in there together, he wondered. Fifteen minutes, twenty? No one could get in there without a key, but how many customers had pulled up to the pumps, then driven off in disgust when no one came out of the station to fill their tanks, or worse, filled up themselves and driven off without paying. This wasn't really his concern, but his unlocked Lexus was. He needed to break this off and get out of there and back on the road before something happened to his vehicle. Then Rick let out a soft moan in appreciation of what Simon was doing to him, and all thoughts of anything other than the man in his hand were gone.

Simon began to drop to his knees but Rick stopped him. "No," he said and opened Simon's shirt. He tugged it off and threw it on top of the toilet tank, then kissed Simon's smooth hairless chest. He took each nipple one at a time in his mouth until they grew as erect as Simon's cock, then Rick stood, grabbed him by the neck, pulled him closer and pressed his lips against Simon's.

Simon opened his mouth to let him in. Their tongues slid over one another and Simon could taste his own cock in Rick's mouth. Rick pulled back and peeled off his own shirt and threw it on top of Simon's. He was thin, but not overly so. His chest was well-defined beneath the wife beater; his nipples, firm and rigid, stood out like tiny mountain peaks. As Simon drew his hand over Rick's belly, he could feel the hard ripples lying just beneath the surface. A tattoo peaked out from beneath the undershirt announced him as BITCH. Grease and dirt stains marked his upper arms.

Rick lifted his right arm and pushed Simon's face in the tangled mass of sweaty hair. "Lick it," he commanded and Simon did as he was told. The pit stunk of sweat both old and new, yet with each pass of his tongue, Simon found himself getting harder. He sucked on the hair, pulling it in his mouth then lapped around the pit until it glistened. He pulled himself back when his glasses became streaked with the sweat and saliva.

Rick gently held Simon's hips and turned them both until Simon's back was against the door. He then removed Simon's glasses, turned and bent to the collection of shirts on the back of the toilet and wiped them on his sleeve. After he did this, he pulled a condom out of his shirt pocket. Rick turned back to him and gently slid the glasses back on his face for him. "Better?" he asked.

"Yeah, thanks." Simon said and swallowed hard. The trickle of fear that had moved through him was now a steady stream. He was nearly naked in a public bathroom with a man he hardly knew beyond the sweet taste of his body. This was a dangerous situation, in the fact they could be caught—though that was slim; a person would need a key to get into the restroom to actually catch them in the act—and that Rick could possibly be something other than what he seemed.

Rick was smaller than Simon, but his hard, lean, muscular body showed Simon that he was strong and could best Simon in any physical competition. If he got it in his head to become physically aggressive, there was not much Simon could do to protect himself, or stop an assault.

But then, Rick had done a stunningly kind gesture by cleaning Simon's glasses for him. He had kissed him, gently, almost lovingly and Simon began to feel more calmness in himself as Rick opened the small condom package and slowly slipped the rubber over Simon's dick, squeezing the end to make sure no air was left in the loose tip. He spat in his palm, rubbed that over the condom, then turned and rested his elbows on the toilet tank. "Fuck me," he said. It wasn't a request.

Chapter 3:
Fading Stains

Simon bent slightly to gain access to the greasy boy's ass, found the sweet tight hole and slowly pushed his cock head against it. Rick gasped as the fat head punctured the opening and Simon could feel the boy's muscles tighten, then go completely loose. He was not a virgin and wanted this as much as, if not more than, Simon.

A bright Aztec sun tattoo blazed up between Rick's shoulder blades and after Simon had slowly fed his fat cock into the boy's sweet, tight ass, he rested a hand over the tattoo and began to work his hips. It was like heaven, clamped in the tight channel, the musky stink of ass and sweat and come all dancing around in his head, while Rick moaned beneath him.

"Jesus, that feels good. Fuck me, man," Rick said and pushed back against Simon.

Simon picked up his speed, his hips a blur against the tile background. His balls slammed against Rick's ass. Rick reached up behind his back, took the hand that covered his tattoo and moved it to the back of his head. He squeezed Simon's hand so it closed, entangling his fingers in the oily, black hair. Then he quickly moved his head forward, letting Simon know he wanted his hair pulled.

Simon did as directed. He snapped at the greasy locks, pulling Rick's head back in the process. "Yeah," Rick yelled.

"You like that?" Simon growled, suddenly realizing exactly what he was doing. He was hurting Rick. He was fucking him with the fierceness of an animal and tugging on his hair as though he wanted to rip it from the roots. He was doing to Rick what Peter had wanted done to him. And he realized he liked it. He liked the dominant role Rick had pushed him into. He liked the feeling of power the

68

aggressive sex was instilling in him. "You like that, you fucking bitch?" He grunted, calling Rick by his tattooed name, and pulled on the hair even harder.

"Yeah. I love it. Hurt me, man."

Hurt me, he had said. Just like Peter wanted to be hurt. He would hurt him. He would hurt him just as Simon had been hurt when he walked out on him. He would show him he could be just as vicious, just as cruel as he had been. He raised his palm to the ceiling and brought it down on Rick's ass. The slap echoed through the small room like a gunshot.

The boy began to buck, slamming his hips back against Simon's crotch. Simon slapped his ass again and again until it became red and warm, all the while twisting his cock in and out of the hot hole. "You like it, greasy boy?" Simon said. "Is this what you wanted me to do? You wanted me to hurt you? I'm hurting you know. Right? I'm doing what you wanted. Is this why you left, 'cause I wouldn't do this? Well, I'm doing it now!" He called out then looked down at the Aztec sun beaming out between Rick's shoulder blades and realized it was not Peter squirming beneath him. For a moment he had been lost in his past, lost to a man who no longer loved him.

What am I doing? he wondered. He wanted to stop this, to pull out of this boy and leave. He wanted to get back in his car and drive home where he could sit and hope Peter would come back to him. He wanted to make dinner for two and forget how liberating it felt to have this mechanic under him, how the surge of power over the boy made him feel more alive than he had since Peter left. He wanted to go back to being alone and miserable because that was familiar, almost comforting to him now.

But he couldn't do that because his body was responding to the boy wrapped around his cock right now. The familiar tingle was coursing through his belly and he could feel his balls tightening to a hard fist as another orgasm worked its way through him.

He felt the come rising in him and knew he couldn't hold off. He pushed himself harder and faster, rocking the mechanic until his head almost hit the wall. The tingle spread through his nuts and down his legs, right down to each toe, then Simon's entire body froze as the orgasm came.

Starlights danced before his eyes as he flooded the condom. Simon heard a loud buzzing as the explosive force of the orgasm numbed his other senses, and in the background, like a whisper, his own voice grunting. His entire body went limp and he fell against Rick, his face pressed against the sun tattoo.

Simon kissed the Aztec sun, lapped at the sweat rolling down from the nape of Rick's neck, as his cock jumped and pumped more juice into the condom until it finally faded. He felt Rick's hand on his head, massaging it, running his dirty fingers through the soft blond hair. Simon pushed himself up and slowly pulled his cock from the boy's hole. He peeled the condom off and tossed it in the toilet.

Rick straightened and turned around. His erection jabbed Simon in the belly.

Simon felt the idea of Peter dissipate, slip away. For six months he had been fixed on the hope that Peter would come back to him, that he would see that Simon's love for him outweighed his need to explore his masochistic desires. Now Simon realized it wasn't just the sex that had split them. Peter simply wanted out and he had used the one thing he thought Simon could not do to free himself. He supposed Simon could not be an aggressive dominant lover, and frankly, Simon thought the same. But now he found he could do it. And he liked it.

If Peter had really wanted to stay with him, he would have given up the idea of a rough sex life, and if Simon had wanted him to stay, he would have given a bigger effort to satisfy him. They both had used the sex as an excuse to end their relationship, he realized. Neither wanted to continue with the other.

Simon felt freer and more liberated than he had in a long time. Yet a kernel of his former lover still held firm. He could feel its power inside him, still controlling him. *How could I live without Peter?* it made him ask himself. How could he go on without the one man he had actually felt something for? He knew, to be truly free from his former lover, he had to take charge.

And so, he pushed Rick back against the wall separating the two stalls, dropped to his knees and pulled Rick down into his throat.

The rankness of his dirty cock coated Simon's mouth. Hot sweat, urine and just a hint of the motor oil that spotted Rick forced a wet retch up through Simon's throat. He pushed it back down and forced that much more of the mechanic into him, until his lips met the tangled mat of pubic hair. He inhaled the boy's odor. Raw, pungent, real. There was no perfume here, no scented soaps or finely trimmed bush. This was a tangled mess of funk and bodily fluids.

"Don't," Rick said. "I'm too close." Rick squirmed and pressed his palms against Simon's forehead, trying to push him back. But Simon ignored him and slid one finger along Rick's balls, tickling the wiry hairs, then back, into the battered yet still suckling hole he had just enjoyed. His finger slid up to the second knuckle, a hot, wet hunger pulling him in, then a sudden vice-like clamp as the sphincter slammed shut and Rick came.

The warm seed painted Simon's throat as he swallowed the sweet, watery liquid and felt the last remnants of Peter leave him. He realized, what went on between Rick and himself in this filthy bathroom—a place he never before could see himself engaging in any intimate contact, much less the rough fucking that had just happened—was more than just sex. It was therapy. He had been freed of the illusion that Peter would come back to him. Free of the restraints of his own sexual proclivities. He could engage in more unconventional sex acts without worrying that he might like it, because he did like it and that was okay. He wouldn't take it too far and hurt the one he was with and he found, through Rick's reaction to the slaps and hair pulling, that pain could be as much a sexual stimulant as a kiss.

Simon worked the cock until it began to grow flaccid in his mouth, then he pulled off it with a slurpy plop. Rick leaned against the wall, panting, his legs, pale, covered in a heavy sprinkling of dark hair, quivered with the rush of the orgasm.

Simon stood, pulled his pants back up to his waist and watched Rick as he gathered himself, slipped into his uniform shirt and tucked it into the Dickies. Rick looked up at him and smiled then quickly kissed him on the mouth. "Gotta go back to work," he said, slipping out of the stall and opened the outside door. A heavy blast of sunlight spilled in the room along with a rush of fresh air.

Simon got dressed and went to the sink to wash his face. His hair was sticky with sweat and the greasy taste of Rick's come was turning sour in his throat. He cupped his hands and drank some of the warm sink water. He checked his wallet, pulled out a pair of twenties for the gas and a business card, then scrawled his name and cell phone number on the back and left the bathroom.

Rick stood outside leaning on the gas pump, drinking soda from a can. He looked up at Simon, then let his eyes fall, suddenly sheepish now that the sex was over. "That's thirty-seven dollars for the gas," he said, returning to the real business. Simon handed him the money and the card. Rick looked at the card, flipped it over to Simon's cell number and smiled. He slipped it in his pocket, then pulled out three ones and handed them to Simon. "Looks like we had the same idea," Rick said and nodded at the money in Simon's hand.

Simon opened the bills. There was a scrap of paper with Rick printed on it and a phone number. "That's my home number. I don't have a cell but I work until six. I'm home after that," Rick told him.

"Cool." Simon looked down at the number, then slipped the money in his wallet.

"How long has it been?" Rick asked.

"What do you mean?"

"Since you last got laid. How long?"

"Six months."

"That's too long, man. Give me a call sometime, maybe we can get a few beers, do this again."

"I'd like that." Simon said, thinking about the two-hour drive he still had to get home. Two hours was a long drive to come back for a quickie. If there was a chance for something more between them, well, then the drive might be worth it. A chance meeting like this was one thing. It was hot and fun and now he was beginning to understand Danny's way of thinking. Not every orgasm had to be another step in a relationship. Sometimes a good fuck could be just a good fuck. It didn't have to mean moving vans and a commitment ceremony.

But to drive back there to relieve a hard-on without a possibility of an "I love you" or even an "I like you" hardly seemed worth the effort.

"I live down the road a bit, at the Elm Street Trailer Park," Rick said. "I got lots of toys. I can trust you with handcuffs, can't I? You don't seem like a serial killer or nothing."

"Yeah, you can trust me," he said and slipped into the Lexus. He slid the key in the ignition, started it and rolled his window down.

"Cool. I live alone," Rick replied, taking a step back from the car. "It sucks, sleeping every night alone. Would spending the night interest you? I mean, if not, we can just fool around, or something." He bit his lower lip with the jagged tooth, reminding Simon of a shy kid asking for a new toy.

"It would interest me," Simon said. He looked at the boy. They were very different people, different classes, not that Simon ever really concerned himself with class. What advantages a man had and what he did for a living didn't matter. It was the man that counted, not what he had or what he did. What little he knew of Rick told him that Rick was probably a good man.

Even with that, though, he couldn't really see this going beyond an occasional tryst. And if it did, well so be it. He wasn't going to plan his future any longer; he had done enough looking ahead since Peter left. He wasn't pining for the past either. All that mattered was the here and now. "I would really like that," Simon said.

"See you around, man," Rick said and nodded his head at Simon.

"I hope so." Simon replied, then slowly drove out of the gas station and back onto the highway. He slipped the paper with Rick's number in his shirt pocket, buttoned the pocket closed, then pulled a Camel from the pack on the seat and lit it.

He inhaled the smoke, the sweet tobacco dancing over his tongue. It was a strong flavor, but it didn't overpower the taste of Rick. He could still sense the boy's sweat and come on his tongue. He liked it.

His cell phone rang and he opened the center console where he had stored it before going into the conference that morning. He looked at the screen. It was Danny. Simon grinned and pressed the green TALK button. "Hey Danny," he said. "Boy, do I have a story for you."

From the Storm

Chapter 1:
In the Tempest

"I'll see you on Monday."

Bailey glanced up from his desk, scattered with papers, case files stacked in every corner. He could never seem to keep it neat like the other defenders in the office. Shelley stood in the doorway to his cubicle.

"Yeah," he replied, momentarily distracted from his files "Have a good weekend."

"Don't work too hard," she said as she left. Bailey laughed, but deep down, he knew he was looking at a long night.

A clap of thunder brought his attention to the gathering storm clouds outside the office window. His eyes itched from the hours he had already spent that day reading the stacks of briefs on his desk. He swore he had gone through every one of them twice—it wasn't the first time he'd been assigned a case where the kid was almost eighteen and the judge wanted him tried as an adult. If he could figure out a deal, the kid might have a chance to start over.

It was after five already, but he wasn't leaving until he found something. Being a public defender wasn't the most glamorous job, and some cases he'd fought had tested his morals. Then there were cases like this; a kid arrested for breaking and entering after running away from foster care for the third time. The ecstasy he'd had on him hadn't helped either. Cases like these were why Bailey had decided to go the public defender route instead of joining a rich, well-established firm.

The air conditioner was on the fritz, had been all day, leaving the whole floor hot and humid. Bailey was sure he looked a mess, brown hair pushed back so many times it stuck up in odd angles.

Appearance was usually the least of his worries, except when it came to the courtroom and looking professional—he was average looking, average height and build, dark brown eyes, and a scar over his eyebrow from the time he'd fallen out of a tree as a kid. His saving grace was that he looked damn good in a suit.

This time, this case, he had to help. If Adam was tried as an adult, he could go to jail for a long time. The felony possession could turn into something much worse. A mark like that on his record would ruin anything else he wanted to do in life.

Bailey's skin was sticky with humidity coming from the rain outside, heat pressing in all around him with no way to get rid of it. Thunder rumbled again behind him; he ignored it, but it was hard as the office got steadily darker and hotter. This case was the only thing on his mind at the moment, but he just couldn't figure it out. Judge Pearson was not one who tended to be lenient toward kids.

Rain battered the windows and his light flickered ominously. Glancing up, he frowned and tried to ignore his growing unease. Bailey had always lived in a large city, growing up in San Diego. He'd stayed there for undergrad, though those years hadn't always been kind. New York, though fundamentally different than San Diego, had its benefits. He'd moved to New York for grad school at SUNY Cortland, and he'd gotten hired at the public defender's office two years ago, after graduation. It was a change from the path he'd once expected to go: his dad had probably been insulted that he'd become a public defender instead of joining the family firm (not that Bailey knew for sure since he hadn't heard from him in years), but Bailey wouldn't have joined even if his dad miraculously apologized for everything. He hadn't become a lawyer just to please his parents or make money.

Rubbing his eyes, Bailey stretched in his uncomfortable chair. The storm shook the windows behind him, gathering strength. Bailey's tie choked him and he tugged it open. The tiny fan on his desk did little more than move the sticky air around. Despite all the things he liked about New York, summer storms were not included.

He dreaded the thought of getting home. There wouldn't be any cabs in the rain and the subway would be crowded and hot at this time of night—rush hour in New York City was always a bitch and lasted forever. It was barely six.

Another clap of thunder shook the office and Bailey jumped, surprised, knocking over the cup filled with pens. They rolled and dropped off the edge of the desk, clattering to the floor. He bent down to them scoop up, looking up sharply when he thought he heard a noise. The worst part of being alone in the building was the irrational fear, the prickle on the back of his neck every time he thought he heard something or someone. He didn't like the idea of the unknown creeping around in the darkness even though he was probably the only one in the office, aside from maybe a janitor. Everyone else had had the good sense to leave.

Bailey wasn't leaving, though, not until he figured out a way to help this kid. He'd been that kid before, the one who had no one to turn to in the darkest moments. He'd been lucky enough that when he had hit rock bottom, it hadn't landed him in jail or worse. Instead, he was simply drowning in student loans, but who wasn't?

"Get a grip," he told himself as he set the pens back in the cup. "You'll figure it out. Maybe we can talk the drug charges down to a misdemeanor."

"Talking to yourself is the first sign of madness."

Bailey jerked, startled as Ian stepped into the doorway. "Hey," he said, shaking away his momentary surprise. "What are you still doing here?"

Ian shrugged, a smirk on his face. His tie was tugged apart as well, the first few buttons of his shirt undone, a glisten of sweat on his forehead.

"Research on the Shale case. The glamorous life of an intern."

Bailey smiled. He remembered those days of endless research and meetings. Not that life had changed much except he got a real salary for his work these days—not all that much of a salary but enough to keep the creditors off his back. Ian wasn't much younger than him, a year or two, finishing up his graduate degree. He was cocky and confident, not to mention entirely too good-looking, with close-cut blond hair, a strong jaw, and a knowing smirk he always seemed to wear around Bailey.

Outside, rain pounded the window and Bailey could hear gusts of wind slamming into the pane.

"You almost done with yours?" Ian asked, rounding the desk and checking Bailey's computer.

Bailey laughed. "Not even close."

"I heard Judge Pearson's a hard ass. You plan on making a plea deal?"

"Depends if Adam's going to be tried as an adult or not." Bailey really hoped Adam wouldn't be—it was his first offense, after all, and he seemed like a good kid underneath the bravado.

Ian slid onto the desk as Bailey sat back in his chair. "What if he is tried as an adult? That'll be a longer sentence, right?"

Bailey sighed, tossing his pen on the desk and gazing at Ian. "Almost definitely a longer sentence if he's tried as an adult, and he'll go to prison rather than juvenile detention. Expunging his record will become nearly impossible, which means a much lower chance of being able to start over once he gets out. The only advantage to being tried as an adult is the right to a jury, which could work in his favor."

"You'll figure it out," Ian said confidently. "You can talk your way out of anything. After all, you talked me into going out with you."

"As I recall, you made a very inappropriate comment about sex at work to me," Bailey said, a smile growing. He left out the part where he had followed Ian into the lobby bathroom afterward and Ian had stuck his hands down Bailey's pants. It had been a damn good hand job and Bailey had jerked off to the memory for a week afterward. They'd been out a few times since, and Ian was becomingly increasingly distracting for Bailey. Not exactly a good thing when he had cases to work on. Luckily, their coworkers remained none the wiser, and Bailey wasn't too keen on finding out what the policies on inter-office romances were.

Ian grinned. "Subtlety is not my forte."

The flirting came easily to Ian; he was much less guarded than Bailey usually was. Even though they'd been out a few times, Bailey wasn't sure what he and Ian were exactly, but they were definitely something, possibly something very good if they could find time outside of work to figure it out.

"How long until you're done here? Does this mean our date is off?" Ian asked, tugging the neckline of his shirt open more in the heat. He grabbed the fan off Bailey's desk and pointed it at himself. With his shirt open, Bailey could see the tiny details in the orchid tattooed on his neck, half disappearing beneath the neckline of his shirt. He tried not to stare, but his mind immediately went to tracing the petals with his tongue.

Tonight was supposed to be his and Ian's third official date, though Bailey doubted there'd be anywhere to go even if he finished his work. Dating was kind of weird for Bailey: most of the time, he met guys on nights out and either didn't see them again, or else they ended up in fuckfest relationships that always ended badly. In undergrad, he'd been solely focused on getting through school without massive amounts of debt, and since his parents refused to pay for a "gay" education once he came out Sophomore year, most of his free time had gone toward doing whatever it took to pay the bills.

Even now, with a steady job and just enough money to afford somewhere to live—even though it was only a shitty studio apartment, not even big enough for a full-size fridge—guys were not a high priority. The last guy he'd dated had been back in grad school. Greg had refused to move to the city with him when he'd suggested it. He'd said it was career differences, but Bailey suspected it was whoever had owned the strange jacket he'd found in Greg's closet the day he moved out. Since then, there had been no one serious. Work came first anyway.

"You knew what you were getting into, dating a lawyer," Bailey said, shaking his head. Ian was still hogging his tiny fan, not that it did him any good anyway. Maybe he could just take the work home. His air-conditioner was a tiny box in his window, but at least it was cool.

"You really care about this kid, don't you?"

"I know what it feels like when people give up on you. Money shouldn't prevent people from having a good lawyer and protecting their basic rights."

Ian smiled. "I thought most lawyers were cutthroat and vicious, you know, the kind I want to be." He leaned in towards Bailey, eyes softening. "But I think what you do is awesome, even if public defenders make shit money."

"I didn't become a lawyer to get rich off other people." Bailey wouldn't exactly say he'd always made the right choices—he had definitely made some terrible ones in the past—but becoming a public defender hadn't been a bad choice. Being a lawyer had always been in the cards, even after his parents had refused to help. "You've got to do what you think is right."

"I completely agree," Ian replied sincerely. He leaned forward, fingers brushing against Bailey's neck. "I think you're amazing, and also that it's way too hot in here."

Bailey agreed, and Ian touching him wasn't making him any less hot, but he still had work to do. Ian's fingers sliding down his collarbone was almost enough to give him pause. If they could get out of there, they could somehow get to Ian's apartment....

"I just have to finish—"

The lights flickered, and with a rumble of thunder, everything went dark.

The computer screen died and his fan spluttered to a stop as Bailey raised his eyes to the ceiling. Every light had gone out, and whatever remnants of air conditioning had been blowing through the office stopped.

"Shit," he breathed, pushing back from his desk. He turned to the window as a bolt of lightning lit up the floor.

"What do we do?" Ian asked.

"Check the stairs," Bailey said immediately, pushing himself up from the chair.

As Ian left to check, Bailey moved out of his cubicle, into the hall where things were pitch black. The only light was Ian's cell phone as he weaved through desks. Fumbling, Bailey pulled out his phone and turned on the flashlight app, glad for the small flood of light so he could at least see where he was walking.

"They're open," Ian said as he came back, his light shining in Bailey's face. "Think we should leave?"

After a moment, Bailey shook his head. "If the power's out, all the traffic lights will be too. The subway'll be chaos. We'll never get a cab. Looks like we're stuck."

Another roll of thunder made Bailey jump and rain battered the window. Bailey told himself that he shouldn't be worried. The power would come back on eventually. He just may never finish going through the files. He had a meeting with the judge in two days.

"Are you okay?" Ian asked.

"I'm fine," Bailey assured him. "I guess I'm not getting any more work done today."

Ian's hand wrapped around his wrist, warm and firm in the light of their cell phones. "How about we get a drink?"

"Doubt there's any good stuff in the kitchen," Bailey pointed out as he followed Ian's cell phone's beam of light toward the kitchenette.

"Guess we'll just have to settle," Ian said, pulling out a couple of bottles of water from the fridge.

"Rule number one of being a lawyer—if you can settle, do it." Leaning against the counter, Bailey set his phone on it so that the flashlight created a bubble of light between him and Ian. Ian set his down as well. With the two phones, it cast a white light over the countertop that dimmed as it climbed up to the ceiling.

"Not great life advice, though," Ian pointed out, taking a swig of his water. "Funny how those things don't translate." He paused, watching Bailey. "What did you mean when you said you know what it's like when you don't have anyone?"

Bailey took a drink, feeling the cold water sliding down his throat. He shrugged. "Let's just say my parents didn't take my coming out so well." Actually, they'd sent him to a counselor, then when it hadn't changed anything, cut him off and he'd been left to struggle to pay for the rest of his undergrad and grad school alone. He hadn't spoken to them in almost five years.

Ian's eyebrows went up. "Well, that's their loss. And apparently the downtrodden of New York's gain."

"They don't all appreciate it," Bailey pointed out. He'd had plenty of cases where his clients despised him. It was his job to help them despite that, no matter how hard it was.

"I'm sure Adam does, in his own surly, teenage way," Ian said simply. After a minute, he sighed and wiped sweat off his forehead. "Jesus Christ, it's boiling."

"I hope we're not stuck here all night."

"Don't worry," Ian said, sliding his hand up Bailey's arm. "We'll find something to do. It could be worse."

"We're stuck twelve stories up with no air conditioning and no lights and no one else in the building." Bailey laughed. "How could it be worse?"

"You could be alone."

"Maybe I'd get some work done," he pointed out, arching an eyebrow at Ian, unable to hide his smile; it was hard enough concentrating on casework when he didn't have hot grad students bending over the copy machine every time he went to print something.

"Do I distract you, *sir*?" Ian smirked and tugged at his tie. "It's too fucking hot in here. I'm getting out of these clothes."

Chapter 2:
Cool Down

Bailey leaned against the counter, tilting his head to the side and enjoying the view when Ian untucked his shirt and unbuttoned it. He grinned as Ian pulled it off, leaving him in a thin under shirt, so thin that Bailey could see the dark outlines of his tattoos. A flush of excitement ran through him as he watched Ian strip. They hadn't quite gotten this far on any of their dates. Not that Bailey hadn't thought about it. He'd thought about it quite a bit in the last few weeks.

"You don't have to be cavalier," Ian said as Bailey stood there, too busy admiring Ian's body to consider joining him. Ian reached for the buttons on Bailey's shirt. A thrill ran through Bailey at the touch. Anytime they touched, whether by accident or design, Bailey got a thrill of expectation. Of course, everything about Ian gave that to him.

Ian was the first person since Greg to make him feel like something more than a one-night stand, which might have been why he hadn't jumped into bed after that first night out. It was different with Ian, even if Ian would leave for school in the fall. Rushing things had never worked out well for Bailey.

He definitely wasn't getting any work done, not that he could without lights or Internet. Bailey snapped out of his reverie a minute later as Ian got the buttons undone. Bailey tugged his tie open enough to yank it over his head and Ian pushed the shirt over his shoulders. He forced himself to stop staring and fantasizing about running his tongue over every inch of the tattoo and Ian's stomach. He planned on doing just that in a minute or two. Air breezed over his arms, and it was a momentary relief.

"Better?" Ian asked.

"Yeah." It was slightly better despite the thunder rumbling all around them, the darkness outside the dim light their phones provided. Ian's face was gilded in blue and white from the light and he smiled at Bailey.

"You look hot," Ian said finally, and Bailey wasn't sure which way he meant it. He didn't move as Ian went to the fridge and pulled open the freezer. Bailey didn't stop himself from staring at his ass. It was a very nice ass.

As Ian rummaged in the fridge, Bailey closed his eyes for a second, trying to remember what being cool felt like, but he couldn't. His mind still lingered on the briefs back in his office, but it became more difficult to concentrate when Ian grabbed a handful of ice and dropped it in a cup on the counter.

"I think we should both cool down," Ian said, coming back to Bailey.

"I don't think the boss would approve," Bailey said, smiling slightly and leaning against the counter.

"Well, I think it's hot in here and you've worked very hard today," Ian replied, cornering Bailey and smirking. Bailey almost groaned, but it was cut off by a gasp as something cold and wet slid along his collarbone, gliding up the bone, sliding up the length of his neck as he tilted his head back, swallowing slowly.

The refreshing coldness only lasted for a second, wherever Ian slid the ice cube, leaving a cold trail behind that seemed to dry within seconds. He felt the brush of Ian's fingers, calloused from his hours plucking at guitar strings. He tried not to shiver, focusing on the way they grazed against his skin.

He felt the ice melting as Ian let it slip down his throat and back to his chest. He breathed out slowly, stretching his neck back and closing his eyes.

It wasn't how Bailey had imagined it, but he'd imagined it in an air-conditioned bedroom, not the tiny office kitchenette where they drank stale coffee and listened to coworkers' gossip.

The ice melted completely, and only Ian's fingers were left, trailing the last bit of water along his collarbone, but when something warmer, softer, pressed against his skin, Bailey's eyes opened.

Bringing up a hand, he slid it into Ian's soft hair as Ian's lips brushed against him. All the blood seemed to be rushing to his cock as Ian's mouth continued its exploration of his collarbone.

"I don't think that's going to help cool us off," he managed to say, biting back a moan at Ian's soft touch. Any lingering worries about the case left him as Ian ran his tongue up his neck and nibbled at his jaw.

"Not supposed to," Ian replied, plucking another ice cube out of the mug and cupping Bailey's jaw. The ice slid against him, shivering cold, a sharp contrast to the heat pressing in around them, thick and muggy.

Bailey kissed Ian first, capturing his lips before he could speak again, licking inside and drawing out a shaky moan. Ian's hand clutched Bailey's neck, the ice cube melting rapidly, cold water sliding down his skin, dripping to the floor.

His cock twitched eagerly when Ian pulled back and grinned wolfishly through the eerie light of their phones. It was finally happening. Ian's hand swept across his stomach, his palm hot as it landed on his hip, fingers pressing into his skin. With his free hand, Ian slid another ice cube to the curve of his neck, cradled there by his hand. Water slithered down his shoulder and onto the floor.

"God," he breathed, breaking the kiss, hands pawing at Ian's undershirt, shoving underneath to get to the skin.

The ice melted and Ian's hand went to Bailey's thigh, sliding up the slick fabric of his dress pants. Fuck, he really needed to get out of those. As far as he was concerned, there was no need for clothes at this point.

Ian tugged at Bailey's shirt, ruffling his hair as he got it over his head. Bailey pulled at Ian's shirt as well, eager to finally get a good look at his body. He wasn't disappointed as the fabric lifted over his head. Bailey had been right—Ian did have more tattoos. From the orchid on his neck, a trail of different flowers formed the tail of an alligator across his chest. For a moment, he was caught up staring at the intricate details he'd be able to see better in more light. Something to look forward to. Three dates and this was the first time he'd seen Ian shirtless. That first hand job in the bathroom had been quick, but this was better. He only wished it could have happened somewhere else; somewhere where the lights worked, where it wasn't a thousand degrees.

For a long moment, Bailey's eyes devoured the tattoo, reaching out and skimming his fingers over the different lines spreading over the skin. Ian's suits covered them, hid them from the partners and everyone else. Bailey was one of the few who got to see them, and even better, touch them.

Reaching over, Ian grabbed another ice cube from the quickly melting pile and brushed it against Bailey's lips. Bailey flicked his tongue out to taste it, cold on his tongue, and Ian watched intently, gaze darkening as he slid it down Bailey's skin instead, brushing over his stomach. Bailey jumped at the coldness tracing his muscles, circling around his bellybutton and brushing to the waist of his pants as it melted.

Bailey moaned, hand tight around the back of Ian's neck, keeping him close as their lips collided, desperate, eager. He didn't want Ian to stop.

"Ian," he breathed, barely able to make his mouth work when Ian's cold, wet hand slid down to his chest, pressing what was left of the ice cube to his nipple. "Oh, shit... yeah."

Ian smiled against his mouth, and Bailey could feel it.

"Shit," Bailey breathed, squeezing his eyes shut for a minute. "Pants?" he asked vaguely, hopefully, reaching for Ian's slacks, but Ian moved faster, yanking Bailey forward by his belt, sliding halfway off the counter as Ian got the belt open, the zipper down, and slipped his hand underneath. His hand grazed down his stomach, wrapped around his cock, and tugged.

Bailey groaned against Ian's neck. Third dates were the best.

"Bailes," Ian said, using that warm, affectionate tone that made Bailey's stomach twist stupidly.

Dragging Ian's mouth to his, Bailey kissed him. This kiss was harder, pushing up against Ian like some horny teenager who couldn't get enough of his hands on his skin. Despite how hot he already felt, Ian's mouth just made him hotter.

Ian's hand tightened around Bailey's cock, stroking slowly, purposefully. Bailey's leg wrapped around Ian's thigh and he groaned into the kiss, mouths pressed together in a breathless exchange of moans, soft, sliding exhales and sharp, sudden gasps.

"Fuck," Bailey breathed when Ian pulled back for half a second, pausing and licking his lips. His head swam dizzily as Ian nuzzled his cheek, drawing him into a slow, burning kiss.

Everything was too warm, heat racing over his skin, panted breath against Ian's mouth as each kiss broke. A second to breathe before their mouths collided again. Over the distant rumble of thunder, Bailey heard Ian's panted breath as they moved together, bodies writhing up. He heard Ian's soft noise, almost a sigh against his lips. Bailey's hand twined into Ian's hair as his hips pushed into Ian's grip.

Ian's mouth collided with his, hot and biting, sucking his bottom lip as Bailey moaned against him, straining in his grip. It wasn't enough, and Bailey opened his mouth to say so, but Ian slid his hand up, jerking Bailey off torturously slowly.

Bailey broke from the kiss with a gasp, head falling back. A roll of thunder shook the room, but he could barely hear it over the rush of blood in his ears, the thudding of his heart against his ribcage.

"Oh, God, Bailey," Ian breathed as Bailey squirmed beneath him.

"Fuck," Bailey muttered. "Ian, fuck." He slipped completely off the counter, standing on his toes. Ian's free hand curled around the back of his thigh, but he didn't try to lift him back onto the counter.

Ian pulled back to look at him, breaking the kiss, leaving them both panting. "Not bad for a third date," he murmured, his hands abandoning their tasks and moving to tug at Bailey's pants.

Bailey could only nod in agreement. It wasn't the third date he'd pictured, but it was ending the way he'd hoped.

Ian slid down slowly, tongue grazing along Bailey's stomach, hands shimmying Bailey's pants over his hips, slipping to the floor. It was going to be a bitch to iron all that, but Bailey wasn't thinking about ironing, not when Ian was on his knees on the ugly linoleum floor. His cock jumped excitedly, expectantly, as Ian traced the lines of his hips.

Bailey said nothing as Ian's mouth enveloped his cock—too hot, too wet, too slick—and he gasped for breath. Anything he might have said would have been inadequate to express the pleasure that rippled through his body as Ian went down on him.

Stretching his neck back, Bailey tried hard not to push his cock into Ian's inviting mouth. Heat rushed to his skin, oppressive as he leaned against the counter, the sharp edge cutting into his back. He would never be able to look at this place the same again. His palms pressed against the counter, gripping tightly as Ian sucked, moving his mouth back and forth over his throbbing cock. He wished the air conditioning would come back on. His skin burned feverishly as he tried to focus, but his mind was fuzzy, and all he felt was hot, Ian's mouth, Ian's hands pushing his legs apart, fingers gliding up his thighs.

Ian moaned around his cock, and Bailey's hips pushed up, following the movement of Ian's mouth. Bailey spent a lot of time, time he should have spent working, fantasizing about things like this, like Ian's mouth on his body, teeth sinking into the skin the way he liked it but never told anyone about.

He let out an embarrassing whimper as Ian took him in deeper, swallowing around his cock. It was too much, too much for Bailey, and he groaned, pushing against Ian's shoulders, trying to warn him.

Ian didn't pull back, despite Bailey's insistence, the way he strained, letting out a choked whimper, body shaking as he came.

Bailey squeezed his eyes shut, gasping for breath as he came, Ian's mouth still around his cock, tongue sliding over the ridges. His hips jerked as the tightness released in his stomach, uncurled slowly as the wave of heat crashed over him and he couldn't hold back.

Sweat beaded on his forehead as he let out a shaky breath, blinking slowly. This was much better than any date could have been. Except, maybe, if they had done it somewhere cooler. Third dates had definitely risen in his estimation.

Ian pulled back, licking his lips and wiping at the corner of his mouth with his hand. He met Bailey's eyes, though, and smiled, pulling himself up by the counter and leaning into him.

"You're so hot," Bailey breathed, kissing Ian softly, reaching between them and pressing his hand into the bulge in Ian's slacks. Ian moaned in appreciation at the touch, shuffling closer to Bailey.

"Yeah, hot," he agreed eagerly, pushing into Bailey's hand.

With a little maneuvering, he got Ian's slacks undone and slid his hand underneath. Ian's cock hardened in his hand, and a ripple of satisfaction ran over him as Ian groaned and shifted into his grip, urging him faster.

"Shit," Ian cursed under his breath. "Bailes...."

Bailey kissed Ian hard, biting down on his lower lip and sucking as he jerked him off, listening to the subtle changes in Ian's breathing, the breathless moan against his skin as his hips jerked and Ian came.

For a long moment, neither of them moved. Bailey's hand was still wrapped around Ian's prick, but he pulled it away slowly, sliding out of his jeans. For a moment, he was sure that this was possibly the best date he'd ever been on, then a crash of thunder so loud it shook the whole building made Bailey jump, heart rising in his throat.

"Jesus," he cursed. He really didn't appreciate the loud, sudden noises.

"It's okay," Ian assured him, stroking a hand down his neck.

Bailey shook his head. "I'm really not that partial to storms."

Ian smiled, running a hand through Bailey's sweaty hair. "It'll be over soon."

Bailey nodded, stealing a kiss. "Then we can plan our next date."

Ian paused thoughtfully. "I was thinking the copy room."

Bailey laughed. "Or we could just go to my place, order pizza, fuck on my oh-so-glamorous futon bed."

"That sounds like an excellent idea, if we ever get out of here," Ian agreed, kissing Bailey soundly.

As if on cue, the lights flickered on above them. Ian looked up.

"Maybe that was the universe's way of agreeing with us."

"Or it was good luck," Bailey said, grabbing his undershirt off the floor and pulling it on. He buttoned his dress shirt, ignoring the wrinkles. "I need to get back to work. No more distractions."

Ian tugged on his shirt and turned back to Bailey. "How about we take the files back to your place and I'll help you?"

Bailey smiled slightly. The case was his, after all, but the one thing he'd learned over the years was to always accept help when it was offered, especially if it came in the form of a hot guy.

"Let's get out of here," he said, heading back to his office and gathering up the files. Ian helped him pack them in his briefcase, brushing his hand against Bailey's as they stepped away. Bailey met his eyes and smiled, heading for the stair door. He wasn't going to let Adam down, but that didn't mean he couldn't have a life as well.

E.E. Grey

If you enjoyed this story, you can sign up for a free membership at ForbiddenFiction.com and discuss it with other readers and the author at the *From the Storm* story page at http://forbiddenfiction.com/story/EEG-1.000186.

We do our best to proof all our work, but if you spot a text error we missed, please let us know via our website Contact Form at http://forbiddenfiction.com/contact.

The Wages of Sin

Chapter 1:
Abomination

I can hear the rumbling of bombs from somewhere north of the city. Washington, D.C. is hunkered down under the onslaught, grudgingly relinquishing the northern suburbs inch by bloody inch to the northern invaders. The vidfeeds from Rockville look pretty rough. Lots of civilian casualties, they say, though it's hard to tell if the Homeland Security techies have doctored the footage. One of the guys down on the sixth floor said he lives in Rockville and they got a couple of stray mortars, but nothing like what we saw on the vids. Regardless of Rockville's fate, it seems clear that the U.S. Army is pretty close to here, firing flock after flock of British-made Bluebird laser-guided missiles into the 'burbs in hopes of pressuring the C.S.A. into withdrawal or surrender. It's a flawed strategy since these guys are fuckin' nuts and don't really care about civilian casualties. When a Churchy dies in the holy war, he or she goes directly to heaven; do not pass St. Peter; do not stand in judgment before the big guy. Fuckin' nuts.

If I sound a little disgruntled for a duly-appointed civil servant with a federal pension minimally funded by the Christian States of America, consider the following facts: I was a career diplomat working in the State Department under Rice and then Romney, recalled from my post in London just before the Partition. I have a PhD from Georgetown, but since my alma mater has lost its accreditation over doctrinal disagreements with the Current Occupant, I am now working for the Department of Christian Policy in a dead-end clerical job editing passport regulations, maintaining low-level international watch lists, and approving student visas (not that there are many of those these days). And last, but certainly not least, I am a deeply-closeted homosexual in a country where homosexuals may legally be put to death without a trial. I think I have a right to sound a little disgruntled now and again.

I hear a particularly loud explosion and a plume of smoke starts to make its way skyward. Somewhere near Chevy Chase, property values have just plummeted.

Before the wars, the building in which I spend my days was a conglomeration of small governmental bureaus, corporate offices, and retail shops, and a hopping place, homosexually speaking. There were at least half a dozen public restrooms where men cruised from early morning to late evening without pause. You couldn't go in the men's room in the food court or the third floor lobby without hearing the rustle of clothing and the clinking of belt buckles, followed by that long, listening silence characterized by held breaths and blinking eyes. And then after a moment or two, if you were deemed harmless, the sounds of sucking and fucking would start up again. It was magical in a way, being surrounded by all those men having sex just a few yards from waiting rooms full of political refugees or college kids bound for semesters in Europe.

Perhaps my memories are tainted, the gilded images of sexual abandon made sweeter by cruel comparison, the darkness of the past decade making the world before seem lighter and freer. But who can say, really. You could ask Larry Craig, but he's on the other side of the fucking Partition, both literally and figuratively, having fled home to Idaho, joining the reconstituted U.S. Senate in Denver as a New Republican. Schwarzenegger calls the NRs a "kinder, gentler form of American Conservatism." I guess what he means is they've left most of the religious wingnuts and the hardcore racists on this side of the Partition so they can afford to be a little more socially inclusive without losing votes. But I'm getting ahead of myself.

The first couple of years after September 11th, things here in D.C. changed slowly, the adjustments seeming calm and natural, but then with the Secession Crisis of 2006, events escalated so suddenly that nobody here on the ground had time to get out of Dodge. By the time I was recalled from (godless) London, the capital was clamped down like an egg in a vice. When the Partition went up a few months later, and the borders were closed for good, the egg transformed into marble, hard and immobile and suffocating.

By the beginning of 2005, the Christian Coalition controlled vocal minorities in both houses of the U.S. Congress. Most Americans were still convinced this was nothing more than politics as usual. Then, the world changed forever. The forty-third president of the republic, flanked by an impressive array of military brass, party leadership, and national religious leaders, formally repudiated the U.S. Constitution and declared "the rebirth of the *true* American republic, a nation unified in its dedication to the implementation of God's law here on Earth."

State governments scrambled to enact bills affirming their allegiance to the C.S.A. or the U.S.A. while pundits and Constitutional scholars argued on network television. At a quickly-convened Constitutional Convention in Denver, the secessionist states reunited under the U.S. Constitution and the hastily redesigned 38-star flag, asserting their rightful claim to the national history and prestige of the former U.S.A.

There were a few naval skirmishes and a couple of spectacular aerial dogfights during the summer of 2006. Conscription began in earnest, but uncertainty prevented the deployment of ground troops. Faced with the prospect of killing other American soldiers in the streets of Washington or Chicago, both sides wondered if U.S. soldiers would freeze.

The whole world waited in stupefying silence as the two Americas stood glowering at one another over the concrete Partition that meandered from Maryland in a jagged line down to Texas. Both sides were armed to the teeth; two nuclear superpowers brimming over with a century's worth of righteous indignation. The Waiting War lasted almost twenty-six months while the two Americas launched international re-branding campaigns, and jockeyed for trading partners, media outlets, and military alliances.

And then at last the smart bombs started to fall on Southern cities.

The bombing raids were heralded as a miracle from God, somehow confirming the righteousness of the C.S.A. cause. Everywhere people talked about the Rapture and speculated on the day or the hour of His coming.

But as the weeks turned to months and the fighting heated up, something started to happen. Belief and exultation started to morph into fear. And fear woke some people up. Finally.

By mid-2009, when the Blue resistance began to rear its ugly head in Atlanta, Birmingham, New Orleans, Dallas, Austin, and finally here in D.C., the egg started to develop hairline fractures. And this shift brought the inevitable breakdown of moral order. When it looked like we might all die, when General Petraeus started talking about tactical nukes and Senator Balder started pushing for an all-out U.S. invasion of the "Occupied South," perceptions about sex here on the other side of the Partition shifted suddenly, at least among the civilian population. We felt the sexual jolt like an earthquake.

When I was in college I remember reading accounts of New York during World War II that described a general spirit of abandon that permeated the bars and the clubs and the streets of the city. *You want to lean me up against that wall and fuck me up the ass? Well, I've never been with a man before, but, what the hell; I'm fuckin' shipping out to the Ardennes tomorrow.*

Likewise here in Occupied D.C. the war had made sluts of us all.

I started seeing young couples making out on the Metro again. Black market bourbon and vodka started appearing at parties and a couple of the dance halls started staying open after ten. People started making the occasional sexual joke in line at the grocery store or in the elevators. I even got invited to a key party up in Woodley Park by this guy I know from the Travel Advisory office.

The suddenness of the shift was so remarkable that the Blues immediately started tweeting about it, claiming that as their guerrilla attacks became more frequent so too did the reports of Levitican Code violations, as if the adulterers and the gender-traitors (homosexuals) and the life-takers (users of contraception) had run into the streets to fornicate to the sounds of automatic gunfire and explosions.

And maybe they had.

There will surely be a future PhD thesis in there somewhere. Refornication: Politico-Social Antecedents to the Sexual Tipping Point Phenomenon in the early C.S.A. period.

For a while, I assumed the shift was an exclusively hetero phenomenon, but I was wrong. The first time I really noticed that the shift included the gays was about a week after the U.S.-backed NOLA Blues seized control of New Orleans. They took over the public works by force and threw open the border to the waiting U.S.

Army. There was an information blackout, even on the internal C.S.A. governmental feeds, but the news was blaring from every major U.S. news site. I had a free-chip Blackberry I'd bought on the black market and I sat in my office with the door locked, watching video of U.S. troops rolling into the Garden District for the second time in a decade, but this time hailed as liberators, the soldiers greeted by cheering crowds waving the old Stars and Stripes and pelting them with Mardi Gras beads and strings of pink azalea blossoms.

I felt the tears streaming down my face and had to log off.

I lay with my head down on the desk for over an hour listening to the sound of my own breathing and feeling sorry for myself. When I finally managed to get my shit together enough to get past the secretaries without too many awkward questions, I told Erika I was going to lunch and headed for the elevators. "Praise be to Him," she called after me, her voice light and sweet.

"Praise be," I called, flashing her a false grin and waving as I fled.

The elevators were state of the art a decade ago, but the company that installed them was on the northern side of the Partition, so service calls were now out of the question. The building manager had hired a couple of guys who used to work for the manufacturer, but the software could not be upgraded and the bugs seemed to multiply as the elevators aged.

On this particular afternoon, they worked perfectly.

I slipped through the open doors and pressed three.

I watched the doors close and wondered why I had pushed three instead of the lobby level. I had a couple of ration credits saved up and there was a newly re-opened Wendy's diagonally across from my building. I'd been smelling the freedom fries for weeks now.

But when the doors slid open on three, I stepped out into the lobby, cutting close to the wall on my right and walking down a narrow strip of carpet that fell outside the range of all four of the ceiling-mounted spypods. I slid along the wall, trying to look nonchalant, nodding to a guy from Engineering and a pair of techies from the State Department data well.

I ducked into the men's room.

It was quiet in the outer room. A row of sinks stood deserted in the flickering light of fluorescents. Half of the bulbs had been removed and all but one of the sinks had been capped. Out of Order signs hung in a neat row above the capped faucets.

I walked across the linoleum, my footsteps echoing angrily in the long empty room.

I pulled open the door to the inner room, tugging past the point of resistance, the door scraping noisily across the battered linoleum. The lights inside glowed dimly; here too many of the bulbs had been removed or never replaced. In the murky half-light I could see a line of six stalls facing eight urinals. A tall thin man in a gray suit stood at one of the urinals, his eyes glued to the wall in front of him.

I prepared to nod to the guy, but he didn't turn around or acknowledge my presence.

I pulled the door noisily shut behind me and made my way across to the row of stalls. I walked down the row, stopping at the second stall from the end and pushing lightly on the door. It was locked. I caught a glimpse of movement through the crack between the door and the frame. I saw tanned skin, dark eyes, dark hair, and a navy blue work shirt that looked like it was unbuttoned from neck to waist. My stomach lurched with excitement.

As expressionlessly as possible, I stepped to the last cubicle and pushed open the door, making a bit of a show of stepping in, throwing the bolt, and settling myself on the toilet with my pants around my knees.

I sat in silence, the lack of sound from the man at the urinals a clear indicator that I had stumbled into something more than an afternoon leak.

I leaned to my right and eased my head down until I could see more of the guy in the next cubicle. He was wearing black work boots and blue uniform pants pushed down low around his ankles. He had muscular calves, hard and tan and covered with thick dark hair. He was sitting with his legs spread wide, but I couldn't see anything more without being obvious.

I sat back up and looked through the crack between the door and the frame and saw that the guy at the urinal had moved over and was standing at an angle, his head turned back to peer into my stall. He was handsome, from what I had glimpsed coming in, with dark hair slicked back and a strong profile with a stubbled jaw line like Clark Kent. From what I could see now, his face didn't really live up to the promise of his profile, but I'd sure as hell let him suck me

97

off. He jerked his head, signaling me to come out, or maybe to let him in.

He shifted his body, giving me a clear view of his cock. It was incredibly long and pale with a pink head. As his long fingers stroked up and down the length of it, the pale foreskin inched up to embrace the spongy head. I could feel my mouth watering.

I slid my hand between my legs and stroked my own erect cock.

The sound of someone yanking the screeching door open startled me so badly I jumped, a jolt of adrenaline searing through my body. My hands started to shake and I looked down at the floor. My eyes settled on the black work boots, motionless at the edge of my vision.

I heard the door to another stall further down the line open and close. The bolt slid into place. There was a rustling of clothing and then silence descended again.

I listened to the hum of the overhead lights and tried to still the thudding of my heart. I imagined the others could hear the telltale pounding of my gender-traitor heart. I wondered if one of them was a DAF officer. The Department of the American Family was tasked with Levitican Code enforcement and they were well known for entrapping the unwary and then issuing execution spot warrants that were carried out by crimson-uniformed members of the Christian Brotherhood.

My mouth was dry; my hands were sweating profusely.

I considered just zipping up and flushing and fleeing, but as the seconds ticked away, I felt my anxiety ease.

I looked toward the urinals but Clark Kent had taken his long dong elsewhere.

I chanced another look under the partition, dipping my head way down this time. I saw the man who had just entered the other stall dropping onto his knees on the floor and jacking himself quietly. He had his back to the toilet and was facing the row of urinals, his cock below the bottom of the door. I looked toward the urinals and sure enough, Clark Kent had wandered down to that end of the room and was standing in front of that other guy's stall, his arm moving in a slow, rhythmic motion that made my cock jump.

My attention was brought back to my own end of the room when I saw the black work boot closest to me tap three times gently on the floor.

Nothing else, just three taps.

I tapped back an answer, my mind racing. If this guy had not busted the other two, he was not DAF, right?

I heard a sound like coins shifting in a pocket and then the guy in blue sank down on his knees, turning his body to face mine. He slid his knees under the partition, his thighs flexed thick and hard as he shifted his weight, pushing further to slide his cock toward me. When his cock slid under the partition, I gasped aloud. I was already up and turning to position myself between his knees when the monster slid into view. He had a thickknobbed head that was purple and big as a plum. It rode a long dark shaft and wore a foreskin that bunched loosely around the mushroom head. When I saw the glistening droplet of precome oozing out of his slit, I forgot all about the DAF and lowered my mouth onto him, sliding the plum between my wide-stretched lips.

He sighed and I swallowed his enormous cock as far down my throat as I could manage.

I was engulfed by the smell of him, sweaty and musky with a strong undercurrent of sex, as if this was not the first time he had had sex today. Intoxicating. I slid him in and out of my throat experimentally, gagging slightly, my muscles completely unaccustomed to his girth. When I felt the gag, I pushed him further down my throat, letting my muscles massage him. The dark curly hair on his muscular thighs scratched against my cheeks.

I slid my mouth up and down the length of him, increasing the rhythm and letting my right hand snake behind his large, low-hanging balls to fondle his asshole. When my finger slid across his anus, I heard him gasp and felt his cock tense in my throat.

A horrific screech sent a panic through us both. We pulled apart and slid back onto our toilets so fast I felt a long string of ropey saliva and precome drip down from my face to my shirt front.

A short figure in a dark suit stepped up to one of the urinals, peed, flushed, and left. The door screeched closed behind him. I looked under the partition and realized the two other guys were now in adjoining stalls at the opposite end of the row. They, too, were looking under the partition. My eyes met Clark Kent's brown eyes. He winked at me. I was so surprised I laughed out loud, and then winked back.

I looked beside me and caught a glimpse of the monster cock's owner. He had a chiseled Italian face, dark eyes and a hairy, muscular chest. He was stroking his cock and before I could say anything, he was on his knees again, pushing his cock back under the partition.

I went down on him with a vengeance, letting my hand stray up his body, sliding along the muscles of his torso, reaching for a thick, hard nipple and twisting it as I felt his body start to convulse. He came in a series of thrusting, pulsing motions that shot come deep down my throat. I sucked until he reached down and touched my chin, his fingers caressing me lightly as he withdrew his cock. He slid back and stood up in his cubicle.

I sat back on the toilet, my own cock rearing up between my legs, and finished myself off in a couple of strokes, sending a torrent of come into a wadded-up ball of toilet paper.

By the time I finished, I was alone in the restroom, wondering if it had all been a dream.

Chapter 2:
Rapture

Over the next few weeks I made a point of running errands throughout the building, stopping along the way whenever I could to survey the men's rooms. I had a lesbian friend named Sarah who worked as a level three accountant. Her office, a satellite of the General Accounting Office, was located on the third floor. We had a mutually-beneficial, publicly on-again-off-again dating relationship, so I spent a little extra time on her floor, taking her flowers a couple of times and then meeting her for lunch, each time slipping into the third floor men's room, but each time finding the place deserted.

The weeks turned to months without another incident. I spent a lot of evenings jerking off to illegal porn or watching live feeds from the U.S. on my black market Blackberry.

With the loss of New Orleans and the critical Mississippi River port, the C.S.A. had escalated hostilities, drafting hundreds of thousands of young Christians into the Army, the Navy and the Cee Bees. The Christian Brotherhood policed the home front while the Army and Navy fought along the borders. As the lists of holy martyrs grew longer, the death of the boys at the front seemed to stimulate the Cee Bees to more violent confrontations here at home.

Clashes between the Cee Bees and the Blues, the most organized of the resistance movements, became more violent. During the week before Thanksgiving 2010, the fighting near DuPont Circle became so bad the Metro station was closed and I had to get off at Farragut North and walk back up Connecticut Avenue to my office. As I approached DuPont Circle that Wednesday morning I stopped cold, my hands shoved in my pockets, my frosty breath suddenly ragged and forced. The fountain in the circle had long ago been drained, the water too precious to waste on frivolities. That morning, the three pale marble maidens, whose lithe bodies represented the sea, the stars, and the wind, were bespattered with great slashes of dried blood, and riddled with bullet holes. The vast basin at their feet overflowed with dozens of bloodied and partially dismembered bodies. The smell of rotting flesh made me gag. I turned away and hurried to the far side of the circle, pulling my scarf up over my mouth and nose and trying not to think of what I had seen.

As I left the circle, I walked under a huge canvas banner bearing the red, white, and blue Stars and Cross of the C.S.A. It had been clumsily hung from a pair of lamp posts facing the fountain. The message in crimson block letters was all too clear: THOU SHALT NOT.

⊐━⊏⊐━⊏⊐━

Now it's January 2011 and the war news is as cold as the air outside, so sad and brittle that the secretaries in the cubicles outside my office have been crying on and off since noon. I am jumpy and having trouble concentrating on the hundreds of emails sitting in my inbox. The power keeps flickering and about an hour ago we stood by the windows and looked up Connecticut, watching a missile strike destroy the Washington Hilton.

I email my secretary Erika a bunch of invoices and set my IM to Away.

I walk down the hallway, hands in my pockets. The Feds have been successfully jamming all of the U.S. wireless internet providers and my Blackberry has been useless for a couple of weeks now. No porn has left me restless, or to be more precise, I'm so horny I can barely see straight. As I head down the hallway, I move my hands around to try to cover the tent in my slacks.

I head down to the third floor on autopilot and duck into the men's room silently, glancing around the outer room and then tugging on the heavy inner door. As the door opens, I find myself staring into the brown eyes of the tall guy from months ago. It's Clark Kent, with the same gray suit and slicked-back hair. His eyes are full and startled, brimming over as if he is on the verge of tears. I take in the tableau before me, my hand frozen on the door handle. Clark is standing with his now-drooping cock hanging out of his fly like an unconscious snake. He has one hand pressed against his stomach, the other held out and away from his body in an awkward, nonsensical gesture. A red-headed man in a blue suit is on his knees in front of Clark, his hand hidden by Clark's suit jacket. Clark's face is frozen in a rictus of surprise.

I am momentarily disoriented. Something is wrong.

I feel my adrenaline spike and start to step back out of the room just as a voice behind me shouts, "Down on the fuckin' ground. DAF! Get down! Get down now!" A heavy body slams into me, knocking me to the floor. Someone is on top of me, wrestling my arms behind me and clamping them together with a plastic strap pulled tight just below my elbows. I squirm to release the pressure on my arms, but a boot kicks me hard in the ribs. I hear rather than feel the sickening crack of bone and know I'm in deep shit.

I turn my head and see Clark dropping to his knees. Sudden realization strikes and I am able to make sense of what seemed merely "wrong" before. The red-headed man on his knees had thrust a knife up into Clark's stomach and sliced across his abdomen. Clark's hand had been holding his stomach together. Now as he dropped to his knees, his hands flew forward to brace himself. There is blood everywhere. I turn my face toward the wall, but I hear the sickening wet splash as his guts spill out onto the dirty linoleum.

I feel someone pulling me to my feet and propelling me through the doorway and out into the main lobby.

"Now what the fuck were you doing here, faggot?" he shouts, shoving me against the wall, my forehead slamming hard against the cold marble. I taste blood on my lips and feel it start to drip from my right nostril.

"I was just going to take a leak," I say, my voice faltering.

The man reaches around and snatches my ID badge off my lapel.

"What are you doing down here on three? No fuckin' johns on ten?"

"I was visiting my girlfriend," I say.

The man grabs my shoulder and flips me around. The pain in my ribs makes my stomach lurch. There are two DAF agents and a trio of Cee Bees in black boots and sleek, crimson uniforms all staring at me like wolves watching a wounded rabbit.

One of the DAF officers scans my implant and checks the information against my ID badge.

"He's who he says he is," he says. "But what the fuck he's doing down here..." He shrugs and walks away.

"Who's the girlfriend?" the other DAF officer asks.

I gulp and tell them her name. One of the Cee Bees takes off down the hallway in the direction of Sarah's office.

The redhead comes out of the bathroom, wiping his hands on a paper towel. He looks me up and down and says, "Girlfriend, my ass."

When Sarah arrives, the DAF guys question us separately for about an hour, knocking us around with an enfilade of rapid-fire questions about our relationship, our families, our apartments, and our church. They cut the plastic cuff from my arms, but force me to kneel on the floor while I answer their questions.

They must eventually be satisfied with our answers, because sometime around 6:30 p.m., they bring Sarah back out where I'm being questioned and leave her sitting uneasily on the edge of a maroon plastic chair. The redhead looks from one of us to the other and shakes his head like we're the saddest pair he's ever seen. He tells Sarah to get the fuck out of his sight.

She starts to protest, glancing at me.

"Get the fuck out of here, you stupid dyke bitch. Or I'll fuckin' sentence you myself."

She blanches, stands, and walks down the hallway with a lot more dignity than I could have mustered.

The other DAF guys and the Cee Bees have wandered over to the elevators and the redhead looks at me one last time. I stagger to my feet.

"I'll get you next time, faggot," he whispers, reaching out and sliding his palm along the front of my slacks. He leaves his hand there long enough to feel my cock begin to stir, then laughs wolfishly and struts over to the elevators with his buddies.

"Praise be to Him," he calls over his shoulder.

"Praise be," I say as he and his buddies step into the elevator.

I stand in the corridor for a long time before I can muster the energy to move.

When I get back to my office, my belongings have been boxed and left in the hallway. My keycard no longer works, so I pick up the box of personal photos, coffee mugs, and resin figurines Erika brought from her vacations to Birmingham and Atlanta and

Jacksonville. My ribs ache dully when I move, but I wonder if maybe they're not broken after all. I look down into the box. The first thing that catches my eye is a stark white business envelope with the C.S.A.A insignia in place of a return address. The C.S.A. Army. Great.

I drop the box on Erika's desk and open the envelope with trembling fingers. The letter notifies me that my official governmental deferment has lapsed, effective immediately. I am directed to report to the Arlington induction center at 0600 the next morning to receive my genetic testing and my assignment for basic training. I stare at the letter for a long time, watching my fingers shake and listening to the soft sound of pop praise music coming from a cubicle somewhere nearby. As one song ends, another—a bluegrass version of the *Battle Hymn of the Republic*—begins and I feel my stomach constrict and churn.

A hand on my shoulder startles me.

"Are you okay, baby?" It's Marva, the elderly office manager; a quiet, no-nonsense black woman with a stern disposition whom I have always suspected of thinking me frivolous and juvenile.

When I turn around to face her, there are tears in my eyes and droplets of blood spotting my shirt and tie.

"Oh, no," she says. "Easy now, baby. Whatever the Lord has in mind for you, I know you have the strength for it." She hugs me and I realize this is the first time anyone has hugged me since I left London.

We stand there for a long time. She rocks me like a baby and my tears start to flow.

"It's okay, Jason, you gonna be alright."

"Miss Marva, I think they broke my ribs," I say at last, unsure what else to tell her.

She pulls back from me and looks me up and down.

"Wait right here," she says, hurrying down the hall to her office and returning with a white metal first aid kit. "I was a nurse in the days before. Now let's get that shirt off and let me have a look."

She eases my jacket off and helps me unbutton my shirt. When I peel back the T-shirt, there is a mottled continent of purplish blue running across my left side.

"Now, that's not too bad," she says, running her long, dark fingers lightly along my skin.

She tapes me up, running a series of long pieces of white tape from my spine to my sternum on my left side. She tells me I can put my shirt back on and gives me three red tablets of ibuprofen. I swallow them dry and then ease back into my clothes.

Marva busies herself with returning items to the first aid kit.

"Thank you," I say, buttoning my shirt and feeling suddenly stronger.

She turns to me and I see the tears in her eyes. "You're a good boy," she says, picking up her first aid kit and turning away. "May the Lord guide you and keep you."

"Thank you, Marva," I say again, watching her go.

A song I don't recognize segues into Michael W. Smith singing *Awesome God.*

I stand in front of Erika's desk for a long time, looking down at the letter and then moving over to the windows to look out over the dark city. The northern horizon is aglow with fire, the sky streaked with tracer fire.

It's after 8:00 p.m. when I finally leave the office. I shred the induction notice and leave the box on Erika's desk.

I tap out my destination on the elevator bay touchpad and it directs me to elevator six. I wait for a beat and then, when the elevator doors open, I step inside.

"This elevator's out of service," a gruff voice says.

"The directory pad sent me here," I say, looking up with annoyance.

I freeze.

The door closes behind me, but the elevator does not move.

I am staring into the dark brown eyes of a beautiful man in navy blue work pants and matching shirt. His dark, curly hair is wavy and lustrous in the full light of the elevator. And suddenly I realize this is the other guy from the third floor restroom.

I glance involuntarily down between his legs, noting the enormous bulge there and remembering the plum-shaped head of his cock.

He eyes me suspiciously.

"What?" he asks.

"You don't remember me," I say.

"Well, I've seen you around here before," he says. "You know, when I'm working on the elevators." He nods at his laptop, which is resting on a small fold-down table and is jacked into the control panel next to the door.

I jerk my head at the spypod and contort my face into a question.

He smiles and taps out a sequence on his touchscreen.

"They're offline," he says, a sly grin sliding across his face.

I nod and then I step toward him, reaching out to stroke his cock through the dark blue material of his pants.

"I sucked you off in the third floor restroom. It was months ago; you might not remember," I say, surprising us both with such a straightforward declaration.

"I remember you," he says, eyes twinkling.

I grin. "And?"

"And now you're coming back for more?" he asks, leaning back against the wall and spreading his muscular legs slightly, pushing his package forward.

"How could I not?" I ask, letting my eyes range over his tight blue uniform, his thick bulging muscles.

I unbuckle his belt, shove his pants down around his ankles, and then ease myself down onto my knees to confront the enormous bobbing head of his cock. I stroke it a couple of times and then slide it between my lips. My body shudders in anticipation and he lets out a low, rumbling groan. I can feel the precome, slick and salty, leaking onto the roof of my mouth and sliding across my tongue.

I grab the base of his cock and stroke him gently. His hands dig into my hair, forcefully adjusting the speed and the angle. It is so rare to have a man's cock sliding across my tongue that I just revel in the feeling of his hot skin inside me and the reek of his sweat invading my nostrils. I push him deeper into my mouth, stretching my mouth as wide as I can and pushing the head of his cock firmly against the back of my throat.

When he comes, he shouts and slams his shoulders back against the wall of the elevator, sending a burst of come shooting across my tongue and down into my stomach. I push my lips against the dark curls of pubic hair and let him grow soft in my mouth, receding at his own speed.

When he finally pulls his cock all the way out of my mouth, letting it dangle limp and long and glistening against his muscular thigh, he leans down and unlaces his boots. He kicks them off and steps out of his pants, easing himself down the wall of the elevator until he is sitting on the ground in front of me, his great muscular legs splayed out on either side of my kneeling form. He unbuttons his blue shirt and lets it drop behind him and then peels off his T-shirt. He is naked except for his blue socks, his body rippling with muscles beneath the olive-complected skin and dark curly hair.

He reaches for my shirt buttons.

I let him unbutton my shirt, and then strip myself naked in front of him.

"What happened to you?" he asks when I peel off my T-shirt and reveal the taped ribs.

"DAF," I say, kicking off my shoes and hurrying out of my pants.

"Fuckers," he mumbles, leaning over and pulling a tiny packet of lube out of his tool bag. "Least they didn't kill ya. Not this time, anyway."

I reach over to stroke his reviving cock.

"The wages of sin," I say.

He smiles at that, his beautiful eyes wet and dazzling.

He lubes me up and I lower myself on top of his enormous cock, wincing as the head slides into me, but soon finding a rhythm that drives waves of dizziness up through my body. He lets me set the pace, leaning back and watching me move. His fingers play along my chest, tweaking my nipples or pressing flat, but gently, against my sternum.

I feel my own excitement rising and I move harder against him. Our bodies are covered in sweat, sliding against each other as we move.

I am riding up and down on him watching his beautiful lips move, his brow curl, and the fingers of his left hand clench and unclench on my thigh.

"Yeah, baby," he whispers. "Yeah. Keep it coming."

I pick up the rhythm, worrying the line between control and surrender, not quite willing to let myself come just yet, though the pounding of his cock against my prostate has me gasping and seeing flashes of white light.

"This is the DAF. You are ordered to cease and desist." A voice booms through the tiny elevator car.

My eyes pop open and I look directly into my partner's startled face.

"Jason Braverman and Daniel Pascal. You are hereby ordered to cease and desist all illegal activities and return the elevator to the first floor lobby immediately."

I look into Daniel's eyes and feel him wilting slightly inside me.

"Holy shit," he says finally.

"Holy shit," I agree.

"What now?" he asks, half to himself.

"Can you override that fuckin' noise?" I ask.

He looks at me for a long time, but then that wolfish grin slides back across his lips. He leans over, pulling his laptop to the floor and tapping out a series of commands.

"Jason Braverman and Daniel Pascal. You are hereby ordered to cease and desist all illegal activities and return the—" The voice stops suddenly.

Daniel leans forward and kisses me for the first time. His lips grind against me and I feel my split lip reopening. I taste blood. My cock jumps angrily and I begin moving again, sliding up and down the length of his monster cock. He wraps his still-lubed fingers around my cock and starts jacking me, slowly at first, but with increasing speed.

"Tell me when you're gonna come, baby," he says, pushing the words into my lips, shoving them between my teeth and pulling me down hard against his cock.

I'm rocking back and forth and starting to grunt with the force and the waves of sensation. I hear him groaning and then he pulls back from me, his low voice saying, "Oh, God, Jason, yes, yes. Oh, God."

And I feel the click and I mumble out "I'm gonna come."

The fingers of his right hand fly to his laptop, touching a sequence of flashing squares, his eyes locked on mine. His left hand strokes my cock, letting the sensation build.

"Me, too," he says, grabbing my chin with his right hand and pushing his mouth back against me.

I feel him start to shoot into me and then I am coming all over his chest and my legs and that's when I feel the elevator start to drop.

I pull my head back, come still shooting from my cock, my stomach lurching as the elevator car accelerates.

"No," he says, "don't pull away." He pushes his lips against mine, his angry, defiant kiss drawing a dribble of blood down my chin as the elevator plunges down too fast to be stopping in the lobby.

If you enjoyed this story, you can sign up for a free membership at ForbiddenFiction.com and discuss it with other readers and the author at *The Wages of Sin* story page at http://forbiddenfiction.com/story/JF1-1.000091.

We do our best to proof all our work, but if you spot a text error we missed, please let us know via our website Contact Form at http://forbiddenfiction.com/contact..

Designated Driver

Chapter 1:
No Parking Zones

In the days before the inebriated had apps to summon a ride home, there were designated drivers...

I knew something was wrong that morning when, slowly coming awake, I didn't immediately know where I was. My sense of direction and place is impeccable, a good thing for a driver. It's not often that I feel lost. I did at that moment. Lost in a bed I didn't know, inhaling smells I didn't recognize. I was wearing a tee shirt and briefs. Socks, too. Which wasn't right either. I sleep in the buff. But what really tipped me off was the bedroom ceiling. I didn't know it.

Then I felt a warm body beside me.

Arthur. It was Arthur. And he *was* naked. No shit, no dream. He had restlessly kicked down the Egyptian cotton sheets allowing me to see him in all his sleeping-prince glory. Tousled black hair, skin a Mediterranean bronze, sculpted shoulders and a chest shaved smooth. Not overly buff, just firm; like his handsome morning hard-on rising out of the black patch of his pubic hair.

I gazed, enthralled, at the sensitive veins and silken gold skin of that beautiful chubby, the darker mushroom head so proudly flared. Saliva pooled under my tongue. And that's when the events of last night returned to me. All of it.

Shit. Oh shit.

Trousers. Where had I left my trousers? Kitchen. That nook of cabinets where it had all happened. My shoes were there, too. Jacket was draped over a chair. I glanced over at Arthur. He was still very much asleep, a winsome smile on his chiseled face. I wanted to kiss those lips. Kiss him awake and suck on his tongue, then nibble my way on down to breakfast.

And that was *not* going to happen. I had to get out before those eyes came open.

But first I had to take care of my own morning wood.

I tiptoed to the bathroom and did my business fast as I could. Then I splashed cold water over my unshaven cheeks. *Wake up, Eric!* I told myself. My mirror image gazed back in dismay. I suppose I'd be called a twink if I was at all cute. Short and skinny is a generous description. A scrawny wimp is more accurate. Basic brown hair, basic washed out complexion. A little bug-eyed. There is nothing at all appealing about me, not even my very average cock.

Which is why I was in the situation I was in now, one I had sworn, on my mother, on my soul, I would never let happen again. But I had, which was giving me profound déjà vu. Three years, and a little under a month ago, I'd woken up in a strange bedroom on a morning not unlike this one. What had happened next was not something I wanted to relive. No way, no how.

I snuck back into the main room. Arthur was curled up with his hands near his chin. I felt my resolution melting and quickly fetched my jeans and shoes out of the kitchen. One shoe slipped and hit the hardwood floors. I winced, but Arthur didn't stir. I ended up with shoelaces between my teeth, brown oxfords swinging as I struggled to get into my pants. Then, without warning, my stocking feet slid out from under me and I stumbled into the bed.

Crap. Crap, crap, crap! My pounding heart spiked as I sat on the mattress. I was such a horrific bundle of nerves that I couldn't even get my damn pants on. I set down the shoes, sucked in some air, and was about to make another go of it when a hand clamped on my bare arm. Arthur had large, strong hands.

"Eric?"

My heart was racing now. Pulse pounding in my ears. Worse of all, I'd started to tremble.

"M-morning, Arthur. Gosh, will you look at the time—"

He didn't let go. If anything, his grip got tighter. I was going to have to face the music. I looked at him over my shoulder. He was frowning and I prayed it was confusion and not anger.

"What happened?"

What happened—Eric

What happened started, for me, long ago. See, I've always been the sort who gets overlooked. Forgotten. Even when I was a kid, neighboring moms and dads would miss me when they passed out cookies. Other kids would reach out and ask, and walk away with two. I'd end up with none.

My parents weren't much better. I'd try to get their attention, and they'd say, "We have to get your brother to soccer practice" or "Can it wait, Eric? I'm working" or "I'm on the phone; be a good boy and amuse yourself." At the dinner table they'd all talk to each other, mom, dad, my big brother, but never to me. On the rare occasions that I tried to enter the conversation, they'd stare at me till I was done, then go right back to whatever they'd been discussing.

Maybe it was because I'd come late into their lives, seven years after my brother who was the family darling. I'd been an unplanned and unwanted extra and remained so as I grew. And it didn't help that I was naturally reticent and quiet.

As for friends... I remember all too clearly that fateful day when the posse of kids I hung with went quiet and looked my way as I approached them. I knew something was up because they usually paid me no mind.

"Hey, what's going on?" I murmured, feeling a sudden tightness in my throat. Why were they all looking at me?

A glance between them, and then Ronnie, the leader said, "We don't want you tagging along anymore. You're no good at sports or anything."

"Yeah," the others agreed.

It was the first time I'd ever felt my stomach drop with dread. It wouldn't be the last. "Did I do something wrong? I won't do it again," I tried.

"Sorry." Ronnie said and led the group away. I never did find out what I'd done to make them cut me out, and I never stopped wondering about it either.

So, okay, kids can be cruel, right? And if that had been all, I might have gotten over it. It wasn't. There was this new kid, Pedro. I saw him standing alone at recess and shyly asked if he wanted to play. He did, that day and the next. At first we were inseparable. We skateboarded together at recess, and always saved each other a place at lunch.

He made other friends, which I didn't mind as it meant I got to share those friends with him. This went okay for a few months. Then I made the mistake of getting noticed. The guys were talking about how annoyed they were with little brothers barging into their rooms, and big sisters having a superior attitude.

"Yeah," I asserted, "my brother... I mean like he always has to be the center of... of everything, you know? He's always ignoring me and..."

The eyes were on me again, the silence deafening. I stopped and shrugged, as if I'd finished. But I felt Pedro's embarrassed shift. The next day, when I came over with my lunch, his friends nudged him, and he put his hand down on the bench.

"Seat's taken," he told me. He never talked or played with me again.

By junior high, I had a pretty good idea of who and what I was. I was the guy who didn't get invited to birthday parties, or movies or sleepovers or trick-or-treating. No one let me join in on the practical jokes or video games. Picked last for the team didn't even begin to cover it. I wasn't picked at all.

By high school I was also pretty sure I was gay, which didn't help me with the shyness, but it did save me from being rejected by girls as well as guys. By graduation, I'd learned two immutable laws: no one, not a group of friends, not even my family, was going to willingly invite me in unless I could be of some use. And if I did get let in, I couldn't ever forget that I was there on sufferance. One slip and I'd be out. Those were the rules. By college, I was living by them.

I came out of the closet, though it hardly mattered. No one who knew me really cared, and my social life remained pretty much the same. If I wanted to see a movie or a band, I went alone. At dances and events, I stood against the wall. Scoping eyes passed over me. It's not that I expected the studs to vie for my favor. All I wanted was to feel I was worth someone's time.

Not that I was completely friendless. Obeying my first law, I'd ingratiated myself with some fellow students by sharing my notes, arranging a study group, and offering to fetch the pizza. I didn't impose, and they tolerated me. They even waved me over now and then when I saw them at a local pub or coffeehouse, allowing me to sit with them.

Which is how, one fateful evening, I ended up at a gay bar seated at a table with Bob. Bob was a handsome black grad student who, like me, was in the architecture department. Bob, however, was at the opposite end of the spectrum: he was enormously popular and social. One of my study buddies was dating one of Bob's buddies and when I entered the bar, my friend summoned me over.

Bob's group was smart and lively and confident. Most were about to get their degree and, like Bob, already had jobs lined up at some firm or company. I sat quietly and, I thought, invisibly, enjoying the laughter and conversation, and Bob's gregarious personality. Being an alcoholic lightweight, I kept to club soda with lime. The rest of the guys challenged each other's stamina with boilermakers. I watched them overturn shots of whiskey into their Coors before swilling the brew. It didn't take long before everyone was three-sheets to the wind.

That's when Bob's attention suddenly fastened on me. "Are you still sober?"

I froze. That kind of question usually meant that I was going to become the night's entertainment, forced to chug till I threw up. And if I wanted to stay in the group's good graces, I was going to have to do it. Rule two: I could not slip up.

"I don't drink much—" I tried, half-heartedly.

"Good!" Bob unexpectedly grinned. "You can drive us home!"

Bob's suggestion was the best stroke of luck that could have happened to me. I may not have had any talent for sports or conversation, but I was a natural when it came to driving; I was not only good at it, I loved it. I would travel around the city in my used Acura, sometimes late into the night, heading down side streets, listening to the radio and memorizing shortcuts.

I drove four of the core members of the group home that night, Bob included. A week later, I was asked to do it again. Bob, I quickly learned, was a hyperactive madman who believed in working hard and playing hard. If he had a weekend free he filled it: dancing, clubbing, poker games. His nights out didn't always involve drinking, but they did involve others and usually required a car. I provided this and did all the driving, which Bob liked. Pretty soon I knew where most of his buddies lived, and I organized the stops to make pick up and drop off more efficient.

Which brings me to blond, blue-eyed Sam. He was almost always the last one I took home because he lived nearest to me. One night, Sam got really wasted. He was barely able to open the car door, and, before I could even drive away, ended up seated on the steps to his apartment trying to find his keys.

I turned off the ignition, got out and took the keys from him. After opening the door to his bachelor pad, I got a shoulder under his armpit and walked him in. Flipping on the light, I maneuvered him to the living room.

"There you go," I said and turned to leave.

"Don't go," Sam asked, pawing after me. "You're cute. Wanna suck my cock?"

That stopped me. I wasn't a virgin, but my few experiences had been quickies in toilets and dark corners. And the desperate guys I had done it with had treated me like I was nothing more than an alternative to their right hand. Now here was Sam, buff and handsome, acting like he actually wanted me. Like he really saw and desired me.

He'd called me "cute." No one had ever said *that* to me.

He was slumped in a chair, drunk as a skunk. I hesitated for about two seconds, then I went to my knees, undid his jeans, reached into his shorts and got out his flaccid dick. It was pale and blue veined, and reeked of sweaty underwear.

"Oh, yeah," he breathed as I took his warm mushroom head into my mouth. "Oh, babe, that's the way I like it."

I felt his hands on my head, stroking. Sucking cock was something I loved doing, and this was the first time I'd had a chance to really indulge in it. It was also the first time that a guy had ever run his fingers tenderly through my hair, as if I were a great lover. Saliva flowed and I slicked down his tool.

"Oh, that's sweet," he said, and a shiver ran up my spine. His cock was growing thick and stiff and I was able to take it down deeper. His juice played over my tongue: salty and bitter, like pretzels and beer.

"So good, so goooooood."

Julian Keys

My own cock was getting hard, throbbing there in my jeans. I was aroused by the cocksucking, but most of all by Sam's words, his hands stroking my neck, his focused attention. On me. *All* on *me*.

I bobbed and slurped, and fondled his nuts through his shorts. Sam continued his endearments.

"You're the best. I love you. Oh, baby—"

He began to fuck my mouth, nearly choking me. Then he grabbed hold of the chair arms. Stiffening, he shot his seed down my throat. I swallowed as much of the glue as I could; the rest dribbled out, wetting Sam's underwear. Resting back on my heels, I wiped my lips with the back of my hand. Sam gazed at me with drunk, lidded eyes. He smiled peaceably.

"That was wonderful," he avowed, and leaned down to give me a very sloppy, very alcohol-fumed kiss. Then he passed out.

Another guy would have been frustrated, but not me. To the contrary, I was elated. I went home, and jerked off while replaying the scene. The memory of Sam's voice calling me "babe" and telling me that he loved me got me so hard, so hot that when I finally came it left me breathless.

Not that I expected Sam to remember any of it, not given how drunk he'd been. And he didn't. The next time I was invited to sit at a table with him, he didn't even glance my way. I suppose if he recalled anything, it was that he'd gotten a blowjob, or maybe he thought he'd just dreamt it. Who had given it to him was likely a blur.

From my end, however, the encounter with Sam had been nothing short of a revelation. It should have been obvious, but it hadn't been to me, not till that night: the drunker the guy, the more likely he was to take notice of me. Simple as that.

I started hanging out in the gay bars, drinking my soda water, and keeping an eye out for lone studs. Whenever I saw a promising one on the brink of inebriation, I offered to drive him home. For his own safety, of course. It worked out pretty well for a while. I made sure I wasn't with anyone too unpredictable, and that the sex stayed safe. And while I might have done the driving, I always followed the drunk guy's directions. Whatever he wanted, he got, and when we were done, I left him safe in bed.

There was a price to pay, of course. None of these guys ever sought me out for a second date. Hell, few of them even learned my name. I'm sure some remembered our lovemaking, but in the cold light of sobriety they wanted nothing more to do with me. I accepted that. I never tried to reconnect with them. That I got their silky cocks for a night, their attention and affection, was more than enough for me.

And then I made a mistake. A bad one.

Chapter 2:
Breaking and Accelerating

Mike. Mike was my big mistake. Roan-haired, red-bearded and pumped, Mike was the sexiest guy in town. Everyone wanted him, but only the best ever got him. Every other week he was with a different stallion. Even college jocks, usually discreet about their sexuality, were willing to be seen with Mike. He'd come into a bar with a blindingly handsome hunk, and they'd drink and tangle tongues until their cocks were bulging.

I use to watch and imagine what it would be like to be noticed by Mike. Then, one night, the night of March 8th to be exact, Mike came in to the bar where I was hanging alone. He ordered a shot of whiskey and made himself comfortable. I thought he might be waiting for someone, but no one showed. He asked for shot after shot, until the bartender, Ken, asked for his keys. Mike surrendered them, then had some more shots. By now he was swaying and looking rather hazy. He demanded his keys back.

The inevitable argument started up between him and Ken.

"They're my keys, you fuck! I'll fuck you up if you don't give 'em back." That sort of thing.

That's when I made my move. "I'll drive him home."

"Oh, hey, Eric." Most of the bartenders knew me by name. I'm sure they also knew what I was up to, but they didn't seem to care. So long as I got the drunks off their hands. Ken certainly looked relieved. "You sure?"

"Who the fuck are you?" Mike demanded.

"Eric's our good Samaritan," Ken said. "He saves guys like you from DUI's."

Mike pondered that, then muttered, "Okay. But I'm still comin' back t' fuck you up!"

Ken rolled his eyes and handed Mike's keys to me.

I got Mike into my Acura and drove him home. I helped him inside, which wasn't easy. He weighed a ton and nearly crushed my spine as he leaned on me. Once inside, however, things went pretty much as planned. He decided he was horny, and that he was going to take my ass. I figured he'd be rough about it and he was. I'd barely gotten the condom on him before he had me on the rug.

"Tell me you wanna be fucked!" he demanded, giving my vulnerable ass a hard slap.

"I wanna be fucked," I yelped, even as he shoved in lubed fingers and stretched my hole. I groaned and wriggled my butt, which got a drunken laugh.

"Beg for it, bitch!"

"Fuck me, please. Please fuck me!"

And then his cockhead was at my entrance, pushing hard and fast enough that I cried out. Pain and pleasure exploded through me as he grabbed me around the waist.

"Fuck! I love fucking twinks!" he growled. "So easy to toss around." Which he pretty much did, all the while banging my ass. He left me with all kinds of rug burns before he finally shot his load.

That's where it ought to have ended, but I was too limp and shaken to move. So I remained, panting on the floor, until Mike hauled me up.

"Let's to go to bed," he said, breathing his liquored breath on me.

"I have to go home."

"Bed." And before I knew it, I was in bed with him. He lay atop me, kissing and cuddling me. Even though I knew he was drunk, it was nice to imagine he actually liked me. Nice to feel safe and cared for in his arms.

I went to sleep. That was my mistake.

The next morning, March 9th, I was woken by a snarl. "What the fuck?" I squinted to see Mike propped up on an arm, red-eyed and glaring at me. The hard light of day was pouring into the room, which probably wasn't helping his hangover.

"Um, good morning," I murmured, and tried to slip out of bed.

He grabbed me by the throat. He had huge hands and I have a very skinny neck. I gasped and tried to pry off his fingers.

"Did we fuck last night?" he demanded.

My heart was racing. I tried shaking my head.

"Did we?"

"Y-you fucked me," I managed to gasp.

He shoved me off the bed. I landed hard and tried to crawl away, but he was already out and standing over me. He was as naked as I was, but he didn't look vulnerable. His fist came down, getting me in the back. I screamed.

Then he grabbed me by my skinny arm, so hard I thought he was going to break it. "I must have been really, really drunk," he said, "and you must have known it, because I don't fuck desperate sluts like you. I don't invite them into my home. I don't invite them into my bed. And I don't let them suck my cock."

"I didn't—you didn't! I mean—."

"I don't fuck their asses either!" Mike backhanded me. Then he kicked and punched, till I was huddled in the corner, protecting my head and shaking. I thought he was going to kill me.

"Get the fuck out!" he barked.

I scrambled for my clothes and got my jeans on before ending up on his front porch.

"You say one word about this to anyone, and you're dead," he promised, and slammed shut the door.

Somehow, I managed to drive myself home. Locked in my student apartment, I checked myself out. There were livid bruises on my arms and back. My lip was swollen and bloody. My one thought was that if I went out like this, I'd be noticed. Everyone would go quiet, and eyes would fix on me in that not-good way.

So I hid in the apartment for the rest of the week. I cut classes and ordered in food, limping about and sleeping badly. Every time I drifted off, I came awake with a start, sure I heard Mike's angry fist hammering on my door.

I never went back to that bar, or any of the bars in town. In fact, the incident shook me so badly that I dropped out of college and moved to another city. Weeks later, when I'd settled in and there were fewer bad dreams. when I didn't jump so much at shadows, I made a vow.

I would never, metaphorically speaking, drive drunk again. On my mother, on my soul. Never again.

About a year and a half after the "event," I was still sober, so to speak. I hadn't visited a bar or club once, and I was gainfully employed parking cars at a midtown lot. Or I was until it closed down so the new owner could build apartments on it. Then I was out and searching for a new job. During one of these searches, while I was having lunch at a burger joint, someone slapped me on the shoulder scaring the hell out of me.

"Eric!" It was Bob. He was dressed in tight Armani jeans and a chic, silk shirt. And he not only remembered me but invited me to join him and his three buddies. They were all about the same age as Bob, all at the start of promising careers, and welcoming enough. One, in particular, caught my eye: shiny black hair, bronze skin and a mouth that smiled warmly.

Arthur.

Once I'd settled in, the usual happened, the guys started talking around or past me. Which was fine, until Bob unexpectedly put his hand on my shoulder and announced, "This here is the best designated driver on the planet."

He might as well have held up an empty chair and said it. I'd faded into the furniture and eyes blinked as the guys tried to remember who I was.

"Really?" Yoshi asked. "How much do you charge?"

Charge?

I'd never really thought about it, but of course there were drivers out there who took a fee for their services. Limo drivers at one end, taxis at the other, and everything else in between. Why not charge for driving people around?

Bob and the others asked for my number, and, being that I was running low on money, I gave it to them. They were my only customers for those first couple of months, which was just as well. They didn't mind piling into the back of my used Acura. Very soon, however, Bob and his buddies were recommending me to others, and my number started making the rounds at nightclubs and bars.

Business picked up, so much so that I rented a black minivan. It could manage eight passengers, had power sliding doors, plenty of cup holders, a CD player and a satellite radio. I stocked it with water and air-sickness bags, a must given my usual customers.

That's how I stumbled ass-backwards into my calling. I wasn't a regular taxi service taking travelers to the airport or shoppers to stores. I was a "designated driver," exclusive to the city's nightlife. My rates were higher than those of a cab, but far lower than those of a limo, as I was neither as utilitarian as the one nor as luxurious as the other. Price depended on number of passengers and hours of service.

Some nights I simply fetched people from the clubs and drove them home. Most evenings, however, I was hired to drop passengers off and then pick them back up at a special time. If they paid extra, I'd wait for them outside or, if they allowed it, sit at a table drinking soft drinks and watching the bachelorettes or birthday boys as they celebrated. Now and then I'd take my clients on a crawl from one bar to another, even out to a late night supper or taco stand.

And, yes, on rare occasions, I ended up helping the none-too-sober to their doors. But that's as far as I went. Once they were over the threshold, they were on their own. I never entered a domicile.

I have stories, of course. The good, the bad, and the bizarre. There were the warm-hearted divorcées who wanted to set me up with one of their daughters, until I confessed my sexual orientation. Then they offered me one of their sons. There was the quartet of elderly barflies who had me play punk music. They liked to lean out the windows screaming the lyrics and spitting at people. There were the football players who drank themselves sick so they could puke on a rival team's goal post. And there were the debutantes who immortalized their coming out by mooning truckers.

Men were more likely to order me around, but also more likely to pay me extra for my trouble. Ladies, who I always helped in and out of the van, thanked me, but didn't tip. My biggest epiphany, however, was that I liked playing chauffer. I liked washing and polishing the van for its evenings out, vacuuming the rugs, and re-stocking the CD selection. I loved knowing all the good short-cuts, and going over maps for the best routes. I liked, as well, feeling that I'd prevented accidents and arrests. DUI laws in our state were strict and it only made sense to have someone like me behind the wheel if liquor was going to be on the menu.

I even enjoyed chatting up my customers who, drunk or sober, were *my* passengers. I took a certain pride in getting them safely to and from their homes.

Strangest of all was that I had regulars, which suggested that some people favored me. Or at least my driving. Among those regulars were Bob and his posse. Sometimes their number swelled as they invited along neighbors, siblings, friends or dates, but most of the time it was just the core foursome: Bob, John, Yoshi... and Arthur.

Arthur. I was mesmerized by his muscled arms, by the way his trousers hugged his butt. He'd brush a black tendril of hair behind his ear and I'd gulp with desire. His voice could raise goosebumps on my flesh, and when those warm, dark eyes fixed on me, my cock would twitch and my pulse would race.

He was perfect casting for the gay wet dream of a classical warrior. Masturbating in the shower, I'd envision him wearing a Spartan helmet and sandals. As hot water dripped off my hard-on, I'd imagine myself his captive. Forced to suck his cock, then, turning round, take it between my spread ass cheeks.

And yes, he was gay. On nights when he alone called me for a ride, he usually fell into the back seat with some sexy twink. The two of them would spend the ride sucking tongues and working their hands down each other's pants. I did my best to keep my eyes on the road and off my rearview. But there was no suppressing a shiver when I heard Arthur say things like: "I'm going to give it to you so hard."

God, what I wouldn't do to have him say that to me. Sober.

I could have passed my feelings off as mere lust, except that when the gang piled into the van, Arthur usually rode shotgun. Which meant I got to know him as a person.

"So, Eric, is this what you wanted to be when you grew up?" he'd ask, and flash that smile of his. Which flustered me. *Why*, I would wonder, *was he wasting his time talking to me?*

"I kinda dropped out of college," I finally confessed on one drive home. "I was taking urban planning."

He perked up. "Really?"

125

"Yeah. I wanted to redesign streets and maps and such. What about you? Did you always want to create affordable housing?"

"Nope. I was into architectural history. Bauhaus. I spent a year in Berlin. I still go back there when I can. I traveled to all the important sites, Weimar, Dessau... explored all the gay nightclubs, too. But I'll save those tales for later." He grinned. "Anyway, one of the original, philosophical intents of Bauhaus was to give everyone cheap, modern housing. What I do now isn't too far from that. And I really like helping people become home owners."

"And meanwhile you rent an apartment?"

He laughed. "I'm waiting for the right guy. How about you? Seems like you're always on the road. Don't you want a real home?"

I shrugged. I daydreamed a lot, but never about anything like that.

As if these short chats weren't torturous enough, whenever I drove the gang, Bob inevitably hired me for the night and invited me to join them. This gave me even more time to agonize over Arthur.

"I never see you with anyone," he remarked to me once.

"Nah," I smiled nervously. Why was he asking me such a thing? "I'm a loner."

"That right?" he murmured. His olive black eyes looked amused, so I guessed he figured the truth, and was probably making fun of me.

The holidays came around, my second as a designated driver. I put lights and a small, festive wreath on the minivan. Between Christmas parties and New Year's Eve, I raked it in. I was so pleased that I took the initiative and mailed out fliers announcing a Valentine's Day special (two couples for the price of one!). That was a great night. I loved watching the handing off of roses and endearments between those I ferried to and from romantic dinners. It made me feel like Cupid.

Hey, if I couldn't get love myself, I could help others get it.

Spring arrived and I felt quite proud of myself. I was making a decent living, I liked the work and I was my own boss. The one bump in the road was that I was still lonely. More lonely than ever. But I held to my vow—no hitting on the inebriated.

And then came Bob's birthday celebration.

—▭—▭—▭—

"What happened?" Arthur demanded yet again. He was kneeling on the mattress, his grip on my arm tight enough to cut off the blood flow.

"Nothing, nothing!" I lied. "You were drunk. I brought you in and helped you out of your clothes. You wanted me to stay and I stayed until I fell asleep."

He was glowering. I wondered if he was suffering from a hangover.

God, please don't let him remember.

"Something happened," he insisted. "Come on. You can tell me while I pee."

He dragged me into the bathroom, keeping a hold of me as he aimed one-handed. "I sleep in my shorts," he went on. "So why would I ask you take off all my clothes?"

"Because you were drunk?"

"God damn it, Eric!" He gave his dick a shake and washed up, again one-handed. "I can tell from that look you're giving me that you don't want to say, but I'm not letting go of you till you do. How fucked-up was I? What embarrassing thing did I do? Or say? Did I propose?"

Don't I wish! "I told you. Nothing happened. You didn't even kiss me." That last was sadly true.

"I can't believe you're shitting me like this." He dragged me back toward the bed and finally released me. "Jesus Christ, you're shaking. What the fuck—?"

His face went ashen. So much so that I thought he was going to throw up. His expression altered from a mix of annoyance and amusement to horror.

"Wait," he breathed. "I remember. I remember what happened. *Everything* that happened."

Oh. Crap.

Chapter 3:
Changing Lanes

What Happened—Arthur

I like twinks. I mean I really like them. I'm fatally attracted to boyish good looks and sleek physiques. And yeah, I enjoy feeling protective and dominant over some little guy. Not that I want him to swoon over my muscles and keep house for me. I just want him to enjoy being lifted into my arms and coddled.

Unfortunately, my track record with twinks isn't so good. They flirt with me, all coy and shy at first and completely at my service in bed. A date or two down the line, however, and they drop the pretense. "Why are you looking at that guy? You should be looking at me," they pout. And "I don't want to go out tonight," or "I hate this place. Take me somewhere better." Once it starts, there's no stopping it: "I didn't order this," "I'm bored," "I've changed my mind..."

The ones that are constantly fishing for strokes are the worst: "I know I'm not very sexy..." or "Sometimes I think people stare at me because they hate me..." Gah! They say things like that and I know I'm supposed to spend the rest of the night catering to their delicate egos.

I suppose it has less to do with twinkness than with the fact that I always go for the beauty queens. Self-centered brats who think their desirability entitles them to use and abuse others and to be a general pain-in-the-ass. Which was why, at the time this all started, I was searching for Mr. Low-Maintenance. Not zero-maintenance. I didn't want a boy who had no opinions or needs. But I was sick to death of the spoilt princes who kept asking if our relationship was "there" yet. Couldn't they just enjoy the ride?

Enter Eric.

The answer to my prayers, though I didn't know it. When I first met him, I hardly gave him a second look. Even after he started hanging out with us, I barely realized he was there. One minute I'd be sure there were four of us at the table, then, with a blink, I'd realize we were five. I'd forgotten to include Eric.

That's how quiet, how self-effacing he was. Finally, nearly a year after he'd joined our little group, I got curious and put an effort into seeing him. He was a smallish, fragile-thin, skater-twink, which was certainly my type, but average in looks. I didn't date average. My competitive streak wouldn't let me. I always went for the prize—the boy with the sultry eyes or a dimple in the chin, the teasing heartbreaker every stud was hoping to fuck.

Eric was... well, nothing special. Still, the more I actually saw of him, the more interested I got. His big, guileless eyes were so honest, and I liked his shy smile, the way he turned his head to hide it. What struck me most, however, was the way he listened. I've never met anyone who hung on words as much as he did. He never entered the conversation, but he took it in, laughing quietly at the jokes.

He was also a darn good driver, able to slip effortlessly in and out of traffic, and parallel park in the tightest of spaces. Maybe that shouldn't have meant anything, but it became symbolic to me. Especially given that he never hotdogged or raced. He was always careful as well as competent, so much so that the rest of us could sit back and relax.

I didn't completely change lanes and consider him seriously, however, until this one, rainy evening. I'd been doing some late-night shopping, and was about to cross the street when it started to pour. So I took refuge under a department store awning and that's when I saw Eric's van. It was parked before a supper club. Eric, an umbrella in hand, was trying to help his passengers, a trio of middle-aged women, out of the vehicle. They were dressed to the nines and anxiously eying the water rushing up over the curb.

"Hang on a minute, Ms. Anders," Eric said to the bleached blonde in front. "Hold the umbrella and allow me." He passed the handle to her, and then he put an arm about her and swung her over the flooded gutter onto the wet sidewalk. Taking back the umbrella, he escorted her to the entrance with its overhang, then went back and did the same with the other two ladies. All of the women were larger and heavier than him, but he put all of his upper body strength into it, and got them down smoothly. Of course, he ended up half-soaked, but that only made the act more gallant.

"I haven't had a man cop a feel like that since my ex carried me over the threshold," the blonde laughed as he brought up the last of the trio.

"Uh-oh, I've been found out," said Eric.

"Isn't it time you stopped trying to pass for gay? Be my houseboy, Eric, I swear, I'll spoil you rotten."

I'd caught glimpses of Eric's shy smiles, but never anything like the genuine grin he beamed at that woman. "That wouldn't be fair to you, Ms. Anders. You deserve a really robust houseboy. Not a wimp like me."

The women chuckled and Eric opened the door for them. "I'll be back to pick you up, ladies. Have a great evening."

I won't say it was a whole different Eric, but it certainly wasn't the same, silent boy who hung out with me and my buds. This one had natural charm, and a vibe that was almost custodial, as if his passengers were his sacred charge. It intrigued me.

I started to really watch Eric, and I began to notice a few things. Like he was always the one who took on the nasty job of looking after the drunk.

"Hey there, fella, easy does it," he'd say when a guy in our group had one-too-many. And he'd assist the poor bastard to the public toilet. I remember seeing him once, holding John's head as he upchucked. Eric had even gotten some paper towels and set them down on the floor so John wouldn't dirty his pants as he knelt before the porcelain altar.

Ditto when he drove us home. "Let me help ya," he'd say, when one of us couldn't quite manage to walk straight. And then he'd put his shoulder under the arm of a bruiser like Bob, who was twice his size, and assist him up two flights of stairs.

And why the fuck were we putting that on Eric? He was the smallest guy in our group. He shouldn't be the one to haul us to our doors.

He fetched us our drinks if there wasn't a waiter, or extra chairs if more were needed. He shifted tables, and even got our coats for us. He called ahead to make reservations at the pizza parlor or to check and see when a band was playing. Yet he never helped himself to a slice of that pizza, never got himself a ticket to the concert.

And the worst thing was: *no one noticed!* It wasn't as if the guys expected Eric to open doors for them, but they didn't thank him when he did. They didn't even acknowledge him. It gave me a weird feeling to watch it. Like he was trying to impress us and couldn't. Or like...

...like he knew he was replaceable. Like if he ever did less than his best, we'd finally notice and give him the boot.

I considered pointing this out to the guys, but I was hardly in a position to cast stones. Time and again, Eric had driven me and some beauty queen home, and each and every time I'd shamelessly made out with my new boy in the backseat. I mean, how brutal was that? *Hey, Eric, take a look at this hottie; let me give you a preview of the amazing sex we're going to have. Too bad you can't even get a mercy fuck.*

Okay. So mistakes had been made, time to fix them. I started by trying to engage Eric in conversation. This turned out to be harder than I thought. He was pathetically eager to listen to what I had to say, but he never had much to say in return. Not, that is, until I finally asked him for driving tips.

"People think you can't get on the freeways after three o'clock," he explained, quite seriously, "But that's not really true. There's this break in the traffic that comes at around four-thirty if you're heading west. East is murder, but west is smooth sailing for about an hour. Then it clogs up again."

"Why is that?"

"The three o'clock traffic sends commuters running for the side streets. Which, then loosens up the freeway. Funny, huh?"

There was that confidence again. I wondered what it might be like to travel with him across country. Or better yet, to take him to Germany and introduce him to the Autobahn. God, wouldn't he love that? I found myself watching his nimble hands, so sure on the wheel. What would they feel like cupping my ass?

"Check this out," Eric said another night, one of the few times he actually spoke first. We were heading down Newberry Boulevard, the hellish part that ran through the commercial district. It had recently been repaved and given islands of concrete and trees, which had significantly improved the traffic.

"Look at the way the islands change the flow. They create private lanes for those wanting the stores. So there's no interference with the main drag." His eyes glowed with admiration. "Such a simple solution. I love it."

A guy who found beauty in traffic flow. How could I not be charmed? Even my initial impression of his attractiveness shifted, going all the way from indifferent to obsessed. What did he look like naked? And would he jump or moan if his nipples were tweaked? Night after night, I'd lie in bed, stroking my stiff cock and dreaming of his bubble butt exposed. I'd imagine myself impaling him, envision the wiry muscles of his back rippling as he undulated.

From the looks Eric gave me, I knew he'd be willing and interested. But his natural reticence made me hesitate. Was it shyness or something more?

"So, what's your type?" I finally asked with false casualness. It was the night of Bob's birthday celebration and I was the first stop, so I was alone with him in the front seat.

He shrugged and kept his eyes on the road. "I'm not picky."

"Come on, Eric. What are you into? Hairy bears? Sculpted jocks?"

He went silent on me, as if he thought I was poking fun at him.

"How about this," I tried, "tell me about the last guy you were with. What was he like?"

I saw his hands tighten on the wheel. "That was a while ago. A one night thing."

A one night thing? I didn't like the sound of that. I wanted Eric for several nights, maybe longer.

"What was he like?"

"Sexy. Rough," he said, and that was pretty much all I got out of him.

We picked up the rest of the gang and drove to a Latin club. Bob had arranged for an intimate bash with an exclusive, curtained booth. There were flights of tequila waiting, four shots for each of us in little flared glasses. They ranged from light to dark gold in color. As we threw back the first of these, my mind wandered back to what Eric had said. I kept replaying it as the waiter brought over small plates of Oaxaca cuisine.

Sexy I could do. And rough if that's what he was into. It wasn't my usual thing, but why not? I watched Eric sipping at his club soda while the rest of us did our second and third shots and nibbled on the food. There were enough servings of petite empanadas and tamales with mole sauce to give each of us a bite, but Eric never asked for his share. He was playing the invisible man again, and doing it all too well. Which, for some reason, angered me.

Down went the last and darkest tequila shot. Damn. That was a good one. We decided it was time to get in some dancing and left the booth. There was a Salsa beat pounding away and we all took our turns partnering with Bob. I bumped up behind him and he laughingly wriggled his ass into me until John stole him away.

I tangoed with a few other guys and a couple of girls, enjoying that wonderful mix of endorphins, tequila and the throb of the music. It was like being inside a great drum. I was about partner up with Bob again when I saw Eric standing on the sidelines. He had a wistful smile on his face, as if he were imagining himself out there with us.

I swung on over and nabbed him. His eyes widened. "Oh, no, Arthur, I can't."

"You're going to have to," I said, spinning him into the middle of that writhing crowd. I got my arm around his waist and pulled him close. He was wearing a thin, designer tee and I could feel the tension in his back, his ribs expanding and contracting with panicked breath. His hands held on to my shoulders for balance. I could feel the heat of his palms through my sleeves.

"There, you see," I murmured, as he started to match my steps. "You can dance." Actually, he could. Not brilliantly, but he was keeping up and he wasn't stepping on my toes. I could smell his clean sweat, see it trickling down from his temples. My shirt was unbuttoned at the top, and I could feel his breath on my skin. I willed him to lean in, to kiss my chest. But he didn't. His head was turned away, as if he were trying to avoid touching his nose to my collarbone.

I ground my hips into his, and was rewarded with a chubby. The music ended just as I was reaching round to squeeze his butt. There was applause, and I heard Eric swallowing hard. His trembling hands fled from my shoulders and I reluctantly let him go.

"Th-the guys are going back to the booth," he pointed out.

Fuck them, I wanted to say. I had a dozen ideas in my head, from dragging Eric to a men's room stall to taking him out into the alley, all of them ending with him on his knees and my cock in his mouth. His expression, diffident and afraid, made me check those notions. I wanted to make love to Eric, not be serviced by him.

There was a second flight of shots waiting at the table, four tastes of different tequilas. Us drinkers gave each shot its due: a lick of salt before we tossed that smooth liquor down, and then a bite of lime to finish it. My aggressive, lustful attitude notched up with each belt.

As we finished up, the waiter brought over a flan with a candle in it. We all sang "Happy Birthday." Bob blew out the flame and got his cheers. He passed around the dessert and Eric got slighted, of course. I saw his gaze shift away. Shit, he didn't even expect to be given a taste!

"Here," I said, spooning some up. I held it out to him, insistent. I couldn't read the look in those gray eyes, disbelief maybe, but Eric took what was offered. The way he licked his lips had me wanting to suck on his mouth and tongue.

"Gentlemen," Bob got our attention by tapping a knife on his plate. "In honor of me, we are all going to have one last shot. A shot of something very special." The bottle he produced was small. It had an odd label, hand drawn and haphazardly glued on; a winged serpent that looked like it came from an Aztec temple. Inside was a clear, pale, yellowy brew.

I didn't know it then, but that strange fuel was going to knock me right into the fast lane with Eric.

Chapter 4:
Fender Benders

"That better not be urine," John quipped about the yellow liquid, and we all laughed. It's what we were all thinking.

"It's mescal," Bob said.

"Where's the warm?" Yoshi asked, peering at the bottom of the bottle. "I mean, worm. Where's the worm?"

"Technically, mescal does not contain a worm. It contains a caterpillar. And the guy who makes this stuff strains out the worms and sells them separately, the greedy bastard."

"Oh." Yoshi was disappointed.

"My uncle gave it to me a few years ago," Bob went on, "He got it in this village that can only be reached by burro. Rumor goes this place makes the most potent mescal on earth. I don't even know if it's legal."

"So it's liquid peyote?" I asked.

"Do not insult my magical mescal," Bob haughtily retorted. "This is not just peyote. If it's as advertised, then there are rare, rainforest herbs and medicines in it."

"Dude," Yoshi was skeptical. "I do not want to puke up my guts while having sweat lodge visions of leopards and shit."

Bob snorted. "You wish." He started to pour it out. "I've been saving this for years, so don't even try to get out of it. Eric," he added, "you'll make sure we don't jump off a building or cut out people's hearts?"

"I'll do my best," he said with a smile.

Yeah, like scrawny Eric could stop us if we decided to go on a rampage. But I doubted Bob's mescal was going to be all that astonishing. And what the hell? It was only a shot.

A shot, I should have remembered, that was going to cap the series of tequila shots we'd been swallowing down all evening.

"To my friends," Bob said, lifting his glass. "Thanks for sharing this with me."

"To Bob for taking us tripping," John joked. "Thanks a lot, friend!" We laughed, clinked glasses, and down went the mescal. It tasted pretty much like tequila, though there must have been some truth to Bob's claims. The flavor hinted of herbs, and something earthy like mushroom.

"I'm not seeing dog yet." Yoshi put down his empty glass. "I mean God. I'm not seeing God."

"Give it time," Bob said, and we went back to shooting the shit. Yoshi was slurring his words and John was swaying in his seat, which after nine chugs of hard liquor, was to be expected. Still, we all knew who we were, where we were and what we were. No one stripped off his clothing and ran out in search of the mothership.

The mescal, alas, had just made us drunker. Nothing more. Or so I thought.

And then I got the telescoping effect. It appeared quite suddenly. One minute I didn't have it, then I did. As if I'd gotten taller and more remote. I was quite pleased with this new ability, and I quickly made use of it on Eric. It was like having an eye doctor click lenses into place. I saw how thick Eric's eyelashes were, the hint of shadow on his chin. I could even see flashes of the future: Eric swallowing down every inch of my powerful cock, Eric under me, squirming and moaning.

There was a gear shift and the languid lust I'd been feeling fired up into a sexual blaze.

John was half asleep by now, and Yoshi was barely able to talk sense. Time to head home. The bill was paid and Eric took care of the valet parking. All we had to do was pile in. To my annoyance, Eric tried to drop me off first.

"I'm not ready to go in," I announced. How could he be so stupid! He knew what I had in mind. He knew I had to be last. I crossed my arms, making it clear I wasn't about to budge. Eric frowned, shook his head, then dutifully headed off to John's place.

"I know your flavor," I murmured to him on the way. He gave me an anxious look, as if worried that anyone should know him so intimately. He helped John to his door, and did the same for Yoshi when we got to his apartment. Bob only needed help separating out the right key for the front door. Then, at last, Eric drove me back home.

"Here we are," he said, pulling up to the curve. I smirked to myself. Eric thought he was getting out of this. He was wrong. As I exited the car, I deliberately stumbled, making like I couldn't walk. As expected, Eric's expression went from anxious to concerned. He hurried around and came up under my arm. Then he hauled me up the stairs to my one bedroom. I leaned on him heavily, and passed him my keys.

"T-there," he got the door opened.

That's when I shoved him in. HA! I shut and locked the door behind us. To my delight, Eric was already on his hands and knees. How thoughtful of him! I unbuckled and unzipped, letting my trousers drop.

"Damn it, Arthur," Eric scrambled up. "I know you're drunk but —"

That's when he saw my hard-on. It was so stiff it nearly ripped apart my shorts. The expression on Eric's face was gratifyingly awed.

"You're going to beg for this, little puppy," I told him with a leer and tugged at his jacket.

"Okay. Okay." The jacket came off and he backed away. "I-I-I'm going to get some caffeine into you. You should take a shower."

He fled into the kitchen. I laughed, then kicked off my shoes, stepped out of my dropped trousers and peeled off socks and shorts. Then, as a finale, I tore open the shirt. It was absolutely great to do that. Just pull it apart. Like Superman. Buttons flew and clattered across the floor.

I glanced down at my naked self. My solid pecs and rock-hard abs. My glorious cock, which was stiff as a pistol. Wow. I was hung like a horse! My telescoping vision went in and out to admire my meaty dick, my brass balls. No wonder Eric was so afraid. Lucky for him, I was a merciful lover. I had every intention of using lots of lube.

"Coffee, coffee—" I heard Eric saying as I stepped into the kitchen. He was digging through a bottom cabinet. I reached up with my telescoping powers to the very top shelving and got down a bottle of vodka.

Eric glanced over his shoulder, saw my nakedness and my giant cock, and jumped. "AH!" he cried, and put his back to the counter. Scared he might be, and rightly so, of such a humongous power tool, but those gray eyes were hungry. He was licking his lips in a way that I knew all too well. Twinks are such sluts.

"Um," he said, as I unscrewed the cap off the vodka. "You don't need any more to drink."

"This isn't for me, you wussy little fuck!" I shoved the bottle at him. "Something to dull the pain and give you courage. You can thank me later."

"I have to drive home," he pleaded.

Merciful, I was. But not that merciful. I put the bottle to his lips. "Don't make me pour it down your throat."

"Okay, okay." He started to take a sip, but I knew that wouldn't be enough. My magnificent broadsword was going to be breaching his most delicate ring of resistance. The pain would be excruciating. I knocked the bottle up and made him swallow down half.

He coughed and cursed, and began to cry. I put aside the vodka. Shit. I didn't want to make him *cry*. Then again, isn't that the way he liked it? Rough? Maybe he was crying because I wasn't being rough enough? How could I remedy that? My telescoping eyes scoped about the kitchen and found the answer. A knife. I snatched it up.

"Time to get started," I purred.

His moist eyes were terrified, but I knew I'd excited him. He had a boner. Oh, yes, he wanted me. "Arthur, for God's sake," he rasped, "put down the knife."

I grabbed his jeans and brought the blade close enough to shave his jaw. Tears were running down his cheeks. I wanted to kiss them off his face, gently, one by one. Instead, I popped his button and got his zipper down. "Get out of these."

Shoes came off, then his jeans. I couldn't help but smile. He had skinny legs and knobby knees. So adorable. Setting the knife aside, I pressed in close and brushed a hand over the outline of his small cock, hot against the fabric of his shorts. Then I reached lower, between his sweaty thighs. He moaned and parted his shaking legs for me, as I knew he would.

"Tell me about your last guy," I demanded, rubbing at him through the cotton. He wriggled and squirmed.

"W-what?"

"Your last guy!" I snapped. "What'd he do?"

Eric flinched. "I-I don't want to talk about him."

"Did he force you?"

His Adam's apple bobbed tellingly. "Yeah," he admitted. "He forced me."

"Like this?"

I slid my hand into his shorts and his breath caught. His nuts were warm and furry. I toyed with them until he was groaning, and then started on his cock. It fit right into my hand. My Eric's dick was the perfect size. And I knew exactly how to arouse it.

"Oh, fuck!" he whispered.

I went exploring. Tears were still running down his face, but he was groaning and writhing under my attentions. And my cock was beginning to drip with lust.

"Arthur, Arthur, you don't want to do this. In the morning—"

I pulled my hand out of his shorts and pushed him down. Down onto those knobby knees, where I knew he wanted to be. My meaty cock clubbed him in the face, but he didn't seem to take any damage. He recovered and stared at it with fear.

"You know what to do."

His lips kissed my shiny tip with all the reverence it deserved. I drew in a sharp breath as the feel of that mouth shocked my groin. And then his warm tongue was bathing my cock, lapping up the pre-come before making its way down my straining rod.

"Oh, yeah," I moaned, as my cock grew achingly hard, "That's my little bitch."

His hands timidly took hold of my hips, which made my heart melt. It was such a sweet gesture. His warm, wet throat swallowed me down as he bobbed forward and back. The sight of my cock sliding between his lips was incredibly hot, especially when he got down to the root, his nose burrowing into my pubes.

He glided back up, his tongue caressing my veins along the way. I could feel my rod pulsing and twitching with ecstasy, with agony, especially when he scraped his teeth very gently on the rim of my mushroom head. Electric shocks flickered up my spine.

Oh, God, he was good. Not just in technique. With my new, telescopic powers I could sense his willingness. I'd been with twinks who liked to show off their artistry, and twinks who sucked on cock as if enjoying a delicious treat. But I'd never been with one so

139

focused on me, on *my* pleasure. Every maneuver, every twist and turn of Eric's was aimed at getting me to my destination. Even his hands, now holding firmly to my ass, seemed to be guiding me higher and higher.

He left my dick to tongue my balls, making my gut tighten. Rough, I reminded myself, and grabbed his hair. He whimpered, but obediently went back to my cock. His mouth and throat were burning hot.

"I want you to be mine, all mine," I said, imagining Eric stripped of his shorts, his body spread. Imagining my thick, powerful cock entering him. Imagining how burning tight he'd be as I pounded away. He'd scream my name, scream for more.

The rolling boil of an orgasm made my muscles clench. I pulled out as my dick began to jerk and spurt with such force I felt my knees weaken. I rode it out, till my cock was spent and starting to flag.

Eric was still staring at it. Gently, I tilted back his chin; jizz glistened on his cheeks and forehead. I was delighted. I'd marked him!

"Now you're mine," I said wetting a paper towel and gently cleaning him off. He was breathing hard and his face was red with shame and stimulation.

"Bed," I told him.

I felt him shivering under my hands. He wobbled as I directed him out of the kitchen and to the mattress. I lay beside him, stroking him, murmuring endearments to soothe his fears. I was going to make us feel so good.

Sooooo good.

The world went dark. Next thing I knew it was morning and Eric was stumbling about, trying to get his pants on. And what the hell was Eric doing in my apartment? Without his pants on? And what was I doing stark naked?

Had something happened? As Eric sat on the bed, I grabbed his arm and asked just that.

Oh, my God, oh, my God, oh, my *God!*

I dropped down onto the bed and lowered my head into my hands as every mortifying detail slammed back into my brain. My God, my God. Why hadn't I drunk less? Eaten more? Refused Bob's magical mescal?

Oh, fuck me. Fuck me. Why had I done what I'd done?

"Arthur, listen to me, please."

My God. I'd threatened Eric with a knife! I'd made him suck my cock... had I forced myself on him in some other way? Or had I just imagined him under me? He was scared of me, scared to death. Was I remembering everything?

"It was just a blow job, Arthur!" Eric said. He sounded like he wanted me to forgive myself. Desperately wanted that. Shit! All those bratty little twinks who could have done with a good scare and I'd abused Eric. Eric, who had no one to stand up for him. Who just had to take it.

What kind of monster was I?

"Can't we just forget this ever happened?" he pleaded.

I met his eyes. Those beautiful gray eyes. I had wanted to make them glow with pleasure. Instead I'd infused them with fear. "Are you out of your mind?" I murmured. How could I ever forget this?

Eric's face paled, so much so I thought he was going to be sick. "Are you... are you going to tell Bob and the others?" he asked.

"You think I'd boast about this?" I was appalled. And then it occurred to me that given last night's performance, he might well think I'd do that. Why not? I could put my own spin on it. Tell all our friends what a desperate, hungry, slut he'd been, how eagerly he'd swallowed my meat. Who would doubt me? Or take Eric's word over mine?

"No, no of course not," Eric said quickly, his manner so mollifying it cut me to the quick. "I never... I mean, of course you don't want anyone to know about being... with me." He said the last word so small, as if deeply ashamed of it. "I won't say anything. I won't do anything you don't want me to do, just..."

Here it came, the price for his silence.

"Just let me walk out of here. I know you want to kick my ass, but, I swear, I never meant to—"

"What the fuck are you talking about?" I shot to my feet. Eric quickly shrunk back. Sweat glistened on his forehead. "Kick your

141

ass? My God, Eric, what did I say to you last night? Why would you think I'd want to hurt you?"

"I-I just know how angry you must be with me."

"Angry with you? The only one I'm angry with is me! I forced myself on you."

It was his turn to look bewildered. "Forced yourself? Is that what you think happened? Oh, geez, Arthur, no. That isn't what happened at all."

"It isn't?" I didn't know whether to be relieved or not. "So...what *did* happen?"

Chapter 5:
Traffic Jams and Detours

What REALLY happened—Eric

I've seen a lot of drunks. Some are so quiet you wouldn't know they were drunk at all. Most become embarrassingly loud and obnoxious. A few are scary and belligerent.

Arthur was stubborn.

I don't think he realized how hard those tequilas hit him. I didn't realize it either, not until the dance. I was watching him move out on the floor, the power in his hips, in his broad shoulders. I was dreaming of what it would be like to dance with him, when his eyes fastened on me. That's when I knew. No one notices me at such times, not unless they're half-gone.

He came up and dragged me into the middle of that writhing crowd. I tried to back out, but his arms clamped round me. He planted his broad hand on my lower back, and directed me about, his breath stirring my hair. His shirt was unbuttoned and my eye was level with that dip in his throat. I stared at the sweat pooling there, inhaling his aftershave. The desire to kiss that spot was so difficult to resist I had to turn my head.

The music beat through my ears in time, it seemed, with the hammering of my heart, and the lights flashed around us. Arthur never let up. With every step his deft hands explored my body and our hips bumped groin to groin, deliberately teasing. I held on to his shoulders, and I tried not to groan aloud as my cock swelled. The desire I felt for him was agonizing. Finally, the music ended, and there I was trembling and gazing up at his face. He looked like he wanted to take me out back and rape me. And I was a breath away from begging him to do just that.

I saw the guys heading to the booth. Thank God! I pointed this out to Arthur and, after a moment's hesitation, he released me and we joined them.

Unfortunately, the guys weren't done drinking. They went through another flight of tequila shots and by the last Arthur was more fixated on me than ever. He insisted that I have a bite of the birthday flan and watched intently as I licked it off the spoon. The custard melted over my tongue, tasting of cinnamon, cream, nutmeg and lime. I had a sudden vision of Arthur kissing those flavors off my lips.

Bob shattered my daydream by bringing forth his mescal. *Uh-oh*, I thought, and discreetly asked the waiter to refill the water glasses. My hope was to hydrate my guys and so prevent vomiting and hangovers. I watched with trepidation as the group threw back those final (please God let them be final!) shots. Luckily, the magic mescal didn't seem to do anything more than make them a bit drunker, and not that much drunker at that. There was no need to haul anyone to the toilet.

Eventually, John started dozing off and Bob reluctantly admitted that it was time to bring the evening to a close. We got into the van. Given how Arthur had been acting, I decided to take him home first. Alas, he was, as I said, a stubborn drunk, and refused to leave. So I had to keep him while I drove the others home.

He was also speaking German.

"*Ich kenne deine Geschmacksrichtung*," he whispered confidentially.

Geschmacksrichtung? Wasn't that an opera with valkyries and stuff?

I dropped off the other guys and took Arthur back to his place. He seemed willing to leave this time, but he couldn't manage to stand up. *He hadn't seemed that drunk before*, I thought with annoyance and went around to help him. He practically fell into my arms. Crap. He was heavy.

What I didn't realize was the son-of-a-bitch was faking it. He pretended he couldn't walk, forcing me to help him to his apartment. But the second the door was open, he shoved me inside. I ended up on the hardwood floors, banging my knees.

"Damn it, Arthur," I said, getting up. "I know you're drunk but —"

I lost the rest as I turned. He was standing between me and the door. He'd dropped his trousers and there was a significant tent in his underwear.

Ah, crap.

"*Hol's Stöckchen, Hundi.*"

"Okay, okay." I shrugged off my jacket. "I'm going to get some caffeine into you and then shove you into the shower." Well, I'd try to shove him into the shower.

I headed into the kitchen feeling more than a little pissed. Why was it that no one thought I was worth fucking until they were drunk? A quick peek into the fridge showed me that Arthur was very health conscious. All the sodas were sugar and caffeine free.

Okay, then, coffee.

Arthur, still by the door, was fumbling around, talking to himself in German.

"Coffee, coffee," I muttered. I found some decaf, cursed, and searched some more. I heard Arthur behind me. There were a surprising number of cabinets boxing us in and he was able to reach the ones up high. Which was exactly what he was doing when I glanced back at him.

He was naked.

And, well, I'm only human. He was... if not exactly as I'd imagined, better than I'd imagined. Smooth bronze skin, toned muscles, powerful legs and arms. His nipples were dark brown and alert. I guessed that he shaved, because except for the hair under his arms, he was smooth almost all the way down. The hair at his crotch was judiciously trimmed to frame his cock.

That handsome, aroused dick.

I was salivating and this was not good. Time to vamoose. Problem was, there was only one way out of that box and Arthur was standing there with an open bottle of vodka. He was close enough for me to feel his heat, to smell his liquored breath. His olive black eyes were glowing like embers.

"You don't need any more to drink," I tried.

"*Iss nich für mich, Mensch, Du... Du Waschlappen!*" he snapped and shoved the bottle at me. "*Iss für Dich. Gegen die Schmerzen und den Mut. Erinner mich später, dass Du mir dafür dankst.*"

"Arthur, I have to drive home."

"*Zwing mich nich, es Dir wo rein zu schütten.*"

He was trying to get the bottle between my lips. I figured I'd better fake a sip, so I took it from him and tipped it. All would have gone well, except that he grabbed the bottom and upended it. A half cup of vodka went down my throat and alcoholic fumes shot up my nose.

I started choking and coughing. "You asshole!"

Arthur set aside the vodka and, to my alarm, snatched up one of those little paring knives. The kind you'd use to slice a kiwi. Only this one didn't look sharp enough to do even that. Still, he might hurt himself.

"*Lass Jucken, Kumpel!*"

"Arthur, for God's sake," I coughed, "put down the knife."

He grabbed hold of the waistband of my jeans, pulling at them. I think he wanted to hold the knife to my throat, but he had it a good foot from my cheek. It was really cute. He was trying so hard to be threatening.

I blinked up at him, tears streaming down my face from all the coughing. The naked man... the warm, hot, sexy, drunk naked man wanted me to take off my pants.

Why not? I asked myself. *He probably won't remember anything anyway. Yeah,* I countered, *and what if he does?*

Arthur pulled hard enough to pop the button and the zipper went down. "*Pack Dich aus.*"

I winced. Fucking things up with Arthur was not an option, but refusing him was becoming pretty impossible. Especially with him waving around that paring knife. I kicked off my shoes and got off my jeans.

He leaned in, pinning me against the counter. I felt him groping downward, and then his hot hand was stroking my cock through my underwear. I bit back a moan. Oh, crap. It'd been so long. My cock twitched with lust and interest.

"Tell me 'bout th' gay—" he said. At last! English! Except that he didn't sound nearly as articulate in English as he had in German.

"What?"

"Your last gay! What'd he do?" I think he meant to whisper this in my ear, but he spit a little in my face instead. I flinched.

My last gay? Guy maybe? Oh. I remembered our earlier conversation. Arthur had asked me about the last guy I'd been with and Mike had flashed to mind. Mike. Crap.

"I don't want to talk about him."

Arthur was caressing my thighs, making me squirm and try to hitch myself onto the counter.

"He for you?" he demanded.

For me? "Um, yeah, he for me."

"Like this?"

His hand went down my shorts and I jumped. *Holy*—

And then he was doing things to me. Things that were wearing away my objections very quickly. He fondled my balls, and oh, sweet Jesus, to have another man touching me like that. He rolled and pulled at them, my cock swelled. I hissed as his thumb teased its way up my straining length, over my sensitive slit. Slick with leaking pre-come, those fingers glided on down under my high nuts and oh, please, back there—

He was at my crack now, delving between my ass cheeks, toying with my tight hole. There was a leering grin on his face. Drunk he might be, but he knew he had me. Tears were running down my cheeks again, tears of desire and need. My cock was aching and my stomach was in knots. Any moment now I was going to break down and beg him to fuck me.

And still he played with me, raking fingernails over the soft flesh between my thighs, hitting the back of my balls with his palm. Circling, maddeningly teasing my hole. My breath was coming so short and fast I thought I was going to faint.

Experience has taught me that you can't reason with a drunk, but I gave it one, last try. "Arthur, Arthur you don't want to do this. In the morning—"

His hand left my ass so suddenly, I cried out in bereavement. And then he shoved me to my knees. His erect cock slapped my face.

"You know what to do," he said.

I could have gotten out of there. I could have darted around his legs and out the door. I didn't. I wanted that velvety cock in my mouth, wanted it too badly to pass it up. Breathing in that delicious fragrance, I went for it. Soon I was lost; drunk on him and getting drunker with every sweet lick and taste. As his cock hardened, I switched from sucking to swallowing, loving how his dick filled my mouth and throat. Then I pulled back, grazed the rim of his mushroom head with my teeth and tongued his slit. The nectar I sipped from there left me thirsty for more. So I took him down again.

I did that for a while, before breaking to lap at his balls. I loved his soft pubic hair, loved his groans and deep breaths, the gyrating of his hips. When he finally touched my head, I whimpered.

Why did he have to be drunk to like me? I wailed inside, and found I was crying. Crap. Years of teetotaling had left me vulnerable to that swig of vodka. It had gone right to my head and turned me maudlin! I sniffled, and took his hot cock back into my throat. Arthur was moaning and saying something, but I couldn't make it out. All I knew was that his fingers were running through my hair.

"I want you to be mine. All mine," he whispered, hips rocking faster. I let him fuck my mouth, loving the feel of his tightening balls knocking into my chin, loving that firm, slippery cock pulsing and twitching against lips and tongue.

Abruptly, he pulled out. I almost fell forward, and then, with a shout, he came. He didn't get me in the eye, but there was a hit to my forehead and a second shot got my cheek and chin. I felt it stick to my skin, warm and thick.

Arthur remained for a moment, holding his dick, which shone like polished bronze thanks to my spit and his sperm. And then his fingers were under my chin and he was tilting up my face. He was gasping for breath, and smiling that lopsided grin.

"Now you're mine," he said. A moment later, he was running water and tenderly, if ineptly, cleaning off my face with a wet paper towel. Which surprised me. I'd gotten it in the face before, and no one, drunk or sober, had ever bothered to do that. That consideration, the look of affection in his dark eyes, shook me.

He's drunk, I reminded myself.

"Bed," he said, pulling me to my feet. Inebriated as he was, he was the one who steered us there. I was too tired. He lay down beside me, studying and stroking my face.

"I'll be as gentle as I can be," he promised.

"Um, thanks," I ventured, with a glance down at his sagging cock. I didn't think it was going to get turgid again, not given the liquor and the blowjob. But even so, Arthur wasn't that much above average in size. Did he think I was a virgin?

He brushed away the hair from my forehead, kissed my neck, caressed my arm. Maybe it was the vodka, maybe it was the long night, the dancing and dealing with Arthur. I was feeling pretty worn out. Probably it was just because he was caressing me. Because I had a very bad crush on him and I didn't want to leave.

Likely, I'm just stupid or suicidal, because I made the *exact* same mistake as last time. I relaxed and fell asleep. You know the rest.

Censoring out most of my feelings and fears, I told Arthur all of this. Then I waited for the axe to fall. He was sitting on the bed, staring at me. He blinked a few times.

"German?" he finally asked.

"German."

To my shock, a huge smile lit his face. "Oh, my God, you're right!" He started laughing. "Shit! I remember! German... and I said... oh, fuck! That's hilarious. And that ridiculous little knife... and oh, my God—" He was laughing so hard now that tears were rolling down his face. "—I thought I was massively hung!"

He fell back, lying on the mattress still laughing. He had me smiling and laughing with him by now. At last he quieted down, chuckling and rubbing at his eyes.

"I'm glad you find it funny," I said, and meant it. Maybe I'd get out of this unscathed.

"You don't understand. I've never been so relieved. I was crazy drunk, not criminally drunk. That mescal on top of the tequila really fucked me up. I better give the other guys a call and make sure they didn't trip out like that."

Shit. My gut dropped. "You're not going to tell them about this, are you?"

He pushed up, frowning. "You said you were okay with what happened. And it *was* just a blowjob. Why are you so scared of it getting out?"

"Because I crossed the line. You were drunk and I... I took advantage of that."

He barked out another laugh at that, which made me flush with mortification. It did sound stupid. Someone like me taking advantage of him.

"Sorry," I said. I'm not sure why I felt so ill at that moment. All in all, I was getting off lucky. The worst that would happen is Arthur would tell the guys and they'd all laugh and I'd have to be a good sport about it. A very good sport.

"Oh, Eric, God, I'm sorry." Arthur was back on his feet, touching my burning face. "I didn't mean to laugh. I didn't realize. You really like me, don't you? And this wasn't just a blowjob, was it? Not for you."

I was trembling now, half out of anger, half out of raw embarrassment. I could hear it now: *How sweet! How cute! Dorky Eric tried to make love to Arthur! Lucky Arthur was drunk at the time.*

"I'm sure I wasn't up to your usual standards," I said bitterly.

He pushed up my chin, making me meet his eyes. "Not that I was sober enough to judge," he said, "but I seem to remember having a very good time."

"Ah." I hated the warm feeling that gave me. "Well, pass it around. Just one more service I provide to regulars. No added charge, of course."

He stiffened, and hurt flickered across his face. Which made me feel bad and damn it, why did I have to feel bad for wounding him? Guys like Arthur, like Pedro and Bob, they had it so easy and they didn't even know it! Friends flocked to them and stuck by them. Guys like me had to work our asses off just to stay on the periphery. We had to take the bruised knees and the drunk sex and the shots in the face. We had to take everyone stomping on our feelings while we tiptoed around theirs.

I was sick to death of it.

"So," he said, and his tone was strangely hard, "if this had happened with one of the other guys, you'd have done the same thing?"

"No," I snapped. "If it'd been one of the others, I'd've have tried harder to get out of the situation. I told you. It's not right if they're drunk."

"What if they're sober?" he asked quietly.

I scowled at him, even as I tried to swallow past the acid lump in my throat. "I'm not stupid, Arthur. I know my place. I'm the bitch. The only reason I haven't been satisfying any sexual needs is because you all can do better than me. But yeah, if you guys ever want me that way, you'll have me. That's what a bitch does if he wants to be kept around. He makes himself useful, and he doesn't fuck up. I understand that."

"That's not fair." He moved in closer, and I barely kept from backing away. "I agree we've never made you feel like part of the gang. But we've never treated you like a bitch, either."

He had his hands on me, running down over my chest. I could feel the heat of his palms through my tee. He pulled it up and I made no protest as he got it off me.

"Do you really think that if we were sober we'd use you like that? Without giving a shit about what you wanted, or how you felt about it?"

My throat was very dry and I couldn't seem to breathe. "No. I-I don't think you'd do that. Not if-if you were sober."

"I'm glad to hear that." He hooked his fingers into my shorts. "Now let me tell you what's going to happen."

Chapter 6:
The Scenic Route

What Happened—Arthur

I had my fingers hooked into the elastic band of Eric's shorts. He had his arms locked in front of him, his skin goosebumped. His shoulders and chest were thin, nearly hairless, the nipples very small and very pink. Below were visible ribs, the dip of his navel, and, finally, the whisper of a treasure trail. I rubbed my knuckles over that faint bit of brown hair, feeling him shiver in anticipation. I could tell he was terrified of what I thought of him, sober and in the light of day.

He didn't have sultry eyes or a dimple in the chin, but I'd never wanted anyone more. And the irony was, he'd as good as told me that he was already mine. I didn't have to do backflips to win Eric. To the contrary, he'd do anything I asked and be grateful for the privilege.

Real challenges happen when no one is looking. I'd worried this morning that I'd been a monster to Eric last night. I hadn't been. But I could be now. There'd be no repercussions. Even Eric would think it fair and right. Only I would know it was wrong.

I'd always assumed I was better than all those brats I'd dated. The ones who thought their desirability entitled them to use and abuse others. Was I?

"We're going to switch places," I told him, moving my fingers around and slipping his underwear down in the back. A glance over his shoulder gave me a beautiful view of his butt, his very small and pert ass. I brushed my thumbs over it, edging toward the crack. Eric's breath was very shallow, his eyes glazed.

"I'm going to drive," I told him, "And you're going to say where we're going."

I brought my fingers around and pulled at the front of the waistband, taking his underwear down to the ankles. His cock, right there before my eyes, was small and tight as a bumblebee with fear. It rested on a tuft of brown hair.

Eric stepped out of his shorts. I crouched there, caressing the back of his legs, breathing on his cock until it started to relax and expand. Then I stood, running my hands up his back and pulling him close. I nuzzled into his neck as I stroked his spine, his ass. His dick swelled some more. My own cock came awake in turn.

"Oh, God," he whispered, his hands holding on to my shoulders just as when we were dancing. His hips began to rock. I nipped and sucked at the tender flesh at his throat, loving the maple flavor of him. I kept fondling his ass.

"You really want me?" he asked faintly.

"Oh, yes. You can't imagine how much."

"Why?"

"Because you never think about yourself," I said, "When you drive, when you make love. You think only of how to please others. I like that. I think you deserve someone who will think about you in turn. Would you like that?"

He swallowed and nodded, his soft head brushing against my shoulder. The heat and friction between us was intensifying. I felt sweat on his lower back and between his ass cheeks. He spread his legs and I touched the back of his low-hanging sac as I explored. He groaned and writhed against me. My dick was thick and aching by now.

Locking my arms under him, I lifted him up and deposited him on the bed. Our hard rods crossed, and rubbed together, which felt so damn good.

"Are we going where you want to go?" I asked.

"Yes," he breathed, "Arthur—"

I kissed him. His lips were very dry, but the tongue that met with mine wasn't. I tasted the tang of his saliva, and hummed a little as he rubbed up against me. Cocks and pubic hair and nuts all pressed together. Hard and silken and pulsing and warm.

Eric was going crazy by now. He bit my lips, sucked at my tongue, roamed his hands over my chest, pinching at my nipples.

Which was incredibly hot, but I was the driver. I broke the kiss, pressing my hand against his chest to hold him back. "Where are we going, Eric," I asked, as his heart beat against my palm. "What happens now?"

-▭-▭-▭-

What Happened—Eric

My body was on fire. Every part of me smoldered, my ass, which Arthur had seared with his touch, my cock, which had flared against his, my lips and tongue which he'd burned. By the time he lifted me onto the bed, I was putty in his hands. He really could have done what he liked. Anything he liked. But he asked me instead, what I wanted. Where I wanted to go.

There was only one answer. Quivering with desire and fear, I rolled over onto hands and knees, and spread myself open to him. There was a knot in my stomach, a terrible mix of the need from my groin and the terror from my gut. I wanted him to fuck me. I wanted it so badly. But most of all, I wanted him to desire me.

I felt the bed shift as he moved to the side, and heard him searching through a drawer. Then the mattress sank as he came up behind me. I felt his hairy knees between my spread thighs, the touch of his warm hands on my hips, and then he was jerking my ass into position. I braced a pillow under my arms, ready.

And then I felt his breath at my crack, and blushed.

"Arthur," I gasped, the knot in my gut tightening up. "You don't have to—"

"*I'm* the designated driver," he growled. "We take my route."

I felt his face between my thighs, the rasp of his morning stubble, which just about drove me nuts. And then his soft tongue was licking my swinging balls. My breath caught. The warmth of that tongue on my sac, shifting my balls, spread through my crotch and I thought I'd shoot right then.

He moved up to tickle my taint, causing me to moan and rock. And all the while I could feel his large, powerful hands on my spread ass-cheeks, holding them captive. I tried to grab my aching cock.

"Don't you touch that!" he commanded, and then his hot, wet tongue went back to that tender area, maddeningly stopping just short of my waiting hole on the upstroke, and my balls on the down. My cock was dripping soaking the sheets with pre-come.

"Oh, Arthur, please, please," he had me begging.

And then his tongue stroked all the way up, hitting my pucker. I was so prepped, so sensitive, I jerked and screamed. His hands gripped my ass, his fingers biting in fierce enough to bruise. My cock was so hard it hurt. And now he punished my little pink hole with that tongue, circling it, caressing it, delving into it. I could feel the sweat trickling down from my lower back and ass.

Finally, he released me and it was almost a relief, I was gasping so hard. I heard the rip of tinfoil, and the sounds of him gloving and lubing up.

"What do you want, Eric?" he said then, "You have to direct me."

I swallowed. *Be of use and don't presume*, those were the rules. I'd broken the first by letting Arthur do all the work. Now he wanted me to break the other one.

"F-fuck me."

"You're the boss," he said, and lubed fingers penetrated me. I expected a quick stretch, but instead he went searching. And then he touched my gland, and my body went to jelly.

"Fuck!" I choked, as his fingers delved deep, fondling and rubbing at that spot. Flickers of delight shot out to my fingertips, pleasure like I'd never known. I undulated, helplessly, groaning and clawing at the bed.

"You're gonna—gonna make me come!"

"Of course I am," he said, slipping out and rising up. I felt his cock at my entrance, and if I could have sucked him in, I would have. I hitched my breath as he entered, gliding in steadily till his pubes were at my ass-cheeks and his balls were hitting mine.

And then he was pounding into me, turning those flickers from my groin into glorious electric shocks.

"D-do you," I breathed, "Do you like it?"

"Like it?" he growled. "God, Eric, I've been wanting your ass for months now. And I love it. I love it and I love you. You're so tight and sweet."

I shivered. "You'll give it to me h-hard?"

In answer he beat his body against me, so powerfully I hadn't the strength to do anything but let him take us where he liked.

"Touch yourself now," he told me. With my face in the pillow, and one arm bracing me, I touched my hard cock. It was slippery wet and so sensitive that I'd barely stroked it before I started shooting.

"Ahhh!" I cried, spitting creamy lines all over Arthur's bedsheets.

"Yeah, baby, that's it! Come for me!" Arthur shouted. I felt my ass clenching about him as my orgasm finished up, and then he, too, went rigid and let loose. He jerked and shuddered, and then, with a great release of breath as if he'd finally reached his destination, he collapsed on top of me.

I remained with my face in a pillow, my body shaking with pleasure and fatigue. Arthur's weight, his warm, sweaty body spooned my back, his heart pounding against me, his gasps coming hard as mine. At last he pulled out, leaving my gut feeling empty. But his hands stayed on me. They were trembling.

I guess... I guess he'd had a good ride, too.

The next time we met with the guys at the hamburger stand, Arthur told them that I had an announcement.

"Eric?" Bob said, brows raised in surprise.

The eyes were all on me and I had to fight to keep my head up, to remember that they weren't unfriendly. "Arthur and I are a couple," I told them.

"What?" Yoshi said, "No way!" and "Really?" John blinked.

"'S true," Arthur affirmed and put his arm around me.

"That's awesome!" Bob beamed and slapped me on the back. "Not that he deserves you. We should go out tomorrow night and celebrate."

Which was Bob all over. Always finding a reason to party. Arthur accepted the invitation on our behalf, but insisted that it be the pizza parlor, no liquor. "You're all going to drive yourselves home," he said pointedly. "The only one getting a ride with Eric tomorrow night is me."

And so it was. We met the next evening for pizza, and when it arrived, Arthur made sure I got the first slice, which made me feel self-conscious.

"It's my job to look out for you," he said. "To make sure you get treated right. That's what boyfriends do."

It was both strange and kinda wonderful. But that wasn't the only surprise of the night. At one point, Bob took Arthur aside, and talked to him quite seriously. "What was that about?" I asked him later, as we were driving home.

"He warned me that I'd better not hurt you," he said, which got a double-take from me.

"What?"

"He knows my track record." Arthur shrugged. "And he doesn't want that for you. He told me that he discussed it with John and Yoshi and they all agree—if I fuck this up, I'll be the one kicked out of the group."

I could hardly believe it, but I didn't think Arthur would lie to me.

"They do see you, Eric," he added. "And they care about you. You're a friend."

Eventually, I came to trust our relationship enough that I told Arthur about my months cruising for drunks, and how it had all ended with Mike. His face was a stone mask when I was done, which scared me.

"I don't do that anymore—"

"Where does this Mike live?" he growled, every muscle in his body taut.

I blinked in shock. "I dunno. It was, God, three years ago."

He pulled me into his arms, holding me tight as if defying anyone to take me from him. "No son-of-a-bitch gets to do that to you ever again. I'll fucking kill him. I swear it."

That was nice to hear. Too nice. "I kinda deserved it."

"The hell you did! *In vino veritas*. It's real easy to do exactly as you like then say, 'Oh, that wasn't me, I was drunk.' Maybe Mike secretly wanted to be with a guy like you, someone he didn't have to impress. Did you ever think of that? His reaction sounds to me like fear for his reputation. God, I wish I could punch his face in!"

"Um—"

"And those other guys—I bet they weren't so smashed. I bet most of them knew what they were doing. Maybe if you'd talked to them afterwards, something more would have happened."

"Maybe," I reluctantly agreed. It certainly had with Arthur.

He encouraged me to go back to school and study urban planning, so I started taking classes during the day while still driving at night. And, as if that wasn't enough, he got Bob and the others to invest in my business. I've got two more vans now, and I'm training drivers, showing them all the shortcuts, teaching them the right way to treat customers.

Odd. The one thing I'd never thought I'd ever be was a boss. Yet here I am, head of the *Designated Driver Company*. People look to me for direction.

Arthur and I still go out clubbing with the guys, and I'm still the designated driver when we do. That's my job and I like it. But when someone can't quite make it to their door, it's Arthur who gets them there. And at the end of the night, I park the car at the house I share with him. Our new home.

Now and then I get asked by friends where the relationship is going. And I tell them: "It's not the direction that matters, it's enjoying the ride." So long as I have Arthur at my side, I'll keep on driving.

And look forward to whatever happens next.

If you enjoyed this story, you can sign up for a free membership at ForbiddenFiction.com and discuss it with other readers and the author at the *Designated Driver* story page at http://forbiddenfiction.com/story/T13-1.000278.

We do our best to proof all our work, but if you spot a text error we missed, please let us know via our website Contact Form athttp://forbiddenfiction.com/contact.

Between Here and There

Between Here and There

Far above the dark expanse of the Delaware River, Avery Williams leans over the bridge's thick metal railing, looking out over both Philadelphia and Camden. The water below is flat and glassy, a mirror bending every point of colored light that it catches, twisting and stretching it. Despite the lack of a breeze, he's still glad he wore a hat—woolen, and knit black; a favorite lately. He likes hiding under it, masking his horribly blond hair. Self-consciously, he tugs the hat down a little farther on his forehead. He can still feel the ends of his hair poking out the edges. Time for a haircut, he thinks... that is, if Timothy lets him. For a while now, Timothy has been the one to call the shots on everything from grooming choices to financial matters. Avery's just along for the ride.

Once, years ago, Timothy was Avery's foster brother. It didn't last long. Soon both of them were shuffled around again to new foster homes, with different foster siblings. That sense of family never left, though. The two boys were survivors, trying to find a place to belong, somewhere to thrive. In some ways, they're still looking. They both aged out of the foster care system. No longer brothers in any technical sense, now they're connected in more intimate ways, belonging only to each other rather than continuing a futile search for that elusive home ever sought in a world that doesn't seem to want them, the children left behind.

There aren't many people out tonight. He's mostly alone, and it makes him feel conspicuous. He pulls at the overlong sleeves of his slim-fitting black shirt, hiding his hands, and he ducks his head to conceal a smile as someone sprints toward him along the Ben Franklin Bridge's walkway, from the Camden side.

"Don't do it!" The teenage boy gasps, hands on knees as he catches his breath, then at his side as a muscle cramps. "Fucker. You have so much to live for! What would your mother think!?"

Avery snorts, "And who's my mother supposed to be?" He turns, leaning back instead of forward on the railing, crossing his ankles, the picture of serenity. His jeans hang low on his lean frame, and with his elbows planted on the railing, the front of his shirt pulls up in front, displaying a tantalizing strip of pale skin between his hips. "Maybe if you weren't so damn *slow*..."

"Slow?" Timothy scoffs, stepping up to Avery, straddling his legs. Usually he makes Avery feel short—at five foot eight he's two inches shorter than Timothy, but convinced he still has one more growth spurt left in him, that the relatives he never met were fantastically tall, even though he has no proof of such a thing. Leaning as he is, Timothy towers over him, so Avery glances up through the long golden bangs he hates, his big green eyes taking over his boyish face. "You had your hand down my pants, then you up and take the fuck off? How am I supposed to run after you?"

"It was pretty funny," Avery grins slyly, sliding up to his feet to use every bit of his height. The glow coming off of Philadelphia on his left makes it look like Oz, a wondrous, magical place—especially compared to darker, seedy Camden on his right. But Camden is his home now. The rent's cheap. The company is good. Letting his lips part softly, his eyes closing halfway, Avery watches Timothy's mouth. Chasing it, he stays a breath away, a smile playing at the corners of his full lips.

"Maybe," Timothy says thoughtfully, his naturally hushed, sandpapery voice like a tickle that races over Avery's skin, "I should keep you on a leash."

"Mm, kinky," Avery purrs, grabbing Timothy brazenly by the crotch. Breathing out a rush of air, Timothy shivers, squints down at him and surges for his mouth. Avery in turn leans back, keeping just out of range, thinking of the random stranger that Timothy blew the other day for a hundred bucks.

"Stop that," Timothy scolds, grabbing Avery by the back of the head, getting hat and hair both, using the grip to pull him into kissing range. The tip of Avery's tongue teases lightly over the center of Timothy's top lip and he tries to jerk away again, but Timothy yanks him close, kissing him deep and dirty until Avery's head spins.

161

They break after long minutes. "When I want to kiss you, you have to let me."

"Oh yeah?"

"Yeah, actually. It's a rule. I just made it."

"Gonna get that tattooed on your arm too? Or maybe you could just write 'property of Timothy' over my ass."

Timothy's eyebrows shoot up. "Can I?"

Avery's response is a deep, rolling chuckle. He undulates forward, dragging in a slow grind against Timothy's groin. It makes Timothy exhale heavily, so Avery does it again but this time Timothy grabs Avery's ass to guide his movements and keep him there. Avery keeps at it until Timothy's dark brown eyes are black with lust, his skin flushed with heat. Then he wriggles away, slipping from his lover's hold and hopping a few feet down the walkway with a bright laugh.

He dashes farther away while Timothy groans and braces a hand on the railing. "How can someone so sweet be so evil?"

"It's a talent?" Avery shrugs. He makes like he's going to run away again, so Timothy fishes something from his back pocket—his wallet. Flipping it open, he holds up one of the pictures held in the plastic sleeve, waving it.

"Avery," he calls in a sing-song voice, and it's mostly that—the music of Timothy's voice, both rough and soft at the same time, that makes him stop and look.

"Oh, you son of a bitch," Avery gasps, startled, his chest suddenly tight, his knees weak. "Gimme that!" He bolts back to Timothy and lunges for the wallet, which Timothy holds away, out over the water. "Give it to me! You have that in your wallet?! You can't do that!"

"Sure I can," Timothy says easily, his smile all sweetness. "What's the matter? It's just a picture of you."

"You know what it is! Give it!"

"No way. It's my prized possession. I told you I was gonna keep it."

"Yeah, I thought you meant keep it in a private place," Avery cries, his face pink with the force of his embarrassment. It makes his lips look dark and sensual, his eyes like jewels, his hair like silk. Timothy drinks in the sight of his prize, while keeping the bait easily out of grabbing range.

162

"Who's going to be looking through my wallet? Huh? Nobody. It's fine."

"That was supposed to be private," Avery says a little breathlessly. His eyes shine wet, and Timothy hooks a hand around Avery's jaw, rubbing over blond stubble. Cars, trucks and motorcycles speed past, blurs of weight, noise and color, inconsequential. The only thing standing still, the only thing here is Avery, close to tears. Timothy lets him grab the wallet and holds Avery's face in two hands instead of one. He turns them, backing Avery up to an alcove, a tucked-away metal door in a tall stone column along the bridge's walkway, leading to God-knows-where, but it takes them out of the line of sight of anyone else that might be near. Hidden in shadows, surrounded by people rushing this way and that, the water sliding by under their feet and the stars spinning in the sky, Timothy kisses Avery. He kisses soft lips and sucks gently on the wicked, hot muscle of his tongue as Avery whimpers quietly and tucks the closed wallet back in Timothy's back pocket. Timothy works open the fly of Avery's pants as they both remember back to that night.

Timothy had been complaining about how he didn't have any decent photos of Avery, so Avery offered to pose for one. Timothy had taken this amazing little blue pill that helped him stay hard for a long, long time, and he made love to Avery over and over again, until he was laying boneless, sweaty, fucked-out and gorgeous on the bed. His eyes half-closed, his skin heated, his lips kiss-bitten, just basking in the afterglow. And Timothy took his picture. Just his face, from the neck up.

It was supposed to be a secret, between only them. Avery doesn't really understand why it hurt to see Timothy wave the picture around like that, but it did. A tear slides down his cheek and his fingers push up the sleeve of Timothy's right arm, tracing carefully the tender, healing skin where Timothy was tattooed a few weeks ago. Avery's fingers map the swollen letters, the A, then the V, the E. That's as far as he gets before Timothy pulls away, sinking down to his knees right there on the bridge. Using his body to protect Avery's modesty, he pulls him out and swallows him down, one hand cradling Avery's erection by the root, the other palming his bottom through his jeans.

Avery groans, letting his head fall back against the metal door. The sound is lost in the chaos of the night. The hot, wet closeness of Timothy's mouth hugs around him. It feels like coming home and then sudden intense suction makes Avery thrust helplessly. Timothy allows it, guiding him into a rhythm. Avery moans louder, the sound breaking off. Sweat beads over his skin, and the unmoving chill of the night balances the heat. Cold outside, hot within. And hot within Timothy. Avery rides him, pushing closer to orgasm. His fingers tangle in the dark-blond, tousled strands of Timothy's hair. He imagines people in the passing cars glimpsing them, there and gone, as they speed past. It gives him a thrill and edges him closer to release. He imagines a cop seeing them, too, and handcuffs, getting brought up on indecent exposure charges. Timothy fondles his balls and Avery moans thickly.

Deciding in a flash, just working on instinct alone, he digs something of his own from his back pocket. Pulling Timothy gently off of him by the hair, Avery croaks, "C'mere. Quick."

Timothy looks confused, but he stands, staying close to block Avery from view. Avery slips something into Timothy's hand. "We need to start using these. Every time. Okay?"

"Okay," Timothy nods. They lock eyes for a moment, and Avery sees the apology brewing, the heartbreak, and the hell of what Timothy has done for them, all of them. The lost and forgotten former brothers and sisters, there and gone, then back together again. That's why Avery turns away, putting his back to his lover, his best friend, his soulmate, and pushes his pants down in back just enough, giving him everything but the chance to say he's sorry.

Timothy moans, stepping up flush to him. He rolls on the pre-lubed condom Avery had passed him and gently, slowly, presses in.

Avery's mouth falls open and the night rips his cry away. For a few minutes there is only the push and pull, the thrumming of movement and racing of life through the bridge, vibrating up through their feet, the sparkle of lights, the bite of the air, the span of the sky overhead. He possesses Timothy, is full of him, aching from it; knowing he's in so deeply, Avery will never be able to get him out, not really.

A hand tugs Avery's dick and he cries out again, coming over the metal door he's pressed against. Timothy works him through it, pounding into him as he tightens up with his climax. Then he twitches, gasping roughly in Avery's ear, filling the condom, holding so tightly to Avery as everything washes away, everything but them.

The condom gets thrown in the river. Timothy zips them both up.

"I love you," Avery says quietly, unable to look at Timothy when he says it.

"I know," Timothy says, just as quietly, glancing around to make sure no police are in sight. "Come on, let's get out of here."

They slowly begin walking back toward Camden, Avery with his hands in his pockets, taking his time, still in a post-coital daze. Timothy watches him constantly out of the periphery of his vision, unable to take his eyes away from the sight of Avery's unintentional beauty. After a while, he slings an arm around Avery's shoulders, pulling him close. They walk like that to the end of the bridge.

"I'm kind of hungry," Avery murmurs, his stomach growling loudly. He's barely eaten all day—the cupboards at home have been empty for a while. No one's gone food shopping or had enough cash to do so, and eating out is too expensive. "How 'bout we swing by Sacred Heart, see if they're still serving dinner?"

Timothy's perpetually sunny face clouds over, his expression darkening. "We can pick up some dinner. I'm not taking you to the fucking soup kitchen."

"Don't worry about it, then. Never mind. I'm getting my paycheck in the morning anyway."

"Hey," Timothy comes to an abrupt halt, stopping Avery too, his arm still wound around him possessively. He closes the circle with his other arm, seeing how thin Avery is and the strain behind his eyes, far too much for an eighteen-year-old. "I'm gonna take care of us. No worries, okay?" The assurance is punctuated with a soft kiss to the furrows of concern in Avery's brow. They smooth away and Avery wraps Timothy in a hug.

"Okay. Sorry, I don't know what's wrong with me." When he pulls away, he's smiling again. "Come on. I'll race you." He fakes like he's going to take off, and at the horror that slackens Timothy's jaw, Avery bursts into wild, free laughter. "Oh my god, you should see your face!"

Rolling his eyes with relief, Timothy hooks his arm more tightly around his companion to rein him in and kisses his temple. "I don't know what your hurry is all the time anyway. You should stop and enjoy things once in a while."

Avery slings his arm around Timothy's waist, leaning on him. They disappear into the starlit night, arm in arm.

If you enjoyed this story, you can sign up for a free membership at ForbiddenFiction.com and discuss it with other readers and the author at the *Between Here and There* story page at http://forbiddenfiction.com/story/LK1-1.000014.

We do our best to proof all our work, but if you spot a text error we missed, please let us know via our website Contact Form at http://forbiddenfiction.com/contact..

Private Security

Chapter 1:
The Night Shift

The worst part of this job, Ryan thought, *is easily the hours, but having to wear this damned tie comes a close second.*

He hooked his finger in the knot and pulled on it, loosening the tie enough for him to breathe, and unfastened the top button of his shirt. This could be considered out of uniform, but the only other person here in the security office was old Bill and he didn't care what you looked like, only that you showed up for your shift on time so he could go home.

"I made a fresh pot of coffee for you," Bill said, and clapped Ryan on the shoulder as he grabbed his time card and punched out for the night.

"Thanks man," Ryan replied as he pulled the stack of textbooks from the backpack he had brought in with him and dropped them on the desk. He never had a great deal of time during the night for studying, but every few minutes he could get in helped.

He poured himself a cup of coffee, mixed in a healthy dose of sugar and powdered creamer, then took it with him on his rounds. He was exhausted, and had been since starting the job. When he accepted the position of security guard for the small company, he had hoped for just a few hours in the afternoon, something he could make a few dollars with after classes, but the only shift available was the graveyard at this warehouse.

In his month-long career as a guard he had gotten maybe five hours sleep a day. He tried to make up for it on his days off, but the constant rotation of his sleep schedule, sleeping days half the week then trying to switch to nights the rest of the time, was wearing on him. He found he was tired all the time, no matter how much rest he got. Living in the dorm didn't help matters any either.

The dorms were quiet during the day, when he was at class; but once lunchtime hit the place was nothing but slamming doors and hallway football games, and it stayed that way until ten at night or later.

To top all this off, he hadn't seen his girlfriend, Jennifer, for more than a few minutes at a time since starting work. He was horny as hell and the quick masturbatory rounds in the shower just barely relieved the physical tension. He desperately needed to touch and be touched in return.

He had met Jennifer during his second year at the university through her twin brother, Justin. Justin had lived in Ryan's dorm building, and the two became close friends, sharing a love of science fiction films. Justin was a hardcore fan, though, where Ryan loved it, but didn't live it. Justin would host weekend-long *Magic: The Gathering* games in his dorm room or *Stargate* marathons, and Ryan would show up dragging in a case of beer, or a bag of weed.

He spent entire weekends in that room with him. Often, the other guys left after a few hours or once the beer was gone, but there was a connection between Ryan and Justin that sometimes confused him, made him wonder who he really was. More than once he woke on Sunday morning with Justin's sleeping body entangled with his, his strawberry blond hair filling Ryan's nose with the scent of green apple shampoo and their dream erections straining against one another.

He hadn't seen Justin since everyone left for Christmas break. Justin had quit school, refusing to come back. Jennifer told him their parents were furious, but what could they do? He was over eighteen and could make his own decisions, no matter how bad they might be. Ryan missed Justin terribly, to the point there was an actual physical ache when he remembered their weekends together. Jenn was frantic with worry about her brother. She hadn't seen him since he left school. Ryan tried to calm her, but he was worried too.

When Ryan first met Jenn he was amazed at how much the siblings looked alike. If the two exchanged clothing they might easily pass off as the other. They both had the same blond hair and blue eyes, and they shared the same smile that not only lit their faces, but their eyes as well. They didn't just smile; they emitted happiness, and it made everyone want to be closer to them.

Now, a month into his new job, Ryan was beginning to question what had attracted him to Jennifer in the first place. Was it her beauty, her intelligence, her joyful, almost giddy disposition, or was it that she reminded him so much of her brother? He found himself thinking of Justin when he was in the shower, releasing his sexual needs. It always started out as Jenn, her face beaming up at him as her long, beautifully tanned legs opened and that lovely spot, moist and inviting, called to him. He would lower his imagined self onto, then into her, almost feeling for real the smooth walls of her vagina hugging his cock, pulling him in deeper and caressing him closer to the inevitable finale. Then, the face beneath him would change, it would grow harder, sharper. Blond stubble would appear along the jaw and the smile would become more mischievous. The legs wrapped around him were just as long and tanned but now, instead of smooth and hairless, they were covered in a thick down of blond hair and fierce runner's muscles stood out along the calves and thighs. And his cock was no longer inside her; it was pressed against Justin's cock, the same strong hardness he had felt in the real world pressing against him as they slept on those science fiction weekends.

This was the point he came. When his imagined self realized it was Justin he was with, his real self lost control and came in the shower.

But Ryan wasn't gay; he couldn't be. He loved women and always had. And he loved Jennifer more than any of the women and girls he had dated before her. He loved the way she made him feel: strong, confident, powerful. Like he had earned her love, even though he had never really done anything to warrant her dedication, except return the same affections.

But these thoughts he had been having of Justin were bothering him. He wasn't cheating on her, not really, not physically, but would she see it that way? Would she laugh and tell him it was okay to fantasize about her twin brother while he jerked off? That it meant nothing. That he was just a sexual being and could appreciate beauty, whether in a man or a woman, just as she sometimes mentioned how gorgeous she found certain women around campus.

Would she understand? More importantly though, did he want her to? Did Ryan want her to tell him it was okay? To give legitimacy to his newly discovered desires.

Besides, just because he fantasizes about Justin doesn't make him gay, right?

Right?

The job itself wasn't difficult; the hardest part was staying awake through the night. Every hour he had to make rounds through the warehouse, checking doors and making sure everything that should be locked, remained so. He didn't dare sleep. If anything happened to the place whilst he was napping he would be fired for not doing the one thing he was paid to do: staying awake and patrolling the grounds. The job might suck, but he didn't want to lose it.

He was actually in pretty good shape tonight, though. His American Lit. class had been canceled and he had been able to catch a few minutes of sleep this afternoon before the roar of the other students in the hall pulled him from his nap. It was Friday night and he knew he could sleep all day Saturday if he wanted, then maybe catch a few hours with Jenn before he had to be back here. He might actually get laid this weekend.

Maybe, if he did get lucky, these thoughts of Justin would end. It was just his sudden lack of sex that was making him think the things he thought in the shower. He wasn't really attracted to Justin. Was he?

He shook his head. No, that wasn't right. Getting off wouldn't stop these fantasy images of Justin naked before him. These thoughts were as old as his friendship with him. They had started almost immediately after they had met. *What is it about him that intrigues me?* he wondered.

The warehouse was a monster of a building. Two stories tall and 50,000 square feet of space, the first floor being the actual warehouse, the second housing offices. When he ran his rounds, it took him about 30 minutes to canvass the entire building, upstairs and down.

He finished his first round then went back to the office to finish his coffee and look through his books. He read a few pages of his Psychology textbook then it was time to head out on his rounds again.

The first floor was secure; nothing had changed since he had been there just an hour before. When he got to the second level though, one of the office doors was unlocked. He had checked them earlier and everything had been locked down then, he was sure of it.

"Hello," he called out, his voice shaking and coming out in barky little squeaks, like a cartoon mouse. *Come on, man up*, he thought. He nearly kicked himself for announcing his presence. If there were a burglar in the room, did he really think the guy would answer him back? He pulled the flashlight from his belt and swung the yellowish beam around the room. There were four desks, each set up alike. A small lamp on the left corner with a small metal trash can on the floor on the right side of each desk. A file cabinet as long as a delivery van stood in the back of the room. There was a door at the back of the room leading to an inner office, probably a supervisor and this was his (or her) secretarial pool. It stood open, which was another oddity. These were usually closed and locked as was everything else in the warehouse.

Nothing seemed to be disturbed in here, though. Perhaps he had made a mistake and only thought he checked the door earlier. Perhaps the month of sleep deprivation was getting to him. He might feel rested now, but there could be a layer of madness growing in him deep, deep down that even the few hours of rest he got today could not dissipate. Maybe he would need a week of rest after this was all over, or several weeks, to feel like himself again.

The room was silent; he could hear nothing but his own heartbeat, now slowing to normal with the excitement of finding an unlocked door fading to the mundane realization that it was not a burglar, but his own error. What would he do if there really was someone, he wondered. The only weapon the security outfit allowed was a stun gun. It was effective; its only drawback was how close you had to be to use it; but it would not keep an attacker down for long. But then, that would be all he would need. Time to get the person subdued and get the police on the phone. If he had to, he could club the guy with his flashlight. It was heavy enough and he was strong enough for it to knock him down, if not out.

The room seemed secure and he was turning to close the door and lock it, when he noticed movement out of the corner of his eye. A flash of movement from behind the back desk on his right side. He swung his flashlight in that direction and caught a quick glimpse of a hand and a richly tanned arm covered in a tattoo of the grim reaper. *Justin*, he thought. Just before leaving school he and Justin had gotten stoned and had thought it would be fun to get matching tattoos. Justin wanted the grim reaper. Ryan wasn't crazy about the idea of one so large, but he agreed because, well, he usually did whatever Justin wanted. Justin just had that effect on him. Justin wanted his on his arm, while Ryan, thinking of future career prospects, opted for his thigh.

The man (Justin?) ducked into the back office, the glass in the door rattling as his foot bumped the corner. Ryan reached behind him and flicked on the overhead lights. The florescent tubes crackled and buzzed over his head and the room filled with the sickly weird glow of the unflattering light. "You might as well come out," he said. "I know you're in there."

Quiet followed, and Ryan took a step forward; his balls pulled up into his body and sweat dampened his back, chest and armpits. Fear was taking him and he had to take deep breaths to calm himself. If the guy had a gun he would lie down for him; he knew that. Courage can only take you so far and he was not willing to die for a dollar over minimum wage. He just hoped the burglar knew this, that he wouldn't shoot first and ask questions later.

The smart thing to do was back out of the room and lock the door behind him, trapping the man inside, then call the police. Let them deal with this; let them take the risk. He began to back step, to move out of the room without turning his back on the inner office door when he saw eyes as wide as saucers shining out of the darkness of the other room. "Ryan?" he heard, and the man stepped into the light.

There was a smile beneath the eyes. A beautifully crafted mouth stretched into a grin that was both friendly and inviting. It was a smile he had seen many times, both in the real world and in his shower stall fantasies. A smiling mouth he had kissed in his dreams and parted with his tongue, and heard call his name not with the curious questioning as it had now, but with the simmering passion of impending orgasm, with the lust of sensations that Ryan brought to it in his dreams.

"J-J-Justin?" he stammered and nearly dropped the flashlight to the floor. "What are you doing here?" he asked. Before Justin could answer, however, Ryan ran to him, pulled him into his arms and hugged him. Justin's body was still firm with the lean muscles along his chest and back that Ryan had felt lying on the couch with him back at school. Ryan inhaled deeply, smelling the body wash Justin had used two, perhaps three days ago lying just under the surface of the natural funk of old sweat clinging to him. The combination actually excited Ryan.

"Ryan, oh Jesus," Justin moaned as he accepted the embrace and returned the same, only his was tighter, more urgent.

"Are you a dream?" Ryan asked, not really expecting an answer. This was his fantasy. He had grown so exhausted he was hallucinating Justin. It was the only explanation for his sudden appearance here at this warehouse.

But, Ryan thought, *if this is a dream, it is the most elaborate one I have ever had.* He ran his fingers through Justin's hair. At school, Justin had kept his hair neat, short. But now it spilled down over his shoulders. And it obviously had not been washed in days, just like the rest of him. Dirty or not, Justin was still stunning.

"What are you doing here?" he asked again as he stepped back, pulling himself from what was, he now realized, Justin's firm grip. "What happened to you?" Ryan asked. *You look like hell,* he thought but didn't say. It wasn't true anyway. Justin was disheveled, a little dirty, but far from unattractive. Ryan did not think Justin could ever be unattractive.

He stepped back again and saw the dark clothes Justin was wearing. Not the light, bright colors he usually wore. He was dressed in dark, nearly black jeans and an equally muted shirt. The clothing was tight against his chest, thighs, and crotch. It skimmed his body like a wetsuit. Ryan glanced at the floor, at the leather satchel half hidden beneath one of the desks. The bag was shut tight, but he could easily imagine what implements might be hidden inside.

"You're here to rob the place, aren't you?" Ryan asked.

Justin quickly looked away from him.

"Is this what you have been doing with your time since you left school? What the hell is the matter with you?" Ryan barked.

Justin swung his eyes up to meet Ryan's. His beautiful blue eyes brimmed with rage. "Fuck you!" he bellowed. "You haven't lived my life. You don't know what I've gone through." Justin stood straighter, the muscles in his chest suddenly pushing at the tight shirt. He seemed to be itching for a fight, something Ryan did not want to join him in. He did not want their first meeting in months to end up in a slug-fest.

"You're right. I'm sorry. Why don't you explain to me what you have been through?" Ryan dropped onto the desktop behind him.

Justin sighed. "I fucked up, Ryan. I got involved with some very nasty people and I owe them money," Justin paused and blinked tears from his eyes. "A great deal of money."

"How much are we talking about?" Ryan asked. The quiver in Justin's voice told Ryan all he needed to know. Justin was scared. Even though he assumed it was Justin's own fault, that he was as much to blame for putting himself in danger as the people after him, Ryan still wanted to help him.

"Ten thousand," Justin replied. "By Monday, or I'm not going to be able to walk for quite a while."

"Shit, man," Ryan groaned. "It might as well be ten million."

"I know. Look, Ryan, just walk away. Do your job just like I wasn't here," he said and cocked his thumb over his shoulder to the office behind him. Inside was a safe nearly large enough to walk into. Its door was shut and locked. "It shouldn't take me too long to get the safe open and be on my way." Justin looked pleadingly into Ryan's eyes.

Ryan's head began to throb as a hot rush of rage tore through him. "Yeah, great idea. And what happens later when you get caught and the police figure out I know you? Don't you think they will assume it was an inside job? I could go to jail with you. I won't do that, Justin."

"Why not? It's your fault I'm in this mess," Justin said, shoving his finger in Ryan's face.

Ryan rose to his feet and pressed his chest to Justin's. Justin did not back away, but leaned in against Ryan, edging him back towards the desk he had just been sitting on. "How do you figure it's my fault?" Ryan asked, the ice thick in his voice.

At that moment Justin deflated. His shoulders sagged and he turned from Ryan, the sadness back in his eyes again. "It just is," he said.

"Then let me help you. But not like this," Ryan said as he stared into Justin's eyes, before he let his attention move down to his lips. They were beautiful lips. Red as strawberries, wet, shimmering even in the unflattering glow of the florescent lights. He thought they would be sweet as strawberries as well. Ryan couldn't take his eyes off them. He had to taste them, feel them against his own lips. Nothing else mattered right now. Not his job, not the break-in. Nothing but those lips and his desire to taste them.

So Ryan did just that. He kissed him and held the kiss until Justin finally, perhaps reluctantly, pulled away. Their eyes locked. The flicker of a smile settled on Justin's mouth. It was an almost satisfied grin, as though he had been wanting to do that for as long as Ryan had. Then his face turned hard again. The anger was back. "You bastard!" he screamed and pushed Ryan backwards. Ryan spilled over the desk, caught his foot in the legs of the chair and slammed to the floor. His head bounced off the thin carpeting and the room spun for a second or two. Everything grew as black as Justin's clothes, and consciousness left him.

Chapter 2:
Getting Dirty

"Ryan? Ryan?"

Ryan opened his eyes, looked up at the ceiling. His head hurt, as did his ankle. He had twisted it on the way down to the floor. "Are you okay?" Justin asked, his face suddenly coming into view as he hovered over him.

"What the hell did you hit me for?" Ryan asked.

"I didn't hit you. I pushed you. Sorry about that." Justin grabbed his arm and pulled Ryan to his feet.

"Hey, I've been hurt worse."

"This isn't the football field, though. I really am sorry."

Ryan stood on shaky legs and steadied himself by leaning on the desk. "I know you are. It's okay Justin, really," Ryan said. He waited until he got his bearings back, then grabbed Justin, pulled him close and said, "Now, where was I?"

"Stop. We can't do this." Justin tried to pull himself from Ryan's hold, but could not break free. Ryan tightened his grip and after a minute or so, Justin gave up his attempt to release himself.

"Why can't we do this?" Ryan asked.

"I'm not gay," Justin replied.

"I know you're not gay. I've seen all the girls you were sleeping with back at school. I kind of envied you with some of them. I'm not gay either, but I want to be with you. I have for a long time. And I think you want to be with me as well."

"Just because I want to, doesn't mean I should."

"So you do want to!"

"I do. I don't know why, but I do." Justin began unbuttoning Ryan's uniform shirt, then slid it from his shoulders and let it pool on the floor at their feet. He slipped his hands beneath the crisp, white undershirt, his cool fingers causing a chill to race along Ryan's belly and chest. Justin looked into Ryan's eyes and they both swallowed nervously at the same time. "Is this what you wanted?" he asked. Ryan couldn't speak. His mouth was desert dry, but he nodded his head that this was exactly what he had fantasized about.

Justin's fingers found Ryan's nipples and teased them until they grew as hard as Ryan's cock had become. God, how Ryan wanted him. He resisted the urge to tear off Justin's clothes and ravish him on the desk. To taste his entire body from ankles to eyelids. Ryan tugged on Justin's jeans, pulling the button loose and sliding the zipper down until his bright white underwear shone out at him. He slipped his hand beneath the elastic band, feeling the shock of pubic hair then the rigid stem of Justin's cock. He was hard and Ryan felt a flutter in his belly when Justin moaned at his touch.

He pulled Justin's cock out, gave it a few tugs, watching as his foreskin slid up over the fat, red head, then pulled away again, leaving the crown slick with precome. Ryan licked his lips, wondering what it tasted like. He had tasted his own semen once, when he was very young and just learning how to masturbate. One quick dip of his index finger in his overflowing belly button and Ryan discovered it was bitter, foul tasting stuff. He had never asked any girl he had been with to take his come in her mouth because of that. Some still did, but not at his insistence. But he had never tasted precome and really had no desire to, until now. He imagined it must taste similar to come, yet he wanted Justin's just the same.

Ryan nuzzled Justin's neck, thrilled by his friend's pleasured moans. He nibbled Justin's earlobe while continuing to fist his cock.

"Oh god, Ryan," Justin moaned. He fumbled with Ryan's uniform pants, tugging them open and letting them slide to the floor. Then Justin had Ryan's cock out and was playing with it just as Ryan was playing with Justin. "I'm sorry I pushed you. I'm sorry you hit your head."

"I told you, it's okay. You didn't hurt me. I understand why you freaked."

"Let me make it up to you," Justin said and before Ryan could comment, Justin was on his knees before him and pulling Ryan's cock into his mouth. Ryan gasped at the sudden wet heat surrounding him. His body went limp and he leaned against the desk before he fell again.

It was obvious that Justin had never done this before. He fumbled his tongue over Ryan's cock in an attempt to imitate what girls had done for him. Ryan didn't complain, though. He knew he would do no better, having never even had the desire to give another guy head before. But he wanted to do this for Justin. And the way Justin looked up at him, the smile in his eyes, the way he struggled to pull Ryan all the way into his throat, Ryan knew the desire to please was not his exclusively. "Does it feel good?" Justin asked, pulling Ryan's cock from his mouth just long enough to get the words out, then went back to it before he got the answer.

"It feels great," Ryan replied. It did, too. It was not the best blowjob he had ever received, but Justin's ambition, coupled with the fact it was Justin doing this for him, more than made up for the inexperience. And there was something truly exciting in knowing he was Justin's first.

Ryan nearly came each time their eyes connected. If he didn't stop him now, he would go over the edge and he might not get the chance to perform the same act on Justin. He desperately wanted to go down on Justin. He hooked his hands under Justin's armpits and pulled him to his feet.

"What's the matter? Did I do something wrong?"

"No, nothing is wrong. It's my turn now." Ryan dropped before him, pulled Justin's pants to his ankles—it was a struggle getting the tight jeans over his well muscled, beautifully rounded butt, but Ryan managed—and inhaled Justin as deeply inside him as he dared.

The several days without bathing had left Justin a little musky, a little funky down there, but Ryan didn't mind. It was very much like the aroma Ryan had inhaled during the hug at the start of the evening, only more pronounced. He had liked that scent and found he loved this stronger version even more. There was a primal feel to it. A feral aroma. And it excited Ryan more than anything he had smelled before. Or at least as much as the scent of a woman in full bloom.

He pulled Justin down, deep into his throat. He fought the gag reflex, struggled to keep his lips buried in Justin's blond bush, but he needed to breathe. He reluctantly pulled back, letting inch after inch of Justin's pale, hard-as-stone cock back out into the office air. It glistened with his saliva. Ryan lapped at it, watching with fascination as Justin's dick bounced and flexed under its own power each time Ryan's lips and tongue made contact. Then he swallowed it once again.

"Oh shit, Ryan," Justin moaned as he curled his hand around the back of Ryan's neck and held him still. He began working his hips, pushing himself deep into Ryan's throat, then back out again, slowly fucking his mouth.

Ryan slid his hands into his own lap and took himself in hand. He slowly pumped himself at the same rhythm Justin was working his mouth. He ran the hand not busy with his cock up Justin's legs. The blond hair ticked against his palm and he ran his fingers in the grooves of the thick muscles along Justin's calves and thighs. He reached around to Justin's butt, massaged the thick globes, and slid a finger between the cheeks. A deep moan slipped from Justin's lips and he began pumping his hips faster. Ryan relaxed his throat and let Justin do what he wanted while jerking himself to the new beat.

"Oh no; I'm going to come!" Justin nearly screamed. He started to pull back, to pull himself out of Ryan's mouth, but Ryan wrapped his free arm around him and held tight. A moment later, the warm splash of Justin's seed coated his tongue and tonsils. It was bitter, but Ryan barely noticed the flavor. He was too busy grunting around the cock in his mouth as his own orgasm painted the carpet between Justin's feet.

Ryan leaned back, letting Justin's still-erect cock slide from his mouth and grimaced at the taste in his mouth. He sat on his knees a moment, while he caught his breath.

After, neither man spoke as they dressed. Ryan glanced at Justin, trying to gauge his feelings about what had just happened, but his body language was as mute as his tongue. Justin finally looked over at Ryan and broke into a wide grin. "That was incredible," he said.

Ryan sighed in relief. For him, it had been better than he suspected it could be. The simple act of pleasuring Justin had felt as good for him physically as the blowjob Justin had performed on him earlier. Getting Justin off, got Ryan off.

"It *was* incredible, wasn't it," Ryan said as he pulled a tissue from a box on one of the desks and cleaned the mess he had made on the carpet. He tossed the sticky tissue in the trash. "Grab your bag; I have to go on rounds."

"So I guess you're not going to let me..." Justin nodded his head at the back office and the safe that hid within.

"No. We are going to have to figure something else out. You don't want to do this anyway. Right? You're a better man than this, Justin." Ryan grabbed his tie and shoved it in his back pocket. He didn't want to fumble with the thing right now. As long as he had it back on before the morning crew showed up, he was safe.

"I don't want to ask my father for help, but I guess I have no other choice." Justin grabbed the leather satchel from beneath the desk and left the office with Ryan leading the way. Ryan locked the door closed behind them and they descended to the first floor. "I didn't want to disappoint my parents. That's why I've been living on the street for the last four months."

"Which would disappoint your father more?" Ryan asked. "You asking him for help, or you getting your kneecaps broken because you were too scared to go to him?"

"I'll drive up there in the morning. Can you come with me? You and Jenn? I don't want to go alone."

Jenn. Ryan had forgotten about her. *Jesus, what have I done?* he asked himself. He had cheated on her. And with her brother no less. This could be the end of them if she found out, and she had to find out. He could not keep something like this from her. He loved her too much to keep her in the dark about this... this revolutionary self-discovery. He liked what they had done and hoped Justin would want to do it again and he couldn't keep this from her.

"Will your father loan you the money?"

"I'm sure he will. I've never been in trouble before. I'm sure he is pissed about me leaving school, but Jenn has him wrapped around her little finger. If I can't convince him I need his help, she will."

"*I'm* still pissed at you for quitting school," Ryan said. The smile he poured down onto Justin never faltered though. "If he can't or won't come up with the cash, we can come up with something."

"Like what? A *Justin fucked up his life* benefit?"

"Maybe. We all make mistakes. It could happen to any of us. The guys at school, they ask Jenn about you all the time. They love you, man," Ryan paused a moment, stared into Justin's deep, blue eyes. "I love you."

Justin laughed. "How do you love me? Romantically?"

"I don't know. Maybe. I've never felt this for another guy before. I've never wanted to be with someone as badly as I wanted to be with you. I want to do this again." He leaned in, kissed Justin. "And again," another kiss, "and again."

What does this make me, he wondered. Those long weekends when they barely got out of each other's sight were the happiest he had ever been with another person, and when Sunday evening arrived and Justin's roommate came back to the dorm after spending the weekend away, forcing Ryan back to his own dorm room, he found sleep difficult. He wanted to be back down the hall, back with Justin, and he would press his own clothes against his face and smell the black cherry air freshener Justin scented his room with.

There was something powerful going on between them. He didn't know exactly what it was, but he liked it. What did this make him? Gay, bisexual, bi-curious? Who cared what he was. They were just labels, to pigeonhole people into categories. He might be sexually attracted to women, but he had never felt such an emotional connection to one as strongly as he did for Justin. He had always loved Justin. From the moment they had met, he wanted to be with him. He was a friend closer than any he had had in high school. The more time he had spent with him, the more attracted to him he became. Did that make him gay? Perhaps, but he didn't care right then what that made him. He liked it. He liked being with Justin and he even liked doing what they had just done. Maybe he was just gay for Justin.

"You are going to have to get out of here soon," Ryan said as he glanced up at the clock on the wall. He was late making his rounds.

"You're not going to turn me in? I don't want you to get in trouble if they see me here on the cameras."

"There aren't any cameras. The owner never installed them because it's cheaper to hire me than it is to monitor the feeds. And no, I'm not going to turn you in to anyone. You made a mistake, but you never had a chance to go through with it, so no real crime has been committed."

"The police wouldn't see it that way."

"Fuck the police. They are just here to protect the rich from the poor anyway." He led Justin toward the security office and the door to the parking lot outside.

"Still the angry idealist," Justin laughed."

"Look," Ryan said, his hand on the door handle. "I need to tell Jennifer about what happened here tonight. I can keep your name out of it but..."

"She will understand Ryan. She won't hate you, or me. It might actually turn her on. She's kind of a pervert that way."

Ryan laughed. "I love her, you know."

"I know. She loves you too," Justin said. "I don't think this is going to bother her that much. She kind of already knows anyway."

"What do you mean?" Ryan pulled on the ring of keys, fit one into the lock on the door leading outside.

"Just before Christmas break, Jennifer told me something that...well, it frightened me. I panicked and left school because of what she said. Don't tell her that was the reason, though. I don't want her to feel guilty about it."

"What did she say?" Ryan turned the key, causing the tumblers inside the door to rattle and fall into place.

"She said that when you and I were together, she saw something in my eyes that made her believe I had a thing for you. She called it a sparkle," Justin laughed. "She is such a girl, but that's what made her believe what I already knew was true. I did have the hots for you; still do. But the thing that scared me? She saw it in your eyes as well. Jennifer thought it was adorable. She actually used that word, adorable. I couldn't stay there, knowing something might happen between us. I'm not gay; I'm not attracted to men...except you."

"So why did this just happen?"

"You live on the streets for a few months; you come to realize what is really important. You are my closest friend, Ryan. I love you, man. I don't know what this is between us, but I like it and would like to explore it more. See where it takes us. If..." he sighed heavily, "that is, if you want to."

"I do want to. I don't know what this is either, but we will figure it out, together."

"And don't feel guilty for my leaving school," Justin said. "It wasn't because of you or what Jenn had said. It was me, my own fear that made me run away. I got scared and I quit school. This was my doing. I made the decision to sell drugs for those guys, and it was my decision to use those drugs rather than sell them. I'm sober now and haven't touched anything in a while, but after I get this mess cleared up, I was thinking about coming back to the university."

"That's great. The dorm is lonely without you."

"I won't be at the dorm. I want to get a place in town. I would like you to move in with me."

"Jenn and I were talking about getting a place off campus. Maybe we could all live together."

"What are you going to do? Bounce from my bed to hers?"

"Maybe. Would that bother you? Do you think Jenn might go for that?"

"She might. She is quite the free spirit. It doesn't bother me. I'm still going to date women, you know. I still love the girls, but I will always have time for you."

Ryan pulled the door open, felt the cool rush of night air flutter over his still bare chest. He buttoned his shirt, pulled the tie from his back pocket and draped it around his neck. "I get out at six. Meet me at the dorm. You can take a shower there before we head to your parents."

"Cool," Justin stepped outside into night. Light was just beginning to illuminate the horizon. It would be morning in a few hours. He began to cross the paved lot to the road when he stopped, turned back to Ryan and said, "I love you, man."

"How did I get so lucky?" Ryan called back, then Justin disappeared around the corner of the building. *How did I get so lucky?* he asked himself again. The two most beautiful people he had ever known loved him. The entire situation was crazy, but he hoped things would work out between the three of them. He wondered if Jennifer would really be okay with this. Justin thought she might. Maybe he was right. If not, there could be some serious heartache in the future. But at least he was secure in the knowledge that he loved them both and that, at least for now, they both loved him. He couldn't ask for more than that.

If you enjoyed this story, you can sign up for a free membership at ForbiddenFiction.com and discuss it with other readers and the author at the *Private Security* story page at http://forbiddenfiction.com/story/PLR-1.000205.

We do our best to proof all our work, but if you spot a text error we missed, please let us know via our website Contact Form atvhttp://forbiddenfiction.com/contact.

Judge Not

Judge Not

Matt yawned, his head drooping towards his desk. The figures in front of him blurred, dancing across the screen, and he rubbed the heel of a hand into the socket of his eye. A headache was building and he groaned quietly. Blinking hard, he took a couple of swallows of the stale, cold coffee sitting next to him before he returned his attention to the screen.

Fifteen minutes later, he admitted defeat, saving everything and finally, finally shutting down the computer. The cleaner had left long ago and Matt wandered through the dark offices. It was always strange being in an office at this time of night; the only lighting the dim orange glow of the security lights, the toxic green of the fire exits. But he wanted to get on; his career was all he had and he wanted to be the best at what he did.

He slipped out, setting the alarm and locking the doors. The night air was cool, damp against his dry skin. Matt turned his face up to the light drizzle, taking a long, slow breath. He wandered along the street, heading for the tube station that would take him out of the city towards home.

People moved swiftly in and out of the station, many heading home, others coming into the city for a night out, others to run the businesses that catered to the night owls that kept the city humming. Matt yawned again as he passed through the ticket barrier, tucking his card back into his wallet. He eyed the escalators, but the soft ping of the lift beckoned him and he slid thankfully into the empty box.

He pushed the button for the lower level, leaning gratefully against the metal wall of the elevator, eyes drifting briefly closed. After the bright lights of the station, the darkness behind his lids was blissfully soothing and he kept his eyes closed as the lift shuddered its way downwards.

Matt rubbed a hand against the stubble that shaded his jaw, debating whether to shower when he got in, or whether just to fall into bed and wake up earlier and shave then. He still hadn't decided —his stomach asking for a third option that involved ingesting something other than coffee and stale Digestive biscuits from the staff room biscuit barrel—when the lift shuddered to a halt and a disembodied voice announced, "Bottom level. Court is in session."

Matt jerked up, staring around. "Bottom level, Earl's Court," the voice announced again. He shook his head, a faint grin curving his lips. Yeah, sleep was going to win out over shaving if he was starting to hallucinate strange voices. The lift doors slid open and he stepped slowly through the opening.

It took a minute for Matt to realise what was wrong, but then it came to him—it was the sound of the place. Instead of the usual hubbub of a busy tube station, Matt could hear the sound of murmured voices from up ahead.

The hallway stretched in front of him was not the usual, white tiled halls of the Underground, but was lavishly tiled in deep green with paler green over the curve of the roof.

Matt turned back just in time to see the lift doors slide closed, the ornate needle above the doors telling him the lift was ascending. He thumped the button for the lift, hoping to summon it back. When the needle shuddered and froze he sighed. Maybe it was broken. Matt knew there were old tunnels, disused stations and platforms spread throughout London. Perhaps he had ended up in one of those.

He ventured forward along the passageway. Perhaps there were stairs up ahead, or maybe some of the people he could hear would help him out. He came to a stop midway along, turning to look at the wall on the far side of the tunnel. He moved closer, bending to peer at some of the tiles on the wall. They were not the same plain colour as the rest of the walls; these were painted with pictures, enamelled in jewel-bright colours.

Matt tilted his head to one side, trying to make sense of the image on the tile in front of him. His cheeks flushed and he jumped back when the image came into focus. Darting a look around, he leant forward again once he realised the hallway was empty.

The tiles all revealed scenes that Matt would never have expected to see in his life, much less in a London subway tunnel. The tile in front of him depicted a woman, tied down over some kind of bench, her ass towards the viewer. She was naked, her legs spread, her position displaying her to perfection. Off to one side stood a masked figure; hand raised above the woman with what looked like a ping-pong bat held in the air.

Matt stared at the next tile. This one had a man, his arms chained above his head, a masked man between his knees. The kneeling man had what seemed to be a phallus protruding from his mask. Two men stood to either side, holding ropes that attached to the standing person's ankles.

Matt glanced at tile after tile. Each one showed varying images of people in bondage, some showed figures being disciplined, yet others depicted various carnal acts that had Matt's blood swirling heatedly through his veins, his cock swelling with interest.

The sound of footsteps approaching along the passageway had Matt leaping backwards away from the wall, straightening his shirt, fingers tugging at the knot of his tie. He pulled his jacket around himself, trying to disguise the evidence of his excitement. He took several steps towards the oncoming footsteps. A man came into view, tall and slender, walking swiftly towards him. There was something unusual about him but before Matt could think about it the man was speaking.

"There you are." He reached out for Matt, fingers closing hard around one of his wrists before Matt could think to move away. Matt stared at the man, eyes wide, as he suddenly turned and started back along the passageway, almost towing Matt behind him. Matt stumbled along behind for a couple of steps before he pulled back as hard as he could.

"What? Who are you? And where are you taking me? And man, let go of my hand! If you just point me in the direction of the exit, I'll see myself out."

The man turned, fixing him with dark eyes. Matt stared, now that he finally had a moment to take in his outfit. He was wearing a suit, but the cut was old fashioned, reminding Matt of old black and white films. He had a thin, dark moustache and his hair was smoothed down and back, exposing sharp cheekbones and those large dark eyes.

"The Court is waiting and we're up next. If you keep the Judge waiting it will not go well for either of us, so come on!" The man tugged at his arm again, already turning away. Matt followed, more out of confusion and curiosity than anything else. The man almost slid to a stop on the tiled floor in front of a large set of doors. He turned to Matt, reaching up to straighten his tie, pulling the knot tight. Suddenly fingers were at Matt's waist and he gave an embarrassing squeak as the strange man tucked his shirt back into his trousers neatly. He fussed briefly with Matt's hair before pressing a long slender finger to Matt's lips.

"Be quiet. Let me do the talking. And whatever you do, do not curse. Oh, and bow to the Judge."

Matt blinked, surprised, confounded and beginning to worry. The man pushed at one of the doors and slipped through the small gap, beckoning frantically to Matt. Matt thought for a brief moment of just turning tail and running back along the corridor, but something had him moving forward. He slid through and the doors slid shut as silently as they had opened. The man curled his fingers around Matt's lower arm, towing him over towards the benches that filled the back area of the large room. He pushed him into an empty row and slid in beside him.

"The Court finds in favour of the submissive and grants her permission to seek a new Dominant. Dominant will be held for three consecutive days and will be banned from searching for a new submissive until nine months from this date."

Matt's gaze jerked up to the front of the room. It looked somewhat how he had imagined a court would look, but there was a set of stocks to one side, a padded bench beside that and an ornate cross fixed to the wall. A slender woman slipped from the bench at the front of the room, curtsying gracefully to the Judge, her head lowered. She exited the room through a small door to the right, another man in an old-fashioned suit following behind her.

Two men in dark leather trousers approached the Judge and slipped shackles around the wrists of the man seated in what Matt had originally thought was the witness box. The man looked shocked at the judgement and then furious as the two guards pulled him from his seat. They stepped back, tugging the man with them, and bowed to the Judge before the man was removed from the room, almost carried out by the other two as he struggled for a moment before spotting the Judge's face and going limp.

"What am I doing here? What is this?" Matt gripped nervously at the strange man's arm as he whispered fiercely in his ear.

"Hush!" The man pressed his fingers to Matt's mouth again, the pads of his fingers rough against the sensitive skin. Matt blinked in surprise at the unexpected contact, face flushing as he fell silent.

A small man—obviously a clerk—his face dominated by wire-rimmed glasses, stood up at the front of the room. His voice was deep and filled the room, surprising Matt when it issued from the man's small frame.

"The Court calls Matt Stephenson."

"But—" Matt's words were cut off as the man, whom Matt guessed was now his lawyer, popped to his feet, pulling Matt behind him. He paused once to whisper swiftly, "Remember to bow."

They approached the Judge and Matt folded himself into a swift bow, keeping his head lowered as he peered up from beneath his lashes. He wrapped his hands together, surprised and disturbed to find his fingers trembling.

"You are Matt Stephenson, age twenty-eight, currently residing at fourteen Elmwood Avenue?"

"Yes, Sir." Matt's voice was small and faint in the large room and he coughed and repeated himself slightly louder as the figure in front of him frowned down at him. Matt dared another look. The Judge's shoulders were broad under a wide, fur-trimmed cloak. Despite the almost archaic cloak he seemed to be wearing a suit under it, the shirt high-collared, a cravat pinned at his throat with a huge ruby pin.

His face was stern and solemn, his features making him more masculine than handsome. He stared hard at Matt and then his lawyer, the dark brown eyes taking in everything. He frowned down at Matt again and Matt could feel a tremor run through him. His lawyer placed a hand at the base of his spine. Matt relaxed into the unexpected touch, finding it oddly soothing and comforting.

The Judge stared at him for another long moment and Matt fought the urge to fidget under the heavy, penetrating gaze. Finally, the Judge nodded slightly to himself before he motioned to the clerk, who now sat at the side of him. The Judge whispered briefly into the clerk's ear before rising to his feet and disappearing through a door behind his seat.

The clerk beckoned to another official and spoke briefly with him. As the official rushed off the clerk announced, "Court is now in recess. Bathrooms are now open and refreshments will be available in the next room. Court will reconvene in one hour."

The clerk approached Matt and his companion. Matt's lawyer inclined his head in a small bow and Matt followed suit. A faint smile flickered across the clerk's face before he moved to the side of Matt and gestured to the door the Judge had disappeared through.

"As this is a new case, His Lordship the Earl will see you in private." Matt felt his companion stiffen slightly beside him before urging Matt towards the door. Matt staggered forward on unsteady legs, his mind beginning to circle frantically. Had the clerk really referred to an Earl? What on earth was going on here and were the police aware that a bunch of weird people had set up a court beneath the tube station?

Suddenly Matt found himself in a much smaller room; the stone walls were draped with fabric, light flickering from an ornate chandelier as well as small sconces on the walls. The Earl was seated across the room in a lushly comfortable chair. Matt stepped forward, his temper beginning to override his confusion.

"What the..." His following curse was muffled by the tight grip of his lawyer's hand as it pressed firmly across his mouth. He struggled against the pressure, eyes wide and frantic.

"I'm sorry, my Lord. A brief moment if you will. This has come as quite a shock to my client."

The Earl waved a negligent hand but his voice was firm as he said, "One moment only, Mr Smith. My time is not yours to waste."

Matt found himself pressed up against the wall of the room, Mr Smith's body leaning hard against him, those dark eyes staring into his own wide green ones. The urge to struggle against him, to fight and then run warred with another unexpected need to submit, to go limp and boneless against the more dominant force.

Mr Smith waited a long moment before he said lowly and firmly, "You need to be calm. Take a deep breath. You do not have permission to speak and I would highly advise against any further speaking out of turn, and especially cursing, unless you wish to be punished here and now. His Lordship is not known for his forgiving nature."

The hand eased off slightly and Matt sucked in a deep breath. "That's it. Good boy. And another... I know this is unexpected." A small snort escaped from Matt, an eyebrow quirking in mocking response. "Okay, perhaps unexpected is not quite the right word, but it is happening and it will happen and the best you can do is keep calm and behave. Things will go much easier for you if you behave."

Matt pulled in another slow breath, inhaling the other man's scent, dark and softly smoky. He felt his cock stir at the pressure Mr Smith was still exerting against him, reacting to the ease with which the man held him up against the wall. A tremor ran through him as he prayed that the other man would not notice his body's betrayal.

His pupils dilated and he let his eyes fall closed as he sucked in another slow breath. Perhaps if he just went along with it all, submitted like they wanted him to, he could get out of here and get home to his nice, safe bed. But definitely not by taking an elevator.

Matt felt the pressure against him ease away and he opened his eyes, shifting away from the wall and moving to stand in the middle of the room as indicated.

"You have not had time to brief your client, Mr Smith?"

"No, Sir. There seems to have been a slight temporal glitch. But he will remain calm and he is most apologetic for his ill-mannered outburst."

Matt nodded his agreement and murmured a soft apology when the Earl's heavy gaze fell on him. The door opened behind them, but Matt kept his eyes fixed firmly on the floor, concentrating on his breathing.

"Ah, Mr Kent. There you are." Matt startled slightly as a voice came from behind him, greeting the Earl. It couldn't be who he thought it was. He let his gaze rise slightly, tilting his head until he could see the new arrival. Two guards had come through the door, but it was the man who accompanied them that drew Matt's attention. His pulse stuttered and jumped as he met the gaze of Thomas, a man he had dated for a while before things had threatened to get out of hand.

Matt had been happy with their occasional nights out, pretending to be friends; long afternoons spent hidden away in his house as

Thomas worked him to the edge of pleasure, held him there before they both spiralled over. Then Thomas had ruined it, had wanted to go public with their relationship, and Matt had still been firmly hidden in the closet. Things had not ended happily.

"Mr Stephenson, Matt. Mr Kent here has accused you of leaving him without permission, also of self-hatred and a fear of being who you truly are. He believes that with a firm hand and some guidance you will be able to come to terms with yourself and thus lead a happier life instead of wasting your youth in an office, burning out without ever being truly happy."

Matt's eyes widened and he turned to Thomas. Thomas stared back him, his eyes sparkling as emotions tumbled across his face. Hurt and disappointment, hope and still, after everything, something deeper, something Matt had never wanted to name. His vision blurred and he shook his head, trying to deny it.

"No, no no no."

"Mr Stephenson, do you deny these charges?"

Matt barely heard the words, his head shaking in denial as long-buried emotions tried to surface once more. Voices continued to murmur in the background, but he paid them little attention, his gaze darting around the room, panic flaring in his chest that his secret was being exposed. His wide eyes always returning to the figure of Thomas, standing there, waiting.

Suddenly, Matt felt hands wrap firmly around each wrist and the air was forced out of him as one of the guards pushed him head down over the back of a settee. Matt's face pressed against the cushions and he jerked, trying to catch his breath. Hands slid in between his hips and the firm back of the settee, making quick work of his buckle, button and zipper.

He struggled hard, his yells muffled against the fabric and cushions pressing against his face. A foot kicked out at his legs, spreading them wide as his clothing was slid over his feet. The cool air against his bare skin had him freezing in fear and anticipation. He pushed up hard with his hands, tilting his head awkwardly in a bid to locate Thomas.

"No! What are you doing? You can't just drag someone down here and... Aaah!"

A line of fire burned across his ass, the crack sounding huge in the small room. "Fucking... goddammit... what the..." His curses trailed off into another yell as the switch fell again, this time slightly lower, bringing another crimson stripe flaring to life. The switch fell again and again as Matt screamed and cursed, moving up and down over the backs of his thighs, the soft swell of his ass.

Finally, the cries turned to soft sobs, to pleading words. The punishment stopped and Matt felt gentle fingers raise his head, fingers softly wiping at the tears that tracked over his temples, disappearing into his hair. Tom crawled onto the sofa, eyes meeting those of the guard standing at ease behind Matt, switch now resting against his leg as he awaited further instruction. Tom lifted Matt's upper body, fingers trailing gently through his hair and down his spine as Matt leaned into him.

Matt pushed back against the sofa with shaking arms, lifted tear-filled eyes, meeting the serious gaze that seemed to see right into his soul. "Thomas, I'm sorry, I'm sorry. Please, don't let them punish me anymore. Oh God, I miss you so much. Please, I'm so sorry." Matt pulled in a harsh breath, his throat raw and burning.

Thomas leant back slightly so that he could meet Matt's tear-filled eyes. "Will you take another five for me, sweetheart? I need to know that you understand why you're being punished, why you're sorry. Tell me why." Matt swallowed hard, lips parting as he tried to speak. His throat still choked with tears, he nodded, lashes falling against flushed cheeks.

"Yes. Okay." The words were barely a murmur against Tom's neck but Thomas heard and nodded to the guard behind Matt, who raised the switch again, bringing it down with perfect precision.

Matt stumbled through his confession as the cane fell, words distorted with tears and soft moans. Thomas continued to cradle him against his chest, counting the last five strikes, murmuring the numbers against Matt's hair.

The deep voice of the Earl came again as Matt's lawyer moved to support him, Tom slipping from the sofa to move round beside Matt. "Your confession has been heard and your pleas have been accepted. We feel that the punishment has been acceptable to all parties. I am happy to hand you over to the care of your Dominant, if you accept him as such. Mr Stephenson?"

Matt turned red-rimmed eyes to Thomas, taking in the long length of his legs, the muscles that used to bunch and twist under his caresses, the strong line of his jaw. Matt stared at Thomas' soft lips, bitten red and swollen. Finally, he looked up, meeting deep blue eyes, his pulse speeding at the heated look, the desire and love that he could read there.

"I do." A low growl ripped out of the blue-eyed man's throat and Matt suddenly found himself plastered against the front of Tom's body, breath escaping in a low moan as Tom kissed him ravenously.

It was not a gentle kiss, too full of teeth and pressure, Tom's tongue thrusting hard into his mouth, seeking out the soft heat, the warm pressure of Matt's tongue. Matt curled his fingers into the firm flesh of Tom's shoulders as the man continued his assault, sucking Matt's lower lip into his mouth before biting gently at the tender flesh. The kiss began to gentle as Matt slipped his hands down the length of Tom's spine, his body curving against the solid support Tom was offering.

Tom pulled back, placing soft biting nips and gentle licking kisses up the length of Matt's jaw. He sucked at the tender spot behind Matt's ear, laughing at the deep groan it drew from Matt.

Matt felt Tom pull back again, chased after his mouth with soft pleas and open-mouthed kisses. He opened dazed eyes, pupils blown wide, mouth parting in a long moan as he saw the naked need in Tom's expression. Tom spun him round and pushed him forward and Matt grabbed at the table in front of him, sliding his palms across the polished surface. Cool fingers traced the scarlet stripes that decorated his pale flesh and Matt sucked in a low breath, a tremulous cry sneaking out.

"Tom, what are—"

"Hush sweetheart, I'm going to take good care of you." Matt heard the sound of a jar opening, then blessedly cool cream was stroked across the abused skin of his ass. Tom's fingers traced each line, moving upwards over Matt's trembling thighs, the ripe curves of his buttocks.

"Open up for me." Tom's voice was dark, heated and rough.

A cool finger traced downwards, circling Matt's entrance. Matt twitched and moaned as it pulled back before it returned, coated with lube. The finger circled again and then pushed slowly inside, Matt's hips curving back to meet it. Matt didn't hear the door open and close as the Earl and his servants left the room, senses swallowed by the feel of Tom's careful fingers opening him up, the soft sounds of Tom's pleasure as he pushed himself deep inside.

Matt braced himself against the table as Tom withdrew and thrust in hard and deep, pulling a broken cry from Matt as pain and pleasure fought within him. The burn of the cane had his skin flushed with blood, nerves firing wildly as his brain tried to catalogue the myriad sensations.

Tom thrust several times, his cock pushing hard up inside Matt, Matt's own cock rubbing against the smooth veneer of table, leaving streaks of clear fluid across the surface. Tom groaned, the sound shuddering through Matt's body.

Matt found himself pulled backward and then Tom was dropping into the chair behind him, pulling Matt down with him. The sudden change in angle, coupled with the stuttering twitch of Tom's hips up against the burning skin of his ass had Matt coming, hard and shocking in its suddenness. His head tipped back against Tom's shoulder in a silent scream, the air forced from his body as it twitched and shuddered.

Matt cried out again as Tom wrapped long fingers around his achingly sensitive cock, pulling every last drop of come from the tip. Tom thrust up twice more, Matt's body contracting tightly around him, pulling his own orgasm from him in a low moan and the sink of his teeth into Matt's neck.

Matt blinked his eyes open, turning to try and see Tom behind him. He could feel Tom's fingers trailing through the liquid mess on his stomach, slipping between his thighs to probe at the sensitive skin there. Tom slipped his sticky fingers inside Matt, working them against the warm inner walls until Matt cried out again.

He slid them out, trailing them over Matt's stomach again, before holding them in front of Matt's mouth.

"You've been a very bad boy. Look at the mess you've made, and here in the Earl's court too. Clean it up."

Matt blinked slowly, meeting Tom's dark gaze with his own. His lips curved at the soft challenge he could see there before his tongue slowly trailed out over his lips, disappearing between them again before it re-emerged to slowly lap at Tom's fingers.

He could see Tom smile softly at him as he licked his fingers clean. Tom turned him and made him lick the table clean too. Matt could feel himself begin to tremble, aftershocks running through his body, tears trailing softly down his face again. He leant against Tom as his Dominant redressed him, easing the fabric over his bruised skin. He curled further into Tom, seeking warmth and comfort as Tom pulled him down beside him on the sofa.

Matt relaxed into the feel of Tom rubbing soothing circles and meaningless patterns along the length of his spine, holding him until the sniffles stopped. Matt closed his eyes as his face was tipped upwards, allowing Tom to place soft kisses on the trembling lashes, the swollen bow of his mouth, his damp cheeks.

"Such a good boy for me. You did so well, baby." The softly murmured words fanned at the small glow in the pit of Matt's stomach, a warm feeling spreading through him as his Dominant took care of him. It had been so long since someone cared for Matt, since someone even asked him how he was and actually cared about getting an answer.

He slipped off the sofa, going to his knees, letting his head fall against Tom's thigh. Feelings rushed through him and he struggled to cope with the sudden reappearance of his past, the events of the past hour.

"I can hear your mind whirling from here, baby. Don't think so hard. I'm here to take care of you now." Tom's fingers slid through his hair, petting at his scalp and Matt slowly let his mind go blank. He rose to his feet at Tom's urging and followed him out of the strange underground court, into the upper part of the station and onto a train.

It was nice to not have to think, to worry about where he's going, what he had to do next. He just had to obey. He felt Tom just behind him, watching over him, taking care of him and Matt realised that all the tension he had been carrying around for months, hell, maybe for the past year had just drained away.

He turned his face to Tom, meeting those rich blue eyes with a soft, shy smile. He leaned in, even though the carriage was nearly deserted at this time of night, and pressed his mouth to Tom's ear.

"I missed you. I missed myself. I never realised how lost I'd gotten until just now. I'm so sorry I did this to us."

"It's okay baby. You've been punished, recognised that you were wrong. We get to start again, you just have to remember what you are." Tom's eyes darkened, his gaze fixing on the still slightly swollen flesh of Matt's mouth.

"Tell me again what you are. Tell me."

"Yours." Matt let his eyes slip closed as the train thunders through the dark, taking him home, finally.

If you enjoyed this story, you can sign up for a free membership at ForbiddenFiction.com and discuss it with other readers and the author at the *Judge Not* story page at http://forbiddenfiction.com/story/KM1-1.000023.

Slow Surrender

Chapter 1:
The Face in the Crowd

Nebula was already crowded that evening when Lucas walked through the door, the dimly lit nightclub filled with music and the sound of drunken laughter. Lucas could feel the heavy bass of the music vibrating through him, pounding in his chest like a second heartbeat.

Lucas gave a quick nod hello to one of the bouncers and spared a moment to snort and roll his eyes at Francisco (aka Whammy Fanny), dressed in cotton candy pink and gyrating up on stage to "Bubblegum Bitch" by Marina and the Diamonds. He clutched his dress bag, makeup case, and wig box close as he weaved through the throngs of sweaty bodies, making his way backstage. Lucas cursed under his breath when the makeup case nearly slipped out his hands because the damn handle had slowly been falling apart. He knew he needed a new one soon, but it would just have to wait.

Lucas was running late but it couldn't be helped. Another barista had been late for their shift, and so Lucas had to stay and cover for them. It sucked, but that's just the way things went sometimes. It wasn't as if he could quit his day job just yet, but he hoped that he could turn drag into a full-time gig someday soon.

There were five other queens in various states of undress when Lucas burst into the dressing room. He laid his dress bag over a chair and then set his other stuff in front of the vanity next to where Andy had set up shop.

"Hey Lucas," Andy said, catching Lucas' eye in the mirror as he continued to contour his jaw line. He was already nearly transformed into Ava Andrews, his glamorous, 1940s pinup style drag persona.

"Hey Andy," Lucas said as he flopped down in the chair next to him and scrubbed a hand over his face.

"Long day?"

Lucas sighed. "You better believe it." Now that he was sitting down he could really feel just how exhausted he was from being on his feet all day.

"Well, save your sob story for someone who wants to hear it," Andy said.

Lucas' eyes widened in mock offense. "But I thought you liked my sob stories."

Andy rolled his eyes. "Stop lazing around and get ready. You're on pretty soon."

"I know, I know," Lucas grumbled as he stood up and started pulling his stuff out. Tired as Lucas was, he knew that as soon as he stepped on that stage, all his exhaustion would fade into the background. Nothing else mattered when he was out there in the spotlight.

"Nice of you to show up," Dorian said as he adjusted his wig; long, wavy, and dyed a rich burgundy color that complemented his brown skin.

"Ah, Dorian. I would say that it's nice to see you, but my mother always taught me not to tell lies."

"Well, it's not like you can even see her underneath all that pancake makeup anyway," Andy chimed in with a little smirk on his face.

"True. I mean, is she beating her face or shellacking it?" Lucas said, stroking his chin and looking pensive, as if it was a serious philosophical question.

Andy mirrored Lucas' expression as he stared at Dorian, who was fully scowling at this point. "Is she a drag queen or a carpenter?"

"Hmm, I think maybe a carpenter. She's certainly got the shoulders for it," Lucas said. This time both he and Andy threw their heads back and cackled.

"Ha fucking ha," Dorian said, but before he could breathe another word a stagehand was poking her head into the dressing room.

"Hella Gaye, you're up next," she said and Dorian got to his feet to go follow her out. He glared at Lucas and Andy as he left, a wicked glint in his eye that said he was definitely going to read them for filth as soon as he got a chance.

"Ah, so the tag team strikes again," Quentin said from his station on the other side of the room next to Long's. Quentin's alter ego was Helena Foster, a pageant queen who was always glamorous and polished. "You know Andy, I like you so much better when your *other* other half isn't around."

Andy was one of the first people Lucas met when he moved to LA, and even though Lucas had only known him for a year, he felt like he'd known him his whole life. Even though they were very different in drag styles, they had quickly become best friends. It felt so natural, the way they just seemed to *get* each other, and the shared wicked sense of humor that made it easy for them to riff off of each other.

"Since we're on the subject of my other halves, did you see John?" Andy asked Lucas. "He said he was going to come tonight."

"No, sorry," Lucas said. "He's probably out there though. I was in too much of a rush to pay attention."

Andy nodded and looked a little disappointed, but seriously he had nothing to worry about; if John said he was coming then he would be there. John and Andy were basically the perfect couple, so in sync with each other that Lucas would have found it sickening if he didn't like both of them so much. John was a nice guy, tall, blond and All-American. A bit of a square, but he knew how to have a good time, too, and was incredibly supportive of his boyfriend. Nebula had drag shows on Wednesdays, Fridays, and Saturdays and John dropped by to show support for his boyfriend at least one night a week.

It all seemed so easy for John and Andy, and Lucas would be lying if he said he wasn't jealous sometimes. Lucas had always prided himself on being tough and self-sufficient. If he wasn't, he never would have had the guts to move to a city where he didn't know a soul and pursue his dream career. But even though he didn't need anyone, that didn't mean that sometimes he didn't want someone. Lucas hadn't had much luck in that department during his two years in LA. He slept with his fair share of guys, but none of them really seemed able to handle Lucas. Just because Lucas was a drag queen didn't mean he was submissive, but when the guys he'd dated finally realized just how dominant he was, they got intimidated and ran. Lucas knew himself well; he was intense, demanding, and uncompromising in his desires. He had fought too hard to be who he was to change it for anyone else. If someone couldn't deal with that, then they weren't worth his time.

Lucas and Andy continued chatting idly as they got ready. Lucas arranged his makeup and brushes, while Andy finished his makeup and started adjusting the victory rolls on his dark-haired wig.

Lucas sat down and stared at himself in the mirror, his bleary, tired eyes taking in his own familiar face: pale skin, angular features, high cheekbones, and sharp green eyes, and messy, medium length auburn hair that was shaved on one side. Lucas quickly pinned his hair back to make it easier to do his makeup and put on his wig later.

His appearance and mannerisms had always made him stand out, an obvious target for nasty taunts and names when he was younger. Back then he'd found himself wishing he was different, more masculine, more normal. But now he owned who he was and he stood out because he wanted to, realizing that the things he'd once looked down on himself for made him a more dynamic performer. If he still sometimes saw flashes of that insecure kid staring back at him in the mirror, he would never say.

"So, what's Miss Bombshell going to do with herself tonight?" Quentin asked Lucas. "Siouxsie Sioux? Annie Lennox 'Sweet Dreams' realness?"

"Ooh, you should do that Bjork thing again," Long said as he dusted his face with more glitter.

"No, not tonight," Lucas said, although he smiled at the memory. It was the most challenging garment he'd ever made. It was a recreation of an outfit she'd worn at an awards show, a skirt and a highly structured, pink iridescent jacket with bisected sphere shapes that almost looked like flowers.

When it came to drag, Lucas was a bit of a chameleon, a shape shifter who could be anyone or anything. He lived for the power, the sheer pleasure of breaking gender apart and putting it back together as he saw fit. He loved to make people do a double take because they weren't quite sure what he was, to watch their expressions go from confusion, to curiosity, to enchantment.

Though he tended towards a more androgynous style, Lucas didn't like to place any limitations on himself. At any given show, he could be a gender-fucking glam rocker, or a goth dressed in lace and fishnets, or a leather-clad evil queen, bent on world domination. Lucas felt free when he did drag, as if there was nothing he couldn't do.

"No, I'm keeping it simpler tonight," Lucas said as he pulled out his black and green wig and placed it on the head form. "A little punk rock, a little club."

"Oh my god, are you going to wear a wig?" Quentin said with an exaggerated gasp. "You might actually look like a drag queen. Well, almost."

Lucas rolled his eyes. "Not every queen has to be fishy. I can do glamour if I want to. I'm just not a one trick pony like some people."

"Yeah, you know *all* about turning tricks, I'm sure."

"What's going on in here?" Francisco said as he stomped into the dressing room and flopped down on a chair.

"Oh, nothing. Just Ursula the Sea Bitch going on about how she's the fishiest queen in the sea again," said Andy. Lucas laughed and turned his attention back to getting ready.

He didn't have as much time as he would have liked, so he set about quickly and methodically putting on his makeup. Before he knew it, he was done with his makeup and slipping into his corset, black leather skirt, and knee high boots. He kept his padding minimal and used tape under his pectorals to create the illusion of a bit of cleavage. He finished it all off by reapplying a bit of his green, iridescent lipstick and putting on his wig: a short, black bob with a green streak running through it.

Lucas stood in front of the full-length mirror, smiling as he gave himself a final once over. He looked stunning, if he did say so himself. He took a deep breath and felt the thrill of adrenaline start to race through him as he started heading toward the stage.

"Hey Lucas," Andy said.

Lucas raised an eyebrow as he turned around to face him.

"Break a leg out there," Andy smirked.

Lucas smirked right back at him. "Oh, I bet you wish I would. But even with a busted leg I'd still never be as busted as you," Lucas said. He never could resist throwing a little shade.

The sound of Andy's laughter echoed behind Lucas as he made his way to the stage. Lucas took a deep breath as he waited in the wings for his cue. He could hear the sound of the crowd laughing at one of Jack's jokes. Lucas rolled his eyes. Jack was a good emcee but he was a bit of a ham, and always talked too fucking much, although the crowd seemed to eat it up with a spoon. Finally, Jack announced the drink specials again and then came the moment Lucas had been waiting for.

"And now ladies and gentlemen, we have a very special treat for you. It's Nebula's very own Bombshell!"

Lucas took a final deep breath as the opening beats of "Fuck the Pain Away" blasted on the sound system.

All of the stress of his day melted away when Lucas slinked out on stage. Though Lucas had performed hundreds of times, there was always something magical that happened when the crowd cheered and the bright lights first hit his face. He let the music flow through him until it felt like it was just an extension of himself, the synthesizers and dirty bass all throbbing in his pulse.

Lucas stalked across the stage like he owned it, a playful yet sultry look on his face as he lip synced along with the song. There weren't a lot of lyrics to memorize for the song, which gave Lucas free reign to focus on dancing and feeding off of the energy of the crowd.

Lucas never felt as powerful as he did on stage; this was what he lived for. He loved the rush of being able to command everyone's attention, the power to hold the audience in the palm of his hand.

When Lucas crossed to the other side of the stage again, he saw John out in the crowd, as if there was ever any doubt he would show up. At least Andy would be happy, though. However, it was the man standing next to John who really caught Lucas' eye.

Who is that? Lucas wondered. The guy was gorgeous: tall, broad, and blond like a fucking Viking. His gaze followed Lucas' every movement intently and Lucas drank it in, feeding off of that energy and throwing himself into his performance even more. The crowd went wild as he gave it his all, gyrating across the stage when the song reached its climax.

The applause was ringing in Lucas' ears as he bowed and headed backstage, but all he could think about was the sharp focus of the mystery man's eyes on him.

Lucas went out into the crowd after his performance and made a beeline for John and Andy when he saw them from across the room. Andy actually looked pretty amazing, with his perfectly-coiffed hair, red lipstick, and the vintage red polka dot bathing suit that showed off his long, long legs and muscular thighs. Lucas, of course, would never tell him he looked great though; it wouldn't do for Andy's head to get too big, now would it?

He could tell from the smirk on Andy's face that he knew exactly what Lucas was thinking. Lucas rolled his eyes and narrowly resisted the urge to stick out his tongue.

"Lucas," John said with a grin. Lucas leaned in and kissed John on the cheek, and this time it was Andy's turn to roll his eyes, though they all knew it was harmless; Lucas had no interest in John as anything more than a friend.

"It's good to see you again. Great job out there by the way."

"Oh, aren't you a doll. I'd pinch your cheeks if I wasn't so sure Miss Ava here would chop off my hands for it," Lucas said, and they all laughed when Andy gave Lucas a playful shove.

"Oh, and this is Connor, one of my buddies from college. He just moved to LA a few months ago."

Lucas gave Connor a once over. The man looked even better up close, in a simple pair of jeans and a black t-shirt that showed off his muscular arms. Lucas was used to towering over people when he was in drag, but even with 3-inch heels, he was only just barely taller than Connor. Connor was beautiful, but with a ruggedly masculine edge: strong jaw with just the right amount of stubble on his chin, long, blond hair pulled back into a ponytail, and baby blue eyes framed by long eyelashes most queens would kill for.

"So, you're Bombshell, right?"

"Ahh, very good," Lucas said with little laugh. "I appreciate a man who knows how to pay attention. Just for that, you can call me Lucas."

Connor smiled, and the way his whole face lit up with it made Lucas a little weak in the knees. "It's nice to meet you, Lucas."

"Likewise."

"You were really great out there," Connor said. "I don't even know how you can walk around in heels, let alone dance so well in them."

"You pay attention *and* you give compliments," Lucas said. "You sure know how to make a girl feel appreciated, Connor."

Lucas gave a quick glance at Andy and John, who were now caught up in conversation with their friend Rebecca and not paying attention to Lucas and Connor at all.

"You know," Connor said as he smiled and leaned in conspiratorially, "I really liked your choice of song."

"Well, you're a man of discerning taste then," Lucas said with a sly grin.

"I'd like to think so," Connor said. Lucas liked the way he laughed with such joie de vivre, his eyes lighting up with open enjoyment.

Maybe Lucas was just imagining things, but it seemed like there was a hint of chemistry between them, a spark that could grow into something more, even if it only ended up being a fun roll in the hay.

Connor seemed like a sweetheart, and Lucas could see why he and John were friends. Lucas didn't usually do sweethearts because they couldn't deal with him, but he thought he might be willing to make an exception in this case.

But before Lucas could say another word to Connor, Andy was patting Lucas on the arm and telling him they needed to head backstage again. Lucas couldn't help but feel a bit disappointed.

"Maybe I'll see you around then," Lucas said as he reached out and tucked a flyaway strand of Connor's hair back into place.

Connor blushed and Lucas barely resisted the urge to laugh at how adorable he was. "Maybe you will."

Chapter 2:
A First Taste

A week later, Lucas was pulsing with adrenaline as he headed back to the dressing room after his first performance of the night, which was to "Elastic Heart" by Sia. He was quite proud of the outfit he'd created to complement the song, his own gothic take on the Queen of Hearts. The whole thing had come together so perfectly, from his black leather boots and gloves, to the red wig and spiky black crown on his head. He couldn't help smiling when he remembered the way the crowd cheered when he finally took his cape off to reveal the deep red and black corset underneath.

Lucas took a swig from a bottle of water and a few deep breaths to calm down from the high of the performance before heading out into the bar to make the rounds and catch up with people. When he stepped into the main area of the club, he spotted a couple of familiar faces. John was there, and he'd brought Connor with him again.

In the week since meeting Connor, Lucas had already pumped Andy for more information about him. Although Andy had rolled his eyes and given Lucas a hard time about it, he ultimately told Lucas a few details. Apparently, Connor was pretty newly out of the closet and had moved to LA from Kansas after some kind of falling out with his family. From what John had told Andy, Connor seemed a lot happier now.

"It's nice to see you again, Connor," Lucas said, after giving John a kiss on the cheek as a greeting.

"Likewise," Connor said as he grinned at Lucas. It tempted Lucas to give Connor a kiss on the cheek, too, just to see what would happen, but he managed to rein himself in. He was still feeling Connor out and didn't want to push too hard.

"Oh, there's Andy. I'll be right back," John said as he started moving through the crowd, leaving Lucas alone with Connor.

Most people would have felt awkward about being left alone in a crowded club with someone they barely knew, but Connor didn't seem bothered at all. There was an easy confidence about him, in his solid posture and effortless smile.

"So tell me, Connor, is LA everything you dreamed of? Enquiring minds want to know," Lucas said as he leaned in a bit closer to Connor.

"Well, it's a lot different than I thought it would be. I was led to believe there would be movie stars everywhere and everyone lived in beach houses," Connor said, and they both laughed.

"I guess your friends and family back home will be disappointed then."

"Oh, I don't know about that. I think Nebula is pretty star-studded," Connor said with a cheeky grin that managed to be intentionally cheesy, but charming.

"Oh, aren't you sweet?" Lucas said as he swatted Connor on the shoulder. Connor grinned, and all Lucas could think about was how good his beautiful, smiling face would look all covered in come. He couldn't help imagining those thick biceps bound by rope, and those muscular legs up on Lucas' shoulders as he fucked Connor to within an inch of his life.

"You were great tonight, by the way. Especially the part when you tossed your cape off. The way you move up there..." Connor said, as he shook his head and smiled. "I don't know how you do it."

"Well, it would be wrong of me to deprive the world of this much fabulousness. I never really did much of the whole coming out thing. As you may have guessed, I've been out since the day I was born," Lucas said with a laugh.

Connor looked at Lucas, his eyes clear with sincerity. "You shouldn't sell yourself short though. You're so... fearless. You are who you are and you don't let anyone stand in your way," Connor said, and something in his tone implied that he didn't see himself in that way. That implication piqued Lucas' curiosity; there was clearly a story there, and Lucas wanted to know what it was.

"But anyway," Connor said, shrugging off his unease, "John's been great at showing me around LA, but maybe you could show me the ropes around here," he said with a lopsided grin.

"Hm," Lucas said, pretending to mull it over. "I suppose it's only right. I am the greatest queen in this castle after all."

Connor laughed, and even though they barely knew each other, Lucas was struck by how much he really did love Connor's smile.

"Then there's no one better to be my guide."

"No, there really isn't," Lucas said. With a smile on his lips, he surreptitiously looked Connor up and down again, considering his next words. Lucas was thoroughly enjoying their back and forth, and he didn't want it to end just yet.

"Maybe we could do a trade of sorts, a bit of my knowledge for a bit of yours," Lucas said and from the look on Connor's face, it was clear he was enjoying their little flirtation too.

"I don't know," Connor said. "I don't know if you'd be interested in any of the things I'm good at. Unless you need a carpenter to build you some cherry wood cabinets."

Lucas laughed. "Probably not, considering the fact that I live in a studio apartment. I didn't know you were a carpenter, Connor. You must be very good with your hands."

"I am," Connor said simply, and Lucas liked the fact that he knew what he was good at and wasn't ashamed to admit it, not bothering to hide behind false modesty.

"And with the way you have to read blueprints all the time, I'm sure you must be very good at following directions."

Connor swallowed hard and stared at Lucas, his cheeks a bit flushed and his lips slightly parted. "I... I am," he said. He seemed both aroused and uncomfortable, and Lucas filed that information away for later.

"Well," Lucas said, moving the conversation along and giving Connor a chance to recover, "I'll let you know if I need any cabinets built, but in the meantime, I'd be happy to tell you all the dirt about Nebula."

Connor chuckled. "I appreciate it."

Lucas smirked. "I would say that I promise not to bite, but that would be a terrible lie," Lucas said as he casually leaned in closer, using his slight height difference to make Connor look up at him. Some guys would have shied away at that point, but Connor's gaze darkened and he leaned in a bit closer to Lucas before seeming to catch himself and pull back.

Interesting, Lucas thought.

Though Connor seemed like a pretty easy going guy, there was more to him beneath the surface. There was a restlessness, something hungry about him that called to Lucas. But there was also an edge of discomfort in Connor that Lucas couldn't quite put his finger on.

"Walk with me, honey," Lucas said, wrapping an arm around Connor to guide him as they weaved through the crowd. He had to lean in close, so that Connor could hear him over the noise in the club, and he relished feeling the heat of Connor's body where it was pressed up against his own.

"You already know John and Andy of course, and how disgustingly cute they are," Lucas said as he pointed at the two of them across the room, laughing about something. "And Andy's drag persona of course, the dated but delightful Ava Andrews. In my completely objective opinion, she's the second fiercest queen here."

"Because I have the privilege of hanging out with number one, right?"

"Ooh, very good. So easily trained," Lucas said with a wicked grin which only grew broader when he felt Connor's slight shiver.

"Up on stage we have Hella Gaye. Gaye as in Marvin and Hella as in bitch moved here from Oakland and brought her tired ass slang with her," Lucas said as he gestured to Dorian dancing around to the latest Beyonce song. "Prides herself on being a dancer, which is all well and good, except for the fact that she does the splits all the fucking time."

"See, there she goes again," Lucas said and he couldn't stop staring at the way Connor's eyes crinkled in the corners when he burst into laughter. "I can't really hold it against her though. After all, if you're good at spreading your legs, then I suppose you should stick to your talents."

Connor laughed again, and the soft warmth of his breath against Lucas' neck gave him goosebumps.

Lucas looked around to see what other queens were out on the floor when he spotted Long.

"That walking disco ball over there is Glittoris." Lucas leaned in and whispered conspiratorially into Connor's ear. "It might come as a shock, but she really, really likes glitter. I'm honestly surprised we don't have to vacuum it out of her lungs every night."

"Okay, so who are those two?" Connor asked when his laughter had died down enough for him to speak again. He gestured at two blondes over by the bar.

"Now these two are interesting. The one in the tacky gown is Helena Foster and the Shakira background dancer wannabe is Maravillosa. Helena has a thing for Cesar," Lucas said, pointing at a muscular bouncer over by the door. "Unfortunately, Maravillosa used to date him and isn't quite over him yet. It was also a particularly messy breakup."

"Damn."

"Exactly," Lucas said. "I already know that's not going to end well. I'm looking forward to pulling out a bowl of popcorn and getting a front row seat."

Connor laughed and looked around the room with wonder. "Wow, it really is like a soap opera."

"Except better, because I'm in it."

"You know, I just realized you haven't told me any of the dirt about Bombshell," Connor said, a playful glint in his eyes.

"Well," Lucas drawled, "even though being devastatingly gorgeous is a full time job, rumor has it that she's got her eye on this guy who's new in town. You know, tall, blond, broad shoulders, sweet smile. Lips that look like they were made to suck cock."

Lucas ran his fingers across Connor's cheek, reveling in the way Connor shuddered at the feel of leather on his skin. He gripped Connor's chin, turning his head just enough to make him meet Lucas' intense gaze head on. Connor flushed and Lucas leaned closer to whisper in his ear.

"But really, that's all I've heard so far. Should we find out what happens next?"

Connor swallowed hard and nodded. Lucas schooled his features, doing his best to contain his excitement.

"That hallway leads to backstage," Lucas said as he pointed it out. "Follow it down to the storage closet, first door on the left. Meet me there in fifteen minutes."

"Okay. Okay yeah," Connor said. He still looked a little dazed, as if his brain hadn't quite recovered from the filth Lucas had whispered in his ear before.

"If anybody hassles you about going back there, let them know that I sent you and that I will be very, very displeased if they interfere." Connor nodded, and Lucas smiled and gave Connor's earlobe a sharp nip before walking away.

Lucas gracefully weaved through the crowd and made his way to the storage room. He was happy to find the room empty except for assorted stacks of boxes and cleaning supplies; if someone else had been there, he probably would have shoved his high heels up their ass and told them to fuck off.

Lucas rested his weight against the door, hiked up his skirt, and set about untucking his cock. This was the reason he usually didn't try to hook up with guys while he was still in drag; having to untuck was such a pain in the ass, especially since he'd have to redo it again soon. Some queens didn't like to fuck in drag at all, and there was nothing sexual about it for them. But Lucas had always gotten a charge out of it and loved being able to tap into the erotic power of his other persona.

The guys Lucas hooked up with tended to fall into one of two categories: "straight" guys who were into drag queens, and "straight-acting" gay guys who gave Lucas the cold shoulder when they found out he was a drag queen because, "no offense," but they were "just not into that". Other than being insanely hot, Connor was interesting because he seemed too self-aware to be in the first category and too attracted to Lucas in drag to be in the second category.

"Mmm," Lucas hummed, because thinking about Connor was enough to get his cock to start waking up. He reached down and stroked himself, slowly working himself up while he waited, occasionally pulling out his phone from where he'd stashed it in his bodice, to check the time.

Sure enough, fifteen minutes on the dot there was a knock on the door.

"What's the password?"

There was a brief pause and Lucas couldn't help but laugh as he imagined the puzzled expression on Connor's face.

"I didn't know there was a password."

"There wasn't," Lucas said, grinning as he opened the door and pulled Connor inside. "I just like keeping you on your toes."

Connor laughed. "I should have known."

"You'll learn," Lucas said, before pressing Connor up against the door and kissing him hard. Connor moaned and kissed back, settling his hands on Lucas' hips to pull him closer. Connor's body felt amazing pressed against his, all those warm, solid muscles. Lucas found himself wishing he had more time to really strip Connor down and get a good look at his body, but this wasn't going to be anything other than quick and dirty. Technically, he shouldn't have been doing this at all, in the middle of a performance night, but the illicitness of it all only turned him on more.

Lucas tangled his fingers in Connor's hair and deepened the kiss as they rubbed up against each other frantically. Lucas was hard as a rock and he could feel Connor's erection through his jeans, pressing against Lucas' thigh. Though it was painful, Lucas managed to pull away from Connor. Rubbing off against Connor felt good, but Lucas was still itching to feel those lips around his cock.

"On your knees. Now," Lucas commanded, and he felt the heady rush of power when Connor obeyed.

"Gorgeous," Lucas murmured as he reached down and ran his fingers through Connor's hair.

"Yeah?" Connor said, and there was a roguish little glint in his eyes. Lucas wanted to put him in his place, so that's exactly what he was going to do.

"Don't get cheeky with me," Lucas said. "You're cute, but you'll never be as pretty as me. Now suck me off."

Connor leaned forward and *God*, the sight of him taking Lucas' cock was so hot that it was almost too much to bear.

"Yeah, that's it," Lucas moaned as he watched Connor bob his head up and down. He was a little sloppy but very enthusiastic once he got into it, like there was nowhere else he'd rather be than on his knees sucking Lucas' cock. He pulled off a couple times to swirl his tongue over the head of Lucas' cock and lick up the underside. The heat of his mouth was exquisite and Lucas knew he wasn't going to last long.

"God, you look so fucking perfect on your knees," Lucas said, and Connor moaned at his dirty praises. His eyes had gone glassy and he looked so lost in it, hips thrusting frantically against nothing as he moaned around Lucas' cock. Lucas took pity on him and pushed one of his legs in between Connor's, so that his shin was pressed right up against Connor's cock.

"Good boy," Lucas said when Connor moaned in appreciation and started grinding his hard cock against Lucas' leg, chasing his own orgasm.

"*Fuck*," Lucas moaned, so close to coming now that he gripped Connor's hair and fucked into his mouth with reckless abandon. Right before his orgasm hit, he pulled out and stroked himself mercilessly, and came all over his hand and Connor's face. Lucas struggled to catch his breath and could only distantly hear the desperate sounds Connor was making over his own heavy breathing. It didn't take long until Lucas could feel Connor's body shake and shiver as he came in his pants.

Connor collapsed against Lucas' thigh and Lucas slipped his fingers into Connor's hair, practically petting him. Connor sighed and leaned into the touch as he tried to calm his breathing. Their eyes met, and even more than the mind-blowing orgasm, it was *this* that got under Lucas' skin: the sight of this strong, beautiful man at Lucas' feet wanting nothing more than to serve, to submit in the way Lucas has always longed for. It was amplified by the look in Connor's eyes as he stared back at Lucas, like he was the answer to a question Connor had never even known how to ask.

"Lucas, where the fuck are you? Aren't you doing another song tonight?" came Andy's voice from down the hall, and the moment was gone.

"Damn it. Apparently I have a job to do," Lucas said wryly and Connor laughed.

"Yeah, I should probably go home and change out of these pants," Connor said, his voice so deliciously raspy from having his throat fucked that Lucas wished he could get hard right now and do it again.

As Lucas helped Connor to his feet, he felt at a loss. He'd hooked up with guys in worse places before, and never worried about saying goodbye. They'd simply just gone their separate ways. But with Connor tonight, things had been different. He couldn't stop thinking about that moment, and wondering just what had passed between them and what it all—

"Lucas!"

"I'm coming, *god* don't get your panties in a twist," Lucas yelled back.

There was no more time to think about it so he settled on giving Connor one last, lingering kiss.

"Don't be a stranger now, Connor," Lucas said with a feral grin that made Connor's breath hitch in the best possible way.

He could taste Connor's lips all the way back to the dressing room.

Chapter 3:
On the Hook

Wednesday night came, and Lucas found himself backstage preparing for the evening's show. He had about 45 minutes or so until he was on and he was nearly ready. Lucas already knew tonight's performance was going to be a lot of fun, and he was looking forward to getting on stage again.

He'd chosen to do "Bulletproof" by La Roux, and would finally get to wear the crazy geometric patterned jacket he'd made, just like one out of the music video. He didn't even need a wig, since his hair was the perfect color and length to style into the dramatic, feathered faux hawk the singer wore her hair in.

Even though he really loved his look tonight, his mind was preoccupied with thoughts of Connor. It was stupid. Lucas had hoped Connor would come to one of the weekend shows, but he hadn't seen that familiar blond head out in the crowd.

He couldn't forget the press of Connor's body against his, his muffled moans, and the way he looked, down on his knees in front of Lucas, like he'd finally found where he belonged.

Lucas sighed. He figured it probably was just a one off. Really, there was no reason to be so disappointed—it wasn't as if it would be the first time.

"What's wrong with you?" Andy asked. "Your face looks more pathetic than usual."

"Well, forgive me for not being all sunshine and rainbows. I'm saving my smiles for people who matter," Lucas said, gesturing out towards the bar.

There was a gleam in Andy's eye and before Lucas could even say a word, he picked up a hairbrush and started singing into it like a microphone.

"Smile, though your heart is breaking... smile, even though it's aching..."

Lucas tried to interrupt, "God, I can't say anything around you," but Andy just kept singing over him and adding an extra bit of vibrato for good measure. "You always do this shit, you're like a shitty jukebox from one of those old fashioned diners."

Andy was the only queen at the bar who sang live, and actually had a great voice, but Lucas would never tell him so. It would only go to his head, and encourage him to sing in the dressing room even more than he already did.

Lucas ignored him, and dug through his bag for a pack of cigarettes.

"Ah, so you're gonna go smoke," Andy said with a disapproving stare.

"Don't judge, just because you and John are all raw vegan paleo gluten-free now or whatever," Lucas said as he glared back at him. In reality, all they had done was a juice cleanse a month ago, but Lucas loved giving Andy a hard time. "I swear everybody in this town is on some weird diet."

"Whereas you're on the standard West Hollywood diet," Andy fired back, making a blow job gesture before breaking into laughter. Lucas rolled his eyes at him.

Andy raised an arm dramatically and starting spinning in his chair, not bothering with the hairbrush this time when he burst into song.

"She is the blow job queen, young and sweet, always on her knees..."

"Oh my god, are you making up songs about Lucas?" Francisco said excitedly, looking over from his makeup station. Lucas groaned when Francisco dashed over and sat down in Andy's lap.

"Okay, keep spinning," Francisco said. Andy laughed and started spinning again, while Francisco raised his arms into the air and added another line to the song.

"Blow job queen, turning tricks since she was eighteen, oh yeah..."

Lucas put his fingers in his ears and tuned them out, as he could really do without the part about how he was having the time of his life.

"You bitches know they get on *their* knees *way* more than I do," Lucas complained when it looked like they were finally finished singing.

"Yeah yeah, we all know what a top you are," Andy said with a roll of his eyes. "Just let the boy have his fun," he continued, patting Francisco on the shoulder; barely twenty-one and the youngest queen of all of them.

"Hey, don't blame Fanny for this. *You're* the one who started it," Lucas said as he pointed at Andy.

Francisco shook his head. "Trying to throw me under the bus? For shame, Ava, for shame."

"Oh shut up both of you. And up with you," Andy said, giving Francisco a playful shove. "Go get your wig on, you know you're up soon."

"Ugh, who died and made you my drag mother?" Francisco said with a smirk, but did as he was told.

"So, back to the subject of blow jobs," Lucas said as he leaned in closer to Andy, "have you heard anything about Connor?"

Usually Lucas didn't care much who knew about his exploits, but he kept his voice low this time. There was something about his encounter with Connor that left him feeling a little raw, and he didn't want the other girls to pick up on it.

"I haven't seen him around, I think he's been really busy with work. I could ask John—"

"No. No, it's fine," Lucas said, silently berating himself for being so dumb. It was just a blow job, nothing more, nothing less.

Andy's brow furrowed in concern, but Lucas stood up to go before he could say anything.

Andy sighed and rolled his eyes. "Fine, go on and smoke your cigarettes, even though you're the one always telling me how bad you want to quit. I nag because I care, you ingrate."

"Thank you, Andy, for being a major pain in my ass again," Lucas said sarcastically.

"I think you mean, 'thank you Andy for trying to help me kick the filthy habit I complain about all the fucking time.'"

Lucas smirked. "There's only one filthy thing in this dressing room, and it sure isn't me."

Andy made an indignant sound and gave him a little shove. "Get out of here, bitch. And if you fall and twist your ankle in those shoes, don't expect me to come rescue you."

Lucas' spirits were lifted as soon as he stepped into the alleyway behind the bar and spotted a familiar blond head through the darkness.

Connor was leaning against a wall and obviously talking to someone on the phone, but he didn't look happy. Lucas couldn't make out anything he was saying, and by the time he'd fully approached Connor the call had ended and he was scowling at his phone before slipping it into his pocket.

"Connor. To what do I owe the pleasure?"

"Lucas," Connor said, his grin so bright it was as if the sun had come out again. "Well, I *wanted* to come check out the show, but I just had to take a call from my boss. We have a demanding client who wants a rush job," Connor said with an annoyed sigh. "I've got to get up at the crack of dawn tomorrow to finish it and I don't even know if we have enough of the right grade of wood at the shop."

"Hm, a 'rush job'? Is that what they're calling it these days?"

Connor laughed. "I swear I'm actually a cabinetmaker, not a hooker."

Lucas looked Connor up and down. "I don't know, maybe you should consider a career change."

Connor laughed again, his cheeks flushing slightly. "Well, thanks for the vote of confidence. I guess."

Lucas pulled out a cigarette and stuck the pack back into his jacket pocket. "You mind?" he said, raising an eyebrow at Connor before lighting it.

"No, go ahead."

When Lucas finished lighting the cigarette, he leaned back and took a drag, sweet relief flooding him. He took another drag, deliberately making his lips cling to the cigarette obscenely as he watched Connor watch him.

Lucas extended the cigarette to Connor, but he shook his head.

"Oh, no I don't smoke."

"Of course you don't. You're a good boy," Lucas said, which made Connor frown.

"Oh, don't be like that. There's nothing wrong with being a good boy. We need at least a *few* decent people in the world, and I know I'm certainly not going to be one of them."

"So I'm taking one for the team then?" Connor said with a laugh, his shoulders noticeably relaxing.

"Exactly," Lucas said. He took another drag of his cigarette and they lapsed into a silence that was sexually charged, but not entirely uncomfortable.

"I see the way you look at me, you know," Lucas said.

"What?"

Lucas smiled and shook his head as he moved in closer. "You're not exactly subtle. But then, neither am I," he said with a laugh as he gestured to his whole get up.

"Ah, subtlety's kind of overrated anyway," Connor said with a huff of laughter.

"My thoughts exactly. No wonder we get along so well." Lucas leaned in a bit closer, and Connor swallowed hard. "See, you're doing it again. Looking at me like you want me to eat you alive."

Connor's breath hitched, and *God* he was so fucking adorable. Lucas was just *itching* to take him apart. He tossed his cigarette to the ground and stubbed it out.

"If this is what you want, then what are you running from?" Lucas asked as he slowly stroked his thumb across Connor's bottom lip. Lucas leaned in slowly, giving Connor one last chance to pull away, if he really wanted to.

He didn't.

The kiss was slow and thorough at first, until Lucas nipped Connor's bottom lip and then shoved him hard up against the wall.

"You're already hard," Lucas said as he cupped Connor through his pants. "Tell me what you want, Connor. If I'm feeling generous, I might even give it to you."

"Everything, *anything*, just... touch me, *please*."

As much as everything and anything sounded good to Lucas too, he knew he'd have to go on stage pretty soon. His tuck also meant that he couldn't get hard, but that didn't mean they couldn't still have some fun. At least now Lucas had the opportunity to scratch the surface on his desire to get his hands all over Connor.

Lucas leaned forward and unzipped Connor's fly, shoving his pants down just enough to pull his cock out.

"Lucas..."

"Shh," Lucas said as he gripped Connor's cock and stroked it a couple times. He'd hoped that Connor would be impressive, and he wasn't disappointed. It was thick and heavy in his hand as he stroked it slowly, precome easing the way with every touch. Connor reached out to touch Lucas too, but Lucas smacked his hand away.

"No, no—I call the shots around here," Lucas teased. He grabbed Connor's wrists and put them over his head, pinned to the wall with one of his hands. It was a hold Connor could get out of easily, if he really wanted to, but Lucas felt certain that he wouldn't even try. Lucas started stroking Connor again, while he nipped at his neck and breathed in the warm, rich smell of wood that clung to his skin.

"I knew you'd be back for more. You want it so bad, don't you?"

"*Fuck*, yes," Connor choked out.

"You have to be quiet so no one sees. Can you do that for me, Connor?" Lucas said into Connor's ear, practically purring. He didn't know for sure, but he thought the fear of discovery was doing as much for Connor as it was for him.

"You're gorgeous like this, you know," Lucas breathed out. "Such pretty lips, and those *eyelashes*. Every queen in the bar would kill for those."

"Lucas," Connor choked out, both embarrassment and arousal in his tone.

"If I could, I'd make you up so pretty. You wouldn't even need much, a little blush, a bit of eyeliner, and lipstick of course, the reddest red that I have," Lucas said before leaning in and capturing Connor's lips in a bruising kiss. Connor gasped for air and stared at Lucas with wide eyes when they pulled apart, his blue eyes nearly blown to black with lust.

"And then I'd push you down on your knees and have you open your mouth and suck me down. Your red lips would look so pretty wrapped around my cock. I already know you're a good little cocksucker, you nice boys always are."

"And then... and then what would you do?" Connor choked out as he fucked into Lucas' fist with increasing desperation.

"And then, right before I came, I'd pull out and paint your face with it."

Connor threw his head back and came right then and there, biting his lips to choke back his hoarse moans. Lucas watched him raptly, drinking in every desperate little sound Connor made.

"Oh no," Lucas said with a smirk as he held up his come covered fingers, "just look at what a mess you've made. I think you'd better clean it up."

"Jesus fucking *Christ*," Connor choked out.

Lucas merely smirked and raised an eyebrow at him. "Well?"

"*Fuck*," Connor said as he leaned forward and did as Lucas asked. It was obscene the way he swirled his tongue and licked up every drop, and Lucas couldn't tear his eyes away even if he tried. Even though Connor was the one all flushed and disheveled, Lucas felt just as wrecked.

"Good boy," Lucas said as he tucked Connor's cock back into his pants. Their eyes met and there it was again—that charge, that *pull*, between them that Lucas couldn't explain. The sound of drunken laughter from a group walking past the alleyway pulled Lucas back to reality.

"Well, I have a show to do and apparently you have a 'rush job,'" Lucas said with a little laugh, "but when you're ready to take it to the next level, you know where to find me." Lucas could feel Connor's eyes on him as he sauntered away, and he couldn't resist a little smirk.

Lucas was a performer and he knew how to read an audience. He could catalogue the look on people's faces when a performance really struck a chord with them, when they were utterly captivated and on the edge of their seats, dying to know what would happen next. Connor's expression tonight had been exactly the same, and Lucas had no doubt that Connor would be back soon.

Hook. Line. Sinker.

Chapter 4:
Soon As I Get You to Myself

Lucas felt a deep sense of satisfaction when he spotted Connor in the crowd at the show on Saturday night. Everything was finally falling into place and now all Lucas had to do was seal the deal.

Grinning, he strutted over to Connor like an animal stalking its prey because he *knew* he looked good tonight in his black leather ankle boots and short black and white patterned dress, showing off miles of long legs. He'd topped the look off with dramatic, smoky eye makeup and a short, blond wig, channeling Robyn a little since he was planning to do "Dancing On My Own" later. The look in Connor's eyes as Lucas approached told him that the outfit was having the desired effect.

"And here I thought that maybe I'd scared you off."

Connor shook his head. "No, I just had a lot to think about. I've never done this before. Not the having sex with guys part obviously, but the... the kinky stuff."

"Is that so?" Lucas said as he leaned into Connor's personal space, using their height difference to make Connor look up at him.

Connor swallowed hard and his gaze was hungry as he looked up at Lucas. "I was thinking, maybe you could come over to my place after the show."

While Lucas was doing a little dance on the inside, he forced himself to stay cool. He wanted to see what it would take to make Connor flinch or back down. He needed to know just how badly Connor wanted what Lucas had to offer him.

Lucas let his fingers dance along Connor's upper thigh, and though Connor's breathing hitched, he didn't look away from Lucas' gaze. He reached up and ran his thumb over Connor's bottom lip and couldn't help the sharp spike of arousal that shot through him when Connor's pink tongue darted out to lick it. Lucas smiled and shook his head at Connor.

"Oh honey, I'm not sure you'd know what to do with me."

Connor swallowed hard but he held Lucas' gaze firmly, a determined glint in his eyes. "Maybe not. But I think you'd know what to do with me."

Their eyes locked and Lucas' whole world narrowed down to the naked longing in Connor's gaze.

"Okay then, after the show," Lucas said. "Where do you live?"

"Silver Lake, not far from here."

Lucas nodded. Silver Lake was close to his own neighborhood of Echo Park. He was grateful that Connor lived nearby and not all the way out in the Valley.

"I'll look for you after the show then. For now, just relax. I have a feeling you're going to need all of your energy later," Lucas said with a sly grin before pressing a kiss to Connor's lips and heading backstage again.

Anticipation buzzed inside Lucas as he remembered Connor's blissed out expression in the storage room and out in the alley, how he gave it up so sweetly with just a bit of coaxing. He might not have done the "kinky stuff" before, but he was a natural. Soon enough, he'd be able to really get his hands on Connor for more than just a frantic hookup.

As far as Lucas was concerned, everything else was just foreplay; tonight they would finally get to the real deal.

When Lucas walked out of the dressing room after the show, Connor was there waiting for him and his face lit up when he saw Lucas. Lucas hadn't changed out of drag, just untucked and slipped on a jacket over his dress. His hands were full of various bags and Connor reached out to take a few from him.

"Let me walk you to your car and then I'll come pull around and you can follow me to my place."

"Mm, such a gentleman," Lucas said, although he sort of wished he'd kept his mouth shut because the other queens started whistling and making catcalls at them. Andy gave Lucas a huge grin and a thumbs up sign and Lucas rolled his eyes. "Come on," he said to Connor as they made the short walk to Lucas' used Honda Civic a couple blocks away.

Lucas popped the trunk and they started putting everything inside. When Lucas went to put his makeup case inside, it nearly fell out of his hands, the damn handle slipping again even though he'd thought he taped it back on pretty good. Thankfully, Connor had good reflexes and caught it in his hands before it clattered to the ground.

"Thanks," Lucas said.

"No problem," Connor said as he really looked at the box. "So this must be where you keep your makeup. Cool logo."

"Thanks, I designed it myself," Lucas said. The logo was simple, just "Bombshell" in jagged block letters with the O made to look like a bomb with a spark and fuse. Lucas had drawn it up when he was in high school, those angst filled years when he'd felt like an outcast and spent his time vacillating between walking around his home town with angry punk rock music in his headphones or crying alone in his room listening to The Smiths.

He could laugh about it now and was glad to have left all that behind, but he'd kept the logo. He wasn't often sentimental, but the logo was a reminder of what he'd been through to get to this point.

"Damn case keeps falling apart though, I keep meaning to get a new one," Lucas said as he shoved it into his trunk. He sat in his car until Connor swung around in his black pickup truck. Lucas followed him for about 20 minutes to a quiet street in Silver Lake.

Parking was actually pretty decent. Lucas was able to find a spot right across the street from the house Connor had pulled up in front of. To Lucas' surprise, Connor didn't walk up the porch into the house, but instead opened the tall wooden gate to the side and led him through a backyard area.

"Ah," Lucas said as he spotted the in-law unit they were headed towards. "This is nice, your own little cottage." It really *would* be nice to have a bit of privacy for whatever activities they got up to that night.

"Yeah, I got lucky," Connor said as they reached the front door. "A couple friends from college live in the main house and were looking for someone to rent the in-law unit around the same time I was planning to move out here."

Connor fumbled with his keys and unlocked the door, flicking on the light switch and leading Lucas inside. Lucas had always been nosy and he couldn't stop himself from looking around. You could tell a lot about a person from looking at their living space.

The living room was small and a bit cluttered. There was a couch, a TV, and a small coffee table with mail and woodworking magazines scattered across it. A couple of dark wood bookshelves were up against a wall. They looked sturdy and well-made, unlike the shitty IKEA ones that Lucas had at home.

"Did you make those?" Lucas asked, gesturing to the bookcases.

"Yeah," Connor said. "I made the coffee table too."

"Impressive," Lucas said as he moved forward, curious to see what was on the shelves. There was a picture of Connor grinning wide with his arm slung over a slightly shorter man with similar features, who Lucas assumed must be his brother. Next to it was another picture of the two of them an older man and a woman, likely their parents.

Otherwise there were some woodworking manuals and other books, tools, and haphazard stacks of DVDs. They were mostly typical dude stuff: a couple Tarantino movies, *Shawshank Redemption*, *Saving Private Ryan*, a few seasons of *Breaking Bad* and —

"*Moulin Rouge*?" Lucas said with a raised eyebrow.

Connor laughed. "Shut up, I like that movie."

"Well, don't tell Andy that. He'll start singing the soundtrack, all the time, and *I'll* be the one who has to suffer backstage."

Lucas turned his attention to the far left side of the room, which was mostly taken up by a small workbench. Unlike the clutter of the rest of the room, the workbench area was neat, and all of the tools there were neatly organized with care. It was obvious that Connor took pride in what he did.

"Reminds me of my own place, except I've got a sewing machine and a bunch of fabric in the corner, instead of a workbench."

"You make your own outfits for your shows? Wow," Connor said, sounding genuinely impressed.

"Oh, don't sound so surprised. You already know how good I am with my hands," Lucas said suggestively before leaning forward and kissing Connor hard; as fun as it was to poke around Connor's stuff, what he really wanted was to get into his pants.

Connor kissed back with equal fervor as he guided Lucas to his bedroom, with Lucas losing his jacket and Connor losing his shirt somewhere along the way.

"God, you're so fucking hot," Connor said when they finally broke for air. He leaned in to kiss Lucas again, but Lucas stopped him with a firm hand on his chest.

"Before we really get started, we should set some ground rules," Lucas said as he sat down on Connor's queen-sized bed.

"I... yeah, okay," Connor said breathlessly, sitting down beside Lucas.

"See the thing is, I know what I like. But what are *you* looking for, Connor?"

Connor paused for a long moment, struggling to put his thoughts together. "I want... I want to just let go of everything. I want you to take control and tell me what to do," Connor said, face flushing a bit and his voice slightly defiant, as if he was afraid Lucas would tell him his desires were wrong.

"You liked it when I pinned you against the wall?"

Connor nodded, as if he didn't trust his own voice right now.

"You want me to push you around and make you beg for it? You want to be a good boy for me?"

"Yeah, and I... I want you to *make* me be good for you if you have to," Connor said and god he was *perfect*. Lucas felt his mouth water at the prospect of breaking Connor in, teaching him how to submit the way Lucas wanted him to, without any bad habits to unlearn.

"I think we'll get along just fine, just follow my lead. If you want me to slow down, say 'yellow' and if you want me to stop completely, say 'red'. Got it?"

Connor nodded.

Lucas gripped Connor's chin hard, forcing their eyes to meet. "I mean it. I want to break you, Connor. But not permanently."

"I understand."

"Good," Lucas said with a feral smile. "Now come here." Connor practically fell into his arms and they started kissing again.

"Mm," Lucas moaned as he ran his hands all over the warm, solid muscles of Connor's arms and shoulders. His skin was deliciously warm and supple, and Lucas loved the way Connor moaned when he raked his fingers down Connor's back. Lucas grabbed a handful of Connor's hair and pulled hard, making Connor hiss as his neck was forced back. He started kissing Connor's neck hungrily, smearing red lipstick everywhere.

"*Lucas*," Connor moaned and arched up into Lucas' kisses. Lucas licked a long stripe up the column of Connor's throat and then pushed Connor away.

Connor was panting and breathless as he stared at Lucas, his neck and kiss-swollen lips streaked with red from Lucas' lipstick.

"Take off your clothes," Lucas said hoarsely.

Connor got to his feet, and though his fingers trembled a little bit at the beginning, he did as Lucas asked, taking off his shoes and jeans quickly and then tossing them aside by his shirt.

Lucas stifled a moan as he stared at Connor, so completely, gloriously naked before him. Connor's whole body was tense, his muscles practically vibrating with need as Lucas' eyes drank him in. Lucas was no weakling, but Connor... Connor could break him in half easily. Yet all Connor wanted to do was to surrender, to give up his power as an offering to Lucas. It was a heady feeling, to say the least.

Connor was all golden skin and powerful muscles, his long, thick cock flushed red and jutting proudly upward. If Lucas didn't want to fuck Connor so badly, he'd get on his knees and swallow it down right now, teasing Connor with his tongue until he begged to come.

Next time, Lucas thought, because he knew this was not going to be enough for either of them. Lucas could tell that he was only scratching the surface of Connor's issues; he looked forward to unraveling them one by one, in all kinds of filthy ways.

Lucas saw the full length mirror hanging on Connor's closet door and he got a wonderful idea.

"Get on the bed. Head down, ass up," Lucas snapped, thoroughly pleased by the way Connor scrambled to obey.

Lucas inspected him, running a finger down Connor's back and making him shiver. He grabbed Connor by the hips and pulled, and Connor followed his lead and scooted back further until his feet were hanging off the bed. When he had Connor where he wanted him, Lucas smacked his ass and spread his legs a little further apart.

"Good. Now arch your back and lift your head," Lucas said. He wanted to make sure Connor would be able to see himself in the mirror. Connor didn't hesitate to meet Lucas' demands.

Lucas had to stifle a moan when he took in the complete picture in front of him. Connor's little hole was fully exposed, and his cock and balls hung heavy between his legs. Lucas moved forward and placed a hand on Connor's ass, making Connor shudder as he slowly ran his fingers up and down the curves. He let his hand dip down to stroke Connor's thick, muscled thighs before slipping between his legs to tease his cock and balls.

"Ohh," Connor moaned, low in his throat, when Lucas gripped his shaft hard and pumped it a few times. He moaned again, this time in protest when Lucas pulled his hand away. Lucas chuckled softly—he would let Connor come eventually, but not without making him work for it.

Lucas licked one of his fingers, and Connor moaned at the wet press of it against his hole. Lucas gripped Connor by the hair and yanked his head back a bit, forcing Connor to look at Lucas in the mirror.

"I was right about you, wasn't I?" Lucas said. "You want to just bend over and take it, don't you?"

"Yes, please," Connor choked out. "I wanted it the moment I saw you."

"Don't worry, I'll take care of you, Connor," Lucas said, his voice low with dark promise.

Lucas let go of Connor's hair and then took off his dress and tossed it aside, leaving him naked except for his high heels.

"Have you ever let a guy fuck you before, Connor?" Lucas said.

Chapter 5:
Behind Closed Doors

Connor's only response was a broken moan that sounded like it had been punched out of him, and Lucas took a moment to revel in it. He felt so powerful, knowing that his words turned Connor on enough to leave him speechless.

"Condoms and lube?" Lucas asked.

"Top drawer," Connor said in a hoarse voice as he pointed to his bedside table. Lucas opened it and fumbled around for what he needed before standing behind Connor again.

Lucas squirted some lube onto his fingers and set about stretching Connor open. Connor was exquisitely tight and hot, and Lucas felt his cock growing harder just from the thought of sinking inside. He petted Connor's back softly while he continued to open him up with rough fingers.

"I bet you finger yourself at night, imagining having a nice, fat cock stretching you open."

Connor didn't speak, but his soft moan gave him away.

"You still haven't answered my question, Connor. Have you ever let a guy fuck you before?" Lucas demanded, and by now he had three fingers up Connor's ass and was fucking him mercilessly.

"I... yes," Connor said as he arched his back shamelessly to get Lucas' fingers deeper inside him. "A few."

"But they never fucked you right, did they? Never gave you what you needed," Lucas said, thrusting his fingers inside a few times before pulling out. Connor moaned at the loss and Lucas only chuckled as he tore open the condom and started rolling it down the length of his dick.

"I bet they were so intimidated by your strength that they didn't know how to put you in your place."

Lucas pressed his hips against Connor's ass in a slow grind before bending over him and leaning down to whisper in his ear. "But I do, Connor. Believe me I do," he said and he felt Connor's whole body shudder beneath him.

"Do it then," Connor demanded, a bit of defiance in his tone. Although Lucas snarled at him for it, he was secretly thrilled by the challenge. It seemed that Connor would not be tamed so easily and it was just as well. That would only make it more satisfying when he made Connor beg and scream his name.

Lucas didn't hesitate any longer; he lined his cock up and slowly fucked his way into the exquisite heat of Connor's body. They both sighed when Lucas finally bottomed out, his balls resting firmly against Connor's ass. He gripped Connor's hips in his hands and started off with long, slow strokes, making Connor feel every inch of him. Connor was so hot and tight inside that a part of Lucas wanted just to rut into him with abandon, but a stronger part of him wanted to savor it. Connor tried to push back against Lucas to get more, but he was met with a firm smack on the ass, reminding him of who was in charge here.

"Lucas," Connor moaned, but Lucas did not change his pace. He just kept fucking Connor with slow precision, forcing him to enjoy the sweet torture of Lucas' cock inside him. Connor's legs trembled a bit with the effort of staying still and taking the fucking Lucas wanted to give him. His breathing was labored and soft, needy moans kept spilling from his lips.

"You see, Connor," Lucas said as he thrust faster, "isn't it so much better to just admit what you want?"

"Yes. Oh god, yes," Connor groaned as he pushed his hips back to meet Lucas' thrusts.

Lucas slapped Connor on the ass, hard, making him yelp. "Look in the mirror, Connor. Look at me," Lucas demanded, as he gripped Connor by the hair and yanked his head back hard. "Look at yourself, bent over like a slut, and getting fucked the way you've always wanted."

And oh, what a sight they were: Lucas fucking Connor hard and Connor bent over and desperate for it beneath him, his golden hair tight in Lucas' grip and Lucas' makeup smeared on his face. Connor was so raw and beautiful and open that Lucas could easily see himself becoming addicted to this.

As Lucas fucked roughly into Connor, his nerve endings were on fire and his blood thrummed with a feverish need to have Connor in every possible way. Lucas felt so wonderfully, incredibly alive. He had finally found someone who could really take it, who could meet Lucas' intensity with his own.

"Harder," Connor said through gritted teeth.

Lucas slapped his ass again, thoroughly satisfied by the way it made Connor yelp. "You don't tell me what to do, Connor," he said, although he did pick up the intensity. It was too good to stop or slow down, and Lucas' own restraint was at the breaking point. He fucked Connor ruthlessly, holding nothing back and making Connor arch and moan beneath him. The room was filled with their desperate moans and the harsh sound of slapping flesh. If not for the fact that Lucas danced around in heels three nights a week, he would have lost all sense of balance and fallen over with the force of fucking Connor.

They stared at each other in the mirror, and Lucas felt terribly proud of his handiwork as he took Connor in. Connor was perfect: messy hair, sweat-streaked brow, smeared makeup, and eyes wide with need as he grunted and pushed his hips back to meet Lucas' every thrust.

Lucas reached down and took Connor's cock in his hand, the shaft heavy and slick with precome as Lucas stroked him hard. "You're so close, aren't you?"

"*Please.*"

"Look at me," Lucas said. "Come for me."

"Oh god," Connor cried out, his pupils blown to black. The muscles in his back went taut with the force of his orgasm, his legs trembling as he came all over Lucas' fingers.

Lucas was not far behind him; the tight clenching of Connor's hole around his cock was too exquisite to resist, and he moaned out his pleasure shamelessly as he came. He collapsed on top of Connor, cock still buried deep inside as they struggled to catch their breaths.

When he finally felt like he could move again, Lucas pulled out, tied off the condom and tossed it into the trash. Weak-kneed and exhausted, they both flopped back on the bed. Connor hummed happily as he wrapped an arm around Lucas and pulled him close.

Though Lucas wasn't usually a cuddler, Connor seemed to crave touch and Lucas felt like he had more than earned it. Aftercare wasn't Lucas' favorite thing in the world, but he wasn't a complete asshole; he wasn't just going to run out on Connor while he was still coming down from the high.

They lay in silence for a while, Lucas running his fingers through Connor's hair slowly to ground him. If he was being perfectly honest, it was also to ground himself. Every time he was with Connor, that spark between them was there and tonight was no exception. Lucas was hard-pressed to remember the last time he'd enjoyed another person so much, and he kept trying to put his finger on what it was about Connor that made him so different.

Lucas loved drag, loved the thrill of the performance, the ability to play around and become someone new. There was nothing wrong with the level of artifice that went into it, because that was a big part of the appeal. But in a world full of masks and personas, Connor was refreshingly straightforward and genuine, and Lucas couldn't help but be drawn to it.

Lucas was so caught up in his own thoughts about Connor that he hadn't noticed the appreciative way Connor was looking at *him*. "That was amazing. God, you are something else."

"Oh, do please be more specific," Lucas said. "I don't know if you know this, but drag queens literally run on praise and adoration. Without them we'll shrivel up and die."

"Well, I obviously can't have you dying on me, so... Well; first of all you're hot as hell. Funny, clever, powerful, talented. But you've got a soft spot too," Connor said with a cheeky grin.

"Have Andy and John spreading lies about me? You think *I* have a soft spot? You're too sweet for this town, maybe you should go back to Kansas."

"Oh god no, I'd never move back. I'm glad to be out here doing my own thing instead of working for my dad's construction company. Plus, being judged and having my life choices constantly scrutinized by family members isn't really my idea of fun," said Connor with a wry smile and a bitter tinge in his voice.

"See, it's much better out here in LA, where you're judged and your life choices are constantly scrutinized by strangers."

"Exactly," Connor said with a laugh. "Hey, I just realized that I don't even know where you're from."

"That's because it's none of your business."

"Oh come on, Lucas. I'm from Kansas. I'm not going to judge you," Connor said, fixing Lucas with puppy dog eyes that he was *not* affected by. No, not at all.

Lucas sighed. "Fine. I'm from New Jersey."

Connor burst out into laughter and Lucas glared at him.

"Shut up," Lucas said with a playful swat. Lucas reached out to run his fingers through Connor's hair and he sighed and arched into the touch. Connor seemed so happy and relaxed. If bossing him around and fucking him got him to this state, Lucas couldn't wait to see what other things they could do. Some of them he felt pretty sure Connor would be into, like being restrained or spanked. Lucas was less sure about what Connor's reaction would be to other things, but he figured he'd never know if he didn't test the waters.

"Remember what I said about putting makeup on you?"

"Yeah, that's not the kind of thing you forget," Connor said.

"Well, the offer still stands if you want it."

Connor shrugged away and refused to meet Lucas' gaze, and Lucas felt genuinely sad for him in that moment. Lucas thought about Connor growing up in Kansas, the family business he'd left behind and the expectations that had likely been wrapped up in it. It was like Connor had made some fucked up bargain with himself, where ignoring his femme side was the price he had to pay for being gay. To be gay was one thing, but to want to wear makeup was a step too far.

"You don't have to be afraid, you know," Lucas said. He mostly kept his tone light but there was a serious undercurrent in it.

Silence hung heavily for a few moments until Connor seemed to recover himself and grinned over at Lucas. "See. Soft spot."

Lucas scowled. "Shut up. I ought to gag you with my panties," he said, which made Connor's eyes widen, obviously liking that idea very much.

"Hey, I know it's late, but you could stay if you want to," Connor said. "I think you wore me out way too much to do anything else, but we could just... talk? Do people even still do that?"

Lucas laughed. "Yes, talking has not yet become obsolete."

Connor breathed an exaggerated sigh of relief. "That's good to know. It's fun talking to you, I don't think I've ever met anyone like you before. I mean, I've met drag queens, but not... you. God, that sounded better in my head," Connor said with a self-deprecating laugh that made Lucas like him even more.

"I leave you tongue-tied, I'm honored," Lucas said, inclining his head in a little bow.

Connor grinned sheepishly. "Cut me some slack, it's almost 3am and my brain is fried. So, what do you say?"

As Lucas stared at Connor's smiling face, there was a part of him that was sorely tempted to take Connor up on his offer. The moment stretched on until Lucas caught himself and snapped out of it. It was better to keep things between them strictly sexual, and he didn't need or want anything more than that. It was better this way, much less chance of disappointment in the end.

"I... I really should be going," Lucas said. Connor nodded, and Lucas hated how knowing he was the one causing Connor's smile to fade made him feel like an asshole.

"But before I do, give me your phone," Lucas said. Connor handed it to him and Lucas quickly added himself as a contact before handing the phone back to Connor.

"I'll walk you to the door," Connor said, getting to his feet and slipping his boxers on.

"Such a gentleman," Lucas said with a little smirk as Connor followed behind him. He gave Connor a lingering kiss in the doorway before stepping out into the night.

"Hey Lucas," Connor called out before Lucas was out of his range of sight. "You don't have to be afraid either."

Lucas didn't reply, but Connor's words rang in his ears the whole drive home.

Lucas groaned with exhaustion when he woke up the next morning, scowling and covering his face from the sun as if it had personally offended him. Bleary-eyed, he reached for his phone to find a text message waiting for him:

—*Hey Lucas, it's Connor*—

Lucas smiled and quickly replied.

—*Hey yourself*—

—*u know, it took me forever to find your name in my contacts. I kept looking under L for Lucas and then I thought maybe B for Bombshell*—

Lucas snickered as he fired off a response.

—I can't believe looking under T for "the greatest person you'll ever meet" didn't occur to you. For shame—

—haha, I know I know. I had fun last night tho—

Before Lucas could respond, another text came from Connor.

—I never would have expected to have such a good time with someone from New Jersey—

"That little bastard," Lucas said indignantly, but there was a grin on his face as he typed a reply.

—you're the worst. I trusted you with my darkest secret and this is how you betray me—

—maybe you'll just have to punish me next time we see each other—

Lucas felt a rush of heat pooling in his belly then because he liked that idea very much. He paused for a moment, thinking of what to say back.

—maybe I will. but in the meantime you can start by bringing me a cupcake from Sprinkles at my next show. and it better be one of the coconut ones—

He was utterly delighted when Connor did.

Chapter 6:
Drawing Closer, Falling Apart

Lucas and Connor settled into a kind of routine, seeing each other about once a week. Connor would hang out at the bar and after the show they'd go to his place, where Lucas would do filthy things to him. Lucas' performances on those nights became a sort of foreplay. He could *feel* Connor's gaze on him as he danced. Their eyes would often meet across the room, and Lucas shivered with pleasure to see Connor so entranced, staring at Lucas as if he were a siren leading Connor to dark places.

They still spent most of their time together having sex, but they texted each other about stupid stuff all the time, and talked on the phone nearly every day. Somehow, between the texts, the calls, the sex and the late night conversations, they'd actually gotten to know each other pretty well.

Lucas knew about Connor's childhood in Kansas and all the trouble he and his little brother Noah used to get into, and his stories about his college days, playing football with John. Lucas still didn't really understand jack shit about woodworking, but he liked hearing the passionate way Connor talked about it, his resonant voice and warm breath against Lucas' ear as they lay next to each other on Connor's bed after sex.

Connor still seemed a bit out of his depth with Lucas' drag, but he was always attentive and genuinely interested when Lucas talked about his upcoming performances and the outfits he was working on. He laughed at Lucas' shit-talking about the other queens at Nebula, and listened curiously when Lucas talked about the history of drag and all of the different styles.

Connor also did nice things for Lucas, from a combination of his submissive streak and his overall kindness as a person. Sometimes it was something as simple as a friendly text when Lucas was having a shitty day. Other times it was running to the store to buy fishnet stockings when Lucas realized he'd left his at home, or bringing Lucas something to eat if he'd had a long day and hadn't had time to grab dinner before racing over to Nebula. Connor always looked so pleased when he made Lucas happy, and Lucas always rewarded him for his service at the end of the night.

The first time Lucas really spanked Connor, it was a Wednesday night and Connor ended up late for the show, because he was working on plans for a construction project. Unfortunately, this meant that he missed Lucas' performance to "Die Young" by Ke$ha, which had been particularly stellar. The crowd had gone wild, dancing and singing along. Lucas was looking forward to punishing Connor for his little transgression.

"Bye Lucas, bye Cupcake," the other queens had called out at the end of the night, when everyone was leaving. Lucas snickered. Connor's cheeks flushed, and he groaned at the nickname. Andy had started calling him that after he brought the coconut cupcake for Lucas, and much to Lucas' amusement and Connor's chagrin, the name had stuck.

"You know, I'm very disappointed that you missed my performance, Connor," Lucas said as they walked out of the bar together toward their respective cars. He wasn't *really* that bothered by Connor's absence, but he saw an opportunity to have some fun with Connor, and he wasn't going to pass it up.

Connor swallowed hard, but he also looked excited as he glanced over at Lucas. "Am I in trouble?"

Lucas grinned. "Oh yes. A whole *world* of trouble."

Thirty minutes later, Connor was completely naked, gulping and flushing so prettily when Lucas took Connor's leather belt and told him to bend over the edge of the bed. Lucas laid into him with precision, laughing and teasing him while Connor squirmed and tried to make himself stay still and take it. Connor's little yelps and the sharp sound of leather smacking his ass were music to Lucas' ears.

Connor's ass was so deliciously red afterwards, Lucas felt like he had no choice but to restrain Connor's wrists with the belt, then pin him face down on the bed and fuck him. Truly, the whole thing was one of Lucas' most inspired ideas and Connor seemed to enjoy himself just as thoroughly as Lucas did.

"Okay, I think I've been thoroughly chastised now. I'll never be late again," Connor said in the aftermath, his eyes bright and warm as he stared at Lucas.

"That's right. I think we both know who wears the pants in this relationship. And the skirts. And the dresses."

Connor laughed and kissed Lucas before flopping back on the bed and telling him about the rich asshole client he'd had to deal with during the day.

"If I didn't take such pride in my work I would have left a few screws loose so that his new cabinet doors would fall on his head when he opened them."

Lucas' eyes widened in mock surprise. "Wishing bodily harm on someone, Connor?"

Connor laughed. "Trust me, you would have too, if you'd been there. I wished I had a little pocket Lucas there with me to keep running commentary."

"See, everybody thinks you're sweet all the time, but I know *all* about your wicked streak. But I suppose you'd have to have one to hang out with the likes of me."

"Yeah, you've been rubbing off on me."

"Oh my god that's terrible. Never say that again or I'll punish you again, and not in the fun way."

Connor grinned and it struck Lucas then that he was comfortable, not just because of the softness of Connor's bed, but because of Connor himself. They were often so in sync when it came to what they wanted to do in bed, but even outside of that they'd settled into a rapport that felt effortless and natural.

"Staying the night?" Connor asked, his low, sleepy voice pulling Connor out of his reverie.

You could stay, a little voice inside him said. He could go into the bathroom, wash off all the makeup, and fall back into bed with Connor. But as much as Lucas liked getting close to Connor, he could couldn't shake the sick panic in his gut, and the fear that everything would fall apart if he really let Connor get close to *him*.

"No, I better head out," Lucas said and as always, Connor looked a little disappointed. Lucas knew that feeling well; he felt the same whenever he asked about putting makeup on Connor and he tensed and shook his head. It seemed they both still had their limits.

"I'll call you."

"You better," Lucas said with a laugh. "I'd *hate* to have to punish you again."

It wasn't until Lucas was halfway home that he realized he'd referred to what he and Connor had as a relationship. He ruthlessly pushed that thought out of his head, both because it made him feel vulnerable in ways he didn't like and because he didn't know what to do with the fact that Connor hadn't corrected him.

"You ready to go?" Lucas asked, as he and Andy finished settling the dinner bill. It was Friday, and they had, as always, dropped their stuff off at the club before having dinner at their favorite Thai place.

The setting sun gleamed against cars racing by as Lucas and Andy started walking back to the bar. They chatted idly, Andy going on about the preparations for the party he and John were hosting the following night and Lucas complaining about asshole customers at the cafe where he worked.

"What else have you been doing with yourself this week, hanging out with Connor?"

"No, he's out of town visiting his family or something," Lucas said with a nonchalant shrug, pretending he didn't have any more details than Andy did. In truth, he knew that Connor had spent the weekend at his cousin Janie's wedding, and now he was helping his dad out with some construction project.

Lucas had laughed out loud at Connor's multiple texts about how ridiculous and tacky the wedding was, complete with pictures of the Pepto-Bismol pink bridesmaid dresses.

—wish you were here to make fun of it with me—

Connor hadn't texted Lucas for a couple of days, but he didn't think much of it. He was probably just busy with his dad.

"Ahh, so that's why you've seemed a little down in the dumps. Life isn't as sweet without your Cupcake."

Lucas rolled his eyes but he couldn't resist a laugh. "You bitches need to stop calling him that."

"Aww, but he does that adorable little half blush half scowl thing when we do."

"I know," Lucas said with a sigh as he remembered the way Connor's skin flushed all over when Lucas was pinning him down and fucking him.

Andy nudged Lucas with his shoulder. "Yeah, how are things going with Connor anyway? Tell me all the dirt."

"My lips are sealed."

"Oh come on, it's Feelings Friday!"

"I can't believe this shit," Lucas said with a long-suffering sigh.

While Lucas was always expressive on stage and enjoyed being over the top, he hated actually talking about his feelings. For some reason Andy thought stuff like that was important, and was always saying annoying phrases such as "don't bottle it up," and "high blood pressure," and "early death."

So Andy had declared every Friday to be Feelings Friday, the one day a week that Lucas had to discuss feelings, or at least actively try to be less evasive. If Lucas didn't already know that Andy's parents were therapists, that would have been a dead giveaway.

"Well, you wanna know how *I* feel? I feel that you and Connor make a cute couple."

Lucas scowled. "That's not a feeling, that's an opinion."

"Nobody's perfect," Andy said with a shrug. "But come on, how does it feel to be actually dating someone and not just hooking up?"

"We're not really dating though. It's... it's not like that."

"Are you fucking serious right now?" Andy said, his eyes wide and incredulous. "You make it a point to see each other regularly, you text or talk on the phone, like, every day, he brings you gifts, you fuck each other exclusively—if that's not dating then I don't know what is."

Lucas looked away, lost in his own thoughts. Andy just walked beside him with a patient silence, while Lucas worked through whatever was on his mind. Lucas couldn't refute Andy's words because they were true; he and Connor *did* do all of those things together.

So he thought about how much he liked being with Connor and how he'd missed him this past week. He thought about the way it felt when Connor smiled at him, about all the incredibly hot sex, and the late night conversations that were equal parts serious and funny.

And then he thought about the ways they'd been keeping each other at arm's length, like how Connor never let Lucas put makeup on him, even though he obviously wanted to try it. Or the way Lucas never stayed the night or let Connor see him completely out of drag.

What are you running from?

Lucas had asked Connor that question several weeks ago, the time he jerked him off in the alley behind the club. Though he knew what Connor was running from, he'd never thought to ask himself the same question.

Lucas had always prided himself on knowing what he wanted and going out to get it. When he was in Connor's bedroom telling him what to do, everything was fine. But outside of that, his feelings for Connor were a twisted knot in his chest that he wasn't quite sure how to unravel, or if he even wanted to.

"Sometimes I'm not sure if Connor likes Lucas or Bombshell," Lucas finally said.

"How did he react the first time he saw you completely out of drag?"

"Well... he hasn't," Lucas said, looking out at the busy street to avoid the sharp look Andy was surely giving him.

"Now, this might sound crazy, but maybe letting him see you out of drag might help answer your question. And then," Andy continued, before Lucas could even get a word out, "okay and this is even crazier, but maybe you could actually talk to him about this stuff, instead of getting caught up in your own insecurities."

Lucas sighed and glared at Andy. "I hate it when you're like this. All..."

"What, logical?"

"I hate you."

"Which is Lucas for 'Andy is perfect and amazing.'"

"Whatever," Lucas said with a huff of laughter.

"You guys are both coming to my party tomorrow night, right?"

"Yeah, Connor said he's coming. He gets back to LA tonight."

Andy grinned. "See, perfect opportunity for you guys to stop being idiots. Feelings Friday is a resounding success!"

"Please shut up now," Lucas said, shoving Andy through the doorway a little as they reached Nebula.

Lucas started getting ready for the show as the other queens began arriving. Before long, the dressing room was as loud and ridiculous as ever, but Lucas couldn't get his conversation with Andy out of his head.

He glanced at his phone a few times before it was time to go on, but there still weren't any new texts from Connor. Part of him worried that something was wrong, but he brushed it off, as anticipation for his performance built up.

He would see Connor at Andy and John's party tomorrow night. Right now, he had a show to do and the audience was out there waiting for him.

John and Andy's party was bustling when Lucas arrived to their house in Silver Lake. Drinks flowed freely. The house was filled with the sound of laughter, and music that was vaguely familiar to Lucas. Probably whatever hipster shit Andy was listening to these days, when he wasn't listening to show tunes.

Lucas had arrived a bit late, hoping that Connor would be there already, but Lucas didn't see him anywhere. Lucas had sent Connor a quick "welcome back" text, but Connor hadn't responded, which only set Lucas more on edge. Before he could go further down the rabbit hole of his own mind, Andy was there hugging him and dragging him further inside.

"I'm glad you made it. You look good, I'm digging the outfit," Andy said as he inspected Lucas' clothes. He'd opted to go for simple: dark blue jeans that fit him just the right way, his leather jacket, and a dark green t-shirt that brought out the color of his eyes. "So, how many hours did you spend picking it out?"

"Shut up," Lucas said, punching Andy lightly on the shoulder.

"Four? Five?" Andy asked, a shit-eating grin on his face.

"One and a half," Lucas finally admitted, which only made Andy's grin widen.

"Now before you ask, no Connor isn't here yet, and yes, you should stop freaking out about it and have a drink. You just got here yourself. I'm sure he'll show up soon."

"Yes, mom," Lucas said sarcastically, and Andy pinched his cheek before wandering off to play host to a couple more people who had just arrived. Because Lucas couldn't help himself, he sent off a quick text to Connor anyway, to ask if he was still coming to the party. A few minutes later, an answer came:

—yeah, I'll be there soon—

Lucas breathed a sigh of relief, and followed Andy's advice. He wandered around the party, chatting with the other queens and their various friends and significant others. When he needed some air Lucas stepped out onto the small patio, shoving his hands into his pockets and staring up at the night sky. He started to pull his phone out and check it again, but he felt someone approach him and nudge his shoulder.

He was pleasantly surprised to find Connor standing there. Lucas grinned as he stared at Connor's broad shoulders and the way his hair glinted under the warm glow of the patio lights.

"Hey you," Lucas said.

"Lucas," Connor said, a broad grin on his face. "It's good to see you. I almost didn't recognize you at first."

"Yeah, I guess you've never really seen me out of drag before," Lucas said before taking a sip of his drink, the taste of vodka a pleasant burn in the back of his throat.

"Well, by all means, let me get a good look at you," Connor said.

Lucas laughed, but he did a slow twirl.

Connor whistled. "Damn, you've been holding out on me. You look great."

"Thanks," Lucas said, and he felt a sense of relief. He even let himself start to hope that maybe this was it. Maybe he'd really found someone who could deal with every facet of him.

However, Lucas' relief didn't last long. He started telling Connor about the goings-on at Nebula while he'd been out of town, and Connor seemed like he was barely there. Nothing like the warm and affectionate person he usually was. Usually the two of them were so comfortable around each other, but everything was so stilted tonight, as if Connor had forgotten how to act around Lucas.

"How was the rest of your trip, besides your cousin's awful wedding? God, those bridesmaid dresses still give me nightmares," Lucas joked. Connor smiled but it didn't reach his eyes.

"It was weird being back. I hadn't been home since I moved away and it was kind of jarring coming back to LA afterwards," Connor said, and Lucas felt a sense of dread in the pit in his stomach.

"Connor, what's wrong?"

Connor shook his head. "Nothing, I think I'm just tired. It's probably jet lag, I think I might go home."

"Oh. I thought we were hanging out tonight," Lucas said, doing his best to keep the hurt and disappointment out of his voice.

"I don't know. Maybe we should take a break for a while, or maybe you could... leave Bombshell at home from now on."

Lucas frowned because this was definitely not was he was expecting. He had been so worried that Connor was more interested in Bombshell than he was in Lucas, but now it seemed like it was the other way around.

"Why?"

Connor sighed. "Now that I've seen you out of drag... you're a good looking guy, Lucas. I guess I just don't really get the whole drag thing. I don't understand why you'd want to dress up like a woman."

Lucas felt his heart sink. Then the feeling was gone, replaced by white hot rage.

"I thought you were better than this," Lucas said flatly.

"Better than what?" Connor asked, his posture now tight and defensive.

"One of those butch 'straight-acting' boys who like to look down on those of us who are more... colorful."

"Look, I'm not trying to insult you—"

"Well, kudos to you for being able to do it so effortlessly then."

"I learned from the best," Connor said, his voice harsh with frustration.

Lucas' sweet submissive boy has left the building. He felt like he didn't even recognize Connor anymore. Lucas poked Connor in the chest hard. "Don't pick a fight with me, Connor. You will lose."

Connor scowled and poked Lucas right back.

"Seriously, what the fuck is your problem?" Lucas said and Connor snapped.

"*My* problem? My problem is all this... all your fucking drag stuff, Lucas. I like you but you get so caught up in it that you don't even think about how it sends the wrong message."

"The wrong message," Lucas said, glaring at Connor so hard that he thought he might burst a blood vessel.

"Come on Lucas, you know exactly what I'm talking about," Connor said. "People see drag queens and effeminate guys on TV all the time, and they think we're all like that. You have to admit that it kind of gives us a bad name. It's just drawing attention to the fact that you're gay."

Lucas stared at him, silently seething as Connor kept talking.

"There are a lot of guys like me, too, who people wouldn't even know we're gay unless we told them," Connor said.

Oh, keep telling yourself that honey, Lucas thought viciously.

"I just don't see why you have to make such a big deal out of everything, and be so out there. Be so, so *loud* about it."

"*Loud*? Oh I'll show you *loud*," Lucas said. He was yelling now and dimly aware that other people were watching, but he was so angry that he didn't care.

"So let me get this straight: we've spent the last couple of months fucking and *now* suddenly you don't like the fact that I do drag. *Now* it's suddenly weird to you. You sure as hell weren't saying that when you were down on your knees for me last week."

Connor looked flustered, his face flushed red with anger and embarrassment. It was obvious that Lucas had struck a nerve and he had no intention of just leaving it at that. He stroked his chin with one hand as he sized Connor up, considering how best to move in for the kill.

"Lucas..."

"Shut up, I'm talking now. Since I'm so fucking *loud*, I might as well live up to the name, right? So what, you played football in college? Good for you," Lucas said, with a few sarcastic, slow claps. "But it doesn't matter how masculine you are. When it comes down to it, none of that bullshit matters. Do you know why?"

"Why?" Connor said through clenched teeth.

"Because you love cock," Lucas said, making Connor gasp as he pressed a firm hand right against Connor's crotch. Lucas wasn't surprised to find it half hard through Connor's jeans.

"You want it in your mouth, up your ass, any way you can get it," Lucas said, making Connor gasp again when Lucas squeezed his cock.

Connor was utterly speechless and his blue eyes were wide. Lucas leaned in close enough to whisper into Connor's ear.

"You act so tough when what you really want is to bend over and take it up the ass like the filthy, needy little slut you are," he said, and he took pleasure in the strangled noise Connor made.

With that, Lucas released Connor's cock and pulled away. "I'm just as much of a man as you are, Connor," Lucas said with a little smirk. "The only real difference between us is that I know who I am and I know what I want. I thought you did too, but you're a fucking coward."

"Oh, *I'm* a coward? You're the one who wouldn't even let me see you out of drag until tonight. You're always hiding behind your wigs and your makeup to keep anybody from getting close," Connor said. It was all Lucas could do not to flinch, because that comment hit a little too close to home.

"You know what? I wish I had done it sooner. Then we could have gotten this whole song and dance over, before you wasted any more of my time."

Connor's fists were clenched and he looked like he was itching to lash out. "You know what? Fuck you."

"You wish," Lucas spat out and he could hear a collective "oooh" from the crowd. He turned around, shoving people out of the way as he left the party.

He didn't look back.

Chapter 7:
Getting to Yes

Lucas didn't talk to anyone the following day, and he wouldn't even answer the phone when Andy called. He stayed at home, and tried to work on a new outfit for his performances. After being forced to use a seam ripper five times to remove stitches he'd fucked up, he realized he was too raw to focus on anything.

The calls from Connor started on Monday, and when Lucas didn't answer, he started texting as well. Other than sending one text saying *leave me alone*, Lucas didn't respond to him. It didn't seem to matter if Lucas was speaking to Connor or not. He couldn't get him out of his head. Much as he hated it, Lucas' mind kept replaying that last night over and over again, sorting through the wreckage.

He was struck by the way Connor had seemed so *off*, his entire affect changed, while he spouted off macho bullshit that didn't even sound like him. The more Lucas thought about it, the more he thought that Connor's trip had had something to do with it, and whatever happened during his visit had really done a number on him. It wasn't right, and it wasn't fair, but Lucas understood it.

But he'd *trusted* Connor. For the first time in a long time, Lucas had let someone get close, and look how everything turned out. So Lucas tried to put the whole thing out of his mind, as if telling himself it didn't matter enough times would actually make it true.

Wednesday rolled around, and in spite of himself, Lucas couldn't help wondering if maybe Connor would come to the show; if he wanted Lucas badly enough to try and really make amends face to face. When he didn't show, Lucas was disappointed, but not surprised. Connor was obviously aware of what he liked, but was too ashamed to admit it. It figured that he'd be too much of a coward to show his face at Nebula again.

Friday evening came. Lucas busied himself getting ready for his second number of the night, while Andy hovered around like a nervous mother hen. Even though Lucas had told him, multiple times, to stop being ridiculous, Andy felt guilty about what happened at the party because he and John had introduced Lucas to Connor in the first place. Unfortunately for Andy, Operation: Cheer Lucas Up wasn't going very well.

Lucas was listlessly staring down at his eyeshadows when Quentin walked into the room, high heels clacking loudly.

"What's the matter, Lucas? Upset because your little cupcake is not so sweet on you anymore?"

Andy crossed his arms and glared. "Helena. There's a time and place for being a bitch and this isn't it."

"We're backstage at a drag club. There's literally no better time or place to be a bitch. But seriously honey, I'm sorry things fell apart. And so *spectacularly* too," he said as he patted Lucas on the shoulder, his condescending tone grating on Lucas' already frayed nerves. Quentin was funny, but *god* he could be such a bitch sometimes, and took a perverse sort of pleasure in kicking someone when they were already down.

Lucas rolled his eyes and went back to looking at eyeshadow, but he could feel Andy's eyes on him. He sensed that Operation: Cheer Lucas Up was about to hit him full force again.

"You know, if you keep moping around like this, you're going to give yourself wrinkles," he said, but Lucas didn't respond. "What? No comeback about how I'm old fashioned? Or how I've got one foot in the grave and Botox is the only thing keeping my face intact?"

"Leave me alone, Ava Anachronism," Lucas said as he tried to focus on picking a lip color.

Andy looked less than impressed. It was a line Lucas had used before, and it was delivered with far more enthusiasm then.

"Wow, a ten dollar word from a two dollar whore. I didn't know you had it in you, I'm almost impressed."

Lucas shrugged.

"You're still not gonna say anything back?" Andy said, his eyes wide and incredulous. "Come on, you *love* throwing shade."

"I know."

"God, you've got it bad don't you?" Andy said, and Lucas could *hear* the wheels in his head turning.

"Don't do it, don't you dare fucking do it," Lucas said with a groan, but Andy had already grabbed a hairbrush and was singing into it.

"You got it, you got it bad—"

"Stop."

"When you're on the phone—"

"No."

"You hang up and then call—"

"*Andy,*" Lucas said, fixing Andy with his most annoyed glare. He laughed at Lucas, but he put the brush down and stopped singing.

Lucas rolled his eyes. "Well, at least you picked a song from this century. Now if we can just get rid of the old lady smell, there might be hope for you yet."

"See? There she is," Andy said with a grin. "There's the bitter bitch we all know and love."

"Speak for yourself," Long said as he walked into the dressing room, sparkling so brightly that Lucas almost wished he was wearing sunglasses.

Andy put his hands on his hips and glared. "Oh come on, can't you see we're having a moment here."

"She can't see anything underneath those cheap eyelashes," Lucas said and both he and Andy burst into laughter.

"Ava, you're next!" a stagehand called out, and Andy straightened up, giving himself a final look in the mirror.

"See, you're gonna be fine, honey," Andy said, patting Lucas on the shoulder. "My adoring public awaits, but you better not be moping again when I get back, you hear?"

"Yes, ma'am," Lucas said, begrudgingly, as Andy walked away.

Lucas went back to working on his makeup and he found that he actually did feel a little bit better. His spirits lifted even more because he could hear Andy out on stage, cackling and singing the hell out of "I Wanna Be Evil". Maybe Operation: Cheer Lucas Up wasn't so bad.

Andy made a beeline for Lucas as soon as he returned from his own performance, his excited footsteps clacking on the ground as ran.

"Lucas," Andy said, excitement in his voice as pulled up a chair and sat down, "you'll never guess who I saw out in the crowd."

Lucas raised an eyebrow. "Who?"

"Connor."

Lucas whirled around to face Andy. "Seriously? Did he come with John?"

"Oh, it's him alright. He's out there by himself too, John couldn't come tonight."

Lucas' heart was racing. He wasn't sure how to feel. It was one thing to ignore Connor's texts and calls, but now he was here in the flesh, out there in the crowd. Lucas couldn't ignore everything anymore. As much as he hated to admit it, there was a part of him that missed Connor and wanted to see him again. But he was still fucking pissed, and his impulse to lash out and really stick it to Connor was strong.

"Hey Andy, can you do me a favor?" Lucas asked, scribbling a song title on a piece of paper. It was a bit of a throwback, not a song he usually did, but he had an opportunity to mess with Connor and he wasn't going to let it pass.

"What are you up to?" Andy asked suspiciously.

"Just a little bit of fun," Lucas said. "I need to finish getting ready, but if you could, please be a dear and take this up to the DJ. I need to change the song for my number."

Andy took the piece of paper and laughed as he looked down and read it. "Hell hath no fury like a drag queen scorned."

Lucas only smiled, feeling very pleased with himself.

When Jack called his name, Lucas stepped onto stage as the lights went dark. He struck a pose and took a deep breath, putting himself into the headspace he needed to perform. His head was clear and he felt calm, yet there was an edge of excitement building. It was as if he could feel the energy of every person in the room, all waiting for him with bated breath.

The spotlight hit him just as the opening notes of En Vogue's "My Lovin' (You're Never Gonna Get It)" blared on the speakers. Lucas smirked as he strutted across the stage, his little black dress showing off his miles of legs. He let the music flow through him as he danced, flinging his long, curly black hair dramatically as he lip synced. The cheers and whistles of the crowd rang in his ears, and some people in the audience were singing along with the song.

When Lucas looked out into the audience, it didn't take him long to spot Connor, who was standing right in the front, on stage left. He watched Lucas raptly, following every movement. Lucas couldn't resist laughing a bit— this was just too good. He mostly ignored Connor, but gave him occasional glances from over his shoulder as he shimmied and shook his body around the stage.

It wasn't until the breakdown that Lucas really let Connor have it. He moved to stage left and crouched down, staring directly at Connor while mouthing the words "never gonna get it" over and over again.

Lucas finished it off by doing something he'd done many times over the past few months: reaching out and brushing back one of Connor's stray hairs. Connor swallowed hard and they stared at each other for a brief moment before Lucas stood up again and stomped away.

At the end of the performance, Lucas took a bow and grinned as the crowd cheered for him. And although he felt amazing, his sense of triumph wasn't as strong as he'd thought it would be. Though Lucas was still pissed at Connor, and had thoroughly enjoyed giving him a hard time, the stupid fucking attraction between them was still there. It really was unfair just how gorgeous Connor was, especially with the way his cheeks were flushed and his lips were parted as he'd watched Lucas on stage.

Adrenaline was still pumping through Lucas' veins when he got back to the dressing room. He was a bit surprised to find it deserted, but he supposed that the other queens must have gone out to mingle with the crowd. Lucas' number had been the last one of the night, after all.

Lucas didn't have much desire to mingle. He was exhausted, and just wanted to get undressed so he could go home and crash. With practiced movements, he took off his shoes, dress, and padding, laying them across a chair. He reached between his legs and took off his gaff, breathing a sigh of relief as his cock was released from its tuck. Lucas sat down and sighed, stretching out his long legs before setting about taking his wig off.

Lucas had just put the wig on a Styrofoam head form when he heard a knock at the door. He stood up and slipped the dress back on to cover himself.

"Come in," Lucas said, eyeing the door suspiciously as it swung open.

It was Connor.

"And just what are you doing here?" Lucas said, crossing his arms and glaring over at Connor.

Connor stood awkwardly in the doorway, so tall and bulky that he barely seemed to even fit. He was holding a big paper bag in his hand, but Lucas couldn't tell what was inside.

"I came to see your show, since you haven't returned any of my calls or texts. I... I haven't been able to stop thinking about you."

Lucas rolled his eyes. "How sad for you."

Connor sighed as he stepped into the room. "Look, I'm sorry about what I said before." He was silent for a few moments, brow furrowed as he struggled to find the words.

"Last week was the first time I've been home since moving to LA. It was weird being around my dad, and all the guys at the construction company, and all the extended family at my cousin's wedding. There are some people who act like I'm a freak or a disappointment for coming out and leaving the family business behind. But I think what's worse are the ones who say they're okay with me being gay, but go on and on about how I'm one of the 'good ones', that I'm still a 'real man' and not one of those freaks who walks around in dresses and makeup."

Connor shook his head and let out a humorless laugh. "But the worst part is that I let it get to me again. I felt like I have something to be ashamed of. And then I brought that back with me and took it out on you."

Lucas paused for a long moment and stared at Connor. "It will take more than that to get back in my good graces, but it's a good start."

Connor nodded and sighed. "I know. We had a good thing going and I fucked it up. But I brought you something, as a peace offering."

Connor reached into the paper bag and pulled out a wooden box and handed it to Lucas. It was sturdy and obviously well-made, but not overly heavy in Lucas' hand. The wood was stained a subtle red color and felt smooth and luxurious to the touch. Lucas held it up to his face and inspected it, the smell of wood reminding him of the way Connor smelled when he buried his nose in Connor's neck.

It wasn't until Lucas opened the box and different compartments fanned out that he realized what it was: a makeup case, a replacement for the one that was falling apart. Lucas closed the box and ran his fingers across the wood again and this time his fingers felt something on the back side of the box. He turned it around to look and there was Lucas' Bombshell logo in beautiful copper inlay.

It was a true work of art, and Connor had obviously put a lot of time and thought into it. Lucas ran his fingers over the smooth lines of the logo again as he struggled to pull himself together. It was quite possibly the nicest gift anyone had ever given him and he had no idea what to say.

"About a month ago I started making a box, but I didn't know what for at first. But as I started working on it, I realized it was for you," Connor said. "That's why I didn't come to the show on Wednesday. I wanted to finish it before I saw you again."

Lucas swallowed hard. "I... it's beautiful. Thank you."

"Lucas, the truth is that I really like you a lot. More than I've liked anyone in a long time."

"But do you like Lucas or Bombshell?" Lucas asked, because he needed to know for sure.

Connor frowned, as if puzzled by the question. "They're both you."

All Lucas could do was stare back at Connor because whatever response he was expecting, it wasn't that.

Connor sighed. "Lucas, look. I like you up on stage and in the bar making fun of everyone. I like you in my bedroom fucking me so hard I can barely think straight and then laying around afterwards talking about everything and nothing. And I liked you in your guy clothes at the party before I fucked everything up and I want to see more of that side of you. Because it's all you, just different pieces of the same person."

For the second time in one evening, Connor had left Lucas speechless. Well, there was no help for it. Lucas knew he was a goner now.

Hook. Line. Sinker.

"Well, I really like you too. A lot," Lucas said, and for once he didn't try to make it sharp and snappy, to dress his words up or hide them behind a joke. He just them lie there, clear and honest, and the way Connor smiled at him then made it all worth it.

There were so many things he liked about Connor, from his refreshing straightforwardness, to the sly sense of humor beneath his earnestness, to the thoughtful streak a mile wide that made him such a sweetheart out of the bedroom—and so beautifully, wonderfully submissive within it.

"I'm still mad at you, though," Lucas said, but he was smiling now.

"I know. So what are you going to do about it?" Connor asked, smiling suggestively back at Lucas.

"Hmm," Lucas said as he stroked his chin. He looked around the room and when his eyes fell on one particular item, he got a wonderful idea. Still, he thought it would be fun to tease Connor a little bit first.

Lucas smirked as he slipped his pumps back on and starting slinking forward, making his way into Connor's personal space. He didn't stop until they were only inches apart and he could feel Connor's body heat. As always, Lucas thrilled at the slight height difference the shoes afforded him, and the way it forced Connor to look up and meet Lucas' gaze.

"Lock the door."

Chapter 8:
True Colors

Lucas' arousal sparked when he saw how quickly and easily Connor obeyed. He could already tell that this was probably going to be the best make up sex he'd ever had.

The other girls were going to be so mad at him, but Lucas didn't really care. He wondered if their absence could be attributed to Andy, who might have seen Connor heading backstage and told all the others to fuck off. Lucas would have to thank him later if that was the case, but there was no time to worry about that now. Not with Connor finally in his arms again as they kissed each other with abandon.

Connor choked out a moan when Lucas slipped a long leg between his, the bulk of Connor's cock warm against his thigh. Lucas himself grew harder with each passing moment, losing himself in Connor's rich, masculine scent and the feeling of those rough, carpenter's hands on his body. Though Lucas had dedicated an entire number to teasing Connor about how badly he wanted it, the truth was Lucas wanted it just as badly. He ached for rough kisses and the sweet roll of their hips grinding. He wanted to take everything Connor had to offer, to fuck Connor so hard, so good that he never shied away from his desires ever again.

Connor shuddered when Lucas slipped his hands under his t-shirt. He seemed to understand what Lucas wanted, pulling away from their kiss just long enough to take his shirt off and toss it aside.

He started trying to kiss Lucas again, but Lucas placed a firm hand on his chest to stop him. Lucas was satisfied with teasing Connor for now; it was time to put his plan into action.

"Go get that brush," Lucas commanded, pointing to the hairbrush over by Helena's station. He knew it was a total bitch move, but he didn't feel that bad about it. Helena was a hateful bitch after all, and Lucas really didn't appreciate her little comment, earlier, about his falling out with Connor.

Connor was breathing hard and his eyes were wide as he handed the brush to Lucas.

"Strip and then bend over my vanity," Lucas said sharply.

"*Fuck.*" Connor swallowed hard and then did as he was told and Lucas watched him appreciatively, enjoying the view. Connor shivered with anticipation when Lucas ran his hands over Connor's ass and gave him a few little warm up smacks.

"I would ask you if you're ready," Lucas said with a wicked grin as he picked up the brush, "but I really don't care."

With that, Lucas swung and delivered the first blow. Connor yelped and the sound of the brush against his bare ass was deliciously obscene as it echoed through the room. Lucas gripped Connor's hair roughly as he kept spanking him, alternating where he struck and how hard so that it kept Connor constantly on his toes. It was so satisfying to see Connor shake and moan and to see his ass get redder and redder after every blow.

Lucas slowed down and settled into a steady rhythm and then started speaking to Connor.

"Next time you have a problem, you come to me about it. Don't go flying off the handle because of some stupid shit your family told you," Lucas said, giving Connor three more rapid smacks.

Connor yelped and then mumbled something under his breath that sounded suspiciously like, "I wasn't the only one flying off the handle."

Lucas yanked his hair hard. "Don't think I didn't hear you. I know you're still pissed that I yelled at you in front of everyone, even though you deserved it."

"You didn't have to—*fuck*, oh god Lucas— you didn't have to be so fucking loud."

"Don't talk back to me," Lucas said with a particularly hard smack, but really that was *exactly* what he wanted Connor to do. They were both still upset about the fight, at least a little bit. Lucas spanking the hell out of him while Connor got to talk back and sass him was a hell of a lot more fun than getting into another argument.

"Oh you were so mad. You totally wanted to hit me."

"I would never, not really. But god, you sure know how—*fuck*—how to rile someone up."

"Yeah, well you humiliated me, you fucking asshole," Lucas said, the last two words punctuated with a hard smack to each cheek.

"You did too," Connor choked out, and by now his eyes were watering. There was something about the particular stinging pain of a spanking that could reduce anyone to tears.

"Well, as long as you don't pull that shit again, we'll keep the humiliation behind closed doors, where you can get off on it like the dirty slut you are."

Connor laughed breathlessly but it quickly turned into a yelp when Lucas struck him again. "Don't pretend you don't get off on it too."

"Shut up now. Enough," Lucas said, and he laid into Connor five more times before putting the hairbrush down. Connor panted, legs trembling slightly, as Lucas stared down and admired his handiwork. Connor and Lucas both moaned as Lucas ran his fingers all over Connor's burning ass.

"Next time I'll use my bare hand, so I can see my handprints all over you," Lucas said as he helped Connor to his feet.

Connor bit his lip to choke back a moan. "Fuck, you can't *say* shit like that."

Lucas only laughed at him. "I can say whatever I want. Now sit in the goddamned chair," he said, pointing to the chair by his own makeup station. "I'm not done with you yet."

Sitting down made Connor wince, but he did as he was told and Lucas sat on his lap and straddled him. He reached behind him, grabbed a tube of liquid eyeliner and then raised an eyebrow at Connor in a silent question. Connor's whole body went rigid as he stared at Lucas, but after a few moments the fight went out of him.

"*Please*," Connor said as his eyelids fluttered shut and he tipped his head back.

"Good boy," Lucas said, as he traced Connor's cheekbone with his thumb. "Now hold still."

Lucas tilted Connor's chin up a little. Connor shuddered at the first brush of eyeliner on his skin.

Lucas laughed and smacked Connor's thigh. "Stay still or you'll look like a fucking raccoon when I'm done."

Connor snorted, but then went entirely still as Lucas really got to work. He finished applying the liner and then artfully added a bit of purple eyeshadow, tilting Connor's head at different angles as needed.

"Open your eyes," Lucas said, so that he could put on the mascara.

God, Connor was gorgeous with the eyeliner on. Lucas didn't think it was possible for his eyes to be any bluer, but the contrast with the black liner made the blue pop out even more.

Lucas had never thought putting makeup on someone could be erotic, but this evening was proving him wrong. Connor's cock was dripping precome and Lucas was so hard he was having difficulty focusing on his task. Luckily for Connor, Lucas was a fucking professional.

When they first met, Connor had told Lucas he admired him for being fearless. Lucas didn't think anyone was really fearless, but he liked to think he was brave. Being brave wasn't really something you were, it was something that you had to actively do.

For Connor, it was admitting that he wanted to submit, even though it wasn't what he was supposed to crave. It was sitting in that chair right now and finally letting Lucas put makeup on him.

And for Lucas... for Lucas it was admitting that he wasn't untouchable, that he felt things deeply. That he cared about Connor, maybe even loved him.

Lucas told Connor to close his eyes again as he moved on to brushing on a little blush. Finally, he pulled out the tube of bright red lipstick and slowly spread it on Connor's lips. When he was all finished, he climbed off of Connor's lap and stood behind him, resting his hands on Connor's shoulders.

"Okay, now open your eyes."

Connor took a deep breath and then finally looked at himself in the mirror. "I... wow," was all he could say. Lucas watched all the different emotions flickering across his face after the initial shock. Wonder, pleasure, and satisfaction were all there but the edges of fear and doubt were still lingering and there was no fucking way Lucas was going to stand for that.

"You look beautiful," Lucas said.

Connor looked away but Lucas grabbed his chin and forced their eyes to meet.

"You do. I mean it, Connor," Lucas said. Lucas had never worn sincerity well, but he could tell how much Connor needed it now.

Connor's shoulders relaxed, and when he looked at himself in the mirror again a slow smile spread across his face.

"Lucas, I... thank you."

"Yes yes, I'm wonderful, I know," Lucas joked. He still was who he was; his ability to tolerate heartfelt moments was low as it was, and he'd reached his limit for the night. "And you, Connor, are the prettiest princess."

Connor laughed. "I thought *you* were the prettiest princess."

"No, I'm not a princess at all. I'm the queen," Lucas said, and they both laughed.

Lucas stared at their reflections in the mirror and was reminded that Connor was still hard, completely naked, and at his mercy. Lucas grinned as he crouched down slightly, loving the way goosebumps formed on Connor's skin as Lucas slowly trailed his fingers down the expanse of Connor's chest.

"I think that maybe you've earned a reward. You'd like that, wouldn't you?"

Connor swallowed hard and nodded, unable to take his eyes off of them in the mirror.

Lucas chuckled and held his palm out to Connor. "Lick it good."

He enjoyed the wet heat of Connor's tongue on his skin, and couldn't help thinking about how good it was going to feel, all wrapped around his cock later.

"Enough," Lucas said as he pulled his palm away and wrapped it around Connor's hard cock.

"Oh god," Connor moaned at the first stroke. Lucas flashed a wicked grin and kept touching Connor with firm, measured strokes. He could already tell that Connor was on the edge and that it wouldn't take long.

"Look at yourself, all dolled up. You look good enough to eat," Lucas whispered into Connor's ear.

"Fuck, *Lucas*," Connor choked out as he stared at their reflections. Lucas couldn't look away either, watching raptly as Connor fell apart under his touch.

"That's it, give it up for me," Lucas said, and Connor was so worked up that he did, shaking and writhing in the chair as he came all over his chest and stomach.

"God, you're so pretty when you come," Lucas moaned into Connor's ear as he watched Connor ride out the last of his orgasm.

"But you know what? I bet you'd look even prettier with your mouth around my cock, wouldn't you?"

"*Yes.*"

"You know what to do."

Connor got out of the chair and then sank down to his knees in front of Lucas. He moaned, soft and hungry, and rested his hands on Lucas' thighs for balance as he took Lucas into his mouth.

"That's it, so beautiful," Lucas said, his voice rough as he stroked Connor's face and hair. Connor kept bobbing his head up and down, as if there was nothing else in the world he would rather do. The image of his red, red lips wrapped around Lucas' cock was even hotter than he could have imagined.

"God, you're so good at that," Lucas moaned. "You look so good down on your knees."

Connor moaned around Lucas' cock, and his cheeks flushed slightly under the praise. Their eyes met and while Connor looked blissful, there was a challenging little glint in his eye that made Lucas laugh.

"You think you can take more then, do you? We'll just see about that."

Without any more warning, Lucas gripped Connor's hair to keep him still while Lucas fucked his mouth with short, powerful thrusts.

"Fuck, *Connor.*"

Lucas knew he wasn't going to last long, not after all the build-up. He felt himself losing control, and all he could do was moan and thrust desperately into the perfect heat of Connor's mouth.

"I'm going to paint your face again," Lucas said, and though he knew he sounded completely wrecked he couldn't find it within himself to care. Lucas pulled out and gripped Connor's hair again to hold him in place before stroking himself hard and moaning brokenly as he came all over Connor's face.

Lucas felt like his legs were going to give out so he managed to collapse on the floor next to Connor. Lucas allowed himself a few moments to catch his breath and enjoy how good Connor looked with his eyes closed and come all over his face.

He reached up and grabbed a box of tissues that were sitting on the vanity and set about wiping Connor's face a bit. Much as he

263

enjoyed this look on Connor, he also wanted Connor to be able open those pretty blue eyes again.

"You ruined my makeup."

"No, I made it better, you ingrate," Lucas said, his eyes wide with mock offense. "You look even prettier now."

Their eyes met and slow smiles spread across both their faces. Connor started to chuckle, and Lucas couldn't stop his own giddy laughter from bubbling up. Bright sounds filled the room as they leaned into each other, laughing so hard that tears burned their eyes. Lucas felt so thoroughly satisfied with how the evening had turned out.

When their laughter finally died down, Lucas surged forward and kissed Connor, wet and messy. Connor kissed back with equal fervor, and Lucas lost all sense of time, forgetting everything beyond the sensation of Connor's lips against his.

"Mm," Lucas hummed as they finally broke for air. He leaned up against Connor and snaked an arm up Connor's back, resting his hand at the nape of Connor's neck. Lucas started running his fingers through Connor's hair and Connor sighed happily, arching into the touch like a sated lion.

Lucas stared at him, taking in the blissful, fucked out expression on Connor's face. That easy confidence was back and he looked more comfortable now, like a weight had been lifted from him. And to Lucas' surprise, he felt the same way.

There was a knock on the door and the sound of someone loudly clearing their throat.

"If you're done defiling the dressing room, I would like to get my stuff and go home," came Dorian's voice. "And for the love of god, please tell me I don't need a Hazmat suit to enter."

"I make no promises," Lucas called out, and he and Connor both laughed as they got to their feet. In the midst of searching for their clothes, Connor paused and rested his hand on Lucas' shoulder.

"Hey, wanna come home with me tonight? And maybe stay the night this time?"

"I... Yeah. I'd like that," Lucas said. "But you're making me breakfast in the morning."

"Of course, yeah," Connor said a bit breathlessly, and *fuck,* Lucas didn't think he was ever going to get over how much Connor loved being told what to do.

They both grinned like idiots the entire time they were getting dressed and straightening up the room. Before Lucas unlocked the door, he leaned into Connor and nudged him with his elbow.

"You know, now that we know how good you look with makeup on, we'll have to see about getting you up on stage someday," Lucas said, and he took great delight in the way Connor shivered at the suggestion.

⌁⌁⌁

Two months later, Lucas took a deep breath, his blood racing with familiar anticipation as he waited to go on stage. Although he'd performed in drag countless times, tonight was special—Connor was standing there beside him, and would be performing in drag for the first time.

"Happy 'Bring Your Boyfriend to Work Day,'" Andy said, as he passed them on his way backstage, after finishing his performance.

"Stop calling it that," Lucas said, but Andy only laughed and kept walking.

Lucas rolled his eyes and then turned his attention back to Connor and smoothing down his leather skirt. His whole ensemble fit perfectly of course, because Lucas had made it himself.

Lucas thought it would be fun to go for a more rock 'n roll look tonight, as they'd be performing to the first song Lucas ever did drag to. With Connor's coloring, he actually made a pretty good Lita Ford —for a guy built like a linebacker—and Lucas had always been able to pull off Joan Jett pretty well.

While Lucas didn't think Connor really wanted to be a drag queen, it was something he wanted to try at least once, now that he felt freer to explore his femme side. Lucas was more than happy to help him with it. Getting ready for the performance had been fun for both of them. Plus, Lucas got to dole out fun punishments and rewards when he taught Connor how to walk in high heels.

"Nervous?" Lucas asked as he rested his hand on Connor's shoulder.

"No, not at all," Connor joked, but Lucas could feel the real thread of tension in him. Lucas gave Connor's shoulder a squeeze and then leaned in close to whisper in his ear.

"You look gorgeous and you'll be fine, honey. And do you know why?"

Connor shook his head.

"Because we're gonna go out there and tear the house down. And then we're gonna go back to your place and I'm gonna strip this off of you piece by piece and fuck you until you scream."

Connor grinned and the worst of his tension seemed to bleed out of him. "I'm looking forward to it."

Before Lucas could reply, the announcer's voice blared on the speakers.

"Up next we have a very special performance for you," Jack said. "Nebula's very own Bombshell, and introducing Ann Munition! I just hope there's something left of the stage once they're done!"

The opening chords of "Cherry Bomb" by The Runaways blared on the speakers and Lucas flashed Connor a wicked grin as they stomped out onto the stage together.

If you enjoyed this story, you can sign up for a free membership at ForbiddenFiction.com and discuss it with other readers and the author at the *Slow Surrender* story page at http://forbiddenfiction.com/story/OS2-1.000211.

We do our best to proof all our work, but if you spot a text error we missed, please let us know via our website Contact Form at http://forbiddenfiction.com/contact.

About the Authors

Jacqueline Brocker lives and writes just north of Cambridge, England. Her short erotic fiction has appeared in anthologies such as *More Smut for Chocoholics* (House of Erotica), *Best Bondage Erotica 2014*, and *Best Gay Erotica 2015* (both from Cleis Press). Her novellas *Body & Bow* and *Gods Among Men*, along with several short stories have been published by ForbiddenFiction. Originally from Australia, when not writing she is a Scottish Country Dancer and a dabbler in foreign languages (current dabblings being German, Korean and Spanish).

Jamie Freeman is a part-time writer with a full-time day job. He dabbles in genre fiction (erotica, gay romance, horror, micro-fiction and literary fiction), reads obsessively, knows every musical theater lyric ever written, and watches more movies in a year than he can count. He's always got half a dozen stories in the works and more lurking inside his head, so stay tuned.

E.E. Grey has been writing for going on eight years, mainly gay romance/erotica novels and short stories. Grey loves to write contemporary fiction with the occasional supernatural influence. In her spare time, Grey enjoys traveling and has visited over twenty countries. Grey also enjoys baking, spending time with friends and pets.

Lynn Kelling began writing in order to tell stories that weren't afraid of the dark, didn't hold anything back and always strived to be memorable, forging lasting attachments between character and reader. Her inspiration comes from taking a closer look at behaviors and ideas lurking at the fringes of life – basically anything that people may hesitate to speak of in mixed company, but everyone wonders about anyway. Her work is driven by the taboo in order to expose the humanity within it. Lynn is an artist, designer and lover of any form of creative self-expression that comes from a place of honesty and emotion, whether it's body art or opera. She has had multiple novels published, has written over 50 works of erotic fiction of varying lengths, and always has several novels in progress.

Julian Keys (also known as Thirteen) is an award winning erotica writer currently being published by both ForbiddenFiction and Beautiful Trouble Publishing. In addition to the gay bdsm Fancy Man series, Julian's work also includes romantic, heterosexual novellas like Valentine Prayers and Pretty as a Picture. Along with editor's choice, year's best and special contest awards, Julian won the Blue Moon award for best M&M 2009.

Dorla Moorehouse makes her home in Austin, Texas, with her spouse and a small menagerie. She has published a number of stories in print and online, and edited Coming Together: Triumphantly. Dorla is currently at work on a manuscript of linked short stories.

Kailin Morgan has been reading for as long as she can remember, devouring everything from horror to classics. After finding fan-fiction she took to writing her own stories like a vampire to the jugular. It was only a short hop from that to writing original fiction and she has been lucky to find a home at ForbiddenFiction, where she is constantly inspired by the other authors. She loves caffeine, words and baking and tries to avoid the Scottish weather as much as possible.

P.L. Ripley is a born storyteller. weaving worlds since he could first express what he saw in his head. Fascinated with human sexuality, erotic fiction is a natural place for him to explore the connection between sexual excitement and our emotional responses to it. He lives near Bangor, Maine with his partner.

Olivia Stone lives and works in the San Francisco Bay Area. She has always been drawn to exploring identity, poking and prodding at the tension between what people show the world and who they really are. Her writing centers around this theme mixed with humor, hot sex scenes, and a lot of heart. In addition to writing fiction, Olivia is also a multi-instrumentalist who writes and records her own music.

About the Publisher

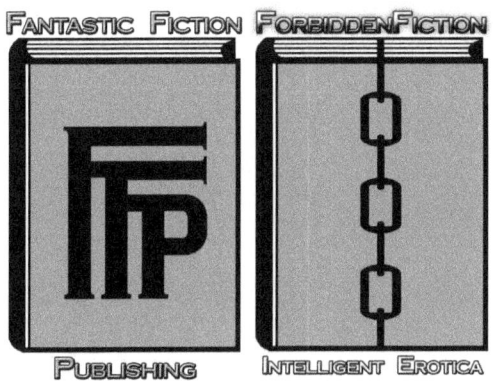

ForbiddenFiction.com is a publisher devoted to writing that breaks the boundaries of original erotic fiction. Our stories combine intense sexuality with quality writing. Stories at Forbidden Fiction.com not only arouse readers through sensations, but also engage them emotionally and mentally through storytelling as well-crafted as the sex is hot.

ForbiddenFiction.com is also designed to be a social reading environment. You'll have fun even if just reading the latest post each day, yet you will have the chance for so much more. Readers and authors can be part of ongoing discussions of specific works and individual authors as well as more general topics.

Sign up for a FREE Membership today at ForbiddenFiction.com